Yesterday's Tomorrow

Yesterday's Tomorrow

~ A Novel ~

CATHERINE WEST

ISBN-13: 9781500564346

Praise for *Yesterday's Tomorrow*...

Brace yourself for a heart-thudding love story amid the raw and real back-drop of Vietnam during one of the most turbulent times in American history. Without question, this is a novel that will woo and win you heart and soul, written by a gifted storyteller who will do the same.

—JULIE LESSMAN, award-winning author of
The Daughters of Boston and *Heart of San Francisco* series

This compelling love story, set against the backdrop of the Vietnam War, transported me through recent history. Catherine West's debut novel is beautifully crafted and thoroughly engaging!

—DEBORAH RANEY, best-selling author of
the *Clayburn Novels* and *Almost Forever*

Catherine West has all-at-once crafted a wonderful story of magnetic cross-appeal for romance lovers, historical fiction lovers, and for fans of stories of international intrigue spiced around a military setting! From riveting tension starting in the prologue, and through the eyes of Kristin Taylor, an independent journalist covering of the Vietnam War while fighting her reluctant attraction for the ruggedly handsome, Oxford-educated war-photographer Luke Maddox, *Yesterday's Tomorrow* is filled with action, emotion, and splendid imagery that captivates the reader from the get-go!

—DON BROWN, author of Zondervan's *Navy Justice* series.

A beautifully told story, crisp and accurate in its detail, filled with emotion and deftly handled by a writer who understands the hope of prayers asked and the beauty of prayers answered, *Yesterday's Tomorrow* is a story to savor.

—LISA WINGATE, national bestselling author of
Larkspur Cove and Dandelion Summer.

I do not exaggerate when I say Catherine West writes an unforgettable and powerful novel with *Yesterday's Tomorrow*. I read the book several years ago and some scenes remain vividly etched in my mind. West is one of my favorite authors because she writes real, she writes raw, and she does it with a mastery of prose that woos readers.

—BETH K. VOGT, author of *Somebody Like You* (PW starred review).

Author Catherine West exquisitely captures the feel of that time and place in the pages of her amazing debut novel, *Yesterday's Tomorrow*. Get ready for an exciting adventure and a heart-pounding ride as you dive into this page-turning story. No doubt this will be the first of many excellent offerings from this talented new author.

—KATHI MACIAS, award-winning author of more than 30 books, including the popular Extreme Devotion series www.kathimacias.com, www.thetitus2women.com

Heartwrenching! Powerful! In *Yesterday's Tomorrow*, Catherine West spans seas and generations to report on the Perfect Love Who will never let go. Don't miss this poignant debut novel.

—PATTI LACY, author of *The Rhythm of Secrets*

TO ALL SOLDIERS EVERYWHERE
The men and women who serve, those who laid down their lives for our
freedom, and those still on the frontlines. You are not forgotten.
"There is no greater love
than to lay down one's life for one's friends."
—JOHN 15:13

Prologue

February 1954.

*D*idn't they know they were shouting so loud the neighbors could hear?

Twelve year-old Kristin Taylor huddled in bed, drew her knees to her chest and clapped her hands over her ears. Through the thin wall she heard Daddy's voice rise and Mom burst into tears. It was past ten o'clock. She was supposed to be asleep, but they'd woken her. Kristin gritted her teeth and began to hum her favorite song, "Somewhere Over the Rainbow."

A moment of peace settled over the brownstone apartment. Kristin smiled and wiped her eyes. It worked every time, even if she couldn't hit the high notes.

Dad started yelling again.

Something smashed against the other side of her wall and shattered. More yells. No way to sleep with this racket going on. She sat up and turned on her bedside table lamp.

Kristin hopped off her bed and pushed her arms through the sleeves of her thick flannel robe. Cold air chased her as she quick-stepped across the faded rug to her dresser. She ran her fingers along the stack of books squashed between two hand-carved wooden bookends. The frayed bindings of *Heidi, Jane Eyre, Great Expectations* and *Pride and Prejudice* and the Bible she'd received at her confirmation shared space with all the Agatha Christie novels Kristin could get her hands on. Every once in a while Mom came in to clean, found them, and threatened to throw them out in favor of books she felt more appropriate, but Daddy wouldn't let her.

"The child has an inquisitive mind, Val. We should encourage that."

"And you do a fine job," Mom retaliated. "She's only twelve years old! She should be reading something more…genteel…what's wrong with The Brontë sisters?"

Kristin remembered the Ian Fleming book hidden under her bed and grinned. Dad snuck it in to her room a couple of nights ago. She'd start it now. Hopefully she could finish the whole story before Mom got her hands on it.

Her eyes landed on the silver framed black-and-white image of Daddy getting his Pulitzer two years ago. They said he was probably the youngest journalist to ever receive the award. At school, they said she should be proud. She was, but Mom didn't seem so happy about it. Everyone wanted Daddy to go all over the world now.

As their shouts died down, she heard the distinct sound of drawers being pulled open and slammed shut. So, he was leaving. Her stomach tightened but she ignored disappointment and tried to imagine her father's exciting world beyond their brownstone apartment. As she waited to see if they'd start up again, a faint cry reached her ears.

Teddy.

Kristin crept down the hall to her brother's room. The lamp on the dresser shed a soft glow over Teddy's round face. He sat up in his bed, fists against his chest. His eyes were scrunched tight—as if that would make them stop. He opened one eye as she entered the room, probably afraid she'd make fun of him for being a crybaby.

Not tonight. Tonight she wanted to cry too.

She skipped over Lincoln logs and Tinkertoys and scrambled up onto the bed beside him, eager to get her cold feet under the covers. "Scooch over."

Teddy's bottom lip quivered but he made a supreme effort to stop crying, and shifted his small frame to give her room in the twin bed. She put an arm around his trembling shoulders and squeezed.

He let out a long sigh matching her own. "Is…Daddy…gonna leave again?"

Hot tears pricked her eyes and told her she wasn't so brave after all. But she couldn't give in. Teddy needed her. Later, Mom probably would too.

"I don't know. I heard them talking earlier. His editor wants to send him to Vietnam."

"Vietnam?"Teddy looked up at her, fresh tears pooling."Where's that?"

Kristin rolled her eyes, but guilt nudged off impatience. He was only ten for crying out loud. Well, almost ten. She couldn't expect him to know everything. "Some place far away."

"Why do they want him to go there?"

"Because the French and the Vietnamese are fighting a big war and they want him to check it out." Because their Dad was the best war correspondent that ever lived. Kristin ran her tongue over her bottom lip. "He has to go talk to some important people and write a story about it."

Teddy shook his head and tugged on his blanket. "Why can't somebody else do it? I want Dad to stay here. Tomorrow's my birthday. We're going to the ice rink, remember?"

"Yeah. I remember."

He shivered and leaned against her shoulder. "But he'll come back, right?"

Kristin screwed up her nose. Couldn't he figure something out for himself for once?

"Kris?"

"What?"

"He'll come back, right? And then we'll go skating?"

She tried to smile but her heart pounded too fast. "Of course he's coming back. He always comes back, dummy."

"You promise?"

She hesitated a moment. What if Dad didn't come back? What would they do then? "I promise. Now can you go back to sleep? It's getting late."

Mom and Dad were arguing again. Their voices seemed louder, closer. Kristin scrambled off Teddy's bed and went to the door. She poked her head out and listened.

"You know why I have to go now," Dad said. "If I wait, my source might be gone. He's only in Saigon a few days."

"I don't like it, Mac." Mom's voice trembled. "You're talking about the CIA, exposing secrets…it's dangerous."

"So is going into a war zone." A door slammed. "But somebody has to do it. Somebody has to tell the truth."

Kristin stepped back as her parents brushed past her. Daddy held a suitcase in one hand, his battered leather briefcase in the other. And his coat was slung over one arm. Would he go without saying goodbye?

Kristin glanced at Teddy, about to tell him to stay put, but her brother was already behind her, standing barefoot in blue cotton pajamas.

She grabbed his hand. "Come on."

Teddy squeezed her fingers so hard she thought he might pull them off. They ran down the stairs and drew up short at the entrance to the living room. The French doors were open. Teddy slammed into her and jumped back with a yelp. Mom and Dad turned their way.

Mom let out a little cry and shook her head, then put her mad face on. "What are you doing out of bed?"

"We couldn't sleep." Kristin pushed hair out of her eyes and stuck out her chin. "You were making a lot of noise."

Mom threw up her hands and huffed as she sank onto the couch. Her dark hair fell around her cheeks and curled on her shoulders. She would have looked pretty if her face wasn't so red and her eyes all puffy.

"I would've woken them anyway, Val." Dad's voice was gruff, but he didn't sound angry anymore.

Mom glared at Dad, pulled at the belt around her green woolen dress and kicked off her high heels. "All yours then, Mac."

Dad set his bags down and released a sigh from somewhere deep inside. His lips stretched apart in a feeble smile. Dark circles lined his brown eyes and stubble covered his jaw. He looked from her to Teddy as if he didn't know what to say.

The air suddenly got sucked out of the room, like someone untying the knot of a balloon. Kristin shook her head and yanked the sash of her robe as tight as it would go.

Dad dropped to one knee in front of them and held out both arms. "Come here."

Teddy ran to him. She knew he would. And he'd probably start blubbering again. Kristin folded her arms and pushed her toes into the rug. The goodbyes were the worst part. Try as she might, in the end she never could keep from crying.

Dad concentrated on Teddy. Her brother always believed everything.

She stood there, like playing statues in gym class, listening while Dad gave his excuses. Teddy would be satisfied with promises of season tickets to the Red Sox and a long train-ride from South Station to Grand Central and back, but she didn't need bribes. She understood his job. Sort of.

Kristin blinked through her tears as her brother threw his arms around Dad's neck and hugged him tight. Then Mom took Teddy by the hand and led him back upstairs.

Kristin shifted, her feet like ice. She should have put on her slippers. Dad's knees creaked as he rose and made his way toward her. He reached for her hand but she tightened her arms. A tear escaped and rolled off down her cheek. Kristin lowered her head.

"Oh, Kris." Dad knelt before her and held her arms. "Sweetheart, look at me."

Kristin slowly raised her chin until she made eye contact. "Sorry."

He lifted an eyebrow. "What do you have to be sorry for?"

She shrugged, but couldn't think of a thing.

Kristin noticed for the first time a few streaks of gray in his hair. His white starched shirt sat open at the collar, a thin black tie slightly askew. Dad's eyes were bright, sad. His mouth lifted in a grin as he wiped a tear from her cheek with the base of his thumb. When she sniffed, moisture shot up her nose. She gave a small involuntary shiver.

"Are you going to Vietnam to write about the war?"

His mouth twitched, like he was surprised she was so smart. Then something chased off the sad look and he smiled. "You're going to make a fine journalist one day, young lady."

Kristin raised her shoulders again and pushed out her bottom lip. "Mom won't let me."

"Sure she will. By then you'll be all grown up. Making your own decisions. Leaving your old man in the dust."

"We could write stories together," she offered. Her grin faltered as she watched his eyes moisten. Kristin sucked in a breath. Dad never cried.

He pulled her to him and rested his lips against her forehead for a moment. "Sounds good to me." He sat back on his heels, solemn. "Look after your brother."

"I always do."

"And don't fight with your Mom."

Kristin looked down, studying the scuffs on his normally shiny shoes. "Kristin?"

"I won't." She met his eyes again and the lump in her throat got bigger. Her skin prickled. He'd left before. Lots of times. But this felt different. "You're coming back, right?"

His face cracked in a funny sort of smile. "Of course I am. But you'll pray for me, every night, just like always?"

"Yeah." She tried to smile back. "God will keep you safe, Dad. He always does."

Kristin rested her head against his shoulder as he hugged her. She inhaled by habit. Tobacco and coffee mingled with the cologne he always wore. She could never remember the name of it, but they got a bottle for his birthday every year. He said he didn't mind, but maybe this year they should do something different.

A flash of headlights chased dust across the room. Dad stood, his smile gone. "There's my cab."

Mom came forward and Dad took her in his arms.

"I'm sorry," they whispered at the same time. Mom stepped back, rested her palm flat against Dad's face. Her cheeks were streaked with tears. His hand came over hers and their eyes met as he pulled her closer and kissed her, a long kiss that seemed to go on forever. Kristin almost felt she shouldn't be watching. But she was glad she was.

"I wish you didn't have to go tonight." Mom said.

"I know." Dad tucked a strand of her hair behind her ear. "War doesn't wait on birthdays, Valerie." Dad pulled on his coat, gave Mom a final kiss and picked up his bags. "I'll call when I can." He turned to Kristin. "Bye, kiddo. I love you."

The little girl in her wanted to run back into her father's arms and beg him not to go. But she wasn't a little girl. She would turn thirteen this year. "Bye, Dad. Love you, too."

Mom walked with him to the door. Kristin raced to the window at the front of the room, pressed her nose against the cold glass and watched him get into the waiting cab.

A light snow swirled around the soft yellow glow of the streetlamp outside their building. Maybe it would storm and his flight wouldn't be able to leave Boston. Kristin pushed harder against the windowpane. It wouldn't matter. He'd get another one. His job was very important. More important than anything else.

Even them.

The taxi pulled out onto the deserted street and Kristin squinted through the window. Her breath made it fog up and she wiped furiously, seeing Dad raise a hand in her direction. She waved back just in time before he drove away.

"The past cannot be erased, nor forgotten. Flash photography; hellish images carved into our minds, emblazoned in our hearts forever. Golden threads try to hold yesterday together, camouflage the pain, and form the foundations for tomorrow. But what of today?"

*Kristin Taylor - **Yesterday's Tomorrow: Vietnam — My Story.** 1974.*

Chapter One

February 1967, Saigon, Vietnam.

Kristin Taylor shuffled along in the line of travel-weary passengers as they exited the plane. She blinked as her eyes adjusted to the daylight, shook off sleep and gripped the handrail of the metal steps. When her shoes hit the tarmac of Tan Son Nhut airport, her hand went to the gold cross around her neck. The intricately carved symbol had been her father's. Kristin never took it off.

I'm here, Dad.

Here to find her brother and make sure he was okay, and to finally finish the story her father started all those years ago.

The one that got him killed.

She rubbed the thick gold between her thumb and forefinger and took in her surroundings. The early morning sun's rays jack-knifed off the tarred surface. Heat sliced through her sneakers and smothered her in its stifling embrace.

Teddy, shipped out three months ago, hadn't been kidding about the weather. Her brother wasn't much for letter writing, and the little correspondence they'd received was hardly forthcoming, but he'd been spot on about the climate.

It *was* hotter than hell.

The pungent smell of gasoline stung her eyes. Kristin pulled on dark sunglasses, tried not to breathe too deeply and looked down the runway. She stepped aside to let others pass as she surveyed the area, the slow thumping of her heart picking up its pace as she began taking mental notes.

Aircraft of varying description lined the blacktop. Everything seemed larger in real life, from helicopters to small fighter jets to the Pan American

Boeing 707 that had brought her here. Gray, green and brown flying machines blended together in an impressive show of US military power.

It was impossible to imagine jumping aboard any of them. Or jumping out.

Army personnel moved smoothly around the aircrafts, refueling and working on engines. Rows of enlisted men lined up to board a larger plane also being loaded with cargo. Soldiers sweating in the heat heaved supplies onto the plane's cave-like interior. Commanding Officers barked like dogs to be heard over the noise as they rounded up their companies. She scanned the groups of soldiers and searched their faces. Some looked anxious, their eyes shifty even as their bodies remained stiff, while others seemed impassive, stone-faced and resolute as they stood between the world they knew and a world gone crazy.

During a lull in the activity on the tarmac, a low rumbling somewhere off in the distance reached her ears. Her throat tightened as she turned toward the outline of mountains beyond the airstrip.

The sound of war needed no introduction.

Kristin caught up with the rest of the arrivals and moved along through Immigration, then pushed through the crowded airport to retrieve her bag. Vietnamese men and women dressed in colorful pajama-like clothing darted in and out of the maze of olive-green and khaki uniforms. Strong scents of heady perfume, spicy tobacco and rancid body odor made a tactile assault on her already queasy stomach.

Signs in Vietnamese were no help, and the quickly spoken foreign tongue on every side of her seemed daunting. Relief cheered her on as she spied the doors that led out of the airport. She put her passport back into the green canvas knapsack on her shoulder and headed for the exit. Her eyes began to water as her body revolted against her present surroundings. She didn't have a clue what lay beyond those doors, but she needed air.

The four journalists she met on the flight stood outside on the pavement and Kristin nodded their way. They'd been in Hong Kong for R&R and had been quite happy to chat with her. Their stories fascinated her. Scared her a little, although she wouldn't admit it. The Frenchman's tales seemed a bit too dramatic. He wore a teasing look the whole time. Caroline, the only female in the group, hailed from England. She worked for a small newspaper that Kristin had never heard of.

Kristin confessed she wasn't working for anyone. Yet. This didn't seem to bother them and they gave her plenty of tips on how to find work.

"Ah, Kristin, *chèrie*." There was an odd comfort at the sound of her name being called in the midst of this foreign chaos. The Frenchman, Jean Luc, lumbered over, carrying two large cases. "Have you got your stuff?"

"This is it." She tugged on a beat-up brown duffel bag. It weighed a ton thanks to her typewriter. It had belonged to her father and she refused to leave it behind. Sweat formed on her brow and a drop rolled down the side of her face.

"You have got a place to stay, *oui*?"

Kristin swiped sweat out of her eyes. "No, actually, I don't." This adventure slowly inched out of her control. "I'll find somewhere." She might afford a couple nights in a hotel room, but that was it. Until she found work, she'd be watching every dime. Or whatever they called the currency here.

Jean Luc took a step back and hissed out air. "Oy." His suitcases hit the ground with a thud and he ran a hand through slick, black shoulder-length hair. A sudden image of him tooling around Provence on a Peugeot made her smile. "Let me talk to my friend." He put two fingers in his mouth and let out a shrill whistle aimed at the group gathered on the far side of the terminal building. "Caroline, sweetie, a minute please…"

The English girl looked their way. Jean Luc pulled a faded red bandana from the chest pocket of his Safari shirt and wiped his brow as he pointed a finger at Kristin. "You don't move, *oui*?"

"*Oui*." Not moving sounded pretty good.

He met Caroline halfway and they engaged in a lively debate. She was fluent in French apparently, hand motions and all. Kristin let her bag slide off her shoulder and positioned herself on the top of one of Jean Luc's large leather cases. Maybe quitting her job at *The Daily* and hopping a plane to Vietnam wasn't the smartest thing she'd ever done. But, despite the sheer exhaustion and more than a little trepidation tailing her, it was arguably the most exciting.

Her mother would by now have found the letter Kristin left her. After countless arguments over Kristin's desire to go to Vietnam, with nothing resolved, Kristin finally decided the best course of action was to simply leave. Guilt plagued her, and the first thing she intended to do once she was settled was to call home and apologize, but that conversation would not be an easy one.

The worst of it though, was that Mom agreed with Kristin's chauvinist pig of an editor. Former editor.

Vietnam was no place for a woman.

Of course she'd pulled the old religious guilt trip. Had Kristin prayed about it? How did she know it was God's will for her to go to halfway around the world, into a war zone no less?

Kristin didn't have time for that crock. God didn't care one way or another. She'd stopped consulting him a long time ago—the day they got the news that Dad had been killed in Vietnam. And years later, once she'd learned what he'd been doing over here on his last assignment, read through the boxes of files her mother stored up in the attic, discovered the story he never got to finish, she vowed to do it for him.

Kristin tied her hair into a ponytail, sweat stinging her eyes. She longed for a cold drink and a few hours of uninterrupted sleep, but wouldn't let her mind go there. She needed somewhere to live and a way to get out beyond the city and do what she'd come here to do.

Find the truth, whatever it was.

And tell it to anyone who would listen.

Jean Luc returned, his sizeable schnozz glowing like Rudolph's. "Okay. We have got a plan."

Caroline stood beside him, a tall leggy blonde with a face so flawless she could be a model, but the wariness in her eyes betrayed the confident smile. "Jean Luc says you need a place to stay."

Kristin nodded. "That's right."

The Grace Kelly lookalike raised a thin eyebrow, lit a cigarette and blew smoke over Kristin's head. "My roomie's gone back to New Zealand. It's a one-bedroom flat, two beds, small kitchen and bathroom, a block away from The Caravelle, a hotel where a lot of the press guys stay. I'm in and out of the city; you'd be on your own a lot. It's not The Ritz, but if you're interested…"

Interested was an understatement. But her savings would last a month or two at best until she got work. "Um. How much…I…"

Caroline smiled. "Oh, that's right. You don't have a job, do you…what was your name again?" She ground her half-smoked cigarette onto the pavement with the heel of her boot, taking along Kristin's last shred of hope.

"Kristin Taylor." She pushed herself to a standing position. Although they were probably around the same age, Caroline gave off an air of superiority she hadn't picked up on earlier. She crossed her arms and shook off insecurity. "I plan to get work as a stringer. I'll have the money." For all she knew, the woman could be psychotic. Kristin ran her tongue over dry lips. But the alternative was…well, there wasn't one.

"You know you'll need press credentials if you want to get anywhere outside the city," Caroline said. "I'm sure something will come up though. Listen, why don't you go have a look at the place? I've got to get to a meeting with my boss, but here…" She foraged in her shoulder bag and came up with a notepad and pen. She scribbled a few lines, then handed over the piece of paper.

Kristin squinted at the barely legible writing. "Thanks, where—"

"Righto, I've got to run. Oh, here's the key, but the apartment should be unlocked. Madame Dupont, my landlady, does laundry for me. She always forgets to lock the door. Just ignore the mess. I'll stop by the flat later and we can chat. Cheerio." Caroline marched off to rejoin her comrades, leaving Kristin to suck air in her perfumed wake.

Jean Luc clapped his big hands together. "*Voilà!* We can share a cab, *oui?*"

"Sure. As long as you know where I'm going." Kristin picked up her bag and allowed a smile. She had a place to stay. Next, a job.

The drive to the apartment building in Saigon turned in to an interminable journey of stopping and starting. The odors inside the beat up blue Renault taxi were almost worse than the airport. Jean Luc grinned and pinched his nose. Kristin leaned a little closer to the open window, seriously wondering about body hygiene in this country.

Men, women and children jostled for space along narrow sidewalks. Peddlers in brightly colored tunics and trousers and large conical shaped hats bowed under the weight of a wooden bar balanced across their shoulders on which a straw basket hung from each side. Avocados piled high in some, while other baskets held bright oranges and some other fruit she didn't recognize.

Her own heavy duffel bag no longer seemed significant.

Tall trees lined the city sidewalks, their lush branches giving much needed shade from the blistering sun. It was odd to see these massive trees in the city, but then again, she hadn't known what to expect. They passed rows of concrete buildings, some almost comparable to what she'd left back in Boston, but no skyscrapers. The architecture, especially the churches and the larger houses, appeared French in design, which made sense given the country's history. The painted shades of blue, peach, pink and yellow put on a happy façade.

She snapped a few photos as they drove. It was tempting to pretend she was merely a tourist on vacation. But this was Vietnam. A place of death—the place her father died—the place where countless others fought for freedom out there beyond the confines of the city. At this very instant men were losing their lives.

Tomorrow she hoped to be taking very different pictures.

As they veered off onto smaller side streets, shops of every description almost sat on top of each other. Striped awnings overhung many of them. They passed a large market where she spotted fruit and vegetable stalls and…oh… Kristin covered her mouth with her hand. What *was* that?

"You don't eat from there. Ever." Jean Luc pointed at the hanging animal carcasses and made a horrible face.

Kristin looked beyond the vile sight and shook her head. "Thanks for the tip, Jean Luc."

As they drove further along, burnt out shops and dilapidated structures here and there revealed the ravages of war and its toll on the city. She turned to him, spider legs crawling up her spine. "I thought Saigon was relatively safe." Her palms were moist against the ripped leather seat of the cab.

The Frenchman grinned and lit a cigarette. "What is relative, *chèrie?*"

Kristin nodded. "You're right." No wimping out. She'd come here to do a job, once she got one, to cover the war. Kristin stared out the window again. The number of vehicles on the roads startled her. Cars, military jeeps and trucks jammed every bit of the asphalt. Pedal-bikes and motorcycles zipped on by, weaving in and out of the traffic. Gasoline fumes took fresh air prisoner and made breathing a chore. The cab inched along until there was a break in the traffic.

Men pushing pedicabs ran along the side of the road. Kristin flinched each time they passed one, thinking the cab would surely hit it, and send the runner and his passengers flying.

Heat emanated through her pores. She hated the cold, but hadn't anticipated the oppression of this sauna-like atmosphere. She should listen to her brother more often. Her fingers slipped into the pocket of her jeans and felt for the thin envelope, his last letter to her before she'd left the United States. She wiped sweat from her brow and frowned. He hadn't revealed his location of course, but she knew he was a combat medic. He could be anywhere. She had to find out where and be able to get in touch. After leaving Mom without saying a proper goodbye, she wanted to be able to tell her Teddy was alive and well.

The cab pulled up outside a large white five-story building with a rounded front. The words *Hotel Caravelle* in large black lettering teetered at the top of the building.

"This is me." Jean Luc gathered his gear and grasped her hand. "Au revoir, *chèrie*. Come for a drink, okay?"

"Cool. Thanks." Kristin watched her only friend in Vietnam disappear through the glass doors of the hotel and fiddled with the cross around her neck. Suddenly she was back in junior high on the first day of a new school, riding the bus for the first time. Alone.

About ten minutes later, the cab shuddered to a stop. Kristin squinted up at the three-storey building in front of her. Distinctly French in architecture, pink paint crumbled in places where the cement had shifted. Two sorry-looking potted palm trees sat sentry on either side of a weathered wooden door. A small brass nameplate read: *La Maison Dupont*.

Good enough. She paid her driver and made her way inside, entered a small living room area and glanced around. Faded wallpaper looked like it had once been pink. A tattered Persian rug curled at the edges lay on the floor in front of the reception desk. Two worn rose-patterned easy chairs were positioned in front of a fireplace. Kristin almost laughed at the sight as sweat dripped down her back.

She peered over a raised wooden desk into a miniscule office. "Hello? Madame Dupont?" Nobody answered except a black cat that jumped down from the counter and prowled around her legs. Kristin cringed and moved aside. "Stay out of my way, cat, and we'll get along just fine."

She called out again but the place appeared deserted. The smell from the full ashtray on the counter tickled her nose but jogged a sudden memory of her father and served up a fresh shot of courage.

Kristin turned toward the only set of stairs in view. Caroline said her flat was on the second floor, first door on the left. She heaved her bag to her other shoulder and went to the darkened stairway, pushing thoughts of *Psycho* from her mind.

The stairs creaked under her. A thin carpet runner proved more of a hindrance, bare in spots and easy to trip over. Nails stuck out of the wood and slowed her down as she picked her way over them. At the top, a long dark hallway stretched out into blackness. Where was the light? Two bare bulbs hung from the ceiling. Finding the switch, she flicked it upward. Nothing.

Kristin squinted at Caroline's instructions in the semi-darkness. Even if she could see the writing, she probably couldn't read it. She stumbled toward the door on the left. Tried the knob and sure enough, it was unlocked.

She found the switch on the wall and thankfully this time the overhead light came on. Kristin let out a low whistle. This was more than just the mess Caroline had warned her about. A hurricane had ripped through the small apartment. That, or her new roommate was a complete slob.

She stepped over piles of clothes and magazines. A large pair of muddy combat boots sat in one corner near the door. She didn't bother to pull up the blinds as she poked through the boxy rooms—a tiny kitchen and one bedroom with two twin beds. She dumped her bag and looked around. One bed was unmade, sheets tangled every which way. The second bed was covered in a light mauve bedspread, what looked to be freshly folded sheets sitting on the single pillow. Heaven.

The battered-looking dresser was cluttered with newspapers, camera film and notebooks. A cramped bathroom tiled in white was next to the bedroom. A shower just big enough for one thin person, a cast iron claw-foot tub and toilet took up most of the space. She didn't dare pull back the shower curtain. Towels lay strewn across the floor. Judging by the musty smell that filled the room, they'd been there a while. But the small circular tiles on the wall sparkled and coaxed a smile. Perhaps she could just live in the bathroom.

Thirst scratched her throat as she retraced her steps to the kitchen. Her hand shook as she turned the tap. It squeaked and sputtered, then spat out a slow stream of water. Kristin frowned at the brown tinge. She washed her hands but decided not to drink it. She'd have to boil water to keep in the fridge. Assuming there was one.

A brief scan of the room revealed a cubic four by four, almost hidden behind the door. Bits of rust showed through the white paint. She pulled the handle, opened the door and quickly shut it again, gagging as the odor of sour milk reached her nose.

Back in the living room Kristin surveyed the mess. Ear-splitting honks from the street below startled her. Closing the window would be out of the question. An upward glance showed her a ceiling fan, and she tugged the cord. The groan and creaks it gave made her jump out of range, but the blades began to move and warm air circled around her. Better than nothing.

Kristin went back into the bedroom, her muscles aching. She stretched her arms over her head and yawned. Maybe she'd take a nap while she waited for Caroline to show up. The empty bed was tempting. Another yawn overtook her. And suddenly sleep was the only thing that made sense.

Luke Maddox entered his apartment, chucked his duffel bag across the living room and shuddered as a yawn escaped him. Jonno sauntered in and gave a low whistle.

"Holy cow, what happened in here? Looks like a tornado hit the place, man."

Luke ignored his friend's observations and made for the kitchen. He yanked on the rusted fridge door, scanned the contents and quickly stepped back. Whatever he'd left in there had died a slow and painful death. Moldy cheese, maybe. Combined with milk—yellow milk, and…well, he didn't know what that was. Something green and slimy, definitely not edible. Only a jug of boiled water hiding on the bottom shelf remained safe. Madame came in to refill it every morning.

He shut the door and let out the breath he'd been holding. "There's no grub. I haven't been home in a while. Sorry." He returned to the living room to find Jonno already stretched out on the couch.

"No sweat. Too tired to eat anyway. I'm just gonna…sleep." Jonno turned on his side, pulled an issue of TIME from under his head and dropped the magazine to the floor.

Luke pushed his fingers through his hair and frowned. Dirt was embedded in his pores. He knew if he looked in the mirror his face would be covered in the red soil they'd ripped over for half the night. He'd shower and get some sleep too.

If he could shut his mind off long enough.

He clenched his jaw and strode to the window, pulled the camera strap over his head and set the Nikon down on the round table. Photographs covered almost the entire wooden surface. He poked at the black and white prints with a grimy finger.

Glancing over his shoulder, Luke saw Jonno's eyes flutter closed. He turned back to the table, pushed the pictures out of the way and retrieved a small leather wallet hidden beneath them. He never took it with him. Couldn't risk losing it.

He flipped it open and allowed his eyes to rest on the familiar smiling images. Melissa's two year-old cheeky grin tugged at his heart. The dull ache in his chest returned.

"Y'all get any good shots yesterday?" Jonno's Southern drawl drifted across the room.

A smile inched up one corner of Luke's mouth and he pushed the wallet back under the other pictures. "Thought you were asleep."

Silence. Another yawn from Jonno.

"Luke?"

"What?" He placed his palms flat on the table and drew in a breath. Exhaustion pummeled him. Couldn't remember when he'd last slept.

"Do you ever wonder if…if it's the right thing to do?"

Luke pulled at the collar of his damp T-shirt and squared his shoulders. It wasn't that he couldn't answer the question. He did answer it, every day, each time he went back out there and stepped into hell. But lately his answers didn't sound as convincing.

His jaw throbbed and he rubbed the bruised spot. He couldn't bring himself to turn around. "I can have you transferred to somebody else. Just say the word."

"Nah." Jonno grunted "Don't sweat it. I'm cool."

"Okay. Sleep. I'm going to shower."

Kristin stirred from deep slumber. She glanced around the room, getting her bearings. Sun filtered through thin curtains, so perhaps she hadn't slept that long. She swung her legs to the floor and leaned over in a long stretch. Then bolted upright.

'You're listening to Armed Forces Radio, Vietnam. Current time is 9.0.0. We're looking for a high of ninety-eight degrees today, folks. Now, here's a little Rolling Stones to get you going this fine morning. 'It's Not Easy'. You all stay safe out there…'

The radio. Kristin ran a hand down her face and let out her breath. Caroline must have arrived. Male laughter filtered through the closed door. And brought some friends back with her.

She worked the kinks out of her neck, pushed herself off the bed and wandered barefoot across the threadbare carpet out into the next room.

"Don't move."

Kristin jumped back and stared into the barrel of a small pistol.

Chapter Two

*T*he man holding the gun towered her and pinned her with an accusatory glare. Air hissed from her lungs as she stared up at him. He was dressed from the waist down in khaki pants, a towel slung around his neck. A large bruise shadowed the right side of his jaw.

"Who are you? What are you doing in here?" His upper lip curled as he snarled the words in a decidedly British accent.

Kristin's knees threatened to give way. Her vision blurred and her throat dried up. She might die of heart failure before he shot her. "I'm… Kristin Taylor. I'm a journalist, from Boston. I—I've been invited."

"Invited by whom?" Two vertical grooves formed between blond brows. He didn't lower the gun.

"Luke! Take it easy, man!" A young black man in Army uniform struggled off the couch behind them. He held up a hand, but remained a safe distance away. Her heart refused to keep still but she forced herself to think. Whoever Luke was, he obviously had no intention of "taking it easy", and G.I. Joe over there wasn't about to help. Kristin veered her gaze back to the small pistol still pointed at her and wondered what her father would have done right about now.

Her assailant ignored the other man's protest. "Who told you to come here?"

"Caroline…" Kristin fished out the scrunched up piece of paper from the pocket of her jeans and frantically tried to make sense of the chicken scratch. Her hands shook so badly she could hardly hold the paper steady. Her earlier thoughts of *Psycho* hadn't been that far off the mark. "… Maddox. We met on the plane. She said she needed a flat-mate. Told me she'd meet me here…I swear I'm telling the truth."

The man stared like she'd spoken in Swahili, then let out his breath in a loud rush of air. He set the gun down on the table and swore. Twice. Kristin's pulse slowed, warm relief rushing through her. So she wasn't going to die this morning. But she kept her eyes trained on him, just in case.

He raked his fingers through his shoulder-length wet hair, and shook his head. "Look, I'm sorry. You're in the wrong apartment. My sister lives next door. First on the left."

"What?" The information filtered through her brain as she allowed her eyes to move around the room. "Are you sure?"

His eyebrows inched even closer together. "Pretty sure this was my place last time I checked, yeah."

G.I. Joe let out a snort and moved toward her. "You okay, ma'am?"

He spoke in a deep Southern accent, and she appreciated the concern in his eyes. He was younger than the tall man, she'd put him at about twenty, if that, barely out of high school. A little stocky, but it suited him.

Kristin nodded. "I'm fine." Still breathing, and not dead.

"You gotta take a sharp turn at the top of the stairs. The door is easy to miss, 'specially in that dark hallway." The young man's dark green fatigues displayed the yellow and green Private First Class insignia on his shoulders.

She remembered the camera equipment and film in the bedroom, and she scanned the photographs covering the table. Maybe this Luke guy was a journalist of some sort, a photographer. Or, given what he'd just put her through, an escapee from the nearest mental institution. If they had such things in Vietnam.

"Who did you say you were again?" Luke's scrutinizing gaze whipped across her face, his mouth set in a frown she suspected to be permanent.

Blood rushed back to her brain. "You just pulled a gun on me. Who are you?"

He stepped back, the barest grin lifting the corners of his mouth. "Luke Maddox. And I thought you were an intruder."

"I gathered that." Kristin processed the last few moments of her life and willed her hands to stop trembling. Nausea attacked without warning and she bent over, palms spread just above her knees. Dizziness swirled and bright sparks flashed before her eyes.

God, please don't let me faint... She made a mental note to write her mother and inform her she'd remembered how to pray.

"You okay?" Luke put an arm out to steady her and she backed off. He raised both hands in mock surrender. "Maybe you should sit a minute."

"I'm fine."

He took her arm anyway, guided her to one of the teak chairs near the window and pushed her into it. She still couldn't focus. The private dashed to the kitchen, returning with a glass of water. Kristin eyed it with suspicion.

"I got it from the fridge. It's fine. I think."

She caught the wary glance he sent Luke's way, but took the glass. "Thank you. What's your name?"

"Private First Class Jonathan Hicks, ma'am. But they call me Jonno." His grin was a wide display of white teeth against his dark skin.

Kristin took a sip of the cold water, tension still gripping her shoulders. "Thanks, Jonno. And you can drop the ma'am."

"Is this your stuff?" Luke Maddox came out of the bedroom with her duffel bag in one hand, her shoes in the other. Kristin could barely nod as he dumped them at her feet. "You should probably go lie down. Next door. You look like you've been dragged through a swamp backwards."

She pushed a few photographs out of the way before putting her glass on the table. "First you threaten to kill me, now you're insulting me?"

Luke cleared his throat, surprise inching over his face. "You want me to apologize again?"

She folded her arms across her chest and pushed down fear. His gun still sat on the table.

"My sincerest apologies, Miss Taylor, for presuming you might be dangerous. Now, if you think you can find your way out...I have things to do." He tipped his head toward the door.

Kristin rose, reached for her bag and forced her body to move. The private was at her side in an instant.

"Let me give you a hand."

"Thank you." Kristin let him heave her bag over his shoulder. "Sorry about the mix-up." She tossed the words in Luke's general direction.

He stood at the window, his back to her. She couldn't pinpoint his age, put she wouldn't put him over thirty. He rested his elbows on the top of the window frame and laced his hands around the back of his damp head, his hair just reaching the nape of his neck.

"Luke's just a little skittish, is all." Jonno's grin made her feel better. "You just flew in, huh?"

"Jonno, the war's not gonna wait for you, mate," Luke said. One foot tapped out an erratic beat on the threadbare rug beneath him.

"Shoot. Won't miss much." Jonno strolled to the door, looking back at Kristin. "You got your kit yet?"

"My kit? Oh, right." He meant the clothes she'd need when she visited the base camps or went into the field. "No. I wasn't sure where to go. I planned to do that today. I arrived last night. I mean this morning." She gave a laugh. "Actually, I have no idea what day it is right now."

"In Vietnam it doesn't matter." The quiet words came from Luke.

Something made Kristin stop again. "Are you a journalist too, Mr. Maddox?"

He made a slow turn and pulled on the towel still draped around his neck. "I'm a photographer." His eyes went to the pictures on the table. "As you may have guessed."

He had to be well over six feet and it was hard not to feel intimidated under the weight of his stare. But he would have information she needed, if he could bring himself to be helpful. Kristin held her sneakers by their laces and twirled them in a wide circle. "Is there a place nearby I can get something to eat?" Food. She'd start there. Maybe she should just wait for Caroline, but her stomach was telling her otherwise.

"Sure. We could take you out," Jonno offered before Luke could speak. "Show y'all around a bit."

"No. *We* could not." Luke gave his counterpart a pointed stare, one eyebrow almost touching his hairline.

Jonno shrugged and rubbed his round jaw. "Well, now if memory serves me correct, Luke, you just about killed the lady. I'd say it was the least you could do."

Luke grunted and shoved his hands into his pockets.

"I'm sure Miss Taylor would prefer to find her own way."

Kristin almost choked on spit. This guy made her ex-boss look like Gloria Steinem. She pushed her feet into her sneakers, not bothering to tie the laces. Getting answers from Luke Maddox was clearly not going to happen. "You're right. I manage to find my way quite well, thank you."

"And do you find 'your way' into men's apartments very often, Miss Taylor?" A hint of a smile teased his mouth.

Tiny needles of heat pricked her face. "I won't be bothering you again, I can promise you that." She reached for her knapsack and started for the door again, but he blocked her path. She didn't stifle her sigh of aggravation. "If you'll let me through…"

He didn't move. "Okay, look, I'm sorry. I've been traveling all night. I may have…over-reacted."

Kristin squeaked. "You could have killed me!"

He leveled his gaze, the smile gone. "I would have gone for the shoulder."

Kristin shuddered and attempted to push past him. He stayed put, studying her with an air of calm. Like he was examining a specimen. "What are you doing in Vietnam?" He shook his head, his upper lip curling again. "Never mind. I don't care. But I'll tell you this; if you came here looking for adventure, this isn't a Debutantes Ball. It's war. Men are being killed out there. As you'll find out, if you stick around long enough. Think you're ready for that?"

"Luke, cut it out." Jonno gave her a sympathetic look.

Kristin squared her shoulders and matched his stare. "I know what to expect."

"Who are you going to be working for?"

"Myself."

He nodded. "A stringer. No papers, press card?" He scratched the blond stubble on his jaw.

"I'll get them."

"Come on, Luke." Jonno moved in and placed a hand on Luke's shoulder. "Be cool for once, huh? We can help her get her stuff and take her out to the 24th." His kind eyes moved over Kristin's face. "If you can get a couple of pieces sold, you'll be on your way. Newspapers are hungry for stories. They don't much care where they come from."

Kristin considered the soldier's offer, but the thought of going anywhere with Luke Maddox clouded her judgment. "Thanks, Jonno, but I'll manage." She walked to the door.

"Hold on." Luke's voice stopped her.

She turned, weariness dragging on her. "What now?"

He lifted his broad shoulders, a thin smile chasing off his scowl for just a moment. "You can do what you want, but we're heading north tomorrow morning. If you'd like some help getting your kit, and a ride, you can come along. If you prefer to go it alone, suit yourself."

Kristin hesitated, almost enticed, but shook her head. No story was worth sharing air space with Norman Bates. "No, thanks. I apologize for intruding." She yanked the door handle and stepped out into the dark hallway, slamming the door behind her.

Early morning heat bathed her like a thick mud bath as Kristin walked the pavements the next day, searching for the shop Caroline told her she'd be able to buy her kit from.

After sleep and a spicy meal at the nearby restaurant Jonno recommended, Kristin had returned to the apartment. The right one, this time, and Caroline finally showed up, with a handsome army captain in tow. Peter something…Kristin couldn't remember his last name.

Caroling laughed about the mix-up with her brother. Kristin didn't relish the idea of running into the man again, but given the options, she accepted Caroline's offer to stay.

Today she was determined not to waste time. She must have turned down a wrong street. If she could get herself to The Caravelle, she might run into Jean Luc. He would help her. As she looked left and right, fear and frustration closed in around her.

A horn's blast came from behind and Kristin jumped, but kept walking. The hotel had to be just around this corner.

"Hey, Miss Taylor!"

Kristin turned. A military Jeep pulled up to the curb. Jonno sat in the passenger seat. Luke Maddox behind the wheel. Jonno waved to her like she was an old friend. "Miss Tay-lah! Over here."

She adjusted her headscarf and let off a bit of tension with a smile. Slowly she approached the vehicle. "Hi, Jonno."

"Where y'all headed?" Jonno wanted to know. His companion looked impatient.

Kristin shifted, sweat sliding down her back. "I thought I'd go over to The Caravelle. Some journalists I met on the plane are staying there."

Luke snorted, his eyes hidden behind a pair of aviator sunglasses. "The Caravelle is the other way."

Of course it was.

"Hey, look," Jonno set his boyish grin on her. "Why don't you just come with us? We can help you get your stuff, and you can ride with us today. What d'ya say?"

Luke huffed and slouched down in his seat.

Kristin narrowed her eyes. She didn't relish the thought of spending a day with The Odd Couple. "Thanks, Jonno, what if you just give me directions?"

Luke swiveled, his shades slipping down his nose. "Are you always this stubborn?"

"Yes."

His mouth stretched into a slow grin. "God help us."

"All right." Kristin sighed and nodded toward Jonno. "I guess some help would be nice."

Jonno hopped out to help her into the front seat. She declined the front and climbed into the back. Luke pulled out and suddenly it hit her. "Hey!" She poked Jonno, shouting to be heard over the noise. "He's not... This is a Military Jeep! Shouldn't you be driving?"

"Yeah!" Jonno laughed as Luke swerved across incoming traffic to get to the opposite side. Once headed in the right direction, stuck behind a bus, Luke glanced over his shoulder. His scruff-covered face revealed a hint of what could be a nice smile. "Welcome to Vietnam, Miss Taylor."

Twenty minutes later, after several traffic jams, near misses and a narrow escape from colliding with a bus, they found parking and walked toward place where they said she'd find everything she needed for the field.

Luke strode ahead down the dusty sidewalk. Kristin gave up on matching his pace. Even though she wore light cotton pants and a sleeveless blouse, moving at any speed in this sweltering climate was torture. She wiped perspiration out of her eyes and plodded on.

Small shops and restaurants like the ones she'd seen on the drive from the airport lined the streets. Women crouched on the sidewalk, cooking over a fire. Thick spicy smoke hung in the air mixing with exhaust fumes somehow prodded hunger. Caroline had scribbled down directions to where she shopped for food, but Kristin hadn't yet been able to crack the code of her new flat-mate's handwriting.

Children darted around the pedestrians. Honks and shouts of impatient drivers added to the pandemonium. She almost tripped over a small child who ran up alongside her, his dirty little hand outstretched. A group of about ten children followed them, chattering away in Vietnamese. They pressed in, surrounding her on all sides. Shabby clothes and bare feet tugged at her heart as their hands tugged on her arms. She faced a sea of toothless grins and wide smiles.

Kristin searched her pockets for anything to give them. Her fingers brushed against her bother's letter, reminding her to ask Jonno about locating him. She found a pack of gum, crouched by the children and began doling out strips.

Luke returned to where Jonno waited, and she heard his low voice rise in warning. She looked up to see Luke waving off a couple of larger boys. One of them fell off the sidewalk. Luke lunged for the boy's arm, pulled him out of harm's way and sent him off with a push and a sharp reprimand. She couldn't make out his words, but heard enough to decide it was hardly fitting language to use in front of a child, even if he didn't understand English.

"Why did he yell at them like that?" She turned to Jonno for help.

"He's telling them to get lost."

"That's ridiculous." Kristin left the kids, looking downward as she sidestepped a bottle. When she glanced up again, Luke stood in front of her, brawny tanned arms crossed, eyes glinting at her over the rim of his sunglasses.

"Problem?"

"What were you saying to that boy? I saw you push him away."

His mouth turned downward. One finger inched his shades up and his eyes went into hiding. "He wanted money. Sometimes a firm hand is the only thing they respond to."

"That's absurd. They're just children." Kristin caught her breath.

Luke sighed and took off his sunglasses. His expression seemed softer somehow. Or she was getting heatstroke. "Look, you may as well get used to the kids. They're everywhere. There's an orphanage around the corner. Another one two blocks away. If you give them anything, they'll never leave you alone."

Kristin shifted under the glare of the sun. "You make them sound like criminals."

Luke put his glasses back on and raked his fingers through his hair. "That's what they are, some of them. Not intentionally maybe, but they're desperate. They'll take whatever you have, whether you give it to them or not." Suddenly he grabbed her arm and yanked her sideways as a bicycle sped past. Kristin stared after it in disbelief. She hadn't even seen it coming.

She looked back at the children who followed them at a safe distance. A little boy ran up to her, his hand outstretched. Kristin hesitated. His protruding belly and soulful eyes were impossible to ignore. Maybe she could give him some money, enough for a meal. She slid her backpack off and opened it.

Luke placed a hand over her wrist and shook his head. "Don't give them anything."

"I can't just pretend they're not there."

"All right. Hey, đi đi!" He yelled in Vietnamese, clapped his hands together and the kids ran off. "There. Now you don't have to pretend." He tipped his head toward the building in front of them. "We're going in here."

Kristin followed him into what looked like a house from the street. Once her vision adjusted to the dim light, she saw a cavernous room with tables upon tables of any item imaginable. A couple of Vietnamese men watched in silence. The musty smelling shop appeared unlike any she'd ever been in. Transistor radios, books, military maps.

Jean Luc had alluded to the black market activity in Vietnam, but she hadn't heard much about it back home. This might be a story.

Kristin lifted an olive green canvas tarp spread over one table. She stared at the row of automatic weapons and pistols hidden beneath it. She poked a finger at what looked to be an M-16, but pulled back when a hand came down over hers.

"Stay away from the toys, Miss Taylor, there's a good girl." Luke placed a hand under her elbow and propelled her in a different direction.

"Where did they get all this stuff?" she hissed.

Luke glanced her way and hiked up an eyebrow. "You don't want to know."

The proprietor hurried over to them and addressed Luke by name. Luke returned the greeting and explained what they needed. After some haggling, they'd talked the old man into what Jonno told her was a decent price for the things she needed. Jungle fatigues in her size, a canteen, a waterproof poncho, helmet and boots. The shopkeeper tried to sell her a pistol, but she'd refused.

Jonno dragged them into a nearby restaurant and they ordered a quick meal. She was going to have to get used the food here too. Once they were on the road again, she examined her purchases and shoved off the thought of wearing some dead soldier's gear. Immediately her thoughts turned to Teddy.

Luke yelled over his shoulder to her as the Jeep sped along the street. "You coming north with us, Taylor? Offer still stands."

Trepidation almost won, but she pushed back doubt and nodded. "Yes, please!" she shouted back.

They screeched to a stop outside the apartment building. Luke hopped out. "Need to grab some more film. Meet us back here in fifteen minutes."

Kristin gathered her things. She'd change clothes quickly, and then it was off...to whatever awaited her outside the confines of the city.

Chapter Three

uke swore as he paced the small square kitchen in his apartment. His job was difficult enough. He didn't have time to play tour guide to some greenhorn reporter fresh off the plane.

He glanced at his watch. Jonno had gone to mail some letters, but would probably be back any minute. Still…enough time…Luke marched to the kitchen and foraged through the cupboards. Where was it? Months earlier, when he'd vowed to change his ways and stay sober, he'd thrown everything out. But he'd missed a bottle tucked behind the pots, found it one day and decided to keep it. For emergencies.

Like now.

His hands shook as he pushed aside a box of saltine crackers. Kristin Taylor was not what he needed right now. The way she'd matched his stare, unflinching. She had no idea what Vietnam was like. What he, Jonno and Caroline, and the men in the field endured here…what she'd soon have to face.

Luke winced at the memory of how close he'd come to actually shooting her.

Ah, there you are…Luke's hand closed around the glass bottle and pulled it off the shelf. Set it down on the scratched Formica countertop and backed up. The light brown liquid inside swirled and settled, beckoning. He folded his arms and set his jaw.

It would certainly make the rest of the day more bearable. Then again, if he went out blitzed, he certainly wouldn't be at his best. That was too dangerous. And he needed new shots to send to Hayden, his boss back in the US. Aggravation tightened the muscles in his shoulders. Maybe he shouldn't have offered a ride to the girl.

Luke grabbed the neck of the bottle, unscrewed the cap and brought it about a half inch away from his lips. Temptation singed his nostrils. The thirst could have him belly-crawling in moments, ready to take him down. He could already taste it…remember what it was like to forget…to feel nothing.

But nothing was ever really gone. The pain always came back, just as strong and often worse. Nothing was strong enough to release the shackles of memories, the aching they caused him every waking moment.

He deserved every bit of it.

Luke took one small sip and let the liquid fire burn down his throat. Then he lowered the bottle and sucked in a long breath.

He moved toward the sink, tipped the bottle upside down and watched the liquor slowly disappear down the drain. Luke closed his eyes. He hadn't prayed in a while. Seemed a good time to start up again.

Kristin stepped out onto the pavement right on time, and spied the dirt-splattered Jeep parked against the curb. Luke and Jonno sat up front, drinking bottles of Coca-Cola. Jonno glanced her way as she approached, his eyes widening under the brim of his cap as he let out a wolf whistle. "Looking sharp there, Miss Taylor."

Kristin noted the scowl garnered from Luke. She gave Jonno a mock salute, then heaved her pack over the side of the Jeep, and climbed in after it. The olive-colored army pants and lightweight cotton shirt were far more breathable than anything she'd brought with her. Plus she wouldn't stand out in the field. Assuming she made it that far.

Luke turned her way. "It'll be better for you to hitch a ride on a Huey or some other bird next time you go out to a base camp. But when you're riding with us, you follow my instructions. If I say get down, you get down. Understand?"

Kristin rolled her eyes. "Despite what you may think, I do know we're not going to Disneyland." She adjusted the leather strap of her camera around her neck and shifted on the hot vinyl seat.

"Do you want to ride with us or not?" Luke growled.

Her heart picked up speed, but her mind raced even faster. He didn't scare her. Much. "Yes. Where exactly are we going?"

"North." Luke shook his head and faced forward, starting the engine. "Do as I say and ask questions later. Got it?"

Luke veered past cars, then stopped in the never-ending line of traffic. He soon changed lanes to pass a truck. He gunned the engine, and Kristin was flung back against the seat. She rubbed the back of her neck. If she endured many rides with this man, she'd soon have a severe case of whiplash. Her hands tightened around the helmet on her lap as they bounced along. "North where? Which camp?" The chance that she might actually find her brother on her first day was slim to none, but Kristin entertained the thought anyway.

"Long Binh." Jonno answered, handing her a dog-eared map and pointing to a spot on it. "24th Surgical Hospital, and base camp for my company. You're gonna love it. It's right on the ocean. We're about an hour or two away, depending on traffic, and…well…other delays."

Oh, she didn't like the sound of that. "Other delays? Like what, exactly?"

Jonno just laughed.

As they drove along Highway 1, she snapped pictures whenever Luke slowed to a suitable speed, which wasn't often. Vietnamese men, women and children walked or cycled along the side of the road. Some of the children waved and shouted at them.

"Hello!" Kristin waved back before she caught sight of the middle finger they were all holding up.

Luke's quiet laughter set Jonno off.

"It's not that funny. Where'd they learn that?" She stared back at the kids still cheerfully giving her the Hawaiian peace sign.

Luke glanced at her in the rear view. "GIs."

Endless strips of green rice paddies stretched around them. Farmers wearing those broad hats worked the fields, driving water buffalo. Mountains rose up to her left, high and lush, bare patches of burnt ground—remnants of war—just visible. Tiny wisps of smoke could be seen here and there filtering through the trees. To the right an ocean of deepest blue came into view. Kristin inhaled salty air mingled with smoke residue. The air, though hot, felt good against her face as they flew past the fields.

That peculiar feeling of playing tourist swept over her again and brought memories of summer holidays spent on the Cape. For all outward appearances, the countryside looked beautiful—a place of peace and harmony. But up in those mountains, the battle raged.

As if in agreement, intermittent explosions could just be heard over the sound of the Jeep's engine. Another loud boom shook the road and Kristin inched down in her seat. This was definitely not a vacation.

After a few hours of driving without a break, the camp came into view. Barbed wire fencing surrounded by sand bags stretched out along the road. Broad loops of sharp metal seemed to run for miles. A couple of watchtowers could just be seen, with a landing strip set at the far end of the camp closest to the base of the mountain. A large hand-painted wooden sign welcomed them to the 24th Surgical Hospital. Luke turned into the gates at breakneck speed. Two GIs nodded acknowledgement as they sped through. At last the Jeep slowed, along with Kristin's heart rate.

Kristin took in her surroundings, scribbling notes as they went. The size of the camp surprised her. There were more buildings than she'd expected, and she noticed the overhead power wires. Long wooden structures with tin roofs were positioned along the roads, sand bags piled high around them too. Vietnamese women hurried by, carrying armfuls of clothes.

Kristin raised an eyebrow. "What are they doing?"

"Laundry," Jonno told her. "They work in the camp, cleaning, keeping house for the officers. We call them Mama-sans."

"Interesting. And they don't mind working for us?" She wondered about welcoming in the enemy, but filed away the thought for future discussion.

Jonno shrugged. "Gotta make a buck. It's better than being kicked out of your hut and having nowhere to go."

GIs strolled along the side of the paved road, some greeted Luke and Jonno by name. They came to a row of several semi-circular buildings constructed of corrugated sheet metal, each one with a large red cross painted on it. Luke brought the Jeep to a shuddering halt in front of it. Another hand-painted sign overhead declared their destination to be "The Army's Best Hospital."

Luke disappeared without a word. Jonno helped her down and grabbed her bag. "I can introduce you to the Colonel if you want. If he's not too busy." He adjusted his cap and gave his Cheshire cat grin.

Kristin took her pack from him. "Sure. That would be great."

She followed Jonno into the medical building, taking mental notes as they walked down a well-lit hall. The strong scent of antiseptic accosted her. She peered into a couple of rooms as she passed, nodding to the wounded men who eyed her with curiosity. A lot of the cots lay empty, folded blankets and surgical trays at the ready in eerie foreboding.

Kristin waited as Jonno rapped on a door at the end of the hall. He entered and she heard a few words being exchanged, then Jonno reappeared, beckoning her in.

He held the door open for her. "Miss Taylor, this is Colonel Maddox."

"Maddox?" Kristin hissed, staring at Jonno. "Is this some kind of army joke?"

Jonno's eyes widened, his grin appearing for a moment. "No Ma'am. The Colonel is Luke and Caroline's dad. They didn't tell you?"

Kristin sighed and shook her head.

Inside the small room, a man in green surgical scrubs looked up from his position behind the desk. He stood as she entered and she saw the resemblance at once. Tall and lean, his silver-streaked hair was the only indication of his age. She'd put him in his late fifties, early sixties at most. Like Luke, he was handsome, but held himself in a more dignified manner. Kristin hoped his personality did not match his son's.

"Miss Taylor, welcome. I'm Douglas Maddox. Most of the boys around here call me Doc. It's a little cliché, I suppose." He extended a hand. Kristin shook it. His glanced at Jonno, who still stood in the doorway. "Where's Luke?"

"Probably getting something to eat, Sir."

The colonel nodded and took his seat again. "Why don't you go join him, then? I'll brief Miss Taylor on protocol here. Dismissed, Private." He indicated the empty chair across from him. "Sit down, Kristin…was it?"

"Yes." Jonno sauntered off and Kristin positioned herself on the metal chair. She ran her tongue over her lips and tasted dirt and sweat.

"Private Hicks tells me you're a journalist, staying at Luke's?"

"No!" Kristin's eyes flew wide. "I mean…I am…in the same building. Though I did somehow manage to wake up in his bed." She clapped a hand over her mouth. What was wrong with her? "It was a mistake…I mean…he wasn't there." Oh, wonderful. "I…I'm sharing an apartment with Caroline."

"I…see…" The colonel's raised brows and slightly amused expression said he wouldn't dare go further on the topic. "How is my daughter?"

"I haven't seen much of her, sir. I've just arrived."

"Ah. Well, she travels around a lot. What paper are you working for?" His smile put her at ease, but the question didn't.

"Well, I'm sort of…on my own at the moment." Kristin balked at her attempt to sound professional. She wasn't sure whether her nerves were due to the fact that he was a colonel or Luke's father.

"So you're hoping to write a few stories and get picked up?" He raised an eyebrow.

"That's the plan." Kristin smiled and waited for him to throw her out.

"Well, good luck to you. I hope you get to stay in-country a while."

"Thank you, Colonel. Would it be all right if I looked around a bit? I promise I won't be a bother."

He held up a hand. "Just as long as you stay out of the way when necessary, and do as you're told, we won't mind you being here. But you will need to get your press credentials if you want to work. You know that?"

"Yes, sir." Exactly how, she hadn't figured out.

"Have you talked to my son? He might be able to be of assistance."

Kristin stifled a laugh. "I'll do that, sir."

"Good. But I'll warn you, if you can't respect orders or I get complaints about you, I'll kick you out. My personnel and the boys we're taking care of here have to come first. Understand?"

"Yes, sir. Of course." Kristin nodded. Okay, down to business. "How many doctors do you have here?"

He leaned back in his chair, pride shining from his eyes. "We're a smaller unit. I've got twenty docs and fifty nurses here at the moment, some of the best in the medical field in my opinion. I'm honored to be working with this bunch."

"And are you pretty busy all the time?"

"Usually. It's worse at night. Not much going on today, but that'll change."

Kristin fired off a few more questions and jotted notes as he talked.

After a while the colonel rounded the desk. "Let me show you around. Did Luke and Private Hicks take care of you in the city? Got you everything you needed?"

She felt a smile pulling up the corners of her mouth. If he considered being held at gunpoint being taken care of… "They did, thank you."

"Excellent. We'll start in Recovery. I've got six men in there today. One head injury, shrapnel burns, nothing major. As I'm sure you know, there's no censorship here. You can write whatever they will publish. But, another warning—some of the men may not want to talk. You need to understand that. What they've seen and heard…well, you'll get an idea soon enough."

Kristin grunted agreement, but a knot formed in her stomach. "Yes, sir." And just how was she supposed to get a story if nobody talked?

A few hours later, Kristin had filled half her notepad and had taken photographs around the camp. Doc left her outside the mess hall, instructing her to get something to eat.

She entered the busy room and looked around. Soldiers, nurses and doctors mingled together, eating and chatting. She nodded in greeting when she saw Jonno, and he made his way over to her. "Are you hungry? Food's not great, but it ain't bad."

Kristin followed him around and took the food doled out to her. Greasy ham, glue-like potatoes, peas, some bread and a Coke. Jonno laughed as she screwed up her nose. But hunger overrode uncertainty and she filled her plate.

Laughter and loud conversation rang through the Quonset hut. They sat at a long wooden table surrounded by soldiers. Most were happy, if not eager to chat with her. The ones she spoke with ranged in age from nineteen to twenty-nine. She learned a few had been drafted, but most enlisted on their own. Some were serving a second tour. Not many of them seemed to discount their presence in Vietnam. And every one of them had a story. Within an hour, she'd filled the other half her notebook.

A few of the men had run into Teddy's company, but none knew him. Kristin scanned the room. As people sauntered in and out of the mess hall, the solitary figure in the corner of the room caught her eye.

Luke Maddox.

He leaned against the table, his boots resting on the bench in front of him. His gaze seemed fixed on the blank wall across the room. A tray of food sat on the table, untouched. Kristin watched him, waiting for him to move, but he didn't.

"What's his story?"

Jonno's soft sigh indicated she'd spoken out loud. "Luke?"

Kristin looked over at him and noted the sad look in his eyes. She nodded, wiping her brow with the back of her hand. Jonno hesitated. For a moment she thought he might give an answer, but he shrugged. "We don't talk about it. And don't you go asking him nothing."

A prickling sensation inched down her spine. She watched in fascination as Jonno worked on a small piece of wood with his army knife. "What are you making?"

Jonno glanced up. "Stick people." He grinned and wiggled the piece of wood at her. "Stick? Get it? Stick people."

Kristin laughed and the muscles in her neck began to relax. "How long have you been over here, Jonno?"

"A year and a half."

"Are you stationed in the city?"

"Yeah. They send me all over. I got stuck running press around. Mostly Luke. But it's okay. Better than being out in the field, that's for dang sho'."

"I bet. My brother's here too. Not exactly sure where though."

"Yeah?" He continued to flick small curls of wood onto the floor. "Maybe you'll run into him, huh?"

"I hope to. Asked a few of the guys already, but nobody knows him." She picked up a piece of the thin paper-like material and curled it around her finger, a flash of Christmas darting through her mind. Mom used to spend hours curling reams of colorful ribbon that she and Teddy would rip off their presents in under a minute. Enough. She couldn't spend all her time thinking about Teddy. Or home. "What part of the South are you from, Jonno?"

"Georgia. Just outside Atlanta." He yawned and rolled his broad shoulders. Then he fished in his pockets and held a small object toward her with a grin. "Here you go."

The wooden carving mirrored her own image with startling accuracy. He'd even painted on brown hair, a pretty close match to hers. The poor thing's mouth was a wide blotch of red—no doubt similar to how she'd looked when Luke Maddox pulled that gun on her.

"Thanks, Jonno. Could you—" She'd been about to ask what the plan was, but Jonno spotted a friend across the room and was off in a flash. She placed her new prized possession into her bag and zipped it up again.

Now what? She glanced at her watch. It was going on seven o'clock. Kristin picked at her meal, ate a bit of the unappetizing food returned her tray to the pile of dirty ones, and eventually rose and walked over to Luke. She dropped her pack on the floor and sat on the far end of the bench. He didn't move. "So. Your father is the Colonel here. Funny how you didn't mention that."

"Must've slipped my mind."

"I'm sure. Are we going back to Saigon tonight?" Kristin asked, forcing a pleasant tone.

"I'm not." He swiveled on the bench, maneuvered his legs under the table and began to turn the pages of a newspaper. She let out a breath. How did he manage to make her feel like an idiot so easily?

"So, I'm staying here then?"

He turned another page and she followed his eyes. The paper was about a week old.

"Unless you want to walk back. It's not a bad jaunt, but in the dark I wouldn't recommend it. VC might getcha."

"Very funny. Where am I supposed to sleep?"

He folded the newspaper and pushed it her way. His eyes roamed over her as he raked long fingers through his mess of straggly hair. "In with the grunts. They won't mind sharing."

"You're kidding me." No way would she share sleeping quarters with these love hungry young soldiers.

"Thought you took any bed you could claim."

She stared at him.

"Could be a story in it for you." Luke's mouth lifted in a grin, a hint of mischief playing in his eyes.

"Ah." Kristin smiled. "Nice to see you've found your sense of humor."

The sparkle in his eyes faded as quickly as it appeared, and his scowl returned. "Nurses' quarters are out back. They'll put you up. Jonno can drive you back tomorrow." He pushed himself off the bench and slung his pack over his shoulder.

"What are you going to do?"

"Work. Probably hitch a ride up to a firebase."

"A firebase? I'd like to go along. When are—"

His laugh cut her off and he wagged a finger in her direction. "No way. I brought you this far. I'm not going to be responsible for you out there. You'll find plenty of stories right here. With any luck, there'll be a dust-off full of wounded soldiers before morning. The ones who can still talk will be all yours. Besides," his grin widened. "It's dangerous out in the field."

Kristin's cheeks burned. "I told you, I don't scare easily. I came here to do a job, Mr. Maddox. I'm more than capable of—"

"Save it, sweetheart." He turned on his heel and strode toward the doors.

Chapter Four

*L*uke yawned, ran a hand over his face then scowled down at his muddy boots. He stood alone in his father's office, hoping to catch a moment with him. His muscles burned and his body begged for sleep.

"Oh good, you're still here."

Luke turned at the sound of Dad's voice. "Yeah. I'll crash somewhere for a couple hours, then get a ride out." He bent to retie the laces of his boots, pulling the frayed strings tight.

"Not taking Jonno with you?" Dad dumped a stack of files on the already cluttered desk.

"Not this time." Luke rose and stretched his arms high over his head, forcing out the tension in his shoulders.

"Be careful." His brow furrowed and Luke choked back a sigh. Dad never stopped fussing. He was worse than a woman.

"I'm always careful." Luke watched the clock on the wall to avoid the worry in his father's eyes. "I gather you met Caroline's new flat-mate."

His father nodded and sank down into the chair behind his desk. "She seems nice enough. And pretty. Driving her up here couldn't have been that painful."

Luke crouched on the floor beside his pack. He foraged through it and checked his equipment. Camera, film…he reached further inside and found his knife. He'd strap it to his ankle later. "She's all right. Got spunk. Once she recovered from our introduction…" He was unable to stay his laughter. "She…uh…sort of wound up in my apartment instead of Caroline's." He heard Dad's short intake of breath and looked up.

"Luke—what did you do?"

"I didn't know who she was." Luke rose, his joints cracking. The memory of the horrified expression on Kristin Taylor's face made him grin again. "I…well, I pulled a gun on her. What was I supposed to do, make her tea?"

Dad raised his eyes to the ceiling and shook his head. "Lord, have mercy on my son."

Luke smiled, swung his pack over one shoulder. "She survived." He checked his watch and then looked back at his father. Apprehension snuck up on him. Dad had that look in his eye.

"Maybe you could help her out. Pass her name along to an editor or two."

"Why would I want to do that?" Luke stepped backward, inching toward the door.

Dad was forever looking out for the underdog. Champion of lost causes. He ran a youth group for years, their basement full to overflowing with teens, most of them rebels, outcasts, looking for trouble. His father found them, drew them in, and gently guided them toward a better path. Then Luke turned thirteen, his mother walked out, Dad joined the Army, and everything changed.

"It's just a suggestion. She seems like a very determined young woman. Asked good questions. Very respectful of everyone, and the boys talked to her. I like her."

"Then you play chauffeur." Luke cleared his throat and ducked out from under Dad's pointed stare. He let out a long sigh. "Fine. I'll think about it." For a millisecond. The less he saw of the aggravating young woman with the penetrating gaze and far too many questions, the better.

His father lifted an eyebrow, a slow smile starting. "You might actually like her if you give her a chance."

Luke snorted. A fly buzzed around him, the low hum annoying. He smacked his hands together, flicking away the now dead object of his irritation. "You've been inhaling too much anesthetic, Doc. Thought you didn't like reporters anyway."

"I don't. But she…she seems different. Sincere."

"Or just stupid." Luke snapped the wristband of his watch. "Miss Taylor is as green as they come. She'll be long gone in a week or two."

Dad laced his hands behind his head and smiled. "I have a feeling she's going to do fine. I just hope she realizes what she's in for."

"Of course she doesn't. None of them do." Luke rubbed his temples, willing his headache away. He needed real food, a full night's sleep and then some. A decent meal around here would take a miracle, and he never slept well.

The young journalist's face flashed across his mind. She had to be younger than him, early twenties, Caroline's age maybe. Headstrong and determined, she didn't have the slightest clue what Vietnam was really like. If she did stick around, that overconfident smile would soon be gone.

"See you, Dad. Take care."

"You too, son. Watch your back. I'll be praying for you."

He agreed with his father on one thing though.

She was attractive.

But even that thought irritated him.

Kristin hid behind the medical building and watched Luke push through the doors. If he was going after a story, well then so was she. He'd have to learn she wouldn't be kept safe.

He moved stealthily through the darkness toward one of the dust-offs—the helicopters—still on the landing pad. He struck up a conversation with two GIs doing repairs on it. She crept forward until she got close enough to hear what they were saying—they wouldn't be taking off anytime soon. Luke let out a low curse and asked the pilot if he could borrow his radio.

Kristin crouched behind some picnic tables and waited, unable to hear anything else. She'd give anything to know who he was calling. The large contraption looked so complicated she wondered how he knew what to do with it.

Luke handed the radio back and strode off in the direction of the camp's perimeter. Kristin quickened her pace and followed him, stopping every time he did, and holding her breath when he turned around. Although hidden in some bushes on the side of the road, she felt sure he could see her. Impossible.

He hovered near the gates of the base camp, crouching down every now and then, scratching the soil with a stick. Kristin's muscles started to stiffen after a while, boycotting her hunched position. Eventually the flash of headlights on the road outside the gates caught her attention. They flashed once then darkness consumed the area again.

Kristin moved to get a better view and her shoelace snagged on a branch. She took a minute to fix the problem then skirted out onto the road again. Luke had disappeared.

Where did you go, Mr. Maddox?

As she debated her next move, a hand clamped around her mouth, preventing her from screaming.

"Do you have a death wish, Miss Taylor?" Luke's warm breath in her ear sent chills down her spine. He held her from behind, one arm pinning her against his chest, the other covering her mouth. She bucked against him, legs flailing. He tightened his hold. "If you kick me again, my gun might accidentally misfire. That would be a shame, considering you've only been in-country what, two days?"

Kristin stopped moving and Luke eased his grip. "When I let you go, you don't scream and you don't run. Got it?"

She nodded. Sinking her teeth into his hand wasn't out of the question.

He released her, stepped back and she stumbled away from him, spitting dirt and who knew what else. "Your hands are filthy."

"I'll wash them next time." The moon slid out from under a cloud and illuminated the dusty road. Luke's eyes glinted in the soft white light as he pushed his pistol back into the holster fastened around his thin waist. "Why were you following me?"

"You said you were going to a firebase."

He gave a low whistle and shook his head. "Didn't my father tell you that you have to take orders?"

"Not from you." Kristin folded her arms. The fire in his eyes threatened to scorch her. The moon disappeared once more and she was grateful.

He rubbed his bearded chin and scuffed the ground with his boot. "I thought you promised you wouldn't be bothering me again. Guess what? You're bothering me."

Kristin ran a hand down her face, pushed hair out of her eyes and summoned calm. "Look, if you could just tell me—"

"Like I said, I won't be responsible for you." Luke shook his head. "Go back to bed. It doesn't stay quiet around here for long."

The thumping of helicopter blades sliced through the calm and woke Kristin from sleep. She tumbled out of her cot and ran after the nurses. The pulsating whir vibrated through her body. Medics sprinted past, their shouts punctured by the noise, yelling out information to the nurses frantically receiving the incoming wounded.

Kristin found herself immersed in the scene being played out before her. It almost felt like watching a movie, but the taste of dirt in her mouth and the throbbing of her pulse smacked of reality.

She set her gaze on the medical building and mustered courage. She had a job to do. Slowly she inched in toward the doors and let herself inside.

The odor of anesthetic clung to the humid air and made her eyes water. Kristin moved out of the way, praying nobody would kick her out. Doctors and nurses weaved around beds with speed and skill amidst the shouts from outside and the groans from the men around them. Their blood-spattered green scrubs gave testimony to the horrors in the room.

Metal clinked as scalpels were passed and trays of surgical equipment wheeled from one bed to the next. Gurneys were pushed in and out as the soldiers were triaged. Agonized moans mingled with the shouted commands from Doc and the other doctors. Above it all, the helicopters kept coming.

The smell of blood and sweat coiled around her and filled her lungs, but she would stay. She wouldn't miss a thing. This was the story. But as another soldier was wheeled past, his body blackened and littered with shrapnel, she felt her courage backing off.

Enough.

Kristin stepped outside and gulped fresh air. Even at night the heat was stifling. Every now and then a breeze lifted off the ocean and engulfed her.

She stood near the landing-pad, shielding her face from flying dirt as yet another helicopter touched down, unloaded the wounded then lifted off as smoothly as it landed.

She returned to the medical building, her pulse racing. Pushed up against a far wall, she witnessed the story unfolding. *The harsh reality of war, what they don't show you on television…* She jumped as Doc slammed through the doors from the operating room, his scrubs stained in dark red patches, barked instructions to one of the nurses and began checking the patients on the cots around her. It was remarkable how they all worked together, moving with such efficiency and care.

When Doc looked her way, his silent warning told her not to start asking questions. So she skirted the perimeter of the long room instead, and took mental notes.

The sounds and smells were making her dizzy. A nurse wheeled another body bag past her and Kristin backed off. How did they deal with this every day? But the instinct to help scraped at her soul and pushed her closer.

"Hey!" One of the nurses she'd bunked with called to her. She stood over a young man who thrashed about in the bed, flinging the IV tube in his arm wildly. Kristin joined her on the other side of him and met the nurse's frantic eyes. "Can you just talk to him? Calm him down? I've given him a sedative. He'll be out soon. I've got to see to the other guys."

"Okay." Kristin reached for the soldier's bloodied hand and mustered a smile. His bare arm displayed a tattoo, a proud symbol of his unit. "Hey, what's your name?" All other thoughts vanished as she focused on his anguished features.

"Corporal Ryan Smith. Am I gonna die?" He stared up at her through wild blue eyes. His face was caked with dirt and blood. A long cut ran the length of his jaw, sutures still oozing. A bloody bandage wrapped around his head.

Kristin wouldn't hazard a guess. She placed a trembling hand on his shoulder. "Take it easy, Corporal."

"They just came out of nowhere! We were on patrol and all of a sudden they started firing at us! We hit the dirt but…oh, man, where's Klein?"

"Klein?" Kristin took a damp cloth from the aluminum surgical bowl beside his bed and wiped his sweaty brow. She looked around for water to give him to drink, but found none within reach.

"Klein, we call him Ozzie, the RTO, he was in back, with the radio…" His words slurred and she leaned in closer to hear him. "I think they got him. I think…they got Ozzie…" His eyes closed and Kristin drew in a breath, panic rising. She reached for his wrist and felt for a pulse. Nice and steady. She almost smiled. He looked about the same age as Teddy.

"RTO?" She looked at the nurse who'd come back over to check on him.

"Radio Telephone Operator. Thanks. I think we're covered here."

Kristin nodded, placed the cloth down and left the young man. Hot tears pricked her eyes. Another man began to yell and she crossed the room to stand by his cot, sweat trickling down her spine. He thrashed around, delirious with pain.

"Hey, there. Hold on. You're safe now." As she took his hand, a vision of her brother in uniform, sprawled across a red dirt road flashed across her mind. She almost saw his face, his eyes wide with fear. Heard the scream rip from his lips.

Nausea rose as the soldier's grip on her hand brought her back to reality. She forced her attention back to him and began to talk again.

Kristin finally stumbled from the tent after what felt like hours. She ran behind the tents, choked on a sob, and retched. Calm, calm, calm…

Her pulse eventually slowed and rational thought returned. She held her head in her hands and willed her mind to stop playing flashbacks. If she was going to survive here, she had to control her emotions.

She'd wanted to see the full truth, the real war.

And, ready or not, she had just found it.

Chapter Five

It seemed impossible that she'd been in the medical building for six hours, but the clock on the wall confirmed it. She now sat in the mess hall with the nurses she'd bunked with, satiated her thirst, but ate little, picking at the food on her plate.

"Thanks for your help in there." Doc stood across the table from her. Bloodstains splattered his green scrubs while exhaustion tinged his features.

Kristin lifted her shoulders. "I didn't do much. You must be wiped out."

His eyes were heavy and bloodshot and he looked as though he might pass out at any moment. "You get used to it. I'll try to nap. No doubt we'll have more company later."

"Is it like this all the time?" She sighed, unable to comprehend it.

The colonel gave a short laugh and shook his head. "That was a slow night, Kristin. Take care now." He patted her shoulder as he passed.

Kristin listened to the conversation around her. The men and women talked of home, of sports and loved ones—anything other than what they'd just gone through. As though they hadn't just operated on countless men with injuries. Men had died in their presence, but they were placing bets on football games.

Kristin made notes and jotted down a few of the nurses' names for potential interviews. Until today, she hadn't known. She'd thought she could handle it, thought she'd been prepared, but the trembling and the nausea she'd experienced told her otherwise. In retrospect, nothing she'd read or seen could have prepared her for this.

Kristin left the mess hall and went outside. The fresh morning air, although hot, revived her a little. She wanted to explore the camp. She took her time, snapped pictures and made notes. She couldn't wait to get back to Saigon and begin writing.

Beyond the buildings, the sound of the ocean intrigued her. As Jonno had promised, the camp bordered on a long strip of white sand and offered a grand view of the South China Sea. Kristin headed along a worn path that led down to the beach. Maybe she could grab a few uninterrupted minutes of solitude before finding a ride back to the city.

"Don't move." Luke Maddox's now familiar drawl brought her to an abrupt halt.

Blood rushed from her cheeks. Not again…

About to turn and give him a piece of her mind, she saw the black snake curled up on the path just a few feet up ahead.

Was it possible to have a heart attack at twenty-four?

Kristin stared down at the reptile that threatened her premature demise.

Rather impressive in size and color, the venomous creature looked peaceful basking in the afternoon sun, but she suspected she'd be done for if it decided to strike.

Suddenly the snake flew up into the air and splattered into bloody bits, showering the sand with its remains. The sound of gunshot sang in her ears and its residue tickled her nose.

She stifled a scream, swiveled and fixed her reluctant gaze on Luke Maddox. "Did you just save my life?"

"Don't worry. I won't tell anyone." He stared at her with what she imagined was disdain. He shifted from one foot to the other, tapping the top of his pistol against the palm of his hand.

She hoped he set the safety.

"Ever see a man step on a land mine, Miss Taylor?"

"No," Kristin squeaked and cleared her throat. What kind of stupid question was that?

"That snake's bite? You'd recover nicely after a few hours. Land mine, not a chance." He shook his head, his lips pressed together. "You're way outside the camp's perimeter. What are you doing out here by yourself?"

"I, uh…I wanted to see the beach." Sweat dripped from her chin. A fly explored the territory around her ears and she swatted it away. "I thought it would be okay."

"Guess you thought wrong." He pushed the gun back into its holster and clucked his tongue. She was beginning to loathe that sound.

Tears of exhaustion threatened to snatch what little dignity she had left and she brushed past him, heading back to camp. "Excuse me."

Luke grabbed her arm, his grip firm, but not rough. "I thought you wanted to see the beach?"

"I did."

"Come on, then. It's this way. This side *isn't* mined." He sidestepped her and led the way down the path. She followed, too afraid not to.

A long stretch of white sand bordered by large gray rocks awaited them. Kristin found a shady spot near a couple of boulders and sank onto the sand with a weary sigh. Luke positioned himself a few feet away.

As she listened to the ocean, her heart found its regular rhythm. Lack of sleep began to tug at her eyes and Kristin blinked under the searing sun. Her gaze veered to the sparkling water. Rushing waves of azure blue crashed onto the beach. She watched the foaming surf roll in and up the shore, pulled back again by some invisible force. For a brief moment, she almost forgot where she was.

Gulls soared overhead, one dropped and soon headed up again, a fish wiggling in its bill. The sun threw golden shards across the sea. Salt spray hit her face, filled her lungs and brought unexpected pleasure.

"It's beautiful." It felt good to smile.

Luke grunted. "The paradox of being in-country."

She nodded. Visions of wounded men re-possessed her thoughts and her smile slipped away. The things she'd seen and heard in the past forty-eight hours hammered at her. She drew her knees up to her chest and placed her head in her hands. If she had been alone, she might have given in to her raging emotions. But with him sitting too close for comfort, she didn't dare.

"My father said you were a big help last night." Luke broke the silence.

"He's kind. I just did what they asked." She shuddered at the memory of the last GI she'd sat with. He'd clung to her, weeping, begging her to get him out of here. To get him home.

"You didn't have to do anything."

A different tone in Luke's voice made her raise her head and look at him.

He stretched out his legs and stared at the horizon. His blond hair lifted in the breeze. Dark shadows circled his eyes, accentuating the haunted look within them.

Perhaps he was more human than she'd given him credit for.

"I've only been in Vietnam a few days and it feels like a lifetime. I have to admit I wasn't prepared for some of what I saw last night." She didn't admit weakness often, and not to a complete stranger, but here, under the heat of the sun, and the strange spell he cast over her, Kristin succumbed.

Luke turned her way and raised an eyebrow. "Were you forced to come here?"

She flinched, but held his stare. "Do you always go for the jugular?"

He flashed a grin and stroked his chin. "Weeds out the wimps a lot quicker." His scrutinizing gaze exposed her, niggled the part of her that was still vulnerable.

"Fair enough." Her cheeks grew warm and she looked away. "I wanted to come. My editor wouldn't send me, so I quit and came on my own."

"You're not the first woman to do that." Luke poked at the sand with a stick.

"I know. Plenty of women have covered the war. Gloria Emerson. Ethel Payne is here. Maggie Higgins, of course." She vaguely recalled her father bringing a few of his colleagues to the house for drinks the year he'd died, and they'd gotten into it, arguing about whether or not women should be allowed to report on the war. Her mother had argued that they shouldn't, but Dad supported it.

He made a point of saving his female colleagues' articles for Kristin, and she'd poured over their stories, amazed at all they had to say. After his death, she'd followed the war more closely, watched as one by one, women began to make their mark on American journalism. Their fierce determination to succeed in the quest for truth spurned her on to follow the trail they had so bravely blazed.

"I loved Dickey Chapelle's writing," she told him. "She was amazing."

"And look what happened to her."

Kristin had just been hired on at *The Daily* two years ago when reports of Chapelle's death rocked the newsroom—the first American female journalist to die during a combat operation.

She swallowed annoyance and shook her head. "She took risks, yes, but she was good at her job, she had a passion for it. I wouldn't be here if I didn't feel the same way. There's no reason a woman can't be a war correspondent. One of these days you boys will realize that."

Luke pitched a stone toward the water and it splashed into an incoming wave. "I doubt it, but go ahead, try and convince us."

Kristin was too tired to argue, her thoughts drifting back to the scenes from the previous night. "I guess I'll get used to it. Seeing…things like I saw last night." Death. She brushed sand off her olive green trousers and rubbed the small grains from her hands. "My brother is out there somewhere. He shipped over here almost three months ago."

"I'm sorry to hear that." His tone softened. "What's his name?"

"Ted Taylor. He's a medic. Wants to be a doctor when he gets out. I don't know his location. He probably doesn't know I'm here yet." She rubbed the top of her nose and battled the fear that always accompanied thoughts of Teddy. Her eyes began to sting again. A change of subject was in order. "Don't you think it's strange, you, your sister and your father all being here at the same time?"

Luke shrugged, picked up a twig and snapped it in half. "It's a strange war."

That it was.

"Why do you carry a gun?"

"To save young journalists from snakes."

"Right. And don't forget threatening young journalists."

He grinned and shoved his fingers through his thick hair. "I thought I apologized."

"Oh, that's what that was." She sniffed and ran a hand over the warm sand, scooping it up and letting it trail through her fingers. "Where did you go last night?"

"None of your business."

Right. "Who do you work for?" She watched him out of the corner of her eye.

A sound close to a chuckle stuck in his throat. "Myself. I freelance mostly. I get a lot of assignments from TIME."

"I see. And where's home for you?"

"Oh, criminy." Luke flexed his arms and stretched them high above his head, pulling one hand down to cover a yawn. "Are you for real?"

"If you want me to shut up, just say so." She smiled and returned to watching the waves roll in and out.

"That would be nice." He cleared his throat and swatted flies away. She angled her head for a better view of the beach and a flash of gold caught her eye. Kristin blinked in disbelief. She looked again to be sure. A thick band of gold sat around the third finger of Luke's left hand.

"You're married?" Her attempt to hide shock failed and he met her inquiring gaze with a scowl. Silence held court for an uncomfortable moment.

"Surprised?"

Kristin opted for silence. She couldn't answer that. And he carried a gun.

"Ah. Speechless at last."

"Sorry for asking."

"I was married. A long time ago."

"Where is she now?"

"Gone." His curt reply warned her not to prod further.

Kristin spied a half-buried shell, picked it up, and turned it over in her hand. Shades of turquoise, pink and silver shimmered under the sun's rays. Her mother had a tortoise shell brush and comb on her dresser back home. When she was little, Kristin loved to use the set on her dolls. She blew tiny grains of sand from the shiny surface of the shell and pocketed it. Then she took off her boots and socks and pushed her toes into the warm sand.

"Kind of easy to forget where you are, isn't it?" Luke pulled a filthy faded blue bandana from his pocket and secured it around his head, lifting a clump of hair off his face.

"Is it?" She turned his way, surprised that he'd spoken out loud her earlier thought, but Luke was stretched out on the sand, his eyes closed.

Weighed down by morbid thoughts and the heat of the sun, Kristin felt sick with exhaustion. She couldn't think about Teddy. Nor did she want to sit here and pass the day with Luke Maddox. She just wanted to pour out her thoughts on paper. It would be a welcome release. "Can I get a ride back to Saigon? I have to write my story."

He opened one eye and stared up at her for a moment. "I suppose you can." That lazy grin spread across his face again and said she was on her own.

Kristin put her boots back on, pushed to her feet and kept a keen eye on the ground around her this time.

"Miss Taylor."

She stopped walking, swiveled and waited. "What?"

Luke came up the path behind her, snapping twigs and kicking rocks out of his way.

He stopped a short distance away, his expression unreadable behind dark glasses.

Then he took off the shades and stepped closer. "Write about it, but don't get too used to it."

His intense gaze shot liquid fire through her and caught her off guard. "Too used to what?" The somber look he wore confused her.

He shaded his eyes with one hand, and for a moment Kristin saw a flicker of life in them, short-lived as it was. "The death. The destruction. It'll take your soul if you let it." He put his shades back on.

She moved up the path in silence, his warning settling in uninvited. A crackling in the bush caught her attention and she jerked her head up. Then froze.

A Vietnamese boy of no more than sixteen, stood in front of them, pointing an alarmingly large rifle straight at her.

She sucked in a breath and all rational thought fled.

Kristin felt the pressure of Luke's hand on her shoulder. "Don't wig out on me. Just. Don't. Move."

The boy shouted something in Vietnamese and Luke yelled back in the same language. Blood pulsed through her as she struggled to stay upright. The sound of gunfire brought her to her knees.

"Get up." Luke grabbed her arm and he pulled her to her feet. The boy lay on the path in front of her. "Let's get out of here. ASAP."

Kristin stared at the dead boy. Blood trickled from a small hole in the middle of his head. A pack of cigarettes had fallen from his shirt pocket and lay on the ground beside him. American cigarettes.

Terror took hold as she tried to wrench her arm from Luke's grasp. "You killed him."

Luke held tight and shook her, his eyes boring in to her. "That was an AK-47. He was about to kill *you*. Did you want me to let him? Then tell him to run back to his commie VC pals and lead them right back to the 24th? Snap out of it!"

He turned her around and pushed her forward. Kristin broke in to a jog, and didn't stop running until she reached the nurses' quarters.

Chapter Six

*B*ack in her apartment, Kristin pounded on the keys of her typewriter until her hands cramped, until she'd emptied her soul of the
sights, sounds and explosion of emotions the past few days in Vietnam had
set off within her. She had her first story now.

All she had to do was sell it.

Caroline brought food, offered alcohol, which Kristin refused, and
read over her shoulder. Told her it was good. Good enough to get picked
up easily. Kristin hoped her roommate was right. Her first week in Vietnam
was drawing to a close and she needed to secure an assignment. Without a
visa…she would soon be here on borrowed time.

Jean Luc offered to speak to his boss on her behalf. She'd given him
her piece and he said he'd get back to her sometime today. Kristin was too
nervous to think about the outcome, so she found cleaning supplies in the
cupboard under the kitchen sink.

She scrubbed the kitchen and bathroom floors on her hands and
knees. Cloroxed the counters and the refrigerator. She even scraped out
black grime from the depths of the old oven that looked like it had
never been cleaned. Folded piles of clothes and placed them on the far
side of the battered couch. Stacked all the magazines and newspapers
fastidiously, and put them on the table. Dusted and even vacuumed the
rug with an ancient Hoover she'd found stashed in a musty closet down
the hall.

By the time Caroline returned from an assignment that Friday afternoon, the place was spotless.

"Wow. Were you a maid in a former life?" Her flat-mate twirled around the living room, her face lit with a smile. Late afternoon sun shone through clear glass of the windows.

"I cleaned up a little. I hope you don't mind." Kristin surveyed the now spic-and-span apartment and allowed a smile. She'd cleaned her surroundings, but couldn't quite erase the memories that muddied her mind. When she closed her eyes at night she still saw wounded soldiers and dead Vietnamese boys.

"Mind?" Caroline grinned, dimples dancing as she dropped on to the couch. "Hey, I ran into Jean Luc on the way home, he said it's a go. They want your story. He got tied up in meetings today, but he said we should all go out to dinner tonight. To celebrate."

"Really?" Kristin gave a whoop, relief surging through her. "I can't believe it."

Caroline laughed and nodded. "Congratulations." Her long flaxen hair hung around her shoulders, pulled off her forehead by a headband. She flashed a smile that would have heads turning from here to the DMZ. "So…now you're not bent over that typewriter and I actually have time to breathe, tell me. You said you went up north, with Luke?"

Kristin slumped to the floor and crossed her legs, rubbing her face with her hands. "Yeah. They offered me a ride and we ended up at the 24th. I met your dad."

"Did you?" Caroline went to the kitchen and clattered about, returning with two glasses filled halfway with a dark liquid. "I haven't seen Doc for a while. How is he?"

"He was very nice. Your brother doesn't take after him at all." Fatigue prevented her from keeping sarcasm in check. Kristin took a sip of the strong brown stuff Caroline handed her. The drink burned all the way down her throat. "What is this? Petroleum?"

Caroline finished her drink in one gulp. "You don't want to know. It's cheap and it's strong. Thought you might want to take the edge off."

"Thanks." Kristin wondered just how often Caroline "took the edge off." She put her glass down on the floor.

"Not much of a drinker?"

"Not really." She'd been drunk once, in college, and woke up so violently ill that she vowed then and there never to drink that much again.

"Vietnam will change that." Caroline reached for Kristin's glass. "Waste not, want not. I'm glad Luke didn't scare you off." Her smile faded. "So… how did you find it, your first taste of war?"

"Um…" Kristin measured her words. "Brutal. Raw. But in a strange way, energizing. Being here is better than being back in Boston writing about the latest sale at Macy's."

"You got that right." Caroline scowled. "The last story I filed before I came over was about a dog show."

Kristin suppressed a yawn and nodded. "Sounds typical. Your father runs a tight ship up there. I didn't really comprehend it, what's going on over here, until now."

"You wouldn't. They don't tell you the real story back home." Caroline mirrored that same haunted look Kristin had seen in Luke. "Anyway." The brilliant smile returned, reminding Kristin of a magazine ad, where all was right with the world. Caroline clinked the two empty glasses together. "I'm going to lie down for a bit. Wake me in an hour and we'll go out. Peter's going to meet us at The Caravelle at seven."

"The captain?" Caroline's boyfriend, apparently. Kristin could have sworn she'd seen a ring on the man's left hand when they'd met briefly on her first day.

"Yes. Oh, there's a party next week at the Embassy. Do you want to come? I can get you in. You might make some contacts."

"Absolutely."

After a delicious dinner and an entertaining evening with Jean Luc and his cronies, Kristin slept well for the first time that week. But her bliss was interrupted by a clattering sound coming from the bathroom. She sat up in bed and listened. Across the room, Caroline huddled under her sheets in peaceful slumber.

"Caroline!" she hissed. Caroline didn't move.

More clattering sent a chill down her spine.

Somebody was in the apartment.

"Caroline, wake up!" Still no movement. "Oh, hell."

Heart pounding, she swung her legs out of bed, flung on her robe, grabbed her flashlight and tiptoed across the room. Light shone from under the bathroom door. A crack in the door revealed the frame of a tall man. She inched closer and pushed the door open with her toe, flashlight held high, ready to bash the intruder over the head.

Luke Maddox turned bleary eyes in her direction.

"What are you doing in here?" she hissed. Fear escalated to anger. "You scared the life out of me!" She lowered her weapon, tempted to hit him anyway.

"Sorry." He squinted under the harsh light of the exposed bulb hanging from the ceiling, leaned back and rubbed his face. Bottles lay scattered on the sink. "I need some aspirin. My head's killing me."

"Then maybe you should stop drinking."

"I haven't been drinking." He shielded his eyes with one hand. "Could you—please…"

Kristin waved him aside and put the mess to rights, handing over the bottle of aspirin. "How'd you get in here?"

"Jimmied the lock." He popped a couple of white pills into his mouth and chewed.

Kristin shuddered, more at the thought of him breaking and entering. He really didn't look too well. She wouldn't address the issue at the moment. "Are you all right?"

He turned on the faucet and splashed water over his face. She held out a towel and he buried his face in it, letting out a long groan. "I just—sometimes I can't sleep. That kid cries all night long."

"What kid?"

"I don't know. Just keeps crying." He released another sigh and pinched the bridge of his nose. Kristin couldn't stifle a yawn and clapped a hand over her mouth.

Luke raised an eyebrow. "Sorry I woke you." He tugged at the collar of his ripped T-shirt and did look apologetic.

"Well, I'm glad it's you and not some thug out to steal all our stuff." Sort of. She saw him to the door. "Get some sleep. At least one of us should."

His bloodshot eyes held hers for a moment. "Saw Caroline today. She told me you sold a piece to that Frenchie's magazine."

"I did." She didn't want to sound too proud, but couldn't stop a smile.

He didn't seem impressed. "If you want a real job, my editor is looking for new stuff. Wants to focus on the war from a different angle. My sister says you're good. I can pass your name along if you like."

Kristin stared back at him, wondering if he was really awake. "To your editor? At TIME?"

He shrugged, giving a lop-sided grin. "If you're not interested..."

"Oh, I'm interested. I'm just...surprised."

Luke rolled his eyes. "You don't have to thank me or anything."

"I...I...thanks." She gripped her elbows, her mind spinning. Suspicion snaked around her and stifled her surprise. "What do you want?"

A hard look froze his face and Kristin wished she could take back her words.

"Not all 'us boys' think women don't belong here, Kristin, nor do we all have ulterior motives." A sad sort of smile touched his lips. "I'll give you Hayden's number tomorrow. You may get a couple of stories as a stringer, no byline as you know, but if he hires you, you'll get accreditation, be able to use the PX. Not sure what the pay will be, but it'll be a start."

"I'm sorry," she choked out. "Really. Thanks."

"Yeah. Good luck." He left the apartment, closing the door firmly behind him.

Lying in bed, all hope of sleep gone, Kristin tried to make sense of Luke Maddox.

It proved impossible.

He'd said a child's cries were keeping him awake. In the time she'd been here, she'd always slept with the windows wide open. She had never heard a child, crying. Not once.

Chapter Seven

Valerie Taylor hurried to get out of the cold and off the busy New York City sidewalk, pushed open the glass doors of the office building and scanned the foyer for the elevators. She shrugged off her camelhair coat and slung it over one arm, clutching her purse in gloved hands. On the ride up to the tenth floor, she rehearsed her speech.

She would not let one of the most influential editors in the news world intimidate her. Oh, he'd been sweet as pie on the phone, very reassuring. But she hadn't been placated. In fact, she'd lost so much sleep the past few weeks that she'd taken the train here last night, booked a hotel room and determined her course of action.

Hayden Thorne would be bringing her daughter home on the next plane.

Their appointment had been scheduled for ten a.m. At ten forty-five, his office door opened. "Mrs. Taylor? Sorry for the wait. I'm Hayden Thorne. Come on in."

Valerie locked eyes with the man in the doorway and all rational thought abandoned her. He leaned against the doorframe, his white shirt rumpled, the sleeves rolled to his elbows, his striped tie slightly askew. He studied her, a hint of a smile curling his lips.

She noticed the scar right away. A faint line that ran from the side of his face, across his jaw and stopped at the edge of his mouth. She shifted her gaze back to his eyes.

A tingling started somewhere deep in the pit of her stomach and her throat went dry.

She hadn't felt such an instant attraction to a man in…well…a very long time.

Not since Mac.

Focus. Think of Kristin. She would not let the man's good looks detract her from her mission. She was almost fifty years old, for heaven's sake. So what if he looked around her age. She rose, gripping her purse as though it were a life preserver, and followed him into his office.

"What can I do for you, Mrs. Taylor?" He pulled a chair out for her and she sat, waiting until he was seated in his own swivel chair across the desk.

"You can bring my daughter home from Vietnam for starters." Valerie drew a shaky breath, smoothed down her hair and hoped her hand wasn't trembling.

He smiled. "Your daughter is a fine journalist. I hired her on that merit. You should be proud."

"She can be a fine journalist here, on American soil. Not half-way around the world in the middle of a war zone." Valerie sniffed her displeasure.

He held up a hand—a ring-less hand—and nodded. "Believe me, I understand. I've got kids of my own. Grown, like Kristin. But since my wife died, I feel even more responsible for them. They don't always appreciate my concern. But there comes a point where we have to let them make their own way."

"I suppose." She fiddled with the gold buttons on her cardigan and picked a thread off her skirt. Then she frowned and made eye contact again. "No. I don't suppose. Not when it comes to life or death situations. Kristin could get killed over there, Mr. Thorne. What with my son being there as well, it's just too much. Too much." She pulled a handkerchief from her purse and dabbed her eyes. Tears came easily these days, but she made no apology. Let him think what he liked.

Hayden Thorne cleared his throat and sat in silence. When she'd composed herself, Valerie met his steady gaze once more.

He narrowed his eyes, his mouth drawn. Then he gave her a sympathetic smile. "I'm sorry. I'm sure it's been very hard on you, being alone."

"How do you know I'm alone?"

What in the world was wrong with her, saying such a thing! Her cheeks grew hot and she lowered her gaze.

His easy laugh filled the office. "Something tells me your daughter got her spunk from you. I've had a few phone conversations with her in the last week or two. She's quite something. Very determined."

"Yes. She is. Sometimes to her detriment." Kristin had called a week ago, elated at getting this job at TIME and the three-month visa that came with it. The salary wasn't much as far as Valerie was concerned, but Kristin crowed at the step-up her career had taken. "She thinks she can make a difference by writing a few poignant stories. As if that will stop the war."

"She may think that." He tipped his head, studying her through kind eyes. "I think she simply wants to tell the truth. It's an admirable goal, Mrs. Taylor."

"So she should risk her life for the truth? I don't…understand that. I never have."

"Your son seems to agree it's worth it."

Valerie looked away. Coming here was a mistake.

"I assure you, I'll do my best to make sure she's watched after. I have some connections. One in particular has given me his word."

Valerie lifted her shoulders and wiped the moisture from her cheeks. She appreciated his earnestness, but it didn't ease her fears. "Can your connections have them stop shelling when she's in the area?" His low laughter made her uneasy. "You're not going to bring her home, are you?"

He gave another complacent smile, running a hand over dark hair streaked with gray. "It's not up to me, I'm afraid. Do you have any idea how many applications we get in a week? Working for TIME is nothing to sniff at."

"I'm well aware of your magazine's reputation, Mr. Thorne. My husband was on assignment for you when he was killed twelve years ago. In Vietnam."

Her words left a heavy silence in the air.

His jaw tightened as he raised a hand to touch the scar on his face. He turned his head slightly. Something in his eyes hinted at old ghosts, sorrow and perhaps fear. The haunted look he now wore disturbed her.

He shifted and settled his direct gaze on her again. "I know that." He rubbed his jaw and studied her for a long moment. "I was there too. And your husband was among my closest friends."

Chapter Eight

Kristin pulled another piece of paper from her typewriter, balled it up and hurled it at the wastebasket in the corner of the room.

She pushed her chair back, put her head in her hands and groaned. Caroline was at another shindig, the location escaped her, but Kristin almost regretted not going. The parties in Saigon were raucous, often extravagant, and went long into the night. You never knew who you might run into. Sometimes Kristin went along to escape her thoughts for a few hours, other times she longed to be alone to process what she was seeing and try to make some sense of it. Tonight she'd chosen solitude, staring at the wall, waiting for words that wouldn't come.

She picked up her mug, drained the last drop of cold tea and made a face. It was almost eleven p.m. No telling when Caroline would be home—if she came home.

In the short time she'd lived here, Kristin realized her life could easily turn into one endless party if she wanted it to. Despite her intentions to stay away from alcohol, she'd found it alarmingly easy to drink away the day's events, flooding her mind with liquor to erase the images of blood, death and destruction. But the illusion of normalcy only lasted for a while. And the war still waged in the morning.

Most of her colleagues worked hard and played harder. Kristin tried to walk a fine line of mediocrity, but as the weeks wore on, it was becoming harder to avoid temptation. There were countless ways to forget the horrors encountered on a daily basis in Vietnam.

Caroline seemed to have mastered most of them.

She pushed her hair behind her ears and stood. She'd make some more tea and then finish the piece. As she headed toward the kitchen, a key turned in the lock on the front door.

Luke entered the apartment, his sister staggering beside him. He met Kristin's eyes and gave a thin smile. He didn't need words to tell her he needed help. She crossed the room, put an arm around Caroline and helped get her inside.

"Just let me go…I'll just…smack him…" Caroline slurred, fixing bleary eyes on Kristin. "The nerve…let me go, I say!" Kristin ducked to avoid one of Caroline's flailing arms.

"Bed is the only place you're going," Luke muttered. Caroline tried to pull away from him and he neatly swooped her up into his arms. In another second her head rolled against his chest and her eyes fluttered closed. Luke grinned. "Thank you, Jesus."

Kristin moved aside to let him pass and continued on through to the kitchen where she put the kettle on to boil. She grabbed a cloth from the kitchen sink and began scrubbing down the counter while she waited.

"Hi." Luke's voice reached her ears and she turned. He stood in the doorway of the kitchen, a beleaguered look capturing his features.

"Is she okay?"

He shrugged. "She and Peter had a fight. He left the party early. She decided to see if she could drink her mates under the table. She lost."

Kristin raised a brow and set to work rubbing imaginary grease off the cupboards. "I'm sorry."

"She'll be fine. Wasn't a great party anyway. You weren't there."

Kristin froze. She almost dropped the cloth she held, took a gulp of air and slowly swiveled to face him. "Pardon?"

Luke's face flushed scarlet. "I meant you weren't there. At the party. Not that it wasn't great because you weren't there. I mean, of course, well…if you had been there it would have been—"

"I'm making tea. Want some? Unless you need something stronger." She put her back to him, unable to stop a grin. Seeing Luke Maddox stumbling over his words was rather enjoyable.

"Nope. Tea. That would be good."

They sat opposite each other at the small table by the window. She sipped the steaming liquid and studied him, suddenly realizing why he looked so different tonight.

He cleaned up well.

Dressed in beige trousers and a navy short-sleeved shirt, his neat appearance proved a nice alternative to his usual dirt-smeared face and filthy attire. Even his wild mop of hair appeared to be behaving this evening, combed down, possibly trimmed. His jaw was smooth, clean shaven.

He cradled the brown ceramic mug between his hands, intent on studying the liquid inside. In the time she'd known him, Kristin observed that he rarely smiled. Not a proper smile anyway. Not the kind of smile that told somebody you were glad to see them.

"You're staring, Miss Taylor."

He'd raised his eyes and she hadn't noticed.

"Yes, I suppose I am. I...hardly recognize you." She took a quick sip of tea and scalded her tongue. He was too good-looking, especially now, when he didn't look like he lived in the jungle.

Luke sipped from his own mug. "So have you recovered from your near death experience?"

Kristin smiled at the question. "Which one?"

His eyes crinkled with a grin. "You do seem to have a knack for attracting trouble."

She flushed under the truth of his words. "Well, thanks for coming to my rescue. Again. I hope you won't have to make a habit of it."

"Guess I'm just a pushover for a damsel in distress." He leaned back in his chair, tiny beads of perspiration dotting his forehead. "How was your week?"

Kristin shrugged. "Not bad. I got the job at TIME. Did you know? I... should have told you, thanked you."

"I heard. Hayden's very pleased with your work. Told me he got you a three-month visa."

Kristin nodded, her cheeks tingling. She longed for a breath of air in the stifling apartment. The moon shone through the open window, covering them in its silvery glow. From where she sat she could see bright stars piercing the darkness. Noise from the traffic and the pedestrians below competed with the music coming from the radio on the table.

"Nice collection of paper over there." He nodded toward the discarded balls near the wastebasket, a grin lifting his mouth. "We should play hoops some time."

She laughed, drawn to this side of him. "So how've you been? Any more headaches? Did you find out which apartment that baby lives in?"

"What baby?"

Kristin drew in a breath and measured his vague expression. "The one that was keeping you awake the night you ransacked my bathroom."

"Oh. That." Luke gave his half-smile but his eyes failed to light. "No. I've been sleeping better. Could be because I'm wiped out."

"I know the feeling." She'd gotten the hang of waiting at the airport for rides on helicopters and had visited several base camps. She'd made friends with a few other journalists, but hadn't seen much of Luke at all. He seemed to disappear for days on end. And people talked. She'd heard him pegged as Agency on more than one occasion now and was beginning to suspect it was entirely possible he did indeed work for the CIA. Which made him all the more attractive. Because he might well provide her with the answers she needed for the story she really wanted to write.

She'd have to be careful. Although he seemed more relaxed tonight, Luke Maddox still made her uncomfortable.

"Kristin." His low voice bounced off the walls and pulled her out of her musings.

"Hmm?" She tightened her hold on her mug, lifted her chin and allowed his intense stare to capture her again.

"You don't have to like me, I can live with that. But you don't need to be afraid of me."

"Who says I'm afraid?" Kristin tried out a laugh that didn't go far.

Luke narrowed his eyes and leaned forward. "I've been in Vietnam a long time. I know fear when I see it."

She smiled and hoped she looked calmer than she felt. "You know I'll figure you out eventually, Luke Maddox."

He angled his head, as though something on the ceiling had his attention. "Did you say you were from Boston?"

"Nice change of subject." Her smile broadened. "Yes. Have you been there?"

"I have indeed. I studied at Harvard. After Oxford."

"You're kidding." Kristin clamped a hand over her mouth. "I mean… I…don't exactly see you as the scholarly type."

He leaned forward again. "How do you see me?"

"How do I see you?" The sudden sparkle in his eyes put her slightly on edge. "I'm not sure." Truth won out. "You're a bit of a mystery."

"Really?" He sat back. "Like an Agatha Christie novel?"

"More like le Carré." Kristin watched him carefully. "The Spy Who Came In From The Cold. It's one of my favorite books."

A hint of a smile crossed his lips. "Mine too."

"So you studied at Harvard and Oxford, yet you're here in the jungle taking photographs of dead soldiers. How'd that happen?"

Luke picked at a scab on his hand and shrugged. "Couldn't decide what I wanted to do, I guess. I'd always loved photography so I figured I'd give it a shot."

"Funny." She wanted to believe him, yet something niggled her, like a tooth on the verge of coming loose that wouldn't quite give. Shouts from the street below interrupted her thought process. The city never seemed to sleep. She put her mug down on the scratched teak tabletop. "So, England?"

"Playing Password again, are we?" The dimple flashing in his left cheek distracted her.

Kristin grinned. She'd always enjoyed watching that show with her Mom. "Well, if you want to go with television shows, I prefer You Bet Your Life."

Luke laughed and pushed fingers through his hair. "All right, Groucho, I'm game. Yes, I was born in England. My mother is English, my father, as you know, American. My parents divorced when I was thirteen. They packed my sister and I off to a dreadful boarding school in the south of England, and we spent summers in the States with my Dad. Got through my teens by the skin of my teeth. Went to University, became a photographer, and here I am. Will that do?"

"I suppose." She doodled on a notepad and thought about Caroline. She could almost relate. Some wounds never heal. "That must have been difficult, your parents splitting up. Do you see your mother often?"

Luke shrugged and put his mug down near hers. "No. We're not exactly on speaking terms."

Kristin raised an eyebrow. "Any particular reason?"

"Let's just say she doesn't agree with my being here." He set his gaze on her again. "Your turn."

"Oh, you don't want to hear about my life. It's very boring." She looked toward the window to escape the indigo eyes that captivated her with no effort at all. Luke's slow laugh drew her back to them.

"Let me guess." He took on a knowing look. "Had a wonderful, but somewhat boring childhood. Excelled in school, made the Principal's list every year, went to some snotty all-girls prep school, and then on to Wellesley, where you graduated Summa Cum Laude. And now you're in Vietnam, determined to make your mark in journalism, having left scores of broken-hearted young men behind you in America."

Kristin choked on her laughter. "Hardly."

"You didn't go to some snotty prep school?"

She lifted a hand in defense. "No, you're right about that. But I went to Princeton. And I didn't leave any broken hearts behind. Except my mother's."

"Really?" His grin told her he didn't believe it.

"Not that it's any of your business."

"Hey, you started it…"

"Touché." She fell silent. "My mother and I aren't exactly speaking either."

"Oh? She doesn't want you here?"

"Nope. Oh, she's not against my having a career. She just doesn't relish the thought of her daughter in a war zone."

"But you came anyway." His eyes clouded over. After a while he cleared his throat, drumming his fingers on the table. "Why?"

Kristin pushed her back against the chair. Nobody had asked her that before. "I want to find my brother."

"Ah. Still no word?"

"Mom has had a couple letters since I've been here, but I haven't located him, no."

He seemed to hesitate. "You know your chances of doing so are—"

"Slim to none. I know. But I won't give up."

"No, I don't suppose you will." His smile sparked feelings in her that she quickly pushed aside. "And the other reason you're here? It's because of your father, isn't it?"

Surprise infiltrated her sorrow like the sun's rays filtering through a dark forest. "You know who my father was?" She tugged at a stray thread on her beige shorts.

"It wasn't hard to figure out. People talk. You're a bit of a celebrity you know." Luke shrugged with that annoying air of nonchalance. "I did a paper on your dad in college. Malcolm Taylor changed the face of journalism. His death was a tragedy."

"I was twelve. It was hard to understand at the time." Kristin felt his eyes on her but looked beyond him at the wall. A painting of Elvis on black velvet pitched precariously from a nail. Each time an explosion rattled the apartment, they waited for it to fall, but somehow it refused to budge. The King's features were mottled with mold—it was disgusting really—but provided such an air of normalcy that neither she nor Caroline would remove it.

"It's still hard to understand," she admitted. "Everything changed. My mother worked as a legal secretary. I went to a private school on scholarship. It was hardly a walk in the park."

"I'm sorry."

Kristin fiddled with the cross around her neck. She saw him studying it. "It was my father's." Two pieces of gold carved to look like tree branches were melded together to shape the cross. She hadn't taken it off since the day her mother gifted it to her, even though she didn't put much stock in the symbol.

"Very unique."

"Yes. He got it from some nun in India. He carried it with him everywhere. Not that it did him any good in the end."

Luke's eyes moved upward and grabbed hold of hers. "Meaning?"

Kristin blew out a breath and ran her fingers through her hair. "I guess when you're twelve, you expect God to follow through for you." She shrugged. "When we got word that he'd been killed, I fell to pieces. But my mother...she went numb. Later, I realized what it was, but, when I refused to get out of bed for a week, she demanded I pull myself together. My father's death was God's will and we mustn't question it." Kristin leaned over her knees for a moment and exhaled. Then she sat up and looked at him again. "I guess you could say I'm still not convinced."

A sad smile crossed his face. "I understand."

Kristin wondered at the untold story in his eyes. "I believe you do."

"Well, that's a bit agreeable, Miss Taylor, isn't it?"

She laughed, twirled the pen around her fingers and waited. He didn't seem in any hurry to go. "How long have you been over here?"

Luke shrugged and mussed his hair. "Too long. I don't keep track anymore."

She nodded and drew two vertical lines on the pad of paper in front of her. "The guys I've talked to…some of them are like that. They don't bother counting days because they're not sure they're getting another one. And some of them can tell you when their tour is up down to the minute."

It was almost impossible to fathom, the sense of duty, of fighting for freedom, putting one's life on the line. Her admiration for the GIs grew every time she went out into the field. "A kid asked me the other day what it felt like, to know I could hop a plane and go home whenever I wanted." Kristin's eyes began to burn. "I couldn't answer him." She marked two horizontal lines across the ones she'd just drawn, put a large 'O' in the center box and put her pen down. "How am I supposed to write about these things? Things I can't even wrap my head around?"

Luke pulled the pen and pad toward him and made an 'X'. "Naught's and crosses. Haven't played this since my boarding-school days."

"X's and O's, you mean." Kristin scratched another 'O'. In two more moves, she'd won. The small victory didn't override the indwelling sadness she'd been pushing down for days.

"Hey." Luke tapped her foot with the top of his boot. "Remember what I told you at Long Binh. You can't do that. You can't take on guilt that's not justified. Not if you want to survive out here."

"You're saying I shouldn't feel? Shouldn't care that boys are dying out there?"

"I didn't say that. Just don't get sucked in. Write from your heart, but use your head. If you want to see your stuff in print, you need to play the game first."

"I don't like playing games."

"Unless the odds are stacked in your favor?" Luke stared at her, about to say more perhaps, but the bathroom door slammed and interrupted the conversation.

Kristin jumped, almost having forgotten Caroline was in the bedroom. The distinct sound of retching reached her ears. "She's going to be hurting in the morning. You know, she…" She stopped herself, catching the look of interest in his eyes. "Never mind."

Luke let out a sigh. "I'm well aware how my sister chooses to live her life. I don't like her choices, but she's a big girl, right?"

Kristin rubbed the gold cross between her thumb and forefinger. "Sometimes I don't think she cares…all the drinking, the men…it's like she's on some mission to self-destruct."

"Aren't we all, in some way or another?"

His quiet words hit home. "I hope not. I hope I never get to the point where I don't care what happens to me."

Luke's grunt of agreement coincided with another low rumble off in the distance. More explosions. Kristin shuddered and closed her eyes.

"Not used to that yet?"

She rubbed her nose and shook her head. "Do you ever get used to it?"

A shadow ran across his face. "In a way, yes. You pretend to anyway. That's what the parties are for. Life's much easier that way, I suppose."

"But it's not real." She pointed to the window. "Out there, *that's* real. That's life and death. Mostly death."

Luke's expression hardened and he scratched his jaw. He ran a long finger over the keys of her typewriter. "You can write from any angle you want, Kristin, but you can't change what's happening around us. You don't believe you can, do you?"

"Of course I don't." Was she that deluded? She heard Caroline's soft groan and the squeak as she got back into bed. "This has gone on so long that nobody back home seems bothered by what's going on over here anymore. Sure, there are those who march around waving peace signs and holding sit-ins, but I don't think they have a clue what it's really like here. Neither do the people who support the war. The whole country is caught up in a political quagmire. If you support this, you're accepting the death of countless men in the name of freedom, if you protest against it you're a peace-loving hippie in bed with the Communists."

Luke nodded. "Damned if you do, damned if you don't."

"Exactly." Kristin sighed and raked her fingers through her tangled hair. "God Bless America."

"Indeed. Well, if it's any comfort, I think you're doing a good job so far. I read your last piece. I thought you portrayed things from the nurses' perspective rather well."

"Thanks." She tried not to show surprise. "I'm never sure what they'll print. No censorship isn't always a good thing. I feel like there's an invisible line I can't cross, things I can't say. Things aren't so black and white anymore, and I don't want to take sides."

"You'll pick a side eventually. It's human nature. Otherwise you walk through life ambivalent. And I can't see you being happy with mediocrity." Luke's steady gaze warmed her cheeks. "So what if, once you get a few things out there, you don't play by the rules? What if you tell the truth?" He gave a wan smile. "If you're going to follow in your father's footsteps, that's the place to start."

"Do you think Hayden will print the truth?" She'd already attended the weekly Army press conferences. They skirted around the truth and rarely gave facts that lined up with what she saw in the field. The journalists in-country labeled the meetings the "Five o'clock Follies".

"One way to find out."

"I can try, I suppose."

"Something tells me you'll do more than that."

The sound of her own laughter jolted her. "Are you giving me positive affirmation?"

"Never." He coughed and lifted a hand to his mouth, but she saw his brief smile anyway.

Kristin sucked in amazement, the shimmer in his eyes spurring it all the more. "You have connections. I'd love to do a few pieces together. I'm sure Hayden would go for it."

The idea wasn't that crazy. She'd seen some of his stuff; he was a good photographer, even if it was just a clever cover. And if they worked together, she could keep an eye on him. Perhaps discover his real story. "What do you think?"

His deep laugh told her exactly what he thought. "I work alone."

Kristin shrugged. "Well, so do I. But I can make exceptions."

"I can't." Luke rose and gave a noisy yawn. "It's late. I'll let you get some sleep. Thanks for the tea."

"Sure." She walked him to the door, hesitating as he paused, crossed his arms and set an inquisitive gaze on her. Kristin narrowed her eyes. She hated it when he looked at her that way. Like he was about to dissect her with a very sharp object. "Was there something else?"

"I don't know. Ever since we met I've been trying to decide whether or not I like you."

"And?" She took a step back, lifting her chin.

Luke grinned. "You're all right, Taylor."

"Thanks. I think." She stiffened and tried not to smile. "And you're not as horrible as I thought you were."

He gave a short laugh, flicking a strand of hair out of his eyes. "I'm growing on you. I can tell."

"Yes. You're growing on me. Like mold." Kristin opened the door for him. "Goodnight, Luke."

"Goodnight, Taylor." He slipped into the hallway and she closed the door against his low laughter. She still wasn't sure she liked him all that much, but she wasn't naïve. Kristin recognized attraction when she felt it. And in this case, it was a dangerous attraction. Luke Maddox was hiding something. She needed to find out what. And if he was CIA, as she suspected, she'd be well on her way to writing the story she'd flown halfway around the world to finish.

Chapter Nine

Luke held his breath as he watched Kristin march down the crowded street. She walked with a determined air that made people get out of her way. Luke recognized her tenacious spirit early on. Most female journalists possessed it, had to really, to survive, but this one… she seemed almost fearless. If she had any idea of the danger she was putting herself in she didn't show it.

He'd already been called in about her. Practically ordered to keep tabs on her, which was the last thing he wanted to do, but the more he tailed her, the more convinced he became that his boss was right. She was probably already onto him. He'd known from the start: Kristin Taylor needed watching.

She stopped outside one of the seediest bars in town and glanced up and down the street. The sun inched down behind the buildings around them and cast an orange hue over the road. The ever-present rumbling from the hills outside the city gave a disturbing air of normalcy.

Luke crouched behind a parked Mercedes on the other side of the road, his eyes fixed on her. Tension wrapped tight cords around his neck as two high-ranking uniformed VCRN officers came into view and headed in her direction.

They exchanged a few words and then Kristin followed them into the bar.

Luke shook his head and let out a low curse. She would get herself killed, no doubt about it. He moved away from the car to stand behind a large rubber tree, the thick smooth trunk providing adequate cover. He still had a clear view of the bar, and her.

They were seated about five tables in. Kristin had her notepad out and wrote furiously while the men talked and drank. He recognized one of the officers and wondered how much she was paying for this little tête-à-tête. He chewed on his bottom lip and debated his next move. When he saw two plain-clothed Americans exit the place a few moments later, his heart stopped.

Oh, God. No. Not now.

A five year-old memory tiptoed around him, taunting, teasing. A strange sense of déjà vu blindsided him like a two-by-four upside the head. But he wasn't standing in front of a decimated Saigon hotel. This was different.

Luke pushed back the eerie feeling, took a couple of deep breaths, and raced across the street, narrowly missing being mowed down by an oncoming military truck. The driver honked and swore but Luke ignored him and kept going. He sauntered into the darkened room and hoped he didn't look like he'd just run the Boston marathon.

The place was dimly lit and crowded with GIs, reeked of smoke and beer and a faint hint of another kind of cigarette a lot of the guys somehow managed to get their hands on. Music pounded from a jukebox in the corner. Vietnamese girls prowled like sleek panthers, looking for prey. One sauntered over to him and placed a hand on his arm. She couldn't have been more than fifteen. Luke shook her off and settled his gaze on Kristin.

Her eyes flew wide as she caught sight of him. Under different circumstances he would have grinned. She made a face and jerked her head toward the door, telling him to get lost. Luke folded his arms and leaned up against the bar. How she'd arranged this meeting was beyond him, but he wasn't about to let it last long.

The soldier seemed adamant on making his point, talking animatedly with his hands. Luke could barely make out the well-rehearsed speech in broken English about the horrors of war and the toll it took on his people. Luke's stomach churned as he glanced down at his watch. He could be wrong, but his gut told him he wasn't.

He always went with his gut.

He had about ten minutes to get her out.

The men stared suspiciously as Luke approached their table, a hint of recognition came over the older one. He said something to his companion and Luke knew there was no time to waste.

He focused only on Kristin and prayed she would understand him. "Ah. There you are. I've been looking all over the city for you! I've got an urgent message for you from home. It's about your brother. You need to come with me. Now."

"What?" Kristin paled. She shot to her feet, alarm freezing her face. Luke nodded and helped her gather up her stuff.

"Sorry, boys. This is a matter of life and death. She'll get back to you." He ignored their startled expressions and propelled Kristin out of the smoky bar. As soon as they hit the pavement, he clamped his hand around her wrist and broke into a run.

"What's happened to my brother?" she yelled, panic clinging to her voice.

"Nothing that I know of." Luke pulled her along faster, his heart thudding against his chest. "But you almost got yourself killed. Just shut up and run!" He yanked her down the muddy embankment and threw her onto the wet grass beside the Saigon River. Kristin raised her head and locked eyes with him.

"Luke! What the…" BOOM! The explosion thundered through the night, shook the ground and sent fiery darts high into the humid air.

Kristin cowered as Luke covered her with his body, her face planted into the wet grass. Shock stole the scream from her throat. The ground heaved under them. Shouts and panic-filled screams filtered down from the street. Sirens blasted and people ran past them. Her heart threatened to leave her chest as she processed the last twenty minutes of her life.

Eventually Luke sat up, his arms dangling over his knees, his head down.

Kristin struggled to sit, wiping mud off her face. She spat dirt and blood. She must have cut herself when she hit the ground. "What just happened?" she breathed out.

Luke jerked his head up, his eyes hooded, haunted. He took deep, shaky breaths, looking as stunned as she felt. "I could be wrong, but I'd hazard a guess that the building just blew up."

Kristin rubbed her aching jaw and squinted.

The hysteria on the street above them lessened to a dull roar. Bits of debris descended from the smoke-filled air, landing on her clothes and the ground around her. Dusk was coming on. Bizarre visions of Fourth of July parties and fireworks played in the recesses of her mind. She brushed off the black bits, Luke's first words coming back to her.

Kristin forced herself to meet his hooded gaze. "You lied to me about Teddy?"

Luke moved closer and placed a hand under her chin. "You're bleeding." He pulled a handkerchief from his pants pocket and wiped her cheek.

Kristin flinched under his touch, her heart still racing. "You…I thought my brother was dead!"

"I'm sorry."

She pushed him with all the strength left in her. Luke said nothing, just shifted away from her. She stared in silence, the cut on her lip stinging. The outline of his face glowed in the twilight, his expression unreadable.

Raging emotions rushed ahead faster than the muddy river beside them. She put her hands up to her face and choked on her sobs.

"I'm sorry, truly." Luke crouched before her, taking her hands in his and pulling them toward his chest, forcing her to meet his eyes. "I didn't know how else to get you out of there. Are you trying to get yourself killed?"

Kristin studied him through a haze of tears. "Were you following me?" The truth slapped her to her senses. "How did you know that building was going to blow up?"

Luke let her go. He stood, angling his neck to one side and then the other. His joints cracked. He shook dirt out of his hair and coughed.

Alarm bells clanged inside her head.

Kristin scrambled to her feet and grabbed his arm. "Talk to me. Who are you working for? Special Ops? CIA?"

"You really did whack your head." He pulled his arm away and picked at his shirt. Dark streaks of mud covered the light blue material. "I told you. I'm a photographer."

Kristin sniffed and rubbed her stinging eyes, acutely aware of his presence.

And the fact that he'd just saved her life. Again.

"I'm not sure I believe that anymore. What do you know about the CIA in Vietnam?"

"Other than the fact that they're here? Everybody knows that. So what?"

She studied him, trying to steady her breathing and walked a little further down the bank, faced the river, her cheeks burning. The rushing river pounded in her ears. An open gutter pipe dumped debris and stinking sewage into the brown water. Every now and then a boat passed, its driver staring at her in eerie silence.

"Why were you meeting with those guys?"

"Those dead guys?" She turned back to face him, her hands still shaking. "I'm working on a story."

He came a little closer. "Drop it, Kristin. Find something else to write about."

"Is that an order?" She turned back toward the river and shook her head. Luke Maddox didn't intimidate her. He had to be working for Central Intelligence or Special Ops…nothing else made sense.

"It's a request. If you continue sticking your nose where it doesn't belong, you'll find yourself enroute back to the States, ASAP."

Kristin swiveled, glaring at him through the semi-darkness. "Or maybe I'll wind up in one of your company torture chambers, huh? Why don't you just tell me the truth, Luke? You know I'll figure out it eventually."

"Okay. You got me." Luke's teeth flashed in the dim light. "I'm a secret agent, a Russian spy. My real name is Vladimir Koskov. I'll tell you all my secrets. But then I'll have to kill you."

His impassive gaze stalled her anger at the boiling point. "You're an idiot." A rat scurried past her feet and she jumped back, her skin prickling. "Can we just get out of here? This place is giving me the creeps."

"After you." He indicated the stairs and she moved toward them.

"For the love of God!" Kristin smacked her hand on the metal railing. "That could have been the scoop of a lifetime."

His eyes flickered and a smile stretched his lips apart. Then his shoulders began to shake. "You're one crazy wench, Taylor." Unfamiliar laughter exploded from him.

A giggle bubbled up from her throat and then another as sudden absurd hilarity took over. "We could have bought it!" She tried to be sober, aware it really wasn't funny.

"You almost did!" Luke tipped his head back and roared. A minute later her laughter was as uncontrollable as his.

Soon they were both laying over the steps, laughing like hyenas, clutching their sides, tears rolling down their cheeks. And she didn't have the slightest idea why.

Chapter Ten

After another grueling week of travel back and forth between Saigon, Long Binh and beyond, Kristin needed a break. On a sweltering Sunday afternoon, she walked the crowded streets of Saigon, venturing into neighborhoods she hadn't yet explored. She found the orphanage by accident.

The run-down building, almost hidden behind large trees, looked like an old church. She read the painted lettering on the beat-up wooden sign above the high gates. "An Lac Orphanage". The wrought iron gates sat open, almost rusted off their hinges.

Chickens pecked about the meager lawn and barefoot children scampered around, playing in the red dirt. Their dark hair shone like black ink. Kristin stood on the sidewalk and watched them, unable to stop a smile.

Through the open windows, she saw a woman teaching a small class of about twelve older children. The younger ones seemed to do as they pleased. They swarmed her as she walked up the front path.

"Thán tử" *Hi*. She practiced the Vietnamese she'd been learning, watching their little faces light up at hearing their own language spoken by her. She lifted the camera around her neck, smiling at their enthusiasm. They bounced and chattered away as she took pictures, until the woman she'd seen through the window came outside.

A welcoming smile stretched across her face. "Hello. Can I help you?"

Startled by the woman's American accent, Kristin faltered. "Hi. I didn't mean to disturb you. I'm Kristin Taylor. I'm a journalist."

The woman drew herself up, folded her arms across her chest, but her smile remained. She had the appearance of a hippie, dressed in a long colorful skirt, peasant blouse and colorful wooden beads around her neck. Her freckled skin was tanned and Kristin guessed her to be somewhere in her early forties. Deep red hair was swept into a bun at the top of her head. "Ah. Another courageous woman come to the battlefields of Vietnam."

"Some days I think I'm more stupid than courageous," Kristin admitted, managing a grin. Two little girls played around her legs, pulling on her pant-leg for attention. She'd stopped at the market earlier and bought fresh tangerines. She fished one out of her bag. "May I?"

The woman nodded and within moments Kristin's supply was gone. The children sat around the small front yard, orange peels flying. The woman gave gentle instruction in Vietnamese and all of the children looked to Kristin and chorused a loud "thank you" in unison.

"That's better." She laughed and extended a hand toward Kristin. "I'm Mary Jo Granger. Would you like to come in?"

Kristin followed her through the house into a warm kitchen. The yellow walls of the small room welcomed her. Checkered curtains in primary colors hung from the long windows. Children's drawings decorated almost every available space. A large poster covered the refrigerator door, The Lord's Prayer written on it in elegant black lettering.

A cast iron pot hung over a fire, its simmering contents filling the air with a spicy aroma. A percolator sat on an old Aga stove in one corner. Mary Jo took two mugs down from a long cupboard and turned to Kristin. "Coffee?"

"Please."

They sat at a long wooden table, burnished with age. Kristin sipped and listened to the children's shouts and laughter. She met Mary Jo's eyes. "How many children live here?"

"Fifty. We're supposed to have a maximum of thirty, but since the war…they keep coming. What are we supposed to do? We're not the only place full to overflowing either."

"Where do they come from?"

"All over—from villages that were either attacked or abandoned—their parents were killed or ran off. We rarely know the full story."

"Villages attacked?" Kristin frowned.

Mary Jo emitted a bitter sounding laugh. "This can't be news to you? Our boys have orders to clear out all the villages. Don't want to risk any of the locals harboring the enemy in their hootch. They go in, burn down the huts and round-up all the men, women and children. Gotta watch for those toddlers with semi-automatics you know."

Kristin fished out her notebook. "Do you mind if I write this down?"

"Write a book if you want." Mary Jo dabbed at her flushed face with a large white handkerchief. "It won't help."

"You never know." Sorrow pricked her at the thought of the children just outside, orphaned forever. "You don't look after them all by yourself, do you?"

"Oh, no. My husband, Bob—he'll be back soon—he and I run the place, but we have four other helpers. Two teach, along with myself. The GIs come and play with the children—some help teach English to the older kids who want to learn. Some of the guys miss their own families, so they come here when they can. We have some support from churches back home in the States, but it's never enough. We try to arrange overseas adoptions, but it's difficult."

"And how did you wind up here?" Kristin asked. An American running an orphanage in the middle of Saigon was the last thing she'd expected to find, but this city was full of surprises.

Mary Jo smiled. "My parents were missionaries. I was born in Thailand. I've only lived in the States about six or seven years, off and on. Bob and I met in college back in the States. He's a pastor. After we married, we moved here to take a church. It was blown up last year. A friend told us about this orphanage. It was in need of new management, and we felt the Lord telling us we were it, so here we are."

"I see." Missionaries. Great.

"What about you, Kristin? What brought you to Vietnam?" Her eyes were kind but displeasure rippled through her tone.

Kristin swallowed, twirled her pencil around her fingers and gathered her thoughts. "I want to cover the war. An opportunity came up for me to do so. So here I am."

"And has it been what you hoped?"

Kristin hesitated. "I'm not sure." She answered honestly. "I don't know what I expected. I've seen so many things already…I'm not sure how to process it yet."

"That might prove impossible."

"Do I understand correctly that you're not a supporter?"

Mary Jo snorted, her expression darkening. "What should I support?" One of the smaller children ran up to her and she lifted the child into her lap, planting a kiss on his forehead. "I don't like senseless death, Kristin. On either side. I'm not so sure God is all that pleased with it either."

A pang of homesickness took her by surprise and Kristin's thoughts went to her mother. She ignored the melancholy feeling and smiled at the child grinning at her from across the table. "There are those who believe the cause is good."

"I'm sure anybody can justify killing a human being if they're hard pressed to." Mary Jo shrugged, and to Kristin's relief her bright smile returned. "Oh, don't listen to me. I'm far too cynical for my own good. I just see the devastating results first hand, as you will. It wears on you after a while."

"Yes." Kristin watched the children out in the yard. They skirted around one another, giggling. "I don't know how to write about this… the atrocities. But people need to know. The lies being told to folks back home…it's crazy…and being here makes it hard to remain neutral."

Mary Jo gave a slow nod. "War is cruel. But I'm sure you'll find most of the boys over here really believe in what they're doing at first."

"They do. Most." Kristin remembered the last few conversations she'd had with some of the GIs. "But they're tired. I don't think anyone thought it would go on this long. Or be this bloody. A lot of them just want to get the hell out." She flinched and put a hand up to her mouth. "Sorry."

Mary Jo laughed. "I've heard the word before, sweetie. Well, we can just keep praying for it to end, but only God knows when it will."

"I hope it does end soon," Kristin mused, thinking of Teddy. "My brother is out there somewhere."

Mary Jo reached across the table and took Kristin's hand. "What's his name?"

Kristin waited for the sour taste to hit her mouth. It didn't come. She measured the sincerity in the Mary Jo's eyes. "His name is Teddy. Theodore, actually. Everyone calls him Ted, except me and my Mom."

"I'll pray he stays safe, honey."

"Thanks. He'd appreciate that. He's big on prayer." Teddy didn't understand her estrangement from God. He'd always gone to church with Mom, believed everything they taught him and latched on with an unshakeable grip.

"And you?" The other woman's eyes were kind, no hint of judgment.

Kristin smiled and lifted her shoulders. "I'm not convinced he's paying that much attention."

"I see." A smile flashed, but she said nothing more. Kristin was grateful. She'd half-expected a lecture on the fires of hell.

It wasn't long before more of the younger children came in to the kitchen to distract them. Moments later, Kristin found herself underneath an old Banyan tree, reading a dilapidated copy of Mother Goose stories to six of them. They huddled in close on both sides. They craved the physical contact. Someone to hug them, tell them they were loved.

The little boy she held was called Tuan. No more than three years old, he'd fallen asleep as soon as Kristin had picked him up and put him in her lap. She wondered how he slept at night, in a crowded bed with other children all around. She smoothed down his glossy black hair, her heart aching. Mary Jo said there were thousands of Vietnamese children displaced, orphaned, sick and wounded as a result of the war. The numbers were staggering. Kristin wondered how they coped, not knowing what tomorrow would bring. Always afraid, wondering if you'd ever have anywhere to call home again.

A commotion at the gate drew her attention. Several of the children scrambled to their feet and ran toward the two men walking down the worn dirt path. The first man she didn't recognize, probably Mary Jo's husband. The tall blond man she recognized at once, and gaped in surprise.

Luke's arms were wrapped around several large brown paper packages. Head tipped back in laughter, he greeted the kids by name as he walked toward the front door. And then his eyes settled on her. "What on earth are you doing here, Taylor?"

Kristin met his startled look and held his gaze, unflinching. She could ask the same of him. "Getting lessons in rocket artillery."

Luke strode over to where she sat, put his bags down and crouched in front of her. His eyes moved from her to Tuan. He placed a hand on the little boy's cheek. A smile crossed his face. "He sleeps too much. He doesn't seem to have the energy the others do."

Kristin wanted to ask what he knew about children, but refrained. There was no telling which side of Luke's personality would show up, and she was not in the mood to be yelled at today.

"How'd you find this place?" His eyes were back on her.

She shifted Tuan from one leg to the other and felt the blood rushing back to the numb side. "Just happened across it. I had no idea I'd see you here."

"Good thing, probably."

She raised an eyebrow. "What are *you* doing here? I thought you didn't like children."

Luke gave a shrug and that half-smile she was getting used to. "I never said that." The twinkle in his eyes disturbed her. It was almost as though he was being…nice. One minute he was chewing her out, the next minute he was saving her life and acting almost human.

The children around her were getting impatient.

"Phó từ. Soon," she told them, pointing to the book, looking up in time to see Luke's eyes widen.

"You speak Vietnamese?"

He couldn't have appeared more shocked if he'd tried. "No, but I'm trying to learn. Is that okay with you?"

Luke shrugged, his face impassive again. "Sure. I'm just surprised. Not many people bother. I didn't think you would." His eyes left hers and returned to the child. Forget nice. He was still an idiot.

"Well, they should bother. This is their country. We're only guests here. You think I should be teaching these kids English instead?"

"No…" He met her eyes again, the usual frown set in place. Then after a minute, his expression changed.

And there it was.

A broad smile stretched his lips wide and brought his dimple out. A smile that said he was glad to see her, and meant it. It turned her insides to jelly, stole rational thought, and made her heart flip. Unbelievable. Even when he was being nice, Luke Maddox upturned her emotions.

"When are you going to stop assuming the worst of me, Taylor?"

"Sorry." She lowered her head and picked up the book she'd been reading. His accusation was too accurate and she couldn't meet his eyes.

Luke got to his feet and moved past her into the building, the children clamoring around him, leaving her and Humpty Dumpty in favor of Luke Maddox and his parcels. She longed to know what he'd brought, but refused to follow him inside. As soon as Tuan woke up, she'd head home.

The other man remained at the gate, picking deadheads off the rosebushes while she and Luke had talked. He now made his way to where she sat.

"Rocket artillery. Ha! Good one." His entire form shook with laughter. He ambled forward and leaned over her, extending a hand. "I'm Bob Granger." Kristin took it, returning his smile. Bob was just a tad taller than his wife, and balding. His thick white beard and jovial twinkle in his eyes made her think of Santa Claus. "You and Luke friends then?"

"Hardly." Kristin's smile faded.

"Oh, he's not so bad once you get past the prickles." He gave another snort of laughter. "Well, Kristin, you're welcome here anytime, honey. If you need a good meal and some half-decent company, you know where to come. Nice to meet you."

"You too."

He sauntered off and let himself into the house. Kristin released a deep sigh.

Not so bad? Right.

Somebody shook her shoulder and woke her from sweet, blessed sleep.

"Taylor? Wakie, wakie."

She opened one eye with reluctance.

"Hey, Tiger, up you come." Luke lifted the little boy out of her lap and handed him over to Mary Jo. Kristin leaned back against the tree again, mildly aware of a scorching heat in her throat and a jackhammer at work in her head. "You awake, Taylor?" He shook her again.

"Hum?" Kristin rubbed her eyes and blinked. Sunlight shot blazing arrows at her. How had she fallen asleep so easily? She pushed herself up and almost had to sit down again. Luke grabbed her arm before she fell.

"Easy, there. You okay?"

"Fine," she mumbled, feeling anything but. She let out a deep breath and drew one in. The fog began to clear. "How long have I been asleep?"

"About an hour, honey," Mary Jo came forward. "I would have come out sooner but we thought you'd gone. You should eat." Concern showed in the older woman's expression. "I've seen your type before. You run on empty, chasing helicopters and ducking hand grenades. Then you crash and burn. Take care of yourself, okay?"

"Thanks. Can I come back and see you again?" Kristin's eyes grew wet. She didn't have the slightest idea why. But something about this place resonated within—the children, the tragedy of it all, and the goodness of Bob and Mary Jo Granger.

Mary Jo took Kristin's hands in hers and squeezed them, her smile warm and comforting. "Come whenever you want. You're always welcome."

Kristin nodded and turned to pick up her backpack but Luke had already hoisted it over his shoulder, his camera bag slung over the other. She pursed her lips and decided not to say anything until they were out of earshot of her new friend. Halfway down the block, she stopped walking and stuck out her hand. "Give me my pack."

He slowed to a stop, gave her the once over and made that horrid clucking noise. "Forget your manners, Sunshine?" His eyes hid behind dark shades, but she was sure they held laughter.

"Give me my pack. *Please*." She glared, hoping he'd get the point and leave her alone. "I can carry it myself."

"I'm well aware of that, but I thought I'd do you a favor. Do you mind?"

"Yes." Kristin coughed. The effort made her headache worse. He raised a blond eyebrow but still held her bag. She coughed again, feeling sicker by the minute. Fine. He could carry it if he insisted.

"You want to get something to eat? Have you had lunch?"

"No." Kristin leaned up against a nearby tree, breathing becoming an effort. Perspiration trickled down her temple. She hated to sweat. And she'd done nothing but since the moment she'd come to this godforsaken country.

Luke pulled out a flask of water and offered it to her. "No, you haven't had lunch or no, you don't want to get something to eat?"

"Both." The warm water wet her lips and satisfied her parched throat. "I don't feel so good."

He held a hand against her forehead and let out a low whistle. "Do you think you can walk home?"

"How far is it?" Thorns scratched the back of her throat. Her joints hurt. Her eyes hurt. Everything hurt. She sank down onto the grass and put her head in her hands.

"Are you lost again, Taylor?" His quiet chuckle wrapped around her and soothed her in an alarming way. As if she wasn't nauseated enough.

She needed sleep. Whatever bug had seen fit to attack her was doing so with a vengeance. As long as she hadn't passed it along to all those kids at the orphanage. She just hoped it wasn't malaria.

"Remind me to get you a map of Saigon for Christmas, okay?"

"Christmas? When's Christmas?" Bob Granger's jolly face flashed before her. Nothing made sense anymore. Christmas was months away, wasn't it? Sweat ran down her cheeks and mingled with tears she had no control over. "I don't want to be here for Christmas. I want…to go home."

There. She'd said it. She wouldn't mean it tomorrow. But today it sounded pretty good. To be in her own bed, Mom baking something delicious in the kitchen, and Teddy out back, mowing the lawn.

Teddy.

"Oh, boy. Listen." Luke crouched in front of her, swaying violently. Or maybe she was swaying. "I'm going to pick you up. Don't scream, okay?"

She couldn't have. The minute he lifted her in his strong arms, her head fell against his shoulder and the lights went out.

Chapter Eleven

Luke stood off to one side and watched the frail-looking Vietnamese woman cradle the dead man in her arms. She wailed and screamed curses at them in her own language. Chickens pecked at the dirt around the macabre scene.

"Maddox. Let's go." The other guys headed for their Jeep while Jonno hung back, watching him.

Two small children ran out of the hut, stared wide-eyed at the blood pooling around their feet. Dogs barked off in the distance. Luke closed his eyes against an assault of memory. Hitting the pavement, staring at the smoldering debris in front of him and shouting and cursing at the gooks, at God. And knowing that every waking moment from then on, he'd seek retribution for what had been taken from him.

He couldn't explain why now, after so many years, this felt so wrong. Nor did he understand why a child's cries still woke him in the dead of night when he knew full well there were no children in the apartment building he lived in.

"Hey, man." A hand clamped down on his shoulder and made him jump. "We're done here. Let's split."

Luke drew in a breath, met Jonno's eyes and nodded.

They drove back mostly in silence. Luke wondered what Kristin was up to today. He'd introduced her to a couple of dust-off pilots and she'd been flying around with them. They were crazy good at what they did and he couldn't wait to read whatever piece she'd come up with after that experience. Providing of course, she survived it.

And why did he care whether she did? She'd been snooping around too much, even sniffed out a couple of his colleagues, started asking them questions. She was wading into dangerous territory, and the rub of it was, he suspected she knew it.

Once he'd discovered she was Malcolm Taylor's daughter, Luke soon put two and two together. If she'd chosen to walk the same path as her father, and all signs said she had, Kristin Taylor would soon be in more danger than he could keep her out of. Snakebites, VC and explosions were nothing compared to what the Agency would do if they decided to take her out.

Luke slammed his hand against the dash of the Jeep, startling Jonno at the wheel. They swerved to one side, but Jonno managed to right them before the vehicle tipped.

"You okay?" His friend shot him a sidelong glance, maneuvering expertly past potholes at breakneck speed.

"Groovy." Luke watched the passing trees as they whizzed along the road. Greens blurred with the blue of the horizon, then merged into green again as they climbed higher up the mountain road.

"Seen much of Kristin lately?" Jonno asked, shifting gears. "She was sick for a while, huh?"

Luke grunted. "Nothing serious. Didn't keep her down for long, unfortunately. She doesn't know when to back off."

"She wants a story. That's her job."

"She'll get more than a story if she's not careful. She'll get a bullet through the head."

Jonno grinned. "Not from you, I hope."

Luke shook his head and hit the dash again. "I can't be in two places at once. I can't be responsible for her. Hayden's asked me to keep an eye on her but for..."

"Hole!" Jonno swerved the Jeep just in time to avoid a large pothole. He maneuvered around it and sped up again. Red dirt flew high into the air and smattered the windshield. "She writes killer stories, no pun intended. Have you read them? The guys love her."

"I've noticed." Luke gnawed on his bottom lip. She *was* a gifted writer. She was blunt without being graphic, honest and forthright. And she connected with the guys out there in a way that he hadn't expected. Everywhere she went she seemed to fit right in. Her wide smile and easy-going manner set everyone at ease. Even the Marines talked to her.

His bet of her giving up after a few weeks had been way off base.

Kristin Taylor was unpredictable. He liked that.

"Being almost fearless in the middle of a war isn't necessarily a good attribute, mate."

Jonno laughed and pressed down on the accelerator. "That's kind of funny coming from you."

Luke pushed aside a low hanging branch as they whizzed past it.

Her hidden agenda worried him. He'd seen her palling around with that French slime-ball who was forever after the company men to give him an exclusive. Of course nobody would.

"Ooo, man. She's got to you." Jonno's laugh hinted of delight.

Luke scowled at his insightfulness, but it didn't surprise him. "Don't be stupid."

"I try not to be, but ya know sometimes it jest comes natural like."

"I never would have guessed." Luke had seen through Jonno's act at their first meeting. He was intelligent and had proven himself invaluable.

"Well, I'll be happy to trail her."

"You're on, Hicks." Luke cracked his knuckles and flinched. "She's definitely not into me."

Jonno spun the steering wheel hard to avoid a boulder in the road. "You noticed?"

Luke couldn't stop a smile. "Kind of hard not to." Then he frowned, checked behind them again. Maybe if he did a piece with her it would get her off his back. He could talk Hayden into it easily enough. He'd done him enough favors in the past.

Luke clenched his jaw, feeling for the butt of his revolver at his side. He shifted as they bumped along the rocky road, and glanced at his watch. An image of Kristin flashed across his mind again.

When he'd walked up the path to the orphanage that day and found her sitting under the tree, Tuan in her lap, his heart jumped. Her long hair fell forward over her shoulders, her face set in an almost serene smile as she read to the children. She seemed to be enjoying herself—until she saw him. Her smile disappeared and her nose wrinkled with that trademark scowl.

It was the last place he'd expected to find her, and the last place he knew she'd expect to see him. But it was almost as though…it was fate or something like it. If he still believed in such things.

He didn't. Wouldn't.

Yet something in him changed that day, and he'd recognized the feeling. Attraction.

Luke hadn't felt it for so long, he'd almost forgotten…but on that day, looking at her, the numbness around his heart began to soften. And since then, watching her around the GIs, seeing her compassion, her outrage and her determination to somehow come through this with her sanity intact, he'd begun to question his own reasons for being in Vietnam.

Luke shook his head. Whatever growing feelings he had for Kristin Taylor would have to take a back seat.

"Luke!"

Jonno's yell startled him. "What?"

"I asked you the same question three times! You going deaf on me?"

"What?"

"How much longer?"

"About ten minutes. Why?"

"I think we have a tail." Jonno's voice dropped as he angled his side mirror. Luke's backward glance confirmed Jonno's suspicions. He grabbed his pistol and moved his foot against the M-16 on the floor of the Jeep. He could reach for it in two seconds if he had to. The Jeep behind them picked up speed and Luke swallowed. Dirt flew as Jonno accelerated.

"I can off road her in two minutes, there's a path up here…"

"Do it," Luke replied as the first bullet ricocheted off the back of the Jeep.

Kristin rifled through the mail after coming in from another week of traveling to various camps. Two letters for Luke. Madame seemed to think they all lived in the same apartment. She separated her mail from Caroline's, then took the two airmail letters addressed to him and marched down the hall. The door to his apartment sat ajar. Kristin knocked, and poked her head around the door. "Luke?"

No answer. The place was still in shambles. Newspapers and magazines were strewn everywhere, camera equipment and photographs all over the table. She craned her neck to look at the pictures.

"Maddox? You home?" She tried again. Both doors to the bathroom and bedroom were closed. Fleeting memories of Luke pointing a gun at her made her hesitate.

She tiptoed around the apartment, searching for family photos, any-thing that would give her more insight on the man who was slowly begin-ning to drive her insane. There were none.

He remained an enigma.

The sound of a door slamming froze her to the spot.

Luke stepped into the living room from the hall. His dirt-smeared face gave away nothing as he dropped his pack to the floor.

"Lost again?"

"Nice to see you, too." Kristin waved the two envelopes at him. "Your mail was in our box. You should keep your door locked."

Luke narrowed his eyes. "Apparently."

He looked bad. "Are you all right?"

He gave his head a shake and fixed her with a glare that would have frozen the Sahara. "You went to Hayden behind my back?" His cheeks darkened and the tendon in his jaw pulsed.

"What?" Kristin drew herself up and stared him down. "About what? I never said anything to Hayden."

Luke raised his eyes to the ceiling. "I just got off the phone with him. He wants us working together. Permanently." His eyes flashed under the overhead light and she knew he wasn't joking.

"I had nothing to do with it. Stop being so moronic. Oh, I forgot. You can't help it."

"Shut up, Taylor."

"Well, I haven't talked to Hayden in a couple of weeks." She huffed out a sigh and dragged her fingers through her tangled hair. "He wants us to work together?"

Luke swore and marched across the room. She heard him banging around in the kitchen. A slow smile slid across her lips. She banished it as soon as he returned.

"You don't have to. You work freelance, right?" Her eyes moved to the vast array of photographs on the table. "Can I have a look?"

"You already have." He moved aside anyway and she walked toward the table.

His talent spoke for itself. The black and white photographs were shockingly graphic. Haunting images of soldiers after battle – the dead littered the ground, their comrades sitting around, stunned expressions on their faces…he had captured the horrors of war.

"You really are a photographer." Kristin reached for another stack of photographs and smiled at the change in subject matter. Jonno goofing off—dancing around camp wearing one of the nurses' caps. Another showed him sprawled over the hood of a Jeep, mouth open in sleep. She grinned. Many of the photos were taken at the 24th Surgical.

"Hey, you got me!" Kristin stiffened, startled to see her own image captured on film. But there she was, crouched beside a group of smiling GIs, notebook and pencil in hand, helmet on her head. Another stolen moment showed her asleep at a table in the mess hall, head down on her arms. She'd just returned from her first overnight trip to a firebase. There had been some heavy shelling and she'd spent hours huddled in a foxhole, under orders not to move. Afterward, it was as though all life had been sucked out of her. Yet another picture showed her laughing with Jonno and Doc, no doubt at one of Jonno's corny jokes.

"Have you been following me around?" Slow heat touched her cheeks.

Luke shrugged, glancing her way. "Didn't think to ask permission."

Kristin flicked through the rest of the pictures. "You're very talented. I wouldn't mind working with you. But since you're clearly not interested…"

Luke brushed past her, stacked the photos and put them into a large manila envelope. His sigh was just audible. "I didn't say no. The money's good."

"Really?" She watched in silence as Luke fiddled with his camera.

"Hayden wants you to call him. But I'm not taking orders from you. Just so we're clear."

"I wouldn't dare, Mr. Maddox. I might get shot."

"Right." His eyes sparkled for an instant before he scowled again. "I need time on my own too."

Kristin raised an eyebrow. "Fine with me."

His jaw twitched and he put his hands behind his head. "I'm not going to be responsible for getting your stories either. I'll take the pictures but you find your own stuff. And please drop the CIA theories or I really will shoot you."

Kristin put her hands on her hips and shook her head. "You're insufferable, Luke Maddox. I'm quite capable of finding my own stories, thank you very much, and I don't care for your assumption. I'm not a child. Is this why your wife left you?"

A look crossed his face that made Kristin regret her words at once. Luke released a long breath, then his eyes pinned her again.

"She didn't leave me. She died."

Chapter Twelve

Kristin recoiled at his words. Her mother always said that her sharp tongue would be the cause of her undoing. She should have heeded the warning.

"I'm sorry. I had no idea." Kristin studied her muddy boots, still reeling. She lifted her head, studied the shadows under his eyes and the tense way he held himself and wondered just how long he intended to run from the pain of his past.

Luke shifted, folded his arms across his chest, looking toward the window for a moment. "It's not something I advertise. I thought Caroline might have mentioned it by now."

"No. She didn't. Luke, I'm sorry...I...didn't mean..."

"Forget it." He raised a hand in dismissal. "I'd rather not talk about it. So, where were we?"

"I think you were making threats on my life. Again."

"Right." An unexpected grin creased his tanned face. "I don't know, Taylor. I might keep you around a little while longer. You just got me a raise. That's gotta count for something." He left her gaping and stalked toward the kitchen.

She grinned, tension slipping away. "You know you're going to have to stop being so charming. I don't think I'll be able to stand it."

Luke returned, holding two bottles of Coke. "Sit."

Charming indeed. Kristin lifted an eyebrow, sending a half smile his way.

He flashed a grin and raised his eyes to the ceiling. "Please. Sit."

Luke shoved aside the paper debris on the couch and she sat. He handed her one of the bottles and positioned himself on the floor in front of her. Kristin wrapped her clammy hands around the cold glass. They drank in silence.

"Have you heard from your brother?"

Kristin spluttered as fizz tickled her nose. Her nerves still jumped every time he opened his mouth. "Yes. He's okay. Didn't say where he was. I'm hoping I'll run into him at some point."

Luke took a long swig, his eyes fixed on her. "Knowing you, you'll get yourself out to every unit between here and the DMZ until you do."

"What's wrong with that? If you're trying to irritate me, you've already succeeded. You don't need to push the limit."

"Do you have a limit?"

Kristin couldn't stop a smile. She was hot, sweaty, probably stunk to high heaven, and still annoyed beyond belief, but something in his tone and the teasing look in his eyes scaled the high wall she'd built around her heart so long ago.

"How about we find some middle ground? I'll try not to annoy you, and you…well…maybe you could just not talk."

Luke ran his tongue over his bottom lip. "Sounds doable. Although I think it might be better if you were the one who didn't talk."

His deep laugh chased away nerves. Kristin placed her bottle down on the floor. "So, truce?" She stuck out her hand.

The overhead fan made the only sound in the room as he regarded her in silence. "Might make life a little dull, don't you think?" His smile broadened and new energy charged through her.

"Oh, don't sell yourself short. I'm sure you'll find some way to aggravate me in less than forty-eight hours, but for now, truce."

"Done." He pushed himself off the floor, stood before her and said nothing for a minute. Then he smiled and took her hand in his. The spark his touch ignited almost made her pull back. But his grip was firm and his eyes held hers. "Something tells me I'll live to regret this, Taylor."

She extricated her hand but returned the smile. "To live is the rarest thing in the world. Most people exist, that is all."

"Oscar Wilde." His dimple came out to play.

"Mmm." She drew her knees up to her chest as he sat down again. "I want change and excitement and to shoot off in all directions myself, like the colored arrows from a Fourth of July rocket."

Luke tapped a finger on his chin for a minute. "Sylvia Plath."

"Impressive, Mr. Maddox."

"Change is the law of life. And those who look only to the past or present are certain to miss the future."

"JFK." Kristin rubbed the cross around her neck and sniffed sudden moisture. "Well. I suppose we could sit here for the rest of the day and throw quotes at each other, but what do you do around here for fun?"

"Oh, it's fun you want, is it?" Boyish mischief crept into his eyes. "Have you ever driven a Jeep?"

An army Jeep sat out front of the apartment building. Kristin didn't know whether it was the same vehicle Jonno drove, didn't care to ask where he was or how Luke happened to be in possession of it.

He waved the keys in her face. "What's the matter, Taylor, you chicken?" His eyes held challenge and she grinned. She'd always wanted to drive a Jeep.

Kristin climbed into the driver's seat. Luke swung his legs over the other side and hopped in. "Go straight down our road and around the block. There won't be as much traffic."

Kristin turned the ignition switch and stared down at the gearshift.

Luke put his hands behind his head and yawned. "You *do* know how to drive a car, right, Taylor?"

"Of course. But…" This didn't look anything like their old Ford station wagon back home.

"Hit the clutch and put her in first. No, not up, down and to the left." His hand came over hers, warm and surprisingly gentle. Kristin suppressed a giggle as the Jeep jerked forward, gave a little shudder and then died.

"What happened?"

"You let the clutch out too fast." He removed his hand and stared straight ahead. "Try again."

She grimaced, flicked on the indicator and pressed her foot down on the clutch once more. She gave it a little gas and they moved forward about two feet. Kristin pressed the gas pedal a little harder and the Jeep shuddered to a stop in the middle of the road. A groan escaped her.

"I give up." A truck rolled past and honked several times, making her jump.

Luke's sigh was long and loud, and aggravating beyond belief. "Let's go, Taylor. We're kind of in the middle of the road here, in case you hadn't noticed."

"I noticed. I don't really need to do this. Can we just switch seats?"

"Nope." He shook his head. "Start her again and don't give it too much gas at first."

A feeble sigh stuck in her throat. Exhaustion took away her spirit of adventure. "Luke."

"Yes?" His wry grin made an appearance and she glowered at him as another vehicle whizzed past, its occupants yelling obscenities at them.

"Luke! Forget it. Get me off the road."

His grin faded, replaced by a stern look as he swiveled to face her. "Say you're out in the middle of Highway 1, and you come under attack. You're the only one not dead or wounded. How are you going to get yourself out of there?"

"Fine." She clenched her jaw and stared at the dash. "I suppose next you'll want to teach me how to shoot that gun of yours."

"Good idea. I'll put it on the calendar. Now, can we get going?"

Kristin started the engine again, depressed the clutch, gave a little gas and drove forward. This time they moved along the road without stalling.

"Excellent." Luke stretched his arms above his head. "We should make it back by breakfast tomorrow at this rate."

"Quiet, I'm concentrating." She hit the gas too hard and slowed a bit, but there was nothing in front of them so she accelerated again. A faint breeze kissed her cheeks and Kristin smiled. She could get used to this.

Luke applauded. "That's more like it. Any idea what the speed limit is around here?"

Kristin shot him a sidelong glance just as a loud honk behind her forced her to slow down. Another jeep pulled up alongside, its occupants, two MPs staring at her, their surprise soon switching to displeasure. Kristin's heart rate tripled.

She pulled over to the curb and put on her best smile. Whatever story she came up with in the next two seconds better be a good one. She looked to Luke for help and her eyebrows arched. He slumped in his seat, his blond head bowed, eyes closed. Horror gripped her, panic hot on its heels. Her passenger had conveniently lapsed into a state of catatonia.

"Oh, come on, don't be an idiot!" she hissed between gritted teeth.

One of the MPs strode around the jeep. He rested his forearms up against her side of the vehicle and drummed his fingers on the metal door. Although he didn't look much older than her, he didn't look happy enough for her to feel at all comfortable in his presence.

"Well, well. What have we here? A civilian operating military equipment? My-oh-my. Name?"

"Kristin Taylor. I'm working for TIME, sir." Kristin cleared her throat as her heart pounded out what could be her final breaths. Her story on POW's might come sooner than expected. Written from first hand experience.

"Bully for you. I don't suppose you have a license to drive this military jeep, Miss Taylor?"

"No, but I…uh…well, he couldn't very well drive it, could he?" She rolled her eyes in disgust as she looked at the 'sleeping' Luke. He let out a little snore for effect. "I warned him he'd had too much, but he never listens…"

"Right. Well, he doesn't have a license either. And the Private who usually drives this joker around would be…where?" A slight grin played around the MP's mouth.

Kristin almost smiled. Freedom lay just around the corner and sounded better by the minute. "Um—he uh, had some urgent business to attend to. He said we should take the Jeep." Hope Jonno's the forgiving kind.

"Get out of here, and off the streets, Miss Taylor. Don't let me catch you driving again."

"No, sir. You won't." Catch me. Kristin pulled out onto the road and breathed a sigh of relief. A snort that soon erupted into a loud round of laughter came from her passenger.

She shot out a hand and clipped him over the head. "That was *not* funny! Do you have any idea how close I came to having a heart attack? And you…you could have stuck your neck out, said something to help me out, but no, you decide to lapse into a coma!"

His mouth fell open, his look of chagrin so put-on she almost hit him again. "So, you're mad?"

"That would be an understatement."

"What happened to change and excitement?"

"Getting arrested wasn't on the list, Luke!"

"Well, you didn't get arrested, did you?" He tipped his head and gave her that I'm-talking-to-a-five-year-old look. "You're getting your knickers in a twist for nothing, sweetheart."

Kristin just about missed the turn off to the other end of their street and the tires screeched along the tarmac as she spun the wheel, causing the Jeep to tip to one side.

Luke's face drained of color. "Are you trying to kill me?"

Kristin pulled into the parking bay outside their building. "It's tempting. And don't call me sweetheart. Ever again."

"So we're going back to being mortal enemies?" He widened his eyes and placed his hands over his heart. "I was just starting to like you, Taylor."

His crushed expression was so insincere that Kristin burst out laughing. "All right, fine. That was fun. Happy now?"

"Delirious." He hopped out and held out a hand as she climbed out of the vehicle. "I haven't eaten yet. There's a nice restaurant just around the block. Care to join me, sweetheart?"

Her indignation was pushed aside by the light in his eyes. And if she were honest with herself, she'd have to admit that right now, she'd like nothing more, so she gave a quick nod before she changed her mind.

Chapter Thirteen

$\mathcal{D}$ays of jostling the other journalists for space on the hot tarmac at the airstrip were wearing on her. Kristin wondered if hanging around helicopters might make her prematurely deaf.

The pilot waved her on board and she shouted her thanks, recognizing him. Familiar faces were always comforting.

Two other reporters jumped into the helicopter after her, and just as they were about to lift off, she saw Luke tussling with Jean Luc for the last spot.

It was high time Luke Maddox showed up. He'd disappeared for so long this time that she wondered if something had happened to him. So far she'd only been able to file one story that he'd actually taken photographs for. Hayden was wondering what was going on.

That was the sixty-four thousand dollar question.

"I'm with her!" Luke's shout got her attention. "We're working together."

Kristin snapped her head up. The pilot turned to her as they loaded the final box of supplies onto the Huey.

"That right, Miss Taylor?"

"Yes, that's right." At least they were supposed to be.

Luke took the vacant spot beside her, hunching his long frame into what looked like a very uncomfortable position. Kristin clenched the sides of the seat and shot him a glare as they took off. The helicopter bumped through cloud cover and Kristin bit her lip. She decided not long after her arrival here that she really hated flying.

She narrowed her eyes and leaned toward him. "Do you have any idea how many times I've waited around for you the past two weeks?"

He fiddled with his camera equipment and didn't look up, but a small grin lifted his features. "I've been busy."

"Doing what, exactly?"

"None of your business."

Kristin wiped her hands over her face, already tired and thirsty, and interminably hot. She'd argued with Hayden over the phone yesterday. He sounded uneasy about printing her last story. She'd given some startling statistics about the war, how many were dying, what the men said. Her facts didn't line up with what the Army touted as truth.

"I thought we had an agreement, Luke," she yelled, "I'm trying to do a job here!"

"So am I! I told you I wasn't going to check in with you 24/7. But I'm glad you missed me."

"Shut up." She wanted to smack him, but the other journalists were already staring, and the gunner at the door seemed a tad too interested in their conversation.

"I'm sorry." Luke stared out the window. "I've had some other stuff to deal with."

"Fine. Just get some good pictures today." Kristin leaned forward to look out of the chopper. Thick clouds of black smoke rose from the lush mountains below. She covered her mouth but it stung her eyes. A loud explosion shook the helicopter and the pilot lifted them above it. The gunner fired off a round and she jumped back.

Luke angled his camera and began to snap. With shaking hands, Kristin fastened her helmet and made sure her flak jacket was secure.

"We've got a hot zone!" The pilot yelled over his shoulder, "I'm gonna go down real fast and get out. Jump or stay on board, it's your call!"

Kristin gathered her things, inched toward the door and made ready to jump when given the signal. Adrenaline pumped through her veins and she swallowed down fear.

"What are you doing?" Luke growled, pulling off his shades. His eyes filled with worry.

Kristin stared. "What do you think I'm doing? Getting out of course."

"Kris...I don't think that's a good idea."

Another explosion sounded, louder than before, and the helicopter lurched to one side. Kristin's stomach went with it. She gripped the handle above her head, steadying herself. The distinct sound of gunfire rattled above the rotors.

"You don't have to come." So much for working together. She scooted over to the side of the helicopter on her bottom, dangled her legs just above the landing skid on her side and waited. Time did not allow second thoughts. Within moments they hovered above the ground and the pilot gave the signal to get out or sit back and stay down.

Kristin pushed off and sailed out of the chopper.

She was already through the trees and digging her hole when she realized Luke was right behind her.

"Incoming! Get down! Stupid reporters—get down!"

Luke pushed her down and covered her body with his as a round of gunfire landed less than ten feet away. Dirt flew high and scattered around them, hitting her helmet like hail. "Remind me to thank you later for getting us killed, will you, Taylor?" His breath burned in her ear and did nothing to soothe her anxious disposition.

"Be quiet," she hissed, straining to see above the dirt hole they lay in. "And get off me. You weigh a ton."

A couple of fighter jets zoomed in and pelted the hill across the plain with artillery. The noise was deafening. Kristin shuddered and drew deep breaths. The enemy within the hills retaliated with a volley of firepower that seemed to go on forever.

Back and forth, back and forth...

At last the land fell into silence. Smoke clouded her vision and her ears rang with the lingering reminder of firepower. Kristin spotted the platoon commander over in the field assessing the situation. She scrambled up and over the red soil embankment and stopped short.

The eerie silence roared victory, but for whom?

When her boot struck something solid, she looked down and jumped back.

All around her lay the fallen.

She stood in the middle of a motionless sea of green fatigues. Splattered blood, flesh, stray helmets and boots littered the muddy ground. Nausea rose, and she knew if she paused long enough to think, she'd throw up.

This was what she'd come here to see, to write about, to experience. Right now it was the last place she wanted to be.

Kristin gasped for breath. Her hands began to shake and she clenched them at her sides. She didn't know which way to turn.

The silence broke as moans and shouts began to fill the air. Young men calling out for help, calling for their mothers—Jesus—anyone. Most of the soldiers closest to her made no noise. Some stared up at her through vacant eyes. Dead or barely alive.

A hand grabbed hers and squeezed, and she jumped again, her nerves raw. "Don't look down. Just keep walking. Straight ahead. We'll get out of here as soon we can." Luke's voice was the only thing that made sense. She gripped his hand and held on. Her body emulated the tremors that shook the ground a short while ago.

"I—can't. I can't move." Tears blurred her vision. This was the worst she'd seen. The worst she wanted to see.

"Come on. Just follow me. I won't let you go." Luke held tight to her hand and pulled her through hell.

Chapter Fourteen

A dinner party seemed like a good idea at the time. A bit of relief from the horrors they encountered out in the field day after day. Now, just an hour before her guests were due to arrive, Kristin wondered at her sanity.

Cooking on a small stovetop with an oven barely large enough to hold the casserole dish she'd borrowed from Madame D. proved more challenging than anticipated. Kristin persevered, sweating and cursing the minuscule kitchen all afternoon.

A tap on the door at six-forty five startled her. "Go away! You're early!" she yelled, looking out of the kitchen as Jonno poked his head around the front door and winked at her.

"I hear there's a five star chef in here. Can I come in?"

"Only if you want to set the table and slice bread." Kristin turned off the burner, smoothed down her blouse and checked her cotton skirt.

Jonno sauntered into the kitchen and let out a whistle. "Wowza, it smells good! Just like home." The wide smile on his face made the afternoon of sweat and frustration worth it.

To her delight, he'd brought her a couple more of his carvings. She displayed her growing collection on her dresser, along with the shells she gathered when she could get down to the beach.

"Let's hope it tastes as good as it smells." Kristin checked the vegetables and opened the oven a crack.

"What're we having?"

"Beef Bourguignon." She screwed up her nose at the potatoes. They were far too big and would take forever to roast. She contemplated taking them out of the pan and boiling them.

"Well, I don't know what that is, but I'm sure it'll be good." He grabbed the cutlery and started for the dining area. Kristin smiled. She enjoyed him. He made her laugh.

Caroline's boyfriend Peter arrived next with a bottle of fine wine and Belgian chocolates. Always the charmer.

Kristin allowed him to peck her on the cheek. He wore civvies and she wondered if this meant Caroline would be disappearing for a few days, as she so often did. "Are you off on leave again? I'm beginning to think the Army never works."

Caroline appeared from the bedroom, radiant in a simple linen dress the color of the ocean and her eyes. Kristin was about to offer drinks when the door opened again.

Luke strode into the apartment. "Evening, all. Am I late?" He pulled a bunch of fresh flowers—a peculiar mixture of purple orchids, pink roses and yellow daises, with twigs of eucalyptus—from behind his back and offered them to Kristin.

Jonno cleared his throat and grinned. Caroline's blatant stare made Kristin's cheeks burn. She blew out a breath and took the flowers. "Well, aren't you full of surprises?"

"You have no idea." Luke smile hinted at more mysteries than she could imagine.

"So what's for grub? C-Rations?" He wandered over to the table and picked up a slice of bread.

"Beef Smorgasbord," Jonno said helpfully. He frowned at Luke. "You know that's rude. We haven't been invited to sit down, let alone said grace yet."

"Nice to see you, Hicks." Luke reached for the large jug of water in the middle of the table, and began to fill the glasses.

"Nice to see you too," Jonno grumbled. "You know if you're gonna disappear for days on end you could at least let me know you're going."

"Yes, dear. I'll be sure to leave a note next time." Luke grinned and Jonno glared.

Kristin found a vase in the kitchen for the flowers. She set the colorful arrangement down on the table. Perfect. "Don't give him a hard time, Luke. Apart from your father, Jonathan is one of the few men I've met in this country who knows how to act like a gentleman. Although the flowers do raise your own standing somewhat."

"*Jonathan?*" Luke whistled. "Taylor, I must say, he's a bit young for you."

"Luke!" Jonno's dark complexion turned even darker.

Luke took a seat at the table, laughter escaping. "Kidding. Okay?"

Caroline took the seat next to Luke. "What's gotten into you?"

"I have no idea what you're talking about." Luke grabbed his glass and gulped water.

Kristin rolled her eyes, went to the kitchen and retrieved her dish from the oven. She reached between them to place it on a corkboard in the middle of the table and pulled her hand back as a word she rarely used slipped out. She'd used a shabby potholder, and the heat of the dish burned through to her skin. She sucked her finger and flinched.

Luke turned in her direction. "Let me see." He grabbed her hand and inspected it like he was a doctor. "Looks all right. Go run it under the tap."

Kristin didn't miss Caroline's look of astonishment. "It's fine, thanks." She yanked her hand from Luke's and sped back to the kitchen to get the vegetables.

"You're awfully concerned," she heard Caroline say. An audible sigh came from Luke.

"Give me a break." His voice lowered and she didn't catch the rest of what he said. Caroline's laughter floated through the apartment. "I think you're a little smitten."

"I can arrange an excruciatingly slow and painful death for you, my dear sister."

"You love me too much."

"Try me."

Kristin cleared her throat as she entered the room, determined to end the fray. "Children, please, that's quite enough. Now, if you're ready to eat, we can begin." Her stern tone incited more laughter but stopped the argument. She took the only empty chair, which happened to be next to Jonno and opposite Luke. They all helped themselves and began to dig in.

Jonno stared them down with a look of disgust. "Don't ya'll think we should ask the Lord to bless the food?"

Kristin smiled. At home Mom would never let them eat without praying first. She looked across the table and caught Luke's eye. Jonno's faith had reminded her of her own upbringing on more than one occasion. "All right. Maybe Luke would say the blessing."

He stared back at her with what looked like mild amusement. "Sure. Shall we pray?" Luke bowed his head.

Kristin choked, but closed her eyes. This would be interesting.

He cleared his throat, and began. "Father, thanks for this food. We ask that you would bless the hands that prepared it, and bless our friends in the fire tonight, God. Just be with all the guys out there. Protect them. And let them kick butt. In Jesus' name, amen."

When she opened her eyes, she found him staring straight at her, a satisfied grin set in place.

"What?" He feigned innocence and she gaped.

"You can't ask God to let them kick butt!" She couldn't suppress a giggle anyway.

Luke shrugged, taking a mouthful. "I can ask God whatever I want. You asked me to pray. I prayed. This is delicious, Taylor. If I'd known you could cook so well, I'd have invited myself for dinner a long time ago."

"I'm sure my brother back home is asking the same thing," Jonno added, shoveling food into his mouth at a rapid rate. "He's a preacher. Best preacher south of Atlanta."

"If I offended you, Taylor, I'm sorry. Okay?" Luke wiped his mouth with the back of his hand, his stare intense.

She drew in a breath and looked away. "You didn't offend me. Forget it."

Luke grunted and continued to eat like he hadn't seen food in a year.

"See? There you go again." Caroline pointed her fork at him, dissolving into laughter. "You're acting—well—human."

"As opposed to what, Caroline? Alien?" Luke glowered and shoved a piece of bread in his mouth.

Kristin began to eat and prayed for the rest of the evening to fly by.

"Anyone need a ride up north with me tomorrow? I'm taking supplies up. I'll probably have room for a passenger or two." Jonno mumbled through bites, on his third helping. Good thing she'd made more than the recipe called for. "Wow, this is really good. My Mama needs this recipe. Miss her cornbread bad, though."

"Where are you headed, Hicks?" Peter asked, draining what was left of the wine.

Jonno swallowed his mouthful and drank some water. "Up toward Da Nang. Maybe for a few days. There's talk of my unit being transferred."

"Da Nang?" Kristin put down her glass. "That's up near the DMZ, right? Why are you going there?"

Jonno shrugged. "We don't ask, we just point and shoot. Maybe they'll let me walk point, huh, Luke?"

"You're not walking point," Luke growled. "You shouldn't even be in Vietnam."

"Ain't you glad I am though?" Jonno shot her a grin as Kristin raised an eyebrow in question, mystified by the altercation.

"I have asthma," he explained. "It wasn't bad until I got here. If I enlisted now, I'd get a 4-F, unfit for service. That's how come I get to play chauffer and run errands. Technically, they could have sent me home, but I wanted to stay and do my tour."

"Why?" Kristin smiled at the serious expression on his face, but the discomfort in his eyes disturbed her. "Why don't you go home, Jonno?"

He shrugged, set down his fork and met her eyes, his smile sad. "I'm a black kid from the South. What do I have at home? I got no money for college. My Mama's got four kids at home and works three jobs. My Daddy ran off two years ago. Crazy as it sounds, I like it here."

"Oh, please." Peter put down his glass. "You people are always wanting us to feel sorry for you," he slurred. "You think whites have it any easier? That there are no poor white people?"

"Peter, for God's sake." Caroline put a hand on his arm. Kristin glanced at Luke and saw his eyes narrow. Peter was probably half drunk when he'd arrived, and now he was definitely over the limit.

Jonno cleared his throat. "I'm not looking for any trouble, Captain."

"No? Just a hand up, right, Hicks? A few years in the army will get you where you want to go? You and your friends can march on Washington 'till the cows come home but you'll never…"

Luke pushed to his feet and placed his hands on the table, towering over Peter. "I suggest you knock it off," he growled. "Now."

"Or what?" Peter stood and threw his napkin onto his plate. "Gonna haul me in for questioning, Maddox? Write me up? Who do you think you're fooling here?"

"Peter, stop it. Just go, sleep it off." Caroline went to him and pulled him from the table. He marched out of the apartment without another word.

"Sorry. I better make sure he gets home." Caroline shot Kristin a despairing look and followed him, shutting the door behind her.

Luke huffed and sat down again, resuming his meal as though nothing had happened.

"Jonno…" Kristin began, desperate to break the uncomfortable silence. Peter's behavior appalled her. Of course she was well aware of prejudice of all forms, but she'd rarely had to deal with it. In her circles back home, she'd never experienced racism firsthand. "I'm sorry. He was way out of line."

"I'm used to it." Jonno flashed his good-natured grin. "Maybe he's right though. Maybe all the marching in the world just won't change the way things are."

"I don't believe that," Kristin said quickly. "I think you have to stand up for what's right, whatever it is, fight against oppression in any form, talk to anyone and everyone until somebody listens."

"You've got that part down," Luke noted, grabbing the last piece of bread.

Jonno laughed, gave Kristin a small smile and settled back in his chair. "Let's be honest, do ya'll think you'd ever invite me for dinner at your house back in Boston?"

"I wouldn't," Luke said, reaching for the vegetables. "But not because you're black. I wouldn't have enough grub for you."

"Good thing, 'cause you wouldn't be able to cook anyways." Jonno laughed and looked back at Kristin. "What about you?"

Kristin's cheeks began to tingle. She pushed her plate away. Jonno didn't mean any harm. He'd just asked a question. But the answer—the truth—smarted.

Jonno's smile faded and he gave his hefty shoulders a shrug. "I'm just messing with you, you don't have to answer."

"No." Kristin shook her head. "No, you're right. I probably wouldn't have invited you for dinner. Not a few months ago. But now," she raised her hands and then slowly lowered them again. Her eyes burned and she waited a moment until she could trust her voice. "You're like family, Jonno. I hope you know that when we do get home, if you need anything, a place to stay, you call me. I mean that."

His incredulous look told her he couldn't quite believe it. Then his mouth stretched into the smile she loved. "Thanks, Kris." As he went back to his food, she thought she caught a glimmer of tears in his eyes.

"So." She turned to Luke, who sat back in his chair watching her in silence. "What was Peter talking about?"

"Ooo, look at the time." Jonno wiped his mouth and shot out of his chair like there was incoming fire. "Thanks for the meal, Kris. I gotta go."

"Hicks…" Luke's low rumble went ignored as Jonno grabbed his cap and lumbered out of the apartment.

And then the lights flickered, went out, and sent the place into darkness.

"Oh, great." Kristin let out her breath. "Another power failure." The candles she'd lit earlier provided some light. She lit a few more and placed them around the room. Music from the radio filled the silence. "Well, that was a disastrous evening." She sat down again and pulled her hands through her hair.

"Not at all. Everything was great. Really." His eyes sparkled in the flickering candlelight, his hard jaw outlined in soft yellow light.

Kristin fiddled with an ashtray, spinning it in a circle. If Peter had continued his tirade, she might have bashed him over the head with it. "I never did like that man. I just hope Caroline will have the good sense to break it off with him"

Luke sighed and rubbed his chin. "She should never have gotten involved with him in the first place. I warned her, but, as you can tell, she likes to do her own thing."

She glanced his way and smiled. "Must run in the family."

"Must do." He pushed his plate to one side and put his hands behind his head.

"They didn't have dessert. I made a pie."

"You did?" Luke's eyes widened with anticipation.

"Yeah. Apple. Took me all bloody day peeling the things too." Kristin clapped her hand over her mouth. She'd definitely been hanging out with Luke too long.

"You don't say?" His laughter bounced around the room. "What are you waiting for, Taylor? Go get your pie."

Kristin got to her feet. Tonight at least, she'd do as she was told.

She finished her small piece and watched Luke devour the rest of it, reminding him to save some for Jonno. "I didn't realize Jonno had asthma."

"Yeah. He should go home, stupid kid."

"And what would you do without your sidekick?" Kristin propped her elbows on the table and rested her chin in her hands, smiling at him.

Luke laughed, and flicked a strand of hair out of his eye. "He's a good friend."

"I know. I'm surprised you've allowed him in."

"I didn't have much choice. He's practically become my shadow."

"He's a decent man."

"Yes." He studied her, a warm expression settling on his face. "What you said tonight, Kristin. It'll mean the world to him. He won't forget it."

Kristin felt her weariness lifting. "I meant it. I wish we didn't live in a world where people are judged by the color of their skin. But maybe things will change one day."

"Maybe." The look in his eyes said he doubted it. Over here, it didn't seem to be a real issue. GIs were brothers, regardless of color or creed. Back home, things were different. But she knew it was something she could no longer ignore.

"Do you think they'll make him fight?" Kristin gnawed on her bottom lip, afraid for Jonno and what he might face.

Luke sighed, his gaze steady. "I doubt it, but with the Army, anything's possible."

She hoped not. If only she could find Teddy. At least make sure he was okay. It was one thing to get letters, but she never knew if the next one would come.

"You talk to you mother yet?" Luke watched her carefully.

Kristin frowned and watched the flame on the candle sway in the soft breeze that came through the open window. "Not really. She writes, about the weather and church, and Teddy. I write back about...the weather. I've only talked to her on the phone once."

"You...uh...ever think she might meet someone? Get married again?"

"My mother?" She laughed off the idea. "No way. She loved my dad. I don't think anyone could replace him."

"Well, not replace him. But you know..."

She sat forward and tried to gauge his expression in the dimly lit room. "My mother enjoys being alone. She has a nice little life, she loves her church, she has plenty of friends."

"Nobody enjoys being alone, Kristin. Not really."

His serious tone disturbed her. Time to end this conversation, whatever it was about. Kristin stood and began to clear the dishes. Luke got up to help.

Under candlelight, she put dishes into the sink she'd filled earlier in the evening, and began to wash the plates. Her thoughts centered on Jonno. What if they did make him walk point? She imagined him wading through rice paddies, rifle in hand, first in line to shoot upon encountering the enemy, the first to die.

She shivered, plunging her hands into the tepid water. Teddy was probably out there, perhaps fighting for his life this very minute. She'd heard little from her brother recently, and despite asking about him everywhere she went, hadn't been able to locate him. It was almost as though he'd vanished. Or worse...

The wet plate slipped out of her hands and fell to the floor, shattered and broke the silence. She swore and Luke glanced her way.

"That was stupid." She grabbed the broom and dustpan from the corner, and began clearing the mess as best she could in the dim light. "I can't see. Stupid lights. Stupid war..."

"Hey. Stop." Luke took the broom from her, leaned it against the counter, and kicked the dustpan away. He placed one finger under her chin and tipped her face toward him. A soft smile touched his lips. "You don't have to be so brave all the time, Taylor. It's okay to cry once in a while."

A strangled sob worked its way out of her. The wall she'd so carefully constructed to hold back her emotions came crashing down like the plate she'd just dropped. Luke said nothing, just pulled her into his arms and let her cry. She didn't know how long she cried, but he simply held her until she was done.

Finally Kristin lifted her chin and blinked up at him. "Sorry."

Luke shook his head. "Don't be."

The moment she'd stepped into his embrace, all rational thought fled, as though it knew it had no place here. His hair was getting long again and a lock of it fell over one eye. Before she thought about what she was doing, she pushed it aside with her finger.

He stood for a long moment, staring at her. Then his hands came to rest around her face. "You do like to live dangerously, don't you, Taylor?"

Kristin allowed her eyes to melt into his, slow heat pooling in the pit of her stomach at the warmth of his touch. She hadn't been sure of much since setting foot in this country, but right now, she knew exactly what she wanted.

She placed her hands over his. "Wouldn't have it any other way."

His fingers worked through her hair and the base of his thumbs brushed away her tears. In the semi-darkness, she could just make out the light in his eyes. She didn't need to see his face to know what he felt. He wanted this as much as she did.

And it scared her to death.

"Luke." She had nothing to say, really, just the need to speak his name. A low growl stuck in his throat as he pulled her closer. Only when his lips brushed against hers did she remember to breathe.

Time stopped. Her arms wound themselves around his neck and she fit neatly against him, as though she always had. Her fingers trailed through his soft hair. His kisses were gentle at first, then more insistent. An urgency rose between them. Kristin accepted his kisses as eagerly as he gave them, with an ardor that shocked her. A minute more in his arms and…

Almost at the same time they pulled away from each other, the lights flickered back on. Uncertainty and surprise crept into his eyes. Being at a firebase in the middle of incoming fire seemed a whole lot less frightening then standing here, waiting for him to speak.

Luke's startled expression revealed everything he didn't say. The back of his hand brushed against her cheek. "That probably wasn't such a great idea."

Kristin couldn't answer him. All she could do was nod, step away and watch him leave her. Moments later she heard his apartment door open and then slam shut, and the sound shook her to the core.

Chapter Fifteen

$\mathcal{T}$he doorbell interrupted Valerie from her morning bible study. She left the kitchen and went to the front door, opened it a crack and stepped back in surprise.

"Mr. Thorne! What on earth are you doing in my neighborhood on a Saturday morning?" She smoothed down her sweater and managed a nervous smile. And then her brain started to work overtime. "Oh, no. It's not... Kristin—" She clapped a hand to her mouth.

He shook his head at once. "No, no. Kristin's fine. I just spoke with her yesterday. I'm in Boston for the weekend, visiting my daughter. She doesn't live too far away so I thought..." He looked relaxed in navy corduroys with a gray sweater over a blue oxford shirt the color of his eyes. "I should have called, but I took a chance you might be home. I wanted to show you something."

"Come in." Valerie ushered him inside, her pulse slowing. Spring had not yet warmed the air, although the crocuses were starting to poke through the dark soil in her small front garden. She led him into the kitchen, pleased with the aroma of fresh baked banana bread and coffee lingering in the air.

He seemed even more so. "Oh, my. Did that just come out of the oven?" His grin widened as he strode across the linoleum to inspect her baking. Valerie laughed and retrieved two mugs from the cupboard.

"Don't you pick at that, Mr. Thorne. I'll slice some up."

"I thought you were going to call me Hayden." He leaned against the counter and watched while she poured the coffee. Valerie handed him a mug and met his eyes.

"I did say that, didn't I?" She gave a little laugh and set to work cutting a few slices of the steaming loaf. He'd been so good about phoning her, at least a couple of times a week, letting her know how Kristin was doing. Last week he'd called three times. After their last conversation, she'd hung up and realized they hadn't talked about Kristin at all.

"Have a seat." She moved toward the square table, put the plate down near him, and pulled out a chair. Hayden sat opposite her and set a manila envelope down on the red Formica tabletop.

He helped himself to a paper napkin and chose a large slice of banana bread. His eyes twinkled when he smiled. "I brought you an early edition. Won't hit the stands until next week, but I thought you might enjoy a preview." He pushed the envelope toward her.

Birdsong filtered through the open window, and the grandfather clock in the hall ticked out time. Soft classical music floated around them from the radio in the living room. Valerie flipped through the glossy pages of TIME with trepidation. The five-page spread wasn't hard to miss.

"You gave Kristin the lead?" She glanced his way, but only for a moment. Her daughter's well-written words soon demanded her full attention.

After Valerie finished reading, she sat in silence, staring at the graphic photographs that accompanied the piece. She drew in a shaky breath and tears pricked her eyes. When Hayden reached for her hand, she jumped and pulled back.

No. This…oh, this was too hard.

She left the table and went to stand at the kitchen sink. With trembling fingers she picked dead leaves off the colorful array of pink and purple violets that sat on the sill, and battled the need to sob.

"Please say something." Hayden's concerned tone brought fresh tears.

Valerie fought for her composure, wiped her eyes and turned to face him. "I'm sorry. It's just that…this is very difficult." She twisted her hands together and gathered her thoughts. "I spent a lot of years fighting with Mac over his occupation. He had some insatiable thirst, drive, whatever you want to call it, to go after the story nobody else would. You know what he was like. Don't get me wrong, I loved my husband, but I didn't always like the choices he made. Story ruled. Everyone else took second place." She sniffed and managed a small smile, wondering at the bitterness she still felt. "Even his family. Sometimes I thought it would have been easier if he'd had a mistress. But I never really tried to understand him. And I prayed our children wouldn't follow in his footsteps."

She released a ragged sigh and returned to the table. His eyes never left her.

"Kristin is so much like him. They were always so close. When he died, it was almost like she shut down. Like a piece of her died with him."

Hayden pulled his chair closer and put an arm around her. Valerie stared at him through a haze of tears. "When she told me she wanted to go to Vietnam, so soon after Teddy left, it was like losing Mac all over again. I was furious with her. I begged her not to go. I didn't understand it then. But now…" She shook her head and met his questioning eyes. "This is where her heart is, isn't it?"

Hayden nodded, one hand covering hers. His thumb made light circular movements over the top of her hand. "I've never seen anyone her age write with such passion, with such authority. From what I hear, she's developed a real camaraderie with the GIs. She's well-liked and respected."

Valerie gave a nod of acknowledgment. "We've never had a great relationship. Lately, I've been asking God to change that. To give me a second chance with my daughter."

"I'm sure He will." Hayden studied her carefully. "You must also trust God to keep her safe, Valerie."

She widened her eyes slightly. "Are you a praying man, Mr…Hayden?"

"I am indeed." He let the information settle, then smiled again. "Kristin has a promising career in front of her. I think your support will mean the world to her."

Valerie acknowledged the twinge of pride that rippled through her as she studied Kristin's by-line. "Who's the photographer? He's good."

"Luke Maddox." Hayden outlined one of the pictures with his finger. "He's…complicated."

"You know him?" Curiosity spurned her on. Something in Hayden's expression changed at the mention of this man's name.

"I've known Luke a long time. He's a good man, but he's suffered a lot. Lately though, he sounds different. Happier." His grin broadened. "I'm wondering if your daughter might have something to do with that."

"Really?" Valerie lifted an eyebrow. "That would be surprising. Kristin doesn't let very many people get too close."

"Neither does Luke."

Valerie enjoyed the look of mischief that crept into Hayden's eyes. She was also enjoying the fact that he still held her hand. When he grew serious again, she felt a pinch of fear.

He sat forward, studying her carefully, as though trying to read her thoughts. Then he smiled. "I'm not one to beat around the bush, so I'll just come right out and say it. I'm extremely attracted to you. I like you, Valerie Taylor, and I want to get to know you better. While I'm thrilled with your daughter's success, I'd much rather talk about us. So I guess I'm wondering if you might like to have dinner with me tonight?"

Valerie blinked, wondering if she'd heard him correctly. Heat rose and filled her cheeks. A smile curled her lips upward, and she nodded. "I thought you'd never ask."

Chapter Sixteen

Kristin sat at the table in her apartment and played ping-pong with her feelings.

Morning sun filtered through the red cotton curtains and cast a bloody glow across the room. She went to the window and pushed back the thin material, let out a tired sigh, sank back into her chair and picked at her toast. Exhaustion overrode hunger and she moved the plate away. She couldn't remember if it was Monday or Tuesday. It was so easy to lose track here.

The memory of Luke's lips on hers still evoked warmth that radiated through every part of her. She wished a thousand times over she had stopped it. But the truth was, she had wanted it. She could no longer deny what she felt for Luke Maddox.

They hadn't talked about what happened between them that night three weeks ago. They worked side by side in silence, joked and threatened each other on a daily basis, but he hadn't come near her again in that way. Then he disappeared again and she hadn't seen him in a week. She swore he was avoiding her.

Kristin glared at a large black fly sitting on her uneaten toast. She'd let her guard down, been swept up in the moment. This put her in the worst possible position. Getting involved with Luke went against all she was trying to do here. If there was one thing Dad had always preached, it was integrity.

With a shaking hand, she reached for the Bible she always placed near her typewriter. Dad's Bible. Mom gave it to Teddy after dad died, and Teddy gave it to her before he left the States.

She never read it. Just having it close by reminded her of her brother and Dad. Both men had stood firmly behind their faith. If Teddy were around to talk to, he'd tell her to find the answers she needed there.

She wasn't so sure. Sometimes her old anger at God curled into guilt and made her wonder if one day He'd get fed up and put her in the path of a grenade just for kicks. And some days she wondered what it would be like to trust Him again.

She flipped through the thin, well-worn pages until she came to Proverbs.

'Trust in the Lord with all your heart and lean not on your own understanding; in all your ways acknowledge him, and he will make your paths straight.'

Kristin closed her eyes. A straight path right about now would be nice. The one she'd chosen to head down had suddenly become very twisted.

A knock on the door startled her and she looked up.

"Kristin, chèrie? Are you at home?"

"Come in, Jean Luc." The Frenchman sauntered into the apartment and she went to greet him. "Where have you been? I thought you'd left us!"

"Ah, non." He kissed her on both cheeks and they sat at the table. "Doing a little research up north. It is getting…how you say…hairy."

"Yes, I've heard." Kristin went to the kitchen and poured more coffee, handing him a mug. "No sugar today."

"What is new?" Jean Luc scrunched up his face and drank. "So. How is our mystery man? I have many meetings now with my Agency contact. He insists that Mr. Maddox is working for them."

Kristin sighed, her chest tightening the way it so often did now when she thought about the story she'd come here to write. "So what if he is, Jean Luc? He's not going to give me any information. Don't we have enough to go ahead anyway?"

"Perhaps. But he is so intriguing, non? A photographer under the cover who sneaks out on the secret missions in the dead of night… fantastique!"

Kristin laughed, her eyes stinging with perspiration. "Let's not get carried away."

He narrowed his eyes and gave a wicked grin. "I think you have a little soft spot, no?"

"No." She answered too quickly and pushed the ashtray toward him as he lit a cigarette. "No soft spot."

Teasing laughter told her he knew better. "Okay, if you say so. Just remember, you came to me for help with this story, oui? You still want to write this with me, chèrie?"

"Of course." Kristin nodded and convinced herself she did. Jean Luc had been in Vietnam several times on other assignments. His knowledge of military personal on both sides, his fluency in French and minimal Vietnamese had come in very handy.

One kiss between her and Luke didn't mean anything. It was just an absurd reaction after a few hellish weeks. They were surrounded by war. Life hung in the balance. They both knew it. People all around them were living the same way. Under the circumstances, it was easy to give in to physical desire.

So many did. The sexual revolution that seemed to be taking over her contemporaries back home in the States had been alive and well in Vietnam much longer.

"I'm fine."

"Good. Well, we have a…how you say…mole…on the inside. He's going to talk. And my editor is very interested. Could be lots of cash in it for us."

Kristin sat up, running her tongue over her lips. "This sounds like it could get dangerous."

"Perhaps. But so is following a platoon around the jungle, non? This has a much bigger payoff, wouldn't you say?"

"If it goes to print, perhaps." She ignored the insistent thumping of her heart and tried to imagine a positive outcome over the decision she'd made. "I'm still in, Jean Luc, don't worry."

"Okay. Maybe you should try harder with your friend, then. You know. Make some…ehm…moves on him." Jean Luc smiled and took a deep drag from his cigarette.

Smoke wafted around her and she batted it away. "Who do you think I am, Mata Hari?" Jean Luc's laughter filled the apartment. Kristin went to the filing cabinet and pulled out a stack of papers. "Here. This is what I have so far. I'll call you soon."

His eyes lit up and he stubbed out his smoke. "Brilliant, chèrie. You will see. This one will be a winner. You're amazing."

Kristin couldn't agree. In fact, she felt anything but.

Later, showered and dressed, Kristin grabbed her bag and headed out on foot for the orphanage. She wasn't in the mood for helicopters and wounded soldiers. Today, she wanted to be with the children.

Mary Jo put her to work like always. Kristin washed dishes, played with the kids, swept the floor—anything she could find to take her mind off Luke.

After lunch, she helped put the younger ones down for a nap while the older group studied around a long table in the dining room, under the direction of Anh, Mary Jo's thirteen year-old Vietnamese adopted daughter.

"Let's sit outside." Mary Jo made tea and they ventured out to the back garden.

Although not large, the garden was beautiful. Bob and Mary Jo had created a natural sanctuary complete with a small water fountain made from a few old ceramic jars. Flowers of every shape, size and color put on a dazzling show and perfumed the air. Velvety roses bloomed from red clay pots, well watered and cared for. Overhanging vines lush with greenery and bright purple flowers crawled up the thick cedar posts of the pagoda Bob built, covered the wooden slatted roof of the structure and provided welcome shade.

They sat on wicker chairs around a tiny metal table. Kristin sipped her tea, enjoying the tranquility and the comforting sound of trickling water. She looked up to find the older woman staring at her.

"You okay, honey? You seem kind of—I don't know, distracted. You aren't getting sick again?"

Kristin shrugged, studying the floral rose pattern on her china cup. There was a chip in the handle and she ran a finger over the unglazed porcelain. "No. I'm fine." How could she attempt to explain her conflicting emotions when she couldn't make any sense of them herself?

"So, you and Luke are working together. How's that going?"

Kristin gave a tired laugh. "It's okay. Luke is…well…Luke." Her cheeks began to burn as she spoke his name. She needed to get a grip. It infuriated her that he intruded on her thoughts with such ease, and with alarming frequency. "He's never around long enough to get any real work done."

"Really? Bob said Luke was awful concerned about you after you landed in that massacre."

"*Was* being the operative word." Kristin squished an ant making its way toward her cup. "Now that he knows I'm not going to fall apart at every horrific scene, he's reverted back to his old charming self."

Mary Jo's smile broadened and her large frame shook with laughter. "Oh, honey. I think you're in trouble, aren't you?"

"I don't know what you're talking about." She laced her hands together and concentrated on the ants on the table.

"I think you do." Mary Jo patted her hand. "We can't always choose the man we fall for, Kristin. Sometimes God does it for us."

Kristin narrowed her eyes, her gut twisting. "Then God would have a rather warped sense of humor in this case. Forget it, Mary Jo, you've got it all wrong."

"Really." It wasn't a question.

Kristin set her jaw and refused to meet Mary Jo's gaze. "You're talking about Luke. The man's a complete Neanderthal most of the time."

The sound of someone clearing their throat caused Mary Jo to swivel in her seat and drew Kristin's eyes to the back door.

Luke stood a few feet away, leaning against the doorframe, his eyes fixed on her.

How fast could she crawl under the table?

Mortified as she was, she couldn't look away, had to force herself to remain seated. He looked like he'd been run over by a tank. A few stitches ran along the side of his cheek. A large purple bruise muddied his jaw, and a bandage was wrapped around his left wrist. The edge of another bandage on his chest could be seen under the collar of the white cotton shirt he wore over khaki shorts.

"Afternoon, ladies." His blond hair hung over one eye as he tilted his head in greeting, a hint of a smile playing on his lips.

Mary Jo let out a squeak and scrambled out of her chair. "What happened to you? Sweetie, you're a wreck!"

"I'll live." Luke bent to kiss Mary Jo's cheek and drew back with a grin. "Us Neanderthals are pretty resilient."

All the blood rushed from Kristin's cheeks and flooded back at furnace heat. She shot a furtive glance at her watch. "I need to get back and finish the story I'm working on." She pushed her chair back as Luke stepped forward, blocking the path.

"Actually, I hoped I'd find you here. I'd like to talk to you." His eyes met hers and he attempted a smile, visibly flinching at the movement. Kristin flinched too.

"I was just leaving. I—I need to—go." She moved around the table but even injured he was too quick for her.

He caught her arm. "It's important."

Mary Jo cleared her throat a little too loudly. "I've got to go check on the children. You two stay out here as long as you like." She bustled inside and Kristin scowled at her back. Then she focused on Luke.

"You look like you had a run-in with Godzilla."

"Feel like it too." He limped to the table and slowly lowered himself on to one of the white wicker chairs, a heavy sigh escaping.

Kristin took her seat again, albeit reluctantly. She couldn't quench the worry at the sight of his bruises. "Are you really all right?"

He glanced her way and met her eyes. "We went up to the Rockpile."

"You went up there without me? When?" She almost shot out of her chair. The place where the heaviest fighting was reported to be taking place…typical. "Why would you do that?"

Luke held up a hand. "Don't start." His eyes were restless. Clearly something significant was on his mind.

Kristin sat back and folded her arms across her chest. "Fine. You can tell me later. So? What's so important?"

Luke set his gaze on her and nodded. Then he let out a long breath. "I wanted to say I'm sorry."

"Sorry for what?"

"For everything. The way I treated you when you first got here. I can be a real jerk sometimes."

"You?" Kristin feigned exaggerated astonishment and watched a grin slide across his mouth.

"You're a hard sell, Taylor."

"So I've been told. Is that it? You wanted to apologize?"

"Yeah. I meant to do this sooner but—I—we got into a spot of trouble up there. Got stuck in the middle of some heavy shelling. I was a little spooked when I got back. I've been home a few days but I...I've been avoiding you."

She gripped the sides of her chair, her stomach churning. "Don't worry, I'm used to it by now." His stare unnerved her. "Stop staring at me."

"Can't help it." The grin stayed this time and Kristin felt the hairs on her arms rise. "You're kind of nice to look at, Taylor."

"Please." She shook her head, but smiled anyway, feeling too warm. "Apology accepted. No need for flattery."

He shrugged but didn't take his eyes off her.

She swallowed and made herself look at him. She'd rehearsed her speech. Best to just get it over with. "Look, about that night—like you said, it wasn't a good idea. I don't have time for relationships—my work comes first. I have no idea why that happened, and with you, of all people, but it's not going to happen again, all right?"

"Pity." His smile widened and alarm coursed through her. Then his face darkened. "What do you mean, 'me of all people'?"

Kristin waved a hand, exasperation threatening to topple calm. "It's not going to happen again and that's the end of it. I'm not looking for a casual one-night stand."

"Neither am I."

He confused her. She knew what men were after. When she'd dated in college, she'd invariably end up running back to her dorm room, seething or in tears. The names they called her still rang in her ears. Eventually she stopped dating altogether. Then they just called her different names.

The ensuing silence threatened to suffocate her and she begged it to.

Luke leaned forward, put his hand on her wrist and gave it a gentle squeeze. "I don't know what guy hurt you, but I'd like to beat his brains out."

The intensity of his words almost frightened her.

"Well, actually it was—"

He grinned wide. "Would you be quiet for a bloody minute and let me talk for once?"

Kristin flopped back in her chair, rubbed her eyes and grimaced. "Sorry. Go on."

Luke coughed and shifted, seeming suddenly uncomfortable. For a moment he played with his thumbs, winding them around each other. "I wanted to tell you...what happened to my wife." He sighed and leaned over his knees, studying his boots for a few long minutes. When he looked up at her again, his eyes shone too brightly. "Frankly, I'm surprised you haven't asked."

Kristin gave a wan smile. "Believe it or not, Luke, sometimes I do know when to keep my mouth shut. Doesn't happen often, you should feel honored."

His grin flashed and faded. "I don't ever talk about it." His voice wavered and he veered his gaze. "But I want you to know."

Kristin swallowed against the unbelievable nerves pelting the walls of her stomach and waited for him to speak again.

At last, his eyes locked with hers once more. A blanket of sorrow seemed to cover him. "I was on..." He let out a breath and stopped. "I was..." His voice trailed off and he looked across the small garden. "I'm sorry. This is hard."

Her eyes traveled to the ring still on his finger as he dragged a hand down his face. Luke clenched his fists and she saw the hard line of his jaw twitching, a trait she now recognized as a hint of approaching anger. But the explosion she expected to follow never came. Instead, a haze that threatened tears covered his eyes.

Kristin bit down on her lip and shifted in her chair. Whatever this story was, it haunted him. "Luke, tell me. What happened?"

His shaky sigh tore at her heart. "All right." He gave a slow nod, crossed his arms on the table, and leaned in. "Almost five years ago, I brought my wife and daughter over here. I was on assignment for TIME. The war was heating up, the press showing more interest. I was only supposed to be here a couple of days, and then we'd planned to travel to Australia for a holiday. I have an uncle there. I went off up to the camp to take some pictures and see my dad, and when I returned the next day, the hotel we'd been staying in was a pile of burnt embers."

"What?" Horror slammed her. "The hotel burnt down?"

His short chuckle reeked of bitterness. "Burnt down, blew up. Whichever descriptive tag you like. It was gone. And so was my family."

"Oh, Luke." Kristin's heart thudded against her chest as she thought of what he must have gone through. What he was obviously still going through. She reached across the small table and placed her hand on his arm. "I'm so sorry."

He lifted his shoulders and let out a long, ragged breath. "It was my fault. I should never have brought them here. Marcia, my wife, wanted to see the war first hand. She was a bit like you in a way. Always wanted to be near the action." His thin smile brought tears to Kristin's eyes.

"How old was your daughter?" The anguish etched on his face tore at her heart. Tears marked his cheeks.

"She was two." His voice shook with emotion. He put his head in his hands. For a long moment, neither of them spoke. The air grew thick with silent sorrow.

Luke sat up and shook himself, running a hand over his wet face. He met her eyes once more, his smile brief. "Melissa. She was a real little imp, had me wrapped around her little finger from her first breath." He shifted, reaching into his back pocket with his good hand. He retrieved a battered brown leather wallet, flipped it open and showed it to her.

Kristin brushed away tears as she stared down at the portrait of a little girl whose life ended far too soon. Her mother's picture was tucked in beside hers. A young woman with straight brown hair and sparkling hazel eyes.

She was beautiful.

Kristin stared at the picture of the little girl again. A sudden vision of Luke foraging around her bathroom that night crossed her mind. He said he'd been kept awake by a child's cry…but perhaps it had been a memory.

She handed the wallet back to him. "I'm sorry. That's such a paltry saying, but…"

"I know." He sniffed. "Nobody knows what to say. That's why I don't talk about it. How do you tell someone you killed your own child? She was the light of my life. If I hadn't been so stupid…"

"You can't blame yourself for what happened, Luke." Kristin flinched at the implication of his words. It all made sense now.

His acrid laugh hung around them. "Easy for you to say."

The fire in his eyes told her not to argue. He carried a load too heavy to comprehend. "Thank you for telling me," she said at last.

Her voice seemed to shake him out of his memories. A conciliatory smile touched his lips. Then he rose and began to pace the square terrace.

"Kristin..." Luke sank down into his chair, meeting her eyes. "I'm not impulsive by nature. Everything I do is calculated. That night at your place..." A slow grin worked its way across his mouth. "Totally impulsive. And extremely out of character for me."

"I'll say." She raised an eyebrow and smiled at the laughter her comment coaxed from him. Too soon the familiar shadow returned to haunt his features once more.

"You have to know," he went on, "despite what you might think, that I do like you. And—I am—attracted to you. Which is sometimes more terrifying than being in a hot zone. But..."

"You're not ready."

Luke nodded and cleared his throat. "I don't think I am."

She understood. Part of her felt grateful. His confession took her off the hook. Yet another part of her just wanted to go home and cry.

His blue eyes sparkled underneath the midday sun that trickled through the vines above them. "Not that I would have had a chance anyway."

"Oh, I don't know about that." Kristin dragged her eyes away from his face and concentrated on the cement terrace below her feet. She stretched out her legs and kicked the tops of her white sneakers together. Life was full of regrets.

"Trust me, my life is far too complicated already."

"I'm sure it is." She rubbed the surface of her thumbnail and picked off a piece of dry skin. "Must be hard working two jobs." She held his hard stare and refused to look away.

A hesitant smile settled on his lips. "I can't tell you what you want me to," he said quietly. "You know that."

As much as she'd longed for this moment, the truth did not hold the victory she'd thought it would. "Trust the instinct to the end, though you can render no reason."

His smile faded. "Whitman?"

"Emerson." She slapped her hands down on her knees. "Anyway. I didn't come to Vietnam looking for romance. I have a job to do, and so do you, whatever it is. I can't afford the energy for anything else."

"I guess that leaves us...where?"

She couldn't tell whether the look in his eyes was relief or disappointment. "Friends?" She smiled at the suggestion, but felt her heart sag.

Luke shot her a wink and a flash of the grin she'd grown remarkably fond of in a short space of time. "If you can stand it."

"I'll suffer through."

He raised an eyebrow. "Caroline will be disappointed."

"She's too busy running after Peter to worry about us."

"Idiot." Luke stood up and gave a loud stretch. "You doing anything this afternoon, Taylor?"

"Nope. I'd planned to hang out here. It's too hot to move much."

"We could take some of the kids to the zoo, if you want?" A smile lit his face and chased away the ghosts.

Kristin nodded, smiled and pushed away any further thoughts of a romantic involvement with Luke Maddox. It would only lead to heartbreak, and she didn't need any more of that.

Chapter Seventeen

Kristin huddled in a chair on the rooftop terrace at The Caravelle. The terrace bar was quiet, hardly anybody about. Kristin was glad. She didn't want company today. She hadn't slept through the night in weeks. Not since they'd landed in the middle of that massacre. Nightmares haunted her. She couldn't get those images of death out of her mind. And then today, the letter from her mother arrived.

She pushed her empty glass away. Her head pulsed, her third headache this week. The heat, the stress, everything was closing in. Her second three-month visa would be up at the end of the week. She'd been in Vietnam for six months. It didn't seem possible.

Time stood still here. The rest of the world seemed to move along at a clip, while everything here, in-country, took place in slow motion.

"God, what am I going to do?" She glanced around, half-expecting an answer. She'd started talking to God again, mostly out of desperation, but the conversations seemed one-sided.

"Do about what?" Luke straddled a chair and sat across from her, his blue eyes unsettled. "You look like you've eaten some bad Bò lúc lắc."

Kristin groaned and put her head in her hands again. "Don't talk about food," she muttered, gripping her empty glass and banging it down on the table.

Luke raised an eyebrow and pried the glass from her hand. He brought it to his nose and sniffed. "What are you drinking, carburetor oil?"

"Not that I've tasted carburetor oil, but I'm sure this comes close."

His laughter rapped on the door of her heart and tempted her to open it just a crack.

"What's so funny?"

"Nothing. How much have you had?"

"Just one. You think I'm drunk?" Kristin stared in disbelief.

Luke shrugged, gazing off into the distant hills as the familiar rumble emanated from them. "It's how most folks deal with things around here."

"As you may have figured out by now, Luke, I'm not 'most folks'. Believe me, right now I'd like to be drunk."

"I still feel like that, almost every day." He sat back in the chair and dragged his hand over his face. "Don't let it get to you, Kris."

Kristin drummed her fingers on the table. "Don't let what get to me? The war? The death? The fact that I have no idea where my brother is—if he's even alive—or the fact that my mother just wrote to tell me she's getting married?" She balled up the airmail letter and threw it down on the table. It bounced off and hit the stone floor.

Luke bent to pick it up, smoothed it out and put it back on the plastic table. "Really? You don't sound happy about it."

Kristin groaned and rubbed her face, willing her tiredness away. Her frayed emotions made it hard to focus on the job she was here to do. When she was out there in the field, high on adrenaline and fear, she functioned without thinking. But here, back in the city, the ceasefire on her soul never lasted long. Mom's news was just what she needed to throw herself a good old-fashioned pity party. "She's getting married to Hayden Thorne, Luke! My mother is marrying my boss. Our boss!" Stupid tears pricked her eyes and she swiped at them.

"What?" Luke stared in astonishment.

"Oh, yes. Apparently she was so distraught about my being here she made quite a nuisance of herself. He started calling, filling her in on how I was doing, then visiting, and that was the start of a grand romance. This is *your* fault!"

"My fault?" His blond eyebrows shot skyward.

Kristin glowered. "If you hadn't given me his name, I wouldn't still be here, and she wouldn't be getting married."

"Oh, I see. Of course." He nodded as though it made perfect sense. "So I should expect an invitation to the wedding?" His grin did nothing to soothe her.

"And what's worse, Hayden's retiring. They're fixing up an old farm-house in Vermont and moving there after they get married."

To his credit, Luke made some effort to hide his obvious amusement. Kristin folded her arms. "Go ahead and laugh. You think it's hilarious. I won't have a home to go back to. She's practically kicking me out onto the streets! I guess I'll just have to become a hippie."

That did him in. He threw his head back and guffawed. Kristin squared her shoulders, gave him a blistering glare and pushed her chair back.

He sobered and grabbed her arm. "Okay, I'm sorry. Sit. I shouldn't laugh. It's just that…how old are you again?" He choked on more laughter and Kristin shook her head, dropping back into her seat.

She shot him an acrid look. "Not that it's any of your business, but I'll be twenty-five tomorrow."

"Tomorrow?" His laughter fizzled and he narrowed his eyes. "You're joking."

Kristin fished out her wallet and chucked it at him. "Check my driver's license if you don't believe me."

"Tomorrow it is," he mused, handing her wallet back. He placed his elbows on the table, resting his chin over his hands. His eyes held hers for longer than she should have allowed. "So. Twenty-five. You're almost ancient."

"Not as old as you. Aren't you pushing fifty?"

"Fifty?" He made a face. "Try thirty. Do I look that old?"

"No." Kristin smiled and felt her pressure lower as she took in the laughter in his eyes. "You look just fine to me."

"That's more like it." He went to the bar and returned with two Cokes. "Don't you have a plan, Taylor? What are you going to do when you go home?"

"I don't know." Kristin pulled at her hair, wiping sweat off her brow. Cigarette smoke from the only other occupied table tickled her nose. "I figured I'd go back to living with Mom and work someplace."

"So you'll just have to get an apartment." As if it were as simple as going to the store for a loaf of bread. "Are you angry with her for finding someone else?"

"Yes! No. Yes." Kristin groaned. The three-year old whiney brat she used to be still lived within her, apparently. "I'm surprised. But I can't blame her for wanting to be happy, I suppose. Hayden seems decent enough. I just wish I could meet him in person before she marries him. They're not waiting for Teddy and I to come home."

Luke nodded, seemed to hesitate, then let out a breath. "When *are* you going home?"

They hadn't talked about it. Their new alliance had brought them closer—sometimes Kristin wondered if it was such a good idea. As each day passed, the more she enjoyed being with him. She told him things she'd never shared with anyone. And she'd noticed a change in him as well, his reticent nature almost replaced by something close to contentment.

When they got along, he was funny, surprisingly sensitive, and nice to be around. When they argued, the chill could be felt for miles. A romantic relationship would be next to impossible. Kristin kept telling herself she didn't want more.

That thought was as far from the truth as the news clips they played back home at The Somerville before the main attraction.

Somehow, in some bizarre twist of fate, she'd been captured by him.

In spite of her resolve, she'd lost the battle when it came to guarding her heart. She couldn't pin down the exact day the crime had been committed, but she knew Luke Maddox had stolen it.

Going home was not something she thought about until she'd looked at the calendar and realized the date was closing in. She couldn't expect Hayden to renew her visa a third time. She'd heard enough of an argument before.

"Kris? When? When are you going home?" Luke's adamant tone brought her back to the moment.

Kristin let out an aggravated sigh. "My second visa is almost up."

"Almost, as in…" His eyes questioned her and she looked away.

"The end of next week, Luke."

The silence between them scared her. She clenched her hands together, watching the tops of her knuckles turn white. Raising her eyes to his, she saw his jaw working, a sure sign of his irritation.

"Well, I guess I'll have to find someone else to spar with." His laugh wavered and dissipated before it began.

Kristin shrugged and managed a grin. "I was thinking of asking Hayden if I could stay."

The thought spoken out loud rang in her ears. Before voicing it, she could have pushed it away, ignored it. Got on that plane and flown home. But she couldn't take it back. Not now when he stared at her in clear surprise, with just the slightest hint of hope shining in his eyes.

Kristin left him and walked to the edge of the terrace. Leaning over the railing, she took deep, calming breaths. The surrounding hills were beautiful. The city, even as crowded and dirty as it was, had somehow captivated her—connected with her soul in a way she could not explain. She loved this country and hated what was taking place in it. Yet, in some strange way, she knew she belonged here.

And then there was Luke…

She heard his heavy steps on the concrete behind her. He placed his hands on her shoulders, gently turning her to face him. In his eyes stirred questions she wasn't sure she had answers to.

"Do you really want to stay?"

She searched his face, desperate for anything that might reveal his heart. "I don't know," she whispered, unwanted tears stinging. "This place— there's just something about it. I can't explain…"

"You don't have to."

She *didn't* have to. She knew he loved the very same things. The natural beauty of Vietnam—rounded emerald hills older than Confucius himself, rich with ancient history that kept account of the beliefs and religions its people followed—the quiet way the villagers spoke as they allowed her into their huts and offered up Vietnamese hospitality—and the children. She loved the children in a way she would never have imagined. And had someone told her a few months ago that she would have anything in common with Luke Maddox, she would have laughed until she cried.

Yet here they were.

Luke's smile was sad as he brushed away her tears with the base of his thumb. "What do you want to do, Kris?"

"I think I want to stay."

"Good. I want you to."

The soft declaration settled in her soul, nudging it ever so slightly toward hope.

His hands moved her hair out of her eyes, and came to rest around her face. He pulled her closer and placed his forehead against hers. He sighed, soft and low, as though he'd given up the fight. And then his lips claimed hers.

His kiss was sweet and lazy, left her breathless, and longing for more.

"Oops." Luke drew back, rubbing his nose against hers.

"What was that?" Laughter caught in her throat as she slipped her arms about his waist. He tightened his embrace and chuckled. She loved the way his eyes caressed her now, filled with a new light that thrilled her.

That she could feel such pleasure in the middle of hell seemed ludicrous.

"I don't know. Let me refresh my memory." His lips found hers again, and she allowed it. One moment in time would not change anything. Or it would.

She didn't care anymore.

Luke stepped back, but didn't release her from the circle of his arms. Mischief played across his face. "I've been wanting to do that again for a very long time."

"Then why didn't you?"

"I have no idea." He traced the outline of her jaw with his fingertip.

Kristin pulled her gaze from him. As much as she wanted to give in to her feelings, something held her back. Luke still wasn't ready for this. He might try and convince her otherwise, but she knew him well enough now to recognize the shadows of the past in his eyes. And he could never be honest with her about what he was really doing in Vietnam. Besides that, she had enough secrets of her own.

He tilted her chin upward until his eyes captured hers. "Talk to me."

"I can't do this." She untangled herself from him and made her way back to the table.

Luke joined her and they sat in silence. Cradling her head in her hands, she drew in a deep breath. Falling apart would do no good. After a while she forced herself to look at him. "I think Hayden will agree to me staying, even to us continuing to work together. But I don't want it to get complicated, Luke…"

"Hey." He held his hands up in front of him. "No complications. I promise."

Kristin accepted the truth. "It's too late. I think I might have some feelings for you, and that scares me to death. I don't want to care this much. Either one of us could be dead tomorrow. And I know what you've been through. I don't want to be…" She clenched her jaw and stared at her hands.

"A replacement." He said it for her.

She met his eyes, and nodded. "I can't compete with your ghosts, Luke. I don't even want to try."

"I know." His eyes were bright, hooded with a sorrow she knew still haunted him. "I'd give anything to be able to tell you you're wrong, that I'm over it, that things will be fine. But I can't." He stretched his hands across the table and she placed hers within them. He held on tight, a smile crossing his face. "Do you understand?"

"I wish I didn't." Kristin's lower lip trembled. "I tried really hard to hate you. I just want you to know that." She attempted to join in his laughter, but couldn't. Her feelings for him ebbed at the surface of her soul.

"I'm glad you don't hate me, Taylor." He lifted her hands and brought them up to his lips.

Kristin wiped her cheeks as he let her go. People were starting to traipse on to the terrace, and she knew the conversation had ended. They'd said all that could be said. But the touch of his lips still burned in her memory.

He mussed his blond hair and nodded to an acquaintance strolling by. "I was going to ask if you wanted to ride up to Dak To tomorrow. Jonno can drive us."

"What's in Dak To?"

"Well, there's a guy I've heard about. He's called Preacher. Supposedly inspiring a lot of men up there. Thought it might make a good story. Bit of relief from blood and guts. Unless you'd rather stay in the city and take a day off."

"No point in taking the day off." Kristin smiled but her eyes smarted. "I hate birthdays anyway."

"Why is that?"

Sorrow made itself at home in her heart once more. "My father was big on birthdays. He'd wake us at the crack of dawn, have presents on the table, then he'd make pancakes. I'm not a kid anymore, but..."

"You still miss him." Luke reached out and took her hand again. The action startled her and she stared in surprise. Tears stung and Kristin blinked them back, already tasting the salt on her lips.

His fingers grazed hers in gentle motion. "I wish I'd had the chance to be that kind of father," he said, his voice hoarse. His words released her tears in full force. He gave her an apologetic look, his own eyes wet.

"I doubt very much you can cook." She brushed her cheeks, her voice still taut with emotion.

"I can't." He laughed and rubbed his face. "I would have tried though."

The thought of him in a flour-covered apron enticed a giggle. The sad moment lifted and she withdrew her hand from his. "What time tomorrow?"

"Early." Luke grinned and pushed his chair back. "Go home and get some sleep, Taylor. I'll see you in the morning."

Chapter Eighteen

Somebody shook her shoulder. Kristin moaned and rolled over. The shaking grew more insistent.

"Kris! Wake up!" Caroline yelled in her ear. "You're going to want to get up for this, trust me."

"Wha—what? What's going on?" Kristin sat up and stared at Caroline through bleary eyes. "What time is it?"

"It's six-thirty."

"In the morning?"

"Yes." Caroline crouched at the side of the bed wearing the stupidest grin on her face.

Kristin scowled, pushing hair out of her eyes. "What is wrong with you? Why'd you wake me up?"

"Because it's your birthday, silly! Come on, up. Come out here." Caroline laughed and skipped out of the bedroom.

Kristin went to the bathroom, washed her face and brushed her teeth, dragged her hair up into a ponytail and pulled her robe on, tying the sash around her waist. She stumbled out into the living room and prayed for coffee.

Kristin gaped at the sight before her.

Luke sat at the table, his legs stretched out, hands clasped behind his head. "Morning, Sunshine. It's about time. Were you planning to sleep all day?" His hair was a mess, his face spotted with flour.

Their old beat-up table resembled something out of a restaurant. Where the white cloth came from, she'd no idea. Juice, coffee, even a few sliced oranges, were all laid out. And there on her plate, sat a stack of steaming hot pancakes that looked remarkably similar to the ones her father used to make. Her eyes moved from the pancakes to Luke.

"Did you…make those?" Kristin clapped a hand over her mouth, her grogginess lifting. She was almost afraid to hear the answer.

"Of course." He folded flour-speckled arms across a very dirty T-shirt and grinned. "Are you going to stand there gawking all day or eat?"

Kristin took a deep breath. If she closed her eyes, she'd be back in bed, dreaming it all. She looked to Caroline for verification.

Her friend's smile was wide as she sat down with her own mug of coffee. "He made them. I talked him through it, mind you. They are actually edible. I've already tried one."

"You made me pancakes?" Kristin stared at Luke again. The evidence sat in front of her.

"If you tell a soul, I'll deny it." Luke laughed and strode around the table. He propelled her to her chair and sat her down, his cheek brushing against hers. "Happy Birthday, Taylor."

Caroline gave a low whistle, a definite gleam in her eyes. "Yeah. Happy Birthday. Pancakes, huh? Wow. Somebody must think you're pretty special."

Kristin pulled herself together and shot Caroline a look of warning which only served to broaden her grin.

"Where's the syrup?" Kristin gulped coffee and surveyed the table.

"Where do you think we are, The Ritz?" Luke flopped into his chair again. "Here's some honey. Best I could do on short notice. Ungrateful wench." His wink forced her to bury her face in her coffee mug.

"I'm very grateful. They're good," she pronounced between mouthfuls.

"This doesn't mean you're moving in, does it?" Caroline arched a thin eyebrow as she gave her brother a suspicious look. Kristin choked on her mouthful and reached for more coffee.

Luke narrowed his eyes. "I do one nice thing and you have us living together? You need to quit pounding out war stories and take up writing romance, sis. Honestly."

Caroline put on a defensive air. "Well, I'm just saying…"

"You're not saying anything because it's my birthday and I get to make the rules," Kristin snapped. "If you want to grab the shower before I get in there, I suggest you run. But save me some hot water."

"You'll be lucky." Luke snorted, enjoying his share of the feast.

"Shut up, you." Caroline smacked him over the head. She leaned over Kristin and drew her into a brief hug. "You should have told me it was your birthday. I'll get you something fabulous this weekend, I promise."

"Thank you. Something expensive," Kristin mumbled, devouring the last pancake on her plate. They would have been better with maple syrup, but Luke was right. You couldn't have everything.

He did allow her to help clear the table, she noticed.

"Ready for Dak To?" Luke asked, washing the final plate. Kristin lifted it from the dish rack and dried it.

"After I shower and get dressed, yeah. How far away is it?"

"A few hours. Okay?"

"Bathroom's all yours." Caroline entered the kitchen, dressed and drying her hair with a towel. "Have a good day. I'm heading out in a minute."

Twenty minutes later, Kristin was ready to go. Jonno met them outside the apartment, laden with more carvings for her collection, and a sweet handwritten card. They were soon speeding around pedicabs and bicyclists, heading north for Dak To.

A couple of hours turned out to be an understatement. But the ride was beautiful, and apart from several nasty potholes that threatened to evict her breakfast, they hadn't encountered any trouble.

They reached the base camp where this Preacher guy was located, and Jonno parked the Jeep. Luke turned to her. "I'll go find him. You two wait here."

Kristin hopped out and surveyed the area, wondering if it would be worth taking notes. The camps she visited were all beginning to look the same. She took some pictures and jotted a few thoughts. A little while later, Luke rounded one of the buildings, a tall, thin soldier loping after him.

One with a familiar gait, and a grin she'd recognize anywhere.

Teddy.

It couldn't be. She was seeing things under the sun's glare.

Seeing what she wanted to see.

Kristin blinked, removed her sunglasses and stared. Jonno looked her way and began to laugh. A gasp shot out of her and her pack slipped from her shaky grasp. She looked again, just to be sure.

And then hurtled herself into her brother's open arms.

Teddy swept her high into the air and spun her around. His deep laughter filled her soul with unbelievable pleasure. Kristin shook her head as he set her down, tears streaking her cheeks.

"Teddy! It's really you!" She squealed and hugged him hard, choking down a sob.

For a long moment they held each other, then Teddy drew back, his wan face beaming. "Happy Birthday, Kris. Figured you'd find me eventually. Have you been getting my letters?"

"Yes, but I've been trying to locate you for ages! I've asked everyone, everywhere I go...how..."

Luke.

Kristin turned toward the Jeep, but it sat empty. She scanned the area, but Luke and Jonno were nowhere in sight.

"They took off toward the mess hall. Let's go sit somewhere." Teddy led her into a courtyard in the middle of the camp, set up around a barbecue pit, a few wooden benches placed in a circle. They sat together on one of the benches.

Kristin studied him, searching for any changes. His lanky frame seemed thinner, dark shadows circled his eyes, but his smile remained as vibrant as she remembered. "Are you all right? Is it okay for you out here?"

He shrugged and rubbed his buzz cut. His eyes still held their old sparkle, but new wisdom lay within them. "It's hard going. I've seen and heard more than I care to remember. But it's okay, I guess. At least as a medic I'm not on the frontlines."

"No. That's good." Kristin sighed, holding his hand in hers. He looked tired. Worn out. And years older. "Do they really call you Preacher?" She wondered now if Luke just made it up, but knowing her brother, it was very likely.

Teddy's face reddened and he grinned. "Yeah. It's kind of an amazing opportunity here. I share my faith, and believe it or not, they talk. I've had guys come from different platoons and seek me out. I don't know. God sells in wartime."

"He does, huh?" Kristin touched the cross around her neck. Mom would be ecstatic.

"What about you?" he asked. "You're working for TIME! I've read all your stories. They're great, Kris. I'm so proud of you."

Kristin smiled, sat back and took in the sight of him. "I've been scared for you."

"Hey." Worry creased his sunburnt forehead. "You're out there too. I pray for you every day."

"Thanks." Her hands began to tremble and she slid them under her legs. "Maybe He's listening. So far so good." Kristin told him of the massacre she and Luke encountered. She could think of it now without tears or feeling—as though it had happened to somebody else. And that frightened her.

Teddy grew serious. "Mom said you were on a three month visa. I guess you got it extended, huh? When are you going home?"

Kristin hesitated, not sure what his reaction would be. "I'm going to ask Hayden if I can stay."

Her brother's eyebrows shot up. "Are you crazy? Why?"

"I have my reasons." She pulled her notepad and pen from her pack and began to doodle. Her brother stayed her hand and made her look at him.

"Are you involved with that guy, Kris?" Teddy's eyes narrowed and he leaned over the table.

She wound her hands together, a slow hammering at her heart reminding her she could not lie to her brother. "We work together. We're friends."

Teddy didn't seem convinced. Worry furrowed his brow. "He's been up here a couple of times. First he came looking for me with the Private. I thought I was in some serious trouble. Last week he came by himself."

"I didn't know." Kristin smiled without meaning to.

Teddy grunted, clearly not as impressed. "Guess he wanted to surprise you." He cleared his throat, his expression serious. For a moment Kristin saw her father staring back at her and had to look away. "Kris, how well do you know him? The guys say..."

"What, Teddy?" She let out her breath, frustration inching closer.

Teddy scratched his nose, pensive. "I've heard he's Agency."

Kristin straightened her back and felt her muscles constrict. Her heart thudded against her chest. "Agency? Like the CIA?" She laughed, pushing up her sunglasses to wipe her damp forehead. "Luke's a photographer. He works for TIME too."

He put a hand on her arm. "You know what I'm talking about, don't you? I can see it in your eyes, Kris. Be straight with me."

She waited a moment, tried to catch her breath and took a swig from her canteen. If there was one person in the world she knew she could trust, it was her brother. "Yeah, okay. He is. I've been writing a story... collaborating with a friend."

His eyes widened and she saw him take a deep, measured breath. "You really are crazy."

"I'm beginning to think so, yes." A rebellious smile slid across her lips even as tears stung her eyes. "I started it a while back, before...before Luke and I...before I really knew him. Teddy, I don't know what to do. It's a good story. It's not going to have a byline. They won't know who wrote it."

"You think not. Kris, this is not cool! You're playing with fire here. And what about him?" He nodded in the direction Luke had gone. "You really want to put him in jeopardy like that? I think he likes you an awful lot. Are you telling me you got involved with him just to get a story?"

"No! I mean...I don't know. Maybe at first. But now..." She put her head in her hands and let out a groan. "I...I'll handle it, Teddy. Maybe I'll just...not do it. You're right, it's crazy. So...look, don't worry about me."

Her brother rolled his eyes. "Sure, I won't worry about you. And the war's gonna end tomorrow. This is about Dad, isn't it? About being the kind of writer he was, would have been, if he'd lived."

"Of course not." She stared at the American flag waving above the roof of the building in front of them. The truth shrank back into the shadows until she could no longer see it.

"It is, Kris. You've been all-fired up about this journalism thing since he died and you know it. But risking your life, just to prove a point, to get back at Mom or God or whatever it is driving you to do this, it's not worth it."

Kristin shook her head and pushed aside the thoughts that plagued her hourly. "This is something I have to do. You wouldn't understand." She met his eyes and felt heat rush her cheeks.

Teddy ran a hand over his head, glanced down at his combat fatigues and nailed her with his eyes again. "I wouldn't?"

Somebody had etched a peace sign into the top of the wooden picnic table. She traced the thick circle with her forefinger, took a breath and let it out as slowly as she could. "I don't want to argue with you. Let's talk about something else."

"Okay." Humor crept in to his eyes and chased away unspoken questions. "Did you hear about Mom?"

"Yep."

"And you're thrilled, I can see." His grin was wicked and Kristin scowled.

"Just because I'm working for Hayden Thorne doesn't mean we know the slightest thing about him."

Teddy sighed and pulled at the collar of his shirt, his face glistening in the heat. "It's not about us, Kris. It's about Mom, her happiness. If she's happy with this guy, then I'm happy for her. I trust her judgment."

"But she's moving to Vermont." She'd known he'd say something like that. "With cows."

His laughter coaxed a smile. Kristin swept her hair up into a bun and secured it with an elastic band. "I just want to know where I'm supposed to live when I get home," she grumbled. "No way am I moving up there."

"Nobody says you have to. You're an adult. Get your own place."

Kristin huffed and pushed her shoulders back. "Now you're sounding like Luke. Don't you think she should have waited, Teddy? Until we were home?"

Teddy sobered and shook his head. "No. We're living in uncertain times, Kris. We're lucky to have had yesterday, and only God knows if we're getting tomorrow. The only day that really matters is today. It's yesterday's tomorrow."

Kristin smiled at the proclamation. Teddy the Profound. "Yesterday's tomorrow. I like that."

"Cool. You can credit me for it when you write that book of yours."

"Maybe." She watched a few GIs stroll along the path across the court-yard. Who knew if they'd be alive tomorrow? She tried not to think about it, but she knew at any given moment she might be in the wrong place at the wrong time, and it would all be over.

"You're right, Teddy. Today is all we have." Emotion caught her unawares, her throat constricted as she took in the conviction in his eyes. "I need to say something to you."

Kristin rose and took slow steps around the bench. Now faced with the moment she'd thought about for years, put off doing and been haunted by, she couldn't quite find the words.

She eased herself back down onto the warm wood of the bench and faced him. "Do you remember the night Dad left, the night he went to Vietnam?"

Teddy's eyes clouded over. "Sort of. He and Mom were fighting. It was my birthday the next day, and he left."

Kristin nodded, let go a shaky sigh. "Yeah. Do you remember…you… you asked me that night, if he was coming back?" She forced herself to meet Teddy's anxious gaze.

He smiled and squeezed her hand. "It was a long time ago, Kris."

"I know. But…I…I told you he was, Teddy. I promised you he was. I promised you. I shouldn't have done that. I'm sorry."

It was out. The memory that disturbed her for years had finally been dealt with. Kristin lowered her head and tasted her tears on her dry lips.

"Kris." Teddy put his arms around her and she leaned in to his embrace. He drew back and stared, his brows knitted together. "You were twelve years old. For all we knew, Dad *was* coming back. I never thought about it. I didn't realize you'd been carrying this around with you…I'm sorry."

Strange relief surged through her and brought a smile. "It's okay. I just…needed to say it. Like you said, we don't know if we're getting tomorrow, right?"

"That's right. We don't." His smile returned, wider than before.

"And you don't want a soul to be lost, huh, Preacher?"

"Right again." He reached for her hands. "Have you stopped being mad at God?"

Kristin veered her gaze, the back of her neck prickling. She pinched her lips together. Where was God in all this madness? The prayers she muttered when she felt the need seemed futile. Since coming to Vietnam, she'd seen nothing to convince her God even existed.

"I'm more confused than ever. You've seen the death, the destruction. How can you sit there, knowing what's going on up in those hills, and tell me God is okay with all this? That He loves us?"

"Kris," he tightened his grip on her hands, his eyes filled with a light she didn't understand. "God didn't make this war. We did." Clear determination and passion shone from his eyes. "When I think about the guys on the frontlines, I can't help but think of Jesus. *'No greater love has a man who lays down his life for his friends.'* That's what the guys out there are doing for us, Kris. None of this makes sense, I know, but it makes even less sense without Him."

Kristin swallowed down her arguments, respect for her brother overriding disbelief. "I love you, Teddy."

And perhaps, in some way, he was right.

Perhaps there really was no greater love.

Perhaps…if she were really being honest…she needed that reminder.

And suddenly her grand plan to expose the CIA shrank under the weight of feelings she held for one particular agent. Feelings she knew she could no longer ignore.

Chapter Nineteen

They rode back to Saigon mostly in silence. Luke was quieter than usual and Jonno didn't attempt to keep up conversation. Kristin didn't want to talk anyway. She had too much on her mind. Although she'd only spent a few hours with Teddy, her spirit had been renewed by his words and his love for her.

Thanks to Luke.

He'd given her what she needed most.

And she didn't know what she was supposed to do with that.

"I'm gonna drop you guys and shove off." Jonno spoke as they neared the apartment building. Luke nodded, stretching his arms behind his head once they rolled to a stop.

Twilight lessened the heat. Kristin gathered up her things and Luke turned from the front seat. "I'm heading over to the orphanage." He hopped out and grabbed his stuff. "Do you want to come?"

"No." Kristin stood on the pavement and shifted her bag on her shoulder, the events of the day pushing her toward the brink of exhaustion. "I'm just going to go upstairs."

Luke blocked her path. "Come with me. You can't sit in your room all by yourself. It's your birthday."

She didn't have the energy for this. "Luke, I don't want to go, okay?"

"No, it's not okay." His eyes glimmered in the dusk, his mouth drawn in a thin line. "You're coming with me."

She shook her head again. "Stop ordering me around. I'm tired. I just want to be alone."

"Don't be stubborn on this one, please?" He took her hand in his, and the knowing look he gave her dragged her heart to her toes.

"You told them it was my birthday, didn't you?"

His eyes danced while a tiny smile played with his mouth. "I might have asked Caroline to get a message over there, yes."

When had she learned to read him so easily?

"You're too much." Kristin tried to sound angry.

"Hey," his tone dropped an octave. "I know you're tired. I'm sure it took a lot out of you seeing your brother again—but if you don't show up, I'm pretty sure Mary Jo will kill me."

"All right." Kristin gave a weary smile, ragged emotion threatening to come out of hiding. She could manage an evening with the Grangers. "Luke."

He put his bag down and reached for her other hand, waiting, concern in his eyes.

Two tears slipped down her cheeks as she stared at him. His mouth edged upward. Kristin felt suddenly exposed by feelings she could no longer control. "Thank you," she whispered. "Today—seeing Teddy, it meant more than you know."

"I'm glad, Kris. I'm glad he's okay." Luke cleared his throat, his eyes clouding. "He seems like a good guy."

"He's the best." She nodded and pulled her hands from his. The street was quiet and she paced up and down outside the apartment building, trying to find the right words.

There were none.

"How long have you been planning this?" Kristin met his eyes, searching their blue depths for the answers she needed.

Luke took slow steps toward her. His face glowed scarlet in the hue of the setting sun. He gave a lop-sided smile, rubbing the back of his neck. "I thought about it for a while, after you wouldn't shut up about him and searched every camp we went to…I found him a few weeks ago. I probably should have told you then…but…I wanted to surprise you. Today seemed like a good day."

She nodded, grateful yet still cautious. "I guess your connections must be better than mine."

A shadow ran across his face and he veered his gaze. "We should get going. You don't want to be late for your own surprise party, do you?" His grin returned and chased away the trepidation she fought.

"Okay. Give me a minute to freshen up." Kristin smiled and let it go.

Perhaps there were things about Luke Maddox she was better off not knowing.

He should say the same about her.

Luke hunched in a garden chair. The party Mary Jo put together came off without a hitch. Kristin gave an Oscar-winning performance as they'd arrived, seeing his father, Caroline, Jonno, and a few of their acquaintances gathered in the garden waiting for her. Almost had him convinced she hadn't suspected a thing.

She was good at that.

The guests were long gone, and Kristin and Mary Jo were inside putting the kids to bed. Kristin seemed to have forged a bond with the children...something else about her that surprised him. He would never have pegged her as the motherly type. But here at the orphanage, the tough exterior she displayed to the rest of the world melted away.

"Hey, man." Bob lowered himself into the chair next to Luke's.

"Nice evening, Bob. Thanks." Luke sighed and stretched out his legs. He felt Bob's eyes on him and waited for the question.

"What's on your mind, Luke?"

The question pulled a smile from him. If there was one person who could see right through him, it was Bob Granger. It had been that way from the first day they'd met.

Luke sat forward, dangling his arms over his knees. A lump rose in his throat and he swallowed it down, anger rising. His solitary existence had suddenly become complicated.

"How long have we known each other?" Bob pressed gently. "A while now, huh, couple of years maybe?"

"Three, almost four. So what?"

"A long time."

Luke tilted his head and took in the grin on his friend's face. Bob shook his head, sobering. "I've seen you at your worst. The first day you stumbled in here half drunk, swearing a blue streak, scaring the kids and Mary Jo half to death…"

"Don't remind me." Luke groaned and shut his eyes against the memory.

"Well, you got through it," Bob said. "You sobered up and you got on with things, didn't you?"

"As best I could. Life goes on, I suppose."

Bob gave a sad sort of smile edging on pity. "It does. But Luke…" He hesitated and Luke narrowed his eyes. "You've just been going through the motions, man. I don't know what it is you're really doing out there, but I know it's dangerous. And I don't think you care. Do you?"

"I didn't."

"Right. You've been living in some sort of self-inflicted hell since I've known you. Even when you're here with the kids, you've never seemed truly happy. Lately, that's changed. I'm starting to see some cracks in that cast-iron shell you've been carting around on your back, my friend." Bob gave a short laugh. "But I wonder if you'll let it continue. If you'll let her in."

Luke pinched the bridge of his nose together with his thumb and forefinger. Were his feelings for Kristin Taylor that obvious?

"I guess that's what I'm trying to figure out, Bob," he admitted, slumping back in his chair. "And I'm not sure I know how."

Bob nodded gravely. "You need to let it go, Luke. What happened to your wife and daughter was a tragedy, but it wasn't your fault. Stop blaming yourself. Stop blaming God."

Luke clenched his fists together and took a couple of deep breaths. "God's easy to blame. He doesn't talk back."

"He'll talk plenty if you'll listen."

"I used to believe that." Luke stared across the moonlit grass, watching the leaves of the trees above them rustle in the breeze. His faith had been strong once. But God let him down. Big time.

"He's still there for you, Luke. He's the only way you'll get through this thing in one piece."

The scent of burning candles hung in the air. The stillness of evening snaked around him, interrupted now and again by the high-pitched chirping of the tiny tree frogs the children loved to chase. Luke sat in silence.

Bob was right.

He just didn't want to hear it. Wasn't ready to hear it.

"Well, I've had my say." Bob squeezed Luke's shoulder. "I'm not going to preach, Luke. But I will ask you to take some time. Go off someplace by yourself. Let this thing go. Make peace with it. Make peace with Him. Until you do, you'll never be ready to move on."

Luke drew in a shaky breath. "I'll think about it."

"Would you let me pray for you?"

Luke fought the urge to refuse. With concentrated effort, he nodded and closed his eyes as Bob began.

When he finished, Luke wiped his eyes and sat back.

It wasn't a quick fix, but it was a start.

"Ah, you're still here," Mary Jo and Kristin came through the kitchen onto the patio. Mary Jo's smile brightened Luke's mood. "Good. I would have asked Bob to run Kris home."

"No need." Luke stood, rubbing the back of his hand across his face. He wondered just how red it was. Maybe in the dim light, they wouldn't notice. "Ready to go?" He glanced at Kristin, ignoring her inquiring gaze.

She nodded and turned to Mary Jo, pulling her into a hug. "Thanks so much. That was a wonderful surprise. The best birthday I've had in a long time."

"We're happy we got to celebrate it with you. I'm so pleased you saw your brother." Mary Jo smiled at Luke. Heat rose to his cheeks and he looked away.

He and Kristin walked back through the quiet neighborhoods in silence. The moon inched out from behind the clouds to light their path. Despite the uncommon calm and beauty of the evening, Luke's heart was heavy. He had too much to say, and few words. It was hard to be near her with so many conflicting emotions battling for first place.

Unable to stand it a minute longer, he reached for her hand and laced his fingers through hers. Kristin didn't miss a step, but he caught the beginnings of a smile as she walked, her eyes glued to the pavement.

A second later he heard gunshot and the unmistakable whizz of a bullet brush past them as he yanked her into the nearest alleyway.

"What's happening?" Kristin stood plastered to the wall behind him, her hand on his shoulder.

"Quiet." Luke held her back with one hand and fired two shots in quick succession—a warning. He caught a glimpse of a shadowy figure dashing across the street and disappearing into darkness. Only then did he let out his breath.

But then he had to face her.

The mix of fear and curiosity on her face made him want to smack her and kiss her at the same time.

He took a step back and slid his gun back into the holster strapped to his belt. His shirt clung to his back, his mouth dry. His heart pounded with the realization that everything in him was ready to dismember anyone who dared get near her.

He'd crossed the line.

"Luke?" She walked toward him, her eyes demanding answers. "Why were they shooting at you?"

He almost smiled. The words he wanted—needed—wouldn't risk riding the rapids of his traitorous emotions. Water dripped from a pipe above them, landing in the gutter, the incessant drip no match for the pounding of his heart. He pulled her into his arms and buried his face in her soft hair.

Then he drew back, met her inquiring gaze and shook his head. "They weren't shooting at me, love. That was for you."

Chapter Twenty

"For me?" Kristin backed up against the wall and stared in clear disbelief.

Luke gripped her arms and forced her to look at him, his nerves singing. "What are you working on?"

"Nothing."

"Tell me the truth. Now." God help him, he couldn't protect her if he didn't know what he was protecting her from.

A stubborn look froze her face. "No, Luke, it's nothing. Let me go." Her eyes flashed a warning through the moonlight. "And tell your goons to back off. I'm not afraid of them."

"You should be." Air hissed out of his lungs and he lowered his arms, resting his hands on her shoulders. "Are you all right?"

"I'm fine." She pushed him aside and marched down the alleyway. Then stopped, turned to face him and ran her fingers through her hair. "This thing with us, Luke. It's not going to work." She scuffed the toe of her boot on the ground and met his eyes again. "It can't."

Defeat jumped him and dragged him down. Luke fought it off, went to where she stood and took her hands in his. She could deny her feelings all she wanted, but the truth shone from her tear-filled eyes.

"It's too late, Kris." He wrapped her in his arms once more and felt her sag against him. A muffled sob escaped and she buried her face into his chest. He held her tight and waited until she could look at him again.

"I don't want to hurt you," she whispered.

"Then don't."

She traced the outline of his jaw with her finger, her eyes steady and full of secrets.

Luke shivered under her touch and captured her hand with his even as he pushed back the knowledge that he was making a huge mistake. He needed to walk away, and now. But he couldn't.

A sliver of light from the street illuminated her face. Her serious expression spoke through the silence that ran between them. Everything he'd learned over the last few years, the skills he'd mastered, the ability to discern a dangerous situation, rocketed through him, demanded that he pay heed and obey.

Luke was suddenly tired of trying to do the right thing.

He walked her to her door and they stood outside. "Are you sure you're all right?"

Kristin flashed that grin he'd come to enjoy so much. "You've got to stop being so nice to me, Maddox. You're ruining your track record."

"Sorry." Luke smiled. A strand of her thick brown hair fell forward and covered one eye. He tucked it back behind her ear, sliding a finger down the side of her cheek. "I have to go away for a few days." As much as he didn't want to leave her, he knew this was something he couldn't put off.

"Oh?" She pulled back, surprise creeping into her eyes. "Where are you going?"

Luke swallowed. The plan had formed as they'd walked home. There was no point in wasting time. "I'm not sure. Somewhere up the coast maybe."

"By yourself?"

"Yes." Luke nodded, running a hand over her hair. It felt soft and smooth, and he loved the way it curled around her face when she allowed it to.

"For work?"

"No." Luke shook his head. "Just for me. I have some things I need to deal with. I want you to lay low while I'm gone. Don't go anywhere."

"Luke." Kristin folded her arms and set her jaw. The familiar stubborn look returned, and defiance glinted in her eyes. He could almost see the wheels turning inside her head. "I'm not going to hide in my apartment. I need to get hold of Hayden, ask him to extend my visa. After talking to

Teddy, I want to do a feature on combat medics. We have no idea what they go through, what they have to endure to save the lives they do... we..."

She was off and running. Luke grinned and shook his head, laughter sticking in his throat.

"What?" She stopped talking long enough to take a breath and give him a sidelong glance. "Sorry. You were saying something about going... when?"

"I think I'll go tomorrow. Sooner the better. All right...if you go anywhere, I want you to fly. The roads are getting too dangerous, and after tonight...well, just don't do anything stupid. Take Jonno along, he'll look after you."

"I can take care of myself."

He smiled at her stubborn look and put his hands on her shoulders. "I know you can. I'm just asking you to be careful. Is that okay?"

"I don't know," she said, her voice suddenly soft, almost shy. She searched his face, looking for answers he couldn't give. "What's this about? What's going on, Luke?"

He shook his head and pulled her against him and held her close. Heard her shuddering sigh as she rested her head against his pounding chest and hugged him, hard, as though it might be for the last time.

Luke pulled back first, cupping her face in his hands, aching to kiss her. "We're a team, remember? Don't go taking up with that Jean Jacques fellow while I'm gone."

"It's Jean Luc." A tiny dimple appeared in her cheek as she smiled up at him. "And don't think I haven't thought about it. He's far more civilized than you."

"Is that so?" He watched her eyes dance under the hall light, noticing the smattering of freckles over her delicate nose. "I'm not so sure he's interested in women."

"That could be why he's avoiding my advances." Her grin told him she teased, but Luke was amazed at the relief flooding through him. As her gray-blue eyes moved across his face he wondered just when they had captured his heart.

"Promise me you'll be careful? Don't go stepping on any snakes or landmines."

Her grin broadened and he swore he saw her blush. "I won't. When will you be back?"

"I don't know." Truly he didn't.

How long did it take to rid oneself of the past?

"Will I see you in the morning?"

"I doubt it. Unless you want me to come wake you." He didn't feel much like smiling, but did anyway. "I'm going to get an early start."

"I don't want to say goodbye." Kristin's voice wavered, her eyes glistening.

Luke shook his head, drawing in a deep breath. "No. Don't do that." He pulled her closer and placed his lips on her forehead for a brief moment. "I want you to be here when I get back, Taylor. That's an order."

Her laughter was like a sweet, unexpected rain shower on a hot summer's day. "Yes, sir. I'll alert the Pentagon. I'm sure they'll get right on it."

"Promise me."

Kristin looked past him, a haunted look shadowing her. "I can't." When her eyes met his again, she gave a sad smile that spoke of things he did not know. "I learned a long time ago not to make promises I don't know that I can keep."

He nodded, unable to take his eyes off her. One thing he knew for sure, no matter where she went, he'd go after her. "If you're not here, I'll find you."

"Not if I find you first." Although she smiled, an obstinate tear escaped and rolled down her cheek.

Luke held her hands in his and brought them up to his lips. The current of feelings running between them felt unlike anything he'd experienced before. He wanted to sweep her up in his arms and never let her go. And perhaps someday, soon, he could do just that. "Good night, Taylor. Get some sleep."

She laughed again, her face lighting. "I will, as long as you don't come rummaging around in my bathroom in the middle of the night."

"I've got my own aspirin now, thank you."

"Well…"

"Goodnight." They spoke at the same time. He leaned in before he could stop himself, kissed her mouth in a way that left little room for doubt as to his true feelings, and watched her let herself into the apartment, a smile spreading across his face. Then he groaned aloud and headed down the hall toward his own apartment, ready to wrestle the demons that came to haunt him nightly.

Chapter Twenty-One

China Beach at dawn. Quiet and deserted, the tourists still asleep after a late night of partying and feasting, nothing moved but the ocean and a few gulls along the shore.

Luke sat halfway up the beach and watched the waves roll in.

His sleep deprived soul felt heavy. Salt spray pricked his cheeks, but the heat of his tears washed it away. The smell of the sea, usually something he loved, taunted him. Reminded him again why he came here a week ago, and what he still had not done. Anger rose and he clenched his fists on the tops of his knees.

"God…" He let out a long, ragged breath, his eyes stinging. "I'm sorry." His hoarse whisper caught in the wind and blew out to sea. "I can't see the good in this. Why did You take them from me? Why? And why can't I let it go?"

Luke cradled his head in his hands and shivered despite the warm ocean breeze. Bob said this wasn't God's fault. That it would never be God's will for him to suffer, or for innocent people to die. Some things just had no answers.

Somehow he had to believe that. The faith he'd once cherished was badly shaken, but not completely gone. Perhaps Bob was right. Maybe his growing feelings for Kristin were all part of that plan.

'All things work together for good, for those that love the Lord and are called according to His purpose.' Romans, eight, twenty-eight. It had been his mantra for many years.

"All right," he said, his voice hoarse. "I don't understand it, but I will accept it. I can't live in the past anymore. Is that what You're telling me?" Luke shuddered, doubt pricking again.

Only the sound of the waves crashing down upon the rocks answered. Perhaps God had turned His back on him. Luke had cursed Him enough times to deserve it.

If he closed his eyes, he could see Marcia. Sixteen and gorgeous, sitting on the dock at the youth camp they'd both gone to the summer they'd met. It had been love at first sight, and they thought they'd have forever.

Forever ended abruptly, five years ago today, in a fiery blast from hell.

The sound of the explosion still lived on inside his head. He'd heard it as he walked back toward the hotel after returning from the 24th. Sweat trickled down his back as he remembered breaking into a run, tearing down those last few blocks, only to find ambulances and a crowd of stricken onlookers.

No survivors.

Nothing for the medics to do. Nothing to even indicate he and his family had ever stayed there. In the seconds it took for the building to fall and crumble, his life had been destroyed.

A sob stuck in his throat. Luke coughed it down, but it refused to be ignored. Images of Marcia and Melissa flashed before him, taking him captive and forcing him to face the truth.

They were gone.

Forever.

Luke's shoulders began to shake as the first sobs tumbled out of him, opening the floodgates to an aching grief that he'd been ignoring for far too long.

"Oh, Jesus, help me…" he whispered into the wind.

Luke pushed himself off the sand as the sun came up.

It warmed his face and dried his tears. With purposeful steps, he walked barefoot until the tepid seawater reached his ankles. He drew his hands together in a slow movement, twisting the gold band on his left hand between the thumb and forefinger of his right. In a moment of anguish that sucked breath from him, he slipped it off.

The ring sat in the palm of his hand, shining under the sun.

"Till death do us part."

The bond was broken—not by choice—but broken nonetheless. He'd loved Marcia as best he could, in his own way. They were young; their marriage had not been an easy one. But he'd never worried about losing her. Never thought he'd had to. Yet at the age of twenty-five, he'd been made a widower.

Now, at thirty, it was time to start again.

With Kristin, if she'd have him.

He brought the ring up to his lips, kissed it, reached behind his shoulder, then, with all his might, tossed the ring high into the air and out to the ocean.

Luke turned and left the beach without watching it hit the water.

Kristin sat alone in the apartment, punched the keys of her typewriter, sweat running down the sides of her face, mingling with her tears. Her fingers were numb, her hands cramping at the slightest movement. The story on the CIA had finally come together. With Jean Luc's sources and her father's old notes, they'd been able to make some startling accusations that she hoped readers would pay attention to.

They hadn't used real names. Jean Luc swore he would be tactful. As far as she knew there was nothing in the piece that would put Luke or his counterparts in immediate jeopardy, and Jean Luc's editor had promised to use an anonymous byline.

So why was she having second thoughts now?

Kristin gave a cry of frustration, ripped the sheet of paper from the platen and tore it in half, buried her head in her hands and let the tears come. Her stomach hurt. Thirst scratched her throat. She hadn't slept through the night in days. The guilt refused to go away.

Aside from seeing her brother, this story had been her main goal, her one purpose for coming to Vietnam. Everything in her wanted to fulfill her father's legacy. To finish the story he started. Finding Luke and eventually working with him had been more of a bonus than she'd imagined.

Falling in love with him hadn't been part of the plan.

Kristin studied the black ink stains on the tips of her fingers and tried to summon calm. She was a journalist. Who wouldn't write a story about the CIA?

The secret interviews she'd conducted over the past few months held all the stuff of the best Fleming novel. Excitement, intrigue, drama and death. Things great stories are made of. The kind of story an editor might pay a lot of money for.

But all the money in the world wouldn't cover the debt of the betrayal she already felt.

Her eyes went to the corkboard on the wall and lingered on the photographs she and Caroline had tacked to it. Luke had taken most of them. They were all good. But one in particular stood out.

They'd enjoyed an afternoon off, just a few days before her birthday, and headed to Long Binh. Kristin had grabbed his camera and put him on the other side of the lens for a change.

His handsome face cracked in a grin as he pointed a threatening finger at her. She'd snapped the shot, tossed the camera his way and run. Luke caught up with her easily, picked her up in his arms and chucked her in to the deliciously cool water, diving in after her.

"You can't outrun me, Taylor," he laughed, shaking water from his hair. "Don't forget that."

No. She couldn't outrun him. Nor could she deprive herself of the intriguing possibilities that lay ahead. At times, her feelings for Luke consumed her, captured every part of her, and filled her with new hope. After the past few days, she'd lay odds on him feeling the same about her.

All right, Luke Maddox. You win.

Kristin brushed tears from her cheeks and made peace with her decision.

She pushed her chair back, slipped on a pair of ratty flip-flops, and raced down the stairs to the foyer. The house telephone sat on a small coffee table by the unused fireplace. With trembling hands she picked up the heavy black receiver and dialed.

He answered on the third ring.

"Hey. It's me."

"Ah, Kristin, chèrie. What is shaking?"

Just her entire body. Kristin paused to catch her breath and sank onto a nearby chair. "I'm not doing the story, Jean Luc. I changed my mind. You'll have to go ahead without me."

"But sweetie, it was a grande collaboration, non? Magnifique! Have they threatened you? They can't do…"

"It's not that, Jean Luc. I'm sorry. I just can't do it."

"Ah. I see." There was a long silence and Kristin wondered if he'd hung up. Then she heard his familiar chuckle. "L'amore, is it not?"

"Something like that." She pushed hair out of her eyes and smiled.

"Sweetie, it is too late. I am sorry. I sent it off last night."

"What?" Kristin gripped the edge of the chair, her throat drying up.

"Yes, it is gone. I thought you were okay with it."

"Oh, God. No. You…you didn't use any names, did you?"

"Non. You have my word, chèrie."

"When will it go to print?"

"Oh, I do not know. Next month, perhaps, my editor, he would not say for sure. I let you know. It's a good story. You stay cool, d'accord?"

"Thanks, Jean Luc." Tension rushed her like the waves on the beach at Long Binh. The dream that had brought her here, spurred her on and kept her going through it all, had just turned into her worst nightmare.

"You want to go where?" The pilot hovered the helicopter over the tarmac of the airstrip.

Luke shifted his heavy bag to his other shoulder and yelled again. "24th Surgical!"

The pilot heard this time and nodded. Luke stepped on the skid, jumped in, greeted the guys on board and settled on the floor near the gunner.

"You going in for pictures?"

Luke stared, confusion rising. "Pictures of…?"

"24th came under attack this morning!" the gunner yelled, shooting spit off the side of the chopper.

"What?" Fear clutched Luke's heart with a vise like grip. "The hospital was hit?" He struggled for breath and prayed he'd heard wrong.

"Yeah, man." The gunner let out a stream of words letting Luke know his feelings about the enemy. It wasn't anything he hadn't heard before. Hadn't said.

"What's the damage?" His father could be dead. Jonno...Kristin...

Before he'd left Saigon for the coast, he'd paid a visit to his colleauges and made it quite clear that if any harm came to Kristin Taylor, he'd have their hides. Still, in this game, few could really be trusted. When he'd returned to the city, he'd gone straight to her apartment, but found it empty. He'd checked the orphanage, but Mary Jo hadn't seen Kristin for a couple of days. She could be anywhere, perhaps even on her way home to the States. All he could do was pray she hadn't been at the 24th.

But Dad would have been...and maybe Caroline.

"Haven't seen for myself, but I hear it's bad," the gunner yelled back.

Luke kept silent vigil as they flew over the beat-up countryside. He held his head in hands and muttered prayers, doubt pricking him every now and again, telling him he was just wasting his time. He'd lost those closest to him before. Of course it would happen again.

After an eternity, the Huey descended onto the airfield of the 24th and the GIs on board began unloading supplies. Luke stood in the middle of the field, put on his shades and surveyed the area. A few of the hootches to his left were blackened, but the hospital looked in good shape. He strode toward the main building. People milled about, but the place seemed eerily quiet for once.

"Luke!" Jonno appeared from the mess hall and lumbered toward him. His usually crisp uniform was dirty and mud streaked his face. Luke stopped in his tracks, his breath coming in short spurts.

He managed a smile as Jonno reached him. "Hey, mate. Are you all right?" Luke swallowed down fear and pounded his friend on the back.

Jonno pounded him in return, his wide grin appearing. "Shoot, yeah. It was a little hairy. They attacked us around midnight. But we got 'em good. Haven't seen that much ammo for a stretch."

"Where's my Dad?"

"Inside. He's cool. Hey, man, you okay? I got freaked when you split."

"Sorry. I'm good. We'll talk later. Glad you're okay." Luke strode off toward the mess hall. He couldn't ask Jonno what he needed to. Didn't want to hear it from anybody but his father.

Luke slammed through the wooden doors and saw his father sitting on the far side of the room with Caroline. "Dad!" Relief rocketed through him.

Three down, one to go.

They both got to their feet as he came toward them. His father reached him first.

"Luke! Thank God. We've been so worried." He pulled him into a long hug. Luke squeezed his eyes shut and allowed the embrace.

The carefully constructed wall he'd hidden his feelings behind for so many years crumbled at the sight of them. Realizing he could easily have lost his father and sister, Luke vowed never to push them away again.

He hugged Caroline and she hugged back, harder than she had in years. "Hi, Lukie."

Luke battled rising panic as his thoughts jumped ahead. "What happened? They told me on the chopper you came under attack. I was frantic!"

Dad pulled a hand over his face and swore, something he rarely did. "They came out of nowhere. Luckily we had a couple of warning shots and were able to get most people into the bunkers—we lost a few boys along the perimeter. During clean up, a round of dust-offs came in. We've been flat out all day…"

Luke gripped his father by the shoulders and met his eyes, almost unable to get the words out. "Where's Kristin?"

Something like a groan came from Caroline but Luke ignored it. What concerned him more was the worry creeping across his father's face.

"She's not here, is she?" Luke asked. "She left, to go back home?"

"No, she didn't leave. She's here, Luke. She, uh…" Dad hesitated, looking at Caroline.

No, no, no. Luke bent over, put his hands on his knees and tried to breathe. He felt his father's hand on his back.

"Luke, she's all right. She got thrown by the blast apparently, but ran around like a paramedic for three hours afterward—you know how she is. Doing everything she could to help. Wasn't until she passed out that we realized she had a nasty gash on her head. She's got a bit of a concussion, but she's all right, son. She's all right."

Luke straightened, each movement agonizing. He wiped a trembling hand across his mouth and sniffed, searching his father's face, and then Caroline's. "Are you sure?" He'd know if they were lying.

"I checked her over myself." Dad drew his brows together in a frown.

Caroline rubbed a hand down his arm, smiling. "You're whiter than a wedding dress. Do you want to sit down?"

Luke shook her off. "Where is she?"

Dad cleared his throat. "She's in Ward One. Sleeping last time I checked so don't…"

Luke didn't give his father time to finish. He smashed through the doors and broke into a sprint as soon as the sunlight hit his face.

Chapter Twenty-Two

Kristin stirred and tried to remember where she was. Gentle pressure on her hand forced her eyes open.

Luke sat on the edge of the army cot, holding her hand, watching her through worried eyes. She took a quick breath, shut them tight then opened them again, just to make sure.

A slow smile started as he came into focus. "Where'd you come from?" She struggled to sit up but Luke put his hands on her shoulders.

"Can't I leave you alone for one minute?"

His stern expression widened her smile. "If you came all the way out here to lecture me, I'm not in the mood. My head hurts."

He lifted her hand up to his lips and kissed it. Then he ran a finger down the side of her cheek, and across the bandage on her forehead. "How do you feel?"

It all came back in a rush. "Stupid idiots attacked the hospital! Can you imagine? Honestly, we were just lucky they're moronic enough to miss, and we got them before they really hit us. Burnt out a couple of our hootches, but I got my pack out in time, thank goodness, and…" Kristin stopped her flow of words as he dissolved into laughter. "What?"

"Nothing." Luke rubbed his face with his hands and gave a snort. "Perhaps we should put you on the front lines."

She sighed, drinking in the sight of him. His eyes, although worried, appeared brighter somehow. His face bore a healthy glow, the top of his nose pink-tipped where skin had peeled off. For the first time since they'd met, Luke seemed rested. And at peace.

"You look good. Where've you been?" She swung her feet over the bed and walked across the ward to where the jug of fresh water sat.

He was at her side at once. "What are you doing? Lie down!"

"Yes, Doctor." She pushed him aside and poured herself some water.

"I thought you might have gone home."

She returned to the bed and stretched out again. "Hayden said I could stay on. He's getting the paperwork through and I should get another visa by the end of the week." Kristin watched the mixture of relief and annoyance cross his face, and her thoughts grew muddled again. "What's that look about?"

"I think you should go." He crossed his arms over his chest, his mouth drawn.

Kristin widened her eyes, a slow pounding beginning in her chest. She ran her tongue over her bottom lip, cracked and peeling from days under the scorching sun. "I thought you wanted me to stay."

"I changed my mind."

His words slapped her, but she didn't allow herself to process them. Maybe she had been off base when she'd ascertained his feelings for her. But then again, maybe he was giving her the way out. She didn't have that much of a concussion.

But she'd already made her decision.

"Well, Luke, I'm not going anywhere. If you don't want to work with me anymore, that's fine, but I'm staying. Whether you like it or not." Kristin set her jaw and met his look of surprise head on.

"You could have been killed today, Kristin! Do you get that? The whole ride here, all I could think, was what if you were dead? What if I'd lost you?" He paced the room like a lion waiting for its next meal. She feared she was it.

"Well, clearly I'm not dead. Don't you think you're over-reacting?"

"No." Luke stopped pacing and pinned her with his eyes, his face still held in a maddening glare. "I'm sorry if you think I'm being ridiculous, but I want you to go home. I'm not going to go through losing the woman I love again. I won't do it." He turned from her and laced his hands behind his head.

So that was it.

Kristin's face grew warm and her anger melted away as his words filtered into her soul. Her hopes and fears collided into an inexplicable jumble of feeling she could make no sense of. Didn't care to. "Can you… uh…repeat that?"

"Repeat what?" he huffed. "I told you. I want you to go home."

"Oh, I heard that." Kristin smiled, her eyes wet, everything else forgotten. "Luke. Come here."

He swiveled to face her, a hesitant smile crinkling his tanned cheeks. In a couple of steps he sat beside her again. Kristin placed her hands on either side of his face. He put his hands over hers and drew her to him, claiming her lips with a kiss that sealed the words he had spoken.

"Tell me what you said again, the other thing," she whispered. He drew her hands down and she laced her fingers through his. She noticed something missing. Kristin turned his hand over in hers and looked down at the white skin where his ring used to be.

"I love you." Luke's voice caught on the words. He grinned like a schoolboy and shook his head, as though he couldn't quite believe it himself. "I'm afraid I've fallen completely, head over heels, insanely in love with you, Kristin Taylor. Is that what you wanted to hear?"

"That'll do." Speech was almost impossible.

Luke's expression darkened. "Well?"

"Well, what?" Kristin giggled, watching his jaw begin to pulse.

Luke scowled. "Usually when somebody says they love you, you're supposed to say it back."

"Oh. Is that how it works?" Kristin laughed at the consternation on his face. She ran her fingers through his blond hair and sought his eyes. "I do love you, Luke Maddox. I think I fell in love with you the first day we met."

"You couldn't have. I almost shot you." He kissed the tip of her nose.

"I must be attracted to dangerous men with a dark side." Kristin emitted a sigh of satisfaction as she wound her arms around his neck. Whatever happened now, they'd just have to find a way to work through it. "I have to admit, I never thought you'd give me the time of day once I figured out I actually wanted you to."

He chuckled, curling her hair around his fingers. "You can be quite aggravating. And, in case nobody's ever told you, you talk too much."

"Only when I have something to say!" Indignation prodded her and she folded her arms across her chest.

Luke rolled his eyes, unwound her arms and took her hands in his. "My love, you *always* have something to say."

"I'm a journalist. I'm supposed to have an opinion."

"True. But you're not always right, you know."

"Says you." A smile stretched across her face, warming her through. It didn't matter what he thought. He was here.

And he loved her.

She studied him, tracing the outline of his face with her fingertip. Her heart, full as it was, ached for what he must have gone through this week. "Was it very hard? Letting them go?"

A bare smile tracked across his face and he looked away for a moment. "Hard, but necessary. I've made my peace with it. I need to move on with my life." Luke pressed his forehead against hers, slipped his arms around her and held tight. "I want you to be a part of that life, Kris. I can't imagine it without you now."

Kristin wrapped her arms across his back, sniffing back tears. Outside, the buzz of incoming choppers reminded her of the world they still lived in. "It's crazy, isn't it? Being so happy in the middle of hell."

He buried his face against her neck and shook his head. "Still thinking too much."

She sat back, loving the new light in his eyes. "I just want you to know that I…I'll respect what you do, Luke. I…" The story she'd written loomed in the back of her mind, a hand-grenade just waiting for somebody to rip the cap off. Honesty and truth tussled with pleasure. Selfish need stepped in and slammed the door on integrity. "Just…be careful, okay?"

His expression never wavered, but the corners of his mouth inched upward. "I can't promise you anything. I think you know that. Is it enough?"

Kristin put her arms around him again and leaned against his chest. "It's enough."

It would have to be.

They left camp in the morning. Rumblings of attempted ambushes were in the air, but Kristin was desperate to head back to Saigon and talked Luke into driving rather than waiting for a chopper. He rounded up Jonno and secured a Jeep despite Doc's protests.

The Jeep barreled along the road at a speed Kristin doubted could get any faster. Having already passed a couple of VC trucks, Jonno wasn't taking any chances. He sped over the potholes as they bumped along the road and Kristin felt sure her head would explode every time he swerved. The way Jonno kept glancing back over his shoulder made her neck prickle. He said something to Luke she couldn't quite hear, but when she saw Luke reach down and come up with an M-16 in his hands, her heart-rate tripled.

"What's going on?" She leaned forward, her hand on Luke's shoulder.

He swiveled slightly, his eyes tinged with worry. "Put your helmet on."

"Okay, but…" She glanced behind them and saw a Jeep in the distance. Too far away to make out faces, but she could tell the occupants weren't military. "Luke…who…"

"Get down, Kristin! Shut up, and get down!"

Kristin heard the first round of gunfire, saw the red soil spurting around them like small geysers as the bullets touched the ground, and she hit the floor of the Jeep. They swerved left and right for longer than she could stand, then everything went black.

The thud of impact brought her into consciousness. Fireworks sounded somewhere around her every now and again, then silence. Prone face down, she shifted on the damp mud beneath her, bombarded by the smell of smoke, dirt and blood.

Fear rendered her unable to do more than glance upward.

A steep embankment faced her. Behind her, tall elephant grass closed her in. She knew it well. Over the weeks of traipsing through it, following whatever platoon allowed her to, she had enough scars from the sharp stuff to remind her of Vietnam for the rest of her life.

Luke…Jonno…lucid thought trickled in and brought a wave of panic behind it. She lay still for a very long time, wondering when it would be safe to move.

A scratching sound startled her and she whipped her head around, coming face to face with Luke as he moved through the grass toward her. He crawled to her, pulled her close, and she allowed herself to breathe again. "Are you hurt? Did you get hit?"

"No, I don't think so," Kristin whispered back, her eyes moving over him. "Are you all right?" Luke spat blood and dirt. Fresh blood dripped from the old gash on his forehead. Kristin fumbled in her pocket and came up with some tissues. She dabbed at the wound carefully. "Are you hurt anywhere else?"

Luke's reply sounded unclear and worry filled her. The setting sun shone through the tops of the trees. Amazingly, she heard birdsong.

"Where's Jonno?" She kept her voice low, too afraid to speak any louder.

Luke shook his head. "I don't know. I have to go find him. Stay here until you hear from me."

"Luke." She gripped his hand, desperate for an ounce of bravery. She didn't want him to leave her alone out here.

He moved within an inch of her and took her face in his hands, his eyes locking with hers. "Don't move. Promise me?"

Kristin summoned all her strength and nodded. "I won't. But you better come back."

Luke pulled his pistol from its holster. He pressed it into her hands. "Sorry I didn't get around to this earlier, but..." He somehow managed to grin, still breathing heavily. "This is the safety, pull it back, hold tight and pull the trigger. If you miss, scream."

Kristin watched Luke crawl up the muddy escarpment. Fear paralyzed her. Kristin closed her eyes. Tears made their way down her face. Her heart pounded and she swallowed, her mouth dry. She'd never felt so alone and so terrified in her life.

She sat in the approaching darkness for what felt like an eternity.

"I know you can do it, Kris. Pray. Pray and God will give you the strength." Teddy's twelve year-old voice crept into her memory. She'd been about to enter the water for the final swim of the State Championship. Although younger, Kristin knew her brother would always be wiser. She'd prayed then, before diving into the water. She hadn't won, but her fear had gone.

She drew in a deep shuddering breath. "God. Please help us. I'm not going to make up any excuses. I've been ignoring You. I'm sorry. But if you could get us out of here…"

"Kris! Come on!" Luke half ran, half fell down the hill toward her. As he reached her, she saw unspoken fear in his eyes. "Come on!" He grabbed her arm and pulled her to her feet. Kristin gripped Luke's arm as he helped her up to the road.

"Did you find him? Is he okay?" *Dear God, let him be okay…*

"He's hit. Bad. We have to get him to a hospital. There's nobody around right now, I think we can make it."

Kristin saw the Jeep halfway down the road. It had fishtailed and now faced the opposite way, which was probably what threw them, but it hadn't tipped over.

Jonno lay near the vehicle, sprawled face down on the red dirt, blood seeping around him. She let out a sharp cry and her fear returned with vengeance.

"Can you help me carry him? Kristin?" Luke snapped his fingers in her face and she nodded, forcing herself to move. Together they lifted him as carefully as they could onto the backseat. Blood splattered everywhere.

Luke grabbed the medical kit Jonno always carried and she watched in amazement as he set to work. He crouched on the backseat next to Jonno and checked his vitals. Luke ripped off his shirt and tied it in a tourniquet around Jonno's leg. Glancing up at her, he indicated the driver's seat. "You have to drive. Get in. Hurry!"

Kristin obeyed without question. "Which way?"

"We're closer to the 24th than the city. Turn around and head back that way. Oh, come on, man…" He bent over Jonno again, wrapping more of the ripped shirt around his wounds.

Too afraid to look back, Kristin started the engine and prayed she would remember what Luke had taught her months ago. Miraculously, the vehicle co-operated. As she turned the Jeep and picked up speed, her heart rate slowed. She could do this.

She *had* to do this.

Jonno's life depended on her getting him back to the hospital.

Kristin pressed down on the gas with all her might and concentrated on the long road ahead. Above the thundering of her heart, all she heard was Luke, talking in low tones to Jonno, and praying over him.

Chapter Twenty-Three

At the 24th, Kristin sat against Luke, his arms securely around her. His steady breathing from behind settled her, soothed her shattered spirit and almost made her believe things would be all right.

Doc had been in surgery with Jonno for over two hours now. Small groups of GIs hung around the mess hall, some huddled in groups, some sat alone. She knew all of them were praying for Jonno to make it. Caroline perched at the far end of their table and smoked in silence. Sorrow hung heavy in the room and Kristin felt the weight of it.

The events of the past few hours continued to assault her. "It's my fault," she whispered, squeezing Luke's thick forearms with her hands. "I should have listened to you. We should have stayed here."

Luke tightened his hold, resting his chin on her shoulder. "It's not your fault. It could have happened anywhere, anytime."

"But I wanted to go back to Saigon. I talked you into it! And that attack…Luke…I saw the men following us. They weren't VC. Were they?"

She heard his tired sigh as he released her, swiveled on the bench and turned her around to face him, his fingers pressing into her shoulders. He shook his head and his eyes blazed into hers. "No. They weren't. But…"

"They were Agency, weren't they? They were after me. Tell me the truth, Luke!"

He held her gaze and tightened his grip. "We're not going to talk about this now. Whatever happens, it isn't your fault."

"He's right, Kris. Don't think about it." Caroline looked over at her through cool eyes. Kristin had no idea how she could she remain so calm when the world around them seemed to be crumbling to pieces.

She couldn't stop trembling. The memory of Jonno sprawled on the red dirt played again and again. "I don't want him to die. God, please don't let him die."

Luke pulled her against him, wrapping his arms around her. Her body felt immobile, encased in concrete. She wanted to cry, needed to cry, but felt numb inside.

She'd almost fallen asleep when Luke shook her some time later. Kristin raised her head and saw Doc heading their way, his expression unreadable, his green scrubs dotted with dark stains. He sat on the bench opposite them, resting his head in his hands for a moment.

"Dad?" Fear laced Luke's voice, and she inched closer to him. Doc looked at them through bloodshot eyes.

Kristin was suddenly back in her living room in Boston. Twelve years old, ripped out of slumber by the sound of her mother's screams.

"He's dead. They killed him…they killed him…"

"We did everything we could. He's still with us, but I'm not sure…for how long. I removed two bullets, patched him up as best I could. Honestly, I can't believe he survived. All we can do now is pray."

"Pray, Kristin. That's all we can do now. Just pray that God will look after us."

Luke nodded, tightening his grip around her.

Kristin blinked back tears, sniffed and dragged a hand across her face. "Praying is a waste of time."

Doc patted her on the knee. "Not always. Are the two of you all right? Were you hurt?" He settled his gaze on Luke, stood to examine the gash above his son's eye. "You need a couple of stitches in that. Anything else?" Luke shook his head, flinching as his father poked and prodded him. "You, Kristin? Any injuries? How's the head?"

Kristin shrugged, unable to answer. The kindness in Doc's eyes was too much to bear. She looked down at the dusty floor beneath her feet.

The others straggled closer, wanting news. She heard Doc repeating what he'd told them, but all she could think was that Jonno would die. He would die and no matter what anybody said, it *would* be her fault. She should be the one laying in that bed, not Jonno.

"I need to see him." Her voice shook as she struggled with the words. She sounded on the edge of hysteria, but she didn't care. "Can we see him?"

"Dad?" Luke turned to his father again and Kristin waited, gulping deep breaths of air. Doc hesitated, looking at her, concern etched into his features.

Caroline moved down the bench and sat next to her, rubbing Kristin's back in a soothing, circular motion. "You need to calm down. If you're going in there, you can't lose it, Kris. He needs your strength right now."

Doc's grave expression told her he agreed with his daughter. "I don't mind you seeing him, Kristin, but I have to warn you, he's not conscious, and he may not come around."

"We understand." Luke got to his feet, took her hand and pulled her up. "Can we see him now?"

Doc nodded and gave a battle weary sigh. "This way."

As they walked down the hall, the sound of choppers overhead reminded her there was still a war being fought out there alongside the one that waged here, in the confines of the hospital.

Kristin didn't know how it was possible, but Jonno looked pale.

His eyes were closed, puffy and swollen, his skin covered in gauze wraps.

Doc left them to go attend to the incoming wounded. The curtains around Jonno's bed were drawn to give them some privacy. Luke leaned against the far wall, staring down at his friend as though he couldn't believe what he saw.

"Luke…" Kristin sank down in the chair beside the bed as soon as the nurse left. Luke crossed him arms and nodded. She looked up at him, desperate for answers. "What's going to happen to him?"

"If he makes it through the next twenty-four hours, he'll be transferred to an Evacuation hospital, and then probably out to Japan. Then they'll send him home."

If he makes it…

Kristin studied the face of the young man who'd come to mean so much to her. "I'm sorry, Jonno," she whispered, half-expecting him to open his eyes and tell her one of his corny jokes. "You hold on. Don't do anything stupid, okay?" She choked on her words and heard a shuddering sigh come from Luke. She clasped Jonno's hand in hers. His skin felt clammy, and he lay motionless. Maybe he could hear her. Maybe if she just kept talking…

Kristin sat up with a start, rubbed her eyes and looked around the small, enclosed cubicle. She'd lost track of time, must have dozed off in the chair.

Luke was gone.

She settled her gaze on Jonno. It didn't look like he'd moved at all. It was almost six in the morning. She let out a ragged breath and rose, her body stiff and sore.

"I'll be back soon," she told him, adjusting the sheet around his chest. Tears pricked her eyes as the probability of his fate began to dawn on her. A lump rose in her throat. She fought it, warding off morbid thoughts. "Don't go anywhere."

As she turned to go, Doc entered the cubicle.

"Any change?"

"No." Kristin watched him examine Jonno, then followed him out into the hall.

"Doc, have you seen Luke?" She kept her eyes on him, taking in the look of trepidation that crept over his face.

He cleared his throat and raked his fingers through his short hair. "He's not here." He put a hand on the door to his office and ushered her in.

"What do you mean he's not here? Where is he?"

Doc stood at the window, his back to her. "He took off a few hours ago, Kristin. He'll be back, don't worry."

Right.

Doc swiveled, and as soon as she met his gaze, she knew. Kristin squeezed her eyes shut and forced air into her lungs. "He's gone to find them, hasn't he?"

He walked to his desk and began sorting papers, tension etched across his forehead.

Kristin pushed fingers through her tangled hair. "Doc, please. You know how I feel about Luke, don't you? Can you at least tell me if he's okay?"

He met her eyes, shook his head, and gave a brief smile. "I do know how you feel. And I know how my son feels about you, Kristin. You've given him reason to live again." He held the look of a beaten man. "But I can't tell you if he's okay. I never know he is until he comes back."

Even though she'd uncovered more than enough evidence over the last few months, she hadn't wanted to believe it. Even as she'd written the story, even as men verified her suspicions, she'd pushed aside the extent of Luke's involvement. She hadn't ever wanted to believe he might be in just as much danger as those men on the front lines. But now she knew. She'd gotten in too deep, waded too far into dangerous waters.

And pulled Luke in right along with her.

Because she knew he hadn't disappeared without reason.

He was seeking retribution.

From the men on his own team.

When Luke returned the next morning, Doc summoned them.

"He's got an infection," he told them, his expression grave. "I was going to transfer him, but then his fever spiked. If you want to see him, you should do it now, while he's lucid. I'm about to give him some fairly strong meds." He paused and dragged a hand down his face, his sigh betraying exhaustion and worry. "Frankly, I'm not sure he'll need them for long. He lost a lot of blood during surgery. His blood pressure's way down, his body's going into shock. I have to be honest with you, it's not looking good."

Luke swore and kicked the toe of his scuffed boot against the concrete floor, his face dark. Kristin saw him ball his fists and take a deep gulp of air. The lump in her throat grew larger and she had to look away.

Doc led them back toward the ward where Jonno lay.

Kristin wanted to run from the room as soon as she set eyes on Jonno.

His pallor was a murky shade of brown, his eyes half-closed. His body shook with fever. As they drew near, he turned his head toward them, his mouth opening in a smile she barely recognized.

"Hey…look…who's…here." He spoke in gasps, reached out a tremulous hand. Kristin shuffled closer as Doc told Luke he'd see them later. Tears burned as his fingers tightened around hers, his face contorted with pain. "It hurts real bad, Kris."

"I know." She was only vaguely aware of the tears slipping off her cheeks and onto the thin white sheet that covered him. "I'm sorry, Jonno. I shouldn't have made us leave. It's my fault. I'm so sorry."

"Aw, Kris." For an instant, the carefree grin she loved returned. "It's cool. It ain't up to you when a man's time to go is. My number came up is all." He shuddered and winced, letting out a high-pitched whine, more like a kitten's mew than a man's cry. She squeezed his hand and willed herself to keep it together.

Luke stood beside her, a strong silent presence she was very much in need of. When she choked on a sob, his arm came around her waist.

"You're going to make it, Jonno," Luke said firmly.

Kristin nodded, needing to agree with him. "They'll give you some meds, you'll rest, and you'll be fine."

"Sure." Jonno nodded, his eyes fixed on Luke now. "But if I'm not, I got some pretty girls up in Heaven to keep me company."

Luke's shaky intake of breath tugged at Kristin's heart. "Yeah. You tell them hi from me, okay, mate? Tell them—I'm okay." Luke's voice shook and he cleared his throat several times. Kristin made a half turn, bringing him in to her view.

Tears slipped down his cheeks. His bottom lip trembled. She put her free arm around his waist and squeezed.

"You two gotta take care of each other…" Jonno's breath came in spurts. He was struggling to hold on, determined to say what he needed to. "I knew it the minute I seen you that first day, Kris, staring him down—I said—that girl—she's perfect for my best friend. I figured ya'll would come to your senses eventually."

Kristin wanted to laugh but her sobs wouldn't allow it. Luke pulled her closer, kissing the top of her head. Jonno's tired eyes fluttered open and closed.

"When you get back home, Kris, go see my sis, would ya? Name's Cassie…she's in New York now. I had them write it down, there…" He grunted, shifting his head toward the small dresser beside his bed, and she saw the notepad on it. "I told her all 'bout you. She'll teach you to make some sweet cornbread."

"Okay." Kristin sniffed and her shoulders began to shake as she battled tears. Jonno's breathing grew shallower, raspy. "Jonno?" She leaned in, placing a hand on his forehead.

"Uh huh." A slow smile spread across his face. "Man, it's pretty over there...aw, he's waiting for me—Jesus. Waiting for me. Imagine that."

Kristin's entire body tingled as she absorbed his words. Even in the midst of this heartbreak, a peace she could not explain flooded through her. "Yes, I can imagine that." She brushed his cool cheek with her lips. "You go on, now." Kristin stepped away from the bed as Luke moved forward, grasping Jonno's hand in his.

"You were the best friend I ever had, mate," he breathed out, somehow managing a smile.

Jonno's eyes fluttered open again. "Don't let her go," he whispered, his voice barely audible. "You—got—your second chance. Don't screw it up."

Luke shook his head, looking back at Kristin through desperate eyes. "I won't. I swear it."

"Good. 'Cause if...I thought...you might...I'd hafta stick around to kick your butt..." Jonno sucked air and wheezed, a horrible rattling sound coming from deep inside his chest.

Kristin shuddered. She'd heard that sound once before, at her grandmother's deathbed. She'd been nine years old, but she'd never forgotten it. She watched Luke close his friend's eyes with his thumb and forefinger. "I'll see you up there, mate." And then he turned to face her. "He's gone."

Kristin moved into his open arms and wept.

They held a memorial service for Jonathan Seymour Hicks down on the beach. His body had already been taken away, being flown back to the States so his family could bury him. Jonno's absence at the 24th Surgical left a gaping hole in the lives of those who'd known and worked with him.

Kristin knew her life would never be the same.

They remained at the 24th for two more days after the service. She saw Luke with his father often, their heads bowed together in prayer, or reading their Bibles. She wished she could gain strength from the source they did, but anger and doubt swayed her all over again.

Why had she even prayed? He was never going to let Jonno live. Just like she had prayed when Dad left for Vietnam. He'd known all along.

Why bother to talk to a God who didn't listen?

Raw unbridled anger settled over her soul, sowing fresh seeds of disbelief.

She and Luke hopped a bird back to Saigon late in the afternoon. Kristin fumbled with the lock on the door to her apartment and pushed it open. She threw her pack to the floor, and sank onto the couch, numb.

"Did you get them?" she asked, wondering at the surprise on his face. "The men you went after? I assume they were your CIA buddies. What did you do to them?"

Luke paced the small apartment, breathing heavily. "Not what I wanted to." Finally he straddled a chair and sat in silence for a long while. "It was an accident, Kris. They only meant to scare you, but their jeep swerved and…"

"Really? Do you people fire off a couple of rounds at whim anytime you want to get a message across?"

Luke picked up his pace again, stopping every now and then to place his hands over his knees and swore. "I want a drink." His honest confession startled her. Kristin looked up, met his eyes and saw unfamiliar fear.

"Don't. Don't do it, Luke, you'll only regret it later."

"You're right. I…" His eyes moved to the direction of the kitchen where Caroline's stash of bottles sat on the counter, as tempting for him as a kid let loose in a candy store.

"Go back to your place." Kristin somehow found the energy to stand and move toward him. "Try to sleep."

He rose and took her in his arms and placed his lips on her forehead. "Would you come with me? I don't...trust myself tonight. I'll sleep on the couch, you can have the bed."

She shivered and drew back, knowing she should refuse, but she didn't want to let him down. And she didn't want to be alone either.

Chapter Twenty-Four

lood covered her from head to toe. Jonno's blood. She stared down at him as horror gripped her, froze her to the spot. But Jonno just laughed. His mouth hung open, white teeth dripped red liquid, his eyes unmoving, fixed on her. His maniacal laughter chilled her to the core.

Horrible creatures of her imagination swooped down, large wings flapping, whipping up wind around her. Sharp talons sank into Jonno's already ripped flesh, pointed beaks pecked at him, tore at his skin. And he continued to laugh.

Kristin bolted upright in bed to the sound of her own scream. Her entire body trembled. Her teeth chattered as she shook off the terrifying image. She pulled the sheet up, clutching it to her chest.

Hard rain pelted the windows of her bedroom. Rain, at last. A cooling breeze filtered through the room. That it would come now seemed right. Rain would clean the road they'd traveled. Wash away all traces of what transpired there, and Jonno would be put to rest. She closed her eyes and took deep breaths, but saw the nightmarish scene again. Another scream ripped through her.

The bedroom door flew open and Luke raced across the room. He sank onto the side of her bed, breathing hard. "What? What is it?" His hands closed around her arms. She caught the glimmer of his eyes through the shadows.

Kristin couldn't speak for a moment, sweat mingling with her tears. "I killed him! I killed him, Luke…I…" Sorrow conquered fear, and harsh sobs wracked her body. She heard his groan as he put his arms around her and held tight, rocking her like he did the children at the orphanage.

"No, Kris. Stop. You're okay. I've got you."

Neither his words nor the gentle tone he used could pacify her. She'd been thrown overboard into a vast, dark ocean, sharks circling. And she'd forgotten how to swim.

At last her sobs subsided.

The steady rhythm of his heartbeat settled her as she rested her head against his chest. It rose and fell with each shaky breath he took. His hands were light as feathers, running up and down her bare arms, willing her back to the safe place inside his embrace. Kristin pressed against him, needing his warmth and strength.

"I think I'm losing my mind," she whispered through the darkness.

"No, you're not. You're fine." Luke pushed her hair off her damp forehead, his eyes locked with hers. Kristin shook her head and looked away, but he gently guided her face back toward him, two fingers pointing at his eyes. "Look here, Kris, right here. You're going to be fine, love. Do you believe me?"

She drew a shuddering breath, fear melting under his touch. She unclenched her fists and relaxed her palms against his broad chest. The feel of his bare skin against hers sent a shiver through her. She moved her hands slowly upward, across his broad shoulders and over his muscled arms.

A shard of moonlight sliced through the darkened room, illuminating his face as she raised her head to look at him. In that one desperate moment she saw everything he needed to say.

Everything he wanted.

And all she loved.

"I should...have listened to you, Luke. I should have left it alone. I'm so sorry." She was desperate that he know her true feelings, how much she loved him still, yet no more words would come. Her eyes and throat burned. She put her arms around his neck and splayed her fingers through his hair, the action comforting somehow, taking her mind off her pain.

Luke brought her closer with one hand, and brushed her tears away with the other, his eyes never leaving hers "I know you are." His voice shook, low and taut with emotion. He kissed her tears away, cradling her face between his hands. "We're in the middle of a war. I don't know what tomorrow will bring, and I can't make you any promises right now. But I want you to know how much I love you. Nothing's going to change that."

Something flashed in his eyes, something she hadn't seen before. In the recesses of her conscience, Kristin felt the shift in the moment, the instant when his embrace evolved from comfort into something more.

Luke slipped his arms around her again. Her heart tightened as a strange and unfamiliar sensation crept through her. When his lips settled on hers and a low groan came from somewhere deep within him as his kisses became more insistent and demanding, she recognized it as her own desire.

It was too easy to forget where they were, all they had gone through, and the pain she still felt. They clung to each other with a desperation she'd never known. With each kiss he gave her, the horror lessened.

Somehow she moved downward on to the bed.

"Oh…love. I should go." His fingers scorched her skin, his tender kisses brushing her cheeks, her nose, then crushing her mouth once more. The need within her heightened, and crossed over into forbidden territory.

Instead of pushing him away, she tightened her arms around him, running her hands over the rippling muscles of his back. "Stay, Luke. I don't want to be alone."

"I can't. We can't…" His breathing unsteady, his words almost inaudible.

Kristin shook her head. "We won't."

He murmured something against her neck, but she didn't hear. The pounding of her heart and the blood rushing through her veins drowned out everything, and took away all rational thought.

A bright sliver of hope, something pure, beautiful and unexpected, burst through the dark cloying mire that had become her world.

He stayed.

And, eventually, they slept.

Luke hardly left her side for a week, holding her through the night as garish dreams sought to steal her sleep and kidnap her mind. As each day faded into dark night, so did Kristin's ability to function normally. The only thing that felt right was being with him, knowing he was there beside her, anchoring her to reality and keeping her safe.

By end of the week, Luke was so worried that he threatened to call a doctor. Kristin forced herself out of bed and promised him she would be okay. Luke left her reluctantly and drove out to check on his father. She refused to go with him. Wasn't ready to face the place where Jonno had breathed his last.

She wrapped her robe around her and stared at her own reflection in the mirror. Her normal healthy glow gone, purplish circles framed her eyes.

As most young girls do, she'd indulged in fantasies of white wedding dresses with flowing trains, pink roses and babies breath. She dreamt of that perfect moment when she'd look into the eyes of the man she loved and know that all was right with the world.

Childhood dreams no longer belonged in the world she lived in.

She dragged the brush through her tangled hair and sighed—a harsh sound that yanked all feeling from her and left her completely empty. A fleeting memory of her mother brushing her hair before she went to bed at night teased and taunted. Strict as she had been, Mom was always there in times of need. Would she want to comfort her now, knowing that Kristin had given herself away without so much as a second thought?

Guilt sidled close and licked her ankles, but she kicked it away.

Nothing about her old life—"the real world", the guys called it— seemed real at all. Some days she wondered if she'd ever lived it.

Her reality came in the form of young men on stretchers, screaming out in pain. Her life meant being surrounded by gunfire, wondering if you'd make it out alive, and watching others die. Day after day, after day. She needed consolation, something normal outside of the hellish scenes she encountered. It didn't seem so strange to want to escape through a few stolen hours of fleeting happiness in the arms of the man she loved.

But when the sun rose each morning, nothing outside the thin walls of her apartment had changed. The sights, sounds and smells of Vietnam had wound their way deep inside of her like the creeping vine that rose up through the city, threatening to take over everything in its path. The more you cut it back, the thicker it grew, bound and determined to smother the life out of whatever it clung to.

The brush she held in her hand fell, clattered into the sink, and Kristin jumped backward, nerves screaming and running for cover. She swallowed down the sob ready to escape, went back to the bedroom and crawled into bed.

Luke stared at his hands, the throbbing in his temples forcing him to close his eyes. It wasn't so much his regrets that bothered him. It was more the fact that he didn't have many.

Bob sat in the chair beside him. A few of the children ran around the garden, laughing and tossing a ball. He caught a glimpse of Mary Jo's red head poking through the window every once in a while. But he hadn't come to play with the kids today. He'd barely managed a smile when they'd surrounded him. Bob sent them off, and he and Luke sat on the terrace behind the house in silence.

Eventually Luke found the words to tell his friend everything. He couldn't pretend guilt or remorse over the choices he had made. Being with Kristin centered him. She was his life raft in a churning sea that wanted nothing more than to pull him down into its dark depths and never let him go.

Luke pushed his hands through his hair, reached down to pick a twig off the damp ground and snapped it in half. "I knew I was taking a risk by getting involved, by letting her in…and I know I've taken it too far… but…God help me, I can't stay away from her." He glanced over at Bob, prepared for judgment, condemnation even, but saw only compassion.

"Do you love her?" Bob stared him straight in the eyes, like he'd done on so many occasions when the truth was needed.

"Yes." Luke nodded, unflinching. Despite it all, he did. "With everything I have left in me." He released a sigh and shook his head. "She just… she got in too deep. And now she's paying the price. I'm worried sick. I think this is it, Bob, the thing that will send her over the edge." He rubbed his arms and pictured the haunted expression Kristin wore since Jonno's death. Luke wasn't sure anything would get her through this. Not even his love.

Despite his own struggles, his own questions and anger, he knew somehow he'd survive this. He couldn't say the same about her.

Bob shook his head, more serious than Luke had ever seen him. "Get her home, Luke. Get her home before it's too late. For both of you."

"How do I do that?" Luke shook his head.

"We pray, and you come up with the right words." Bob sat forward, his eyes wet. "You've both endured enough. It's time you left this war alone, Luke."

He sat for a long while, contemplating the conversation.

Finally Luke left the orphanage, Bob's words weighing heavy on him.

Back at the apartment, Luke pushed open the door to the bedroom. Despite telling him she was going out to work this morning, Kristin was back in bed.

"Hey. You awake?" He knelt at the side of the bed, running a hand over her head. Kristin stirred and rolled over, staring up at him through wide eyes.

Haunted eyes—red-rimmed and void of all sparkle.

She opened her mouth, but then drew it closed in a thin line, folding her arms across her chest. As if that would keep him out of her heart.

Kristin curled onto her side, unmoving, her eyes on him, questioning, like she expected him to have a miraculous remedy for her pain. Luke tried to smile, but the moisture in his eyes betrayed him. "How can I help you, Kris?"

Kristin stretched out her hand until her fingers touched his face. "You can't."

Luke sniffed, covered her hand with his own, and brought it to his lips. "I love you, you know. I can't stand this."

She lay still for a long while, her breathing steady. Tears escaped from the corners of her eyes, stealing off down the sallow cheeks. His heart tore in half as he brushed them away.

Never in his life had he known such a powerful force, such a compelling need to be near her, to be with her. His feelings overpowered reason, bolted the door against logic, and defied any argument he'd previously made against the validity of them.

"I'm not going anywhere, love," Luke whispered, leaning over her. Her eyes slid toward his, almost unbelieving. He touched her forehead with his lips, then sat back on his heels. "But it feels like you are. Like you're slipping away from me, to some place I can't go. I don't want to lose you. Tell me what to do."

"Nothing. There's nothing *to* do." She sighed, sat up and pulled her robe around her. "I'll get over it. And we'll go on like nothing happened. Right?"

Get over it? Luke watched her carefully, saw her somehow summon hidden strength from somewhere, and envied her. "Okay."

He wondered if he should say more, press the issue, but fear of what her response would be prevented him. "Why don't you get up, take a shower. Then maybe we could go for a walk…go get some dinner. How does that sound?"

She nodded, impassive, as though all her enthusiasm for life had somehow been stolen from her by the same evil that had taken Jonno from them. "I don't think I could eat, but I'll keep you company. Tomorrow I think I'll see if I can get up to the Rockpile. I still need to file a story from there."

"Kris…" He hesitated, his fingers closing around her slender arm. She wasn't ready for that. But her eyes narrowed into stubbornness, a spark of her old fire lighting them for an instant. Luke leaned in and kissed her cheek. Maybe she did need to work. Maybe that would bring her back to him. "All right. I'll go with you."

"If you want." She nodded, tearful again. For a brief moment, he wondered if things would ever be the same between them. He drew in a breath, rose, and left her.

Chapter Twenty-Five

Strength came from somewhere. Kristin locked her nightmares away and tried to go on like nothing had happened. Tried not to re-live that day on the road or the consequences that stemmed from it. Eventually she learned to function around her nightmares. She plunged back into work as though it would save her somehow, present her with some magic formula that would help her forget everything they'd experienced over the hellish past few weeks.

"Kristin!"

As she walked past Doc's office at the 24th, she heard him shout her name. Kristin turned and headed back down the hall. She'd just been dropped off after spending two nights at a firebase with some of the nicest guys she'd met here. Incoming sniper fire forced them to put her out of commission. She'd wanted to stay, insisted on it, but hadn't been strong enough to fight the Platoon Commander who'd scooped her up under one arm and thrown her into the waiting Huey as bullets ricocheted off the ground around them. Thoughts of how many of those men were still alive plagued her.

Dirty and hot, she wanted a shower more than anything, but couldn't very well ignore the colonel. She retraced her steps and entered his office, and stopped short. Luke sat with his father.

They'd seen little of each other lately. Luke seemed to throw himself into work as well, taking jobs that sent him to places she refused to think about. It was almost as though being apart made it easier.

She'd heard nothing from Jean Luc lately, and inwardly thanked God for that. The last thing she needed now was for their story to come out.

She knew it would, eventually. And the fallout would be far worse even than this insurmountable guilt that had moved into her soul and secured squatter's rights.

Pulling her hair up into a knot at the back of her head, she settled her eyes on Luke. "When did you get here?"

"About a half hour ago." He looked tired, worn-out, and filthier than her.

Kristin folded her arms across her chest and studied him. "You okay?"

"I'm cool." The slow grin she loved appeared for an instant.

She let out her breath. "Good. So," she turned to Doc, managing a smile. "You yelled?"

He nodded, rising. "Your editor has been trying to reach you. He couldn't get you at the apartment, so he tried here. I said I'd have you call him when you got in. You can use my phone. I've got rounds." He left them, closing the door behind him.

Kristin scowled at the telephone, and then at Luke, a sense of foreboding settling in. "What do you think he wants?"

"Only one way to find out."

Kristin sank into Doc's chair and patched the call through. A few minutes later she heard Hayden Thorne bellowing down the line. "When's the last time you talked to your mother? Do you know she thinks you're dead? I've tried telling her you're not, shown her your articles, but she's driving me crazy..."

Kristin bit down on her lip and held the receiver away from her ear. She'd last talked to her mother...she couldn't remember. Hayden's booming voice came through loud and clear and rang around the room. Luke chuckled and Kristin threw a pencil at him. He indicated the phone, and she realized it was now silent.

"Sorry, Hayden. I'll send her a telegram today. There's been a lot going on."

"Well, I'm sure. Just as long as you're okay. You are okay, aren't you?"

She closed her eyes against the question, images of gunfire, out-of-control jeeps and muddy roads covered in blood clouding her vision. "Sure, Hayden. I'm cool."

"Right. Well, I gotta tell you, honey, those last few stories you sent me—pretty gory stuff."

Kristin nodded, looking down at the wooden desk. The top was scratched, covered in writing. A mess of gibberish, scrawled initials and dates that made no sense to anyone save the author. Just like the pieces she had sent to Hayden.

"I can't print them, Kristin. They're too graphic."

Kristin pushed her chair back in one swift move. "Where do you think I am, Hayden? This isn't some county fair, you know. I'm in the middle of a war—a god…" She pressed a hand to her mouth in effort to stop the flow of words. Luke raised an eyebrow. She shook her head.

"Kristin, I don't like your tone." The edge to Hayden's voice startled her and she glared into the receiver.

"Well, try this. I thought you wanted to print the truth! You want a newsreel version, get someone else. Readers deserve to know the real story."

"And a mother deserves to read about heads being blown to bits under sniper fire, and go to bed wondering if it was her son? *No*, Kristin. And there's something else."

Kristin clenched her fingers around the phone and waited.

"A story has come out, some small magazine in Paris. Well, I'll just get to it. Rumor has it that you collaborated on this story about the CIA. It's pretty detailed. I've already been questioned and they're not happy. Do you want to tell me about that?"

Detailed? She turned her back toward the wall and away from Luke. "I don't know anything about it."

Hayden let out a muted curse. "You better be telling me the truth. I've got the CEOs breathing down my neck over this. You know this is my last week here. I'll tell them as far as I know you had nothing to do with it. In the meantime, send me another orphanage story. They like those. And start packing. I'm bringing you home."

"What?" Her own shriek shocked her, Luke too. He came to where she stood, questioning her with his eyes. Kristin waved him off, sucked in air and sank into the chair again. "I have another month, Hayden. You can't do this!"

"I can. I should never have extended your visa the last time you asked. Two weeks, honey. If you're not on that plane, I'm coming to get you myself." The click of the receiver and the monotonous dial tone that followed left her cold.

Luke took the phone from her hands. "What's going on?"

"Hayden is bringing me home. In two weeks. And he won't print my stories. That's it. I'm done." She pounded her fist on the desk and swore. "I need to get out of here. I can't think." She brushed past him, slamming the office door behind her.

Luke waited until his father returned and filled him in. "She's over the edge, Dad. I don't know what to do." That was a lie. He knew exactly what to do. He'd just been avoiding the truth, hoping things would get better.

Doc leaned forward, met Luke's eyes, and shook his head, worry etched into his features. "She needs to go home, Luke. The sooner the better."

First Bob, now Dad. Finally Luke nodded. "I know. You're right. I just…"

"Luke!" Dad's eyes blazed with a fire Luke hadn't seen in a long time. "You're a professional. You can see it as well as I can. If you love her like you say you do, you'll make sure she gets on that plane."

Luke swallowed down the urge to throw something. They were right. Kristin needed to get out of Vietnam, but he didn't have to like it. The thought of remaining here without her was not something he wanted to entertain.

"Luke?"

"What?" He didn't like that look, the one Dad wore when he'd already made up his mind on something.

"I think you should go with her."

Luke stared, words bashing about in his brain as he tried to make sense of the statement.

Dad nodded, his eyes serious. "You've been here too long, son. You've done your bit. Don't you think it's time?"

Again, Bob's words were mirrored.

Maybe God was trying to make a point.

A deep sigh escaped him and Luke pulled his hands behind his head. He never contemplated leaving. Just pushed through the days with unyielding determination. His existence had become a matter of putting one foot in front of the other. Thoughts of building a life outside of the one he'd created here terrified him. It wouldn't be easy, but not impossible. He could do it if he really wanted to.

If.

His eyes stung with unwanted emotion, but he nodded. "I'll think about it."

Chapter Twenty-Six

A week later, Kristin sat alone in the mess hall at the 24th, brooding over a cup of sludge-like coffee. The smell nauseated her and she pushed the Styrofoam cup away. Contempt for Hayden Thorne boiled in her. She'd managed to extend her stay on his good graces before, but those days were gone. He wouldn't back down. Next week she'd be on a plane back to the States. She couldn't bear to think about it. She hated that she had to go home with so much left here to say.

And then there was Luke.

The doors to the mess hall slammed open. Luke crossed the room in long strides.

Her heart leapt but she battled an urge to run in the opposite direction. Every time she saw him, she felt sure he'd read their story and would accuse her of writing it. She still hadn't seen the printed version, but everything in her knew that Jean Luc had changed it. All she could do was pray that it didn't put Luke in jeopardy. Still, part of her rose up in defense of what she'd done. Everything they'd uncovered and written had been the truth. Even Luke would have to admit that.

"If I didn't know better, I'd start worrying about you making moves on my Dad you're out here so often." He stood before her, a soft smile settling on his lips.

Kristin pushed to her feet, slinging her backpack over one shoulder, relieved at the absence of anger or accusation in his tone. "Don't fancy me for a stepmother?"

Spending time at 24th Surgical had little to do with Douglas Maddox. It had to do with the men and women here—most of whom she'd unintentionally grown close to—people who'd worked with Jonno and been his friends. Memories bound them. She found comfort by surrounding herself with those who'd known and loved him. And missed him. Luke knew why she kept coming back here as well as she did. They just didn't talk about it.

He held out a hand. "Let's take a walk."

Kristin left her bag in a corner of the room and they headed down to the beach in silence. The waves crashed against the rocks, salty spray flying around them. She breathed in the soothing scent of the sea. As usual, the sun warmed her tired soul. But her joy came from being with him.

Not that he would know it.

She'd done her best to avoid him. Couldn't find the words to explain how she felt. Didn't know how to tell him all she needed to. She'd even tried putting things down on paper, but came up empty. Her future career as a writer suddenly seemed doubtful.

Luke hadn't said a word, yet each time he caught up with her, the sorrow in his eyes deepened.

He stopped walking, and reached for her hands. "Kris…" Hesitation settled in his tone, his face marked with regret. "I know you think you're not finished here, that you still have stories to tell. But I have to agree with Hayden this time. You've had enough. You need to go home."

Kristin searched his eyes, hoping to find something that hinted at the joke he made. She saw nothing. "Haven't we had this conversation?"

He shook his head. "This is different. Everything's changed. *You've* changed. Can't you see that?" His tone implored her to see reason, yet she battened down the hatches of her heart, and refused.

Kristin left him and walked along the sand toward the ocean. Salt spray smacked her face and she breathed deeply. She wrapped her arms around herself and shuddered. It didn't matter how fiercely she fought against the truth, sooner or later, it would catch up with her.

Sleep had become a precious commodity. Emotions seemed out of reach—framed and hung on the wall of her memories. At some point, she'd inoculated herself against them. He was right.

She *had* changed.

Luke came up behind her, pulled her into his embrace and held her close. She placed her hands over his arms, leaned back against him and continued to watch the waves, allowing the sound of their rhythmic ebb and flow to mesmerize her and lift the dark shroud that covered her.

Kristin swiveled in his arms, studying him for a long moment. "We're not going to win this war, are we?"

She saw him chew on his bottom lip, his eyes shifting from her to the water. Then he shook his head, catching her eyes with his again. "In my opinion, no. It doesn't look good."

"But you're going to stay." Kristin maneuvered out of his embrace and walked further down the beach, her boots sinking into the sand.

For days now, since Hayden's phone call, she'd dreaded this moment. Talk of the future. Too afraid to ask, and terrified to hear the answer, she'd run from him. She'd played cat and mouse, neatly extricating herself from anywhere he happened to be. She hadn't thought about what she would do when it came time to say goodbye.

"Kristin, wait!" Luke caught her, and stood before her, his blond hair shining in the sun, his eyes more piercing than she'd ever seen them, begging her to cease the futile isolation she'd mastered. "Stop running away! Do you have any idea what you're doing to me? You're leaving at the end of this week, Kris. Don't you want to spend time with me? What's going on with us? Have things changed so much that you can't stand to be in the same room as me anymore?"

His words pelted her like tiny stones, chipping away at her hardened heart. Kristin's bottom lip began to quiver and she drew in a breath, squeezing her eyes shut for a moment. "No. Nothing's changed, Luke. I love you so much...I almost can't stand it." Her voice sounded hoarse, unused to speech. Hot tears pricked her eyes as she watched the anger in his face drain away. "I'm scared to go home. I don't know how to go back there and try to live a normal life." She let her hands rise and fall. "What's normal after Vietnam?"

They shared a brief smile and she shook her head. "I'm trying to figure out how to leave. How to say goodbye to Mary Jo and Bob....and...to those kids." Kristin tasted the salt of the sea and the tears on her lips. She yearned to just sit down and sob, but in all honesty, she no longer thought herself capable.

She took in everything about him, the fine lines that played around his eyes when he smiled, the way his jaw clenched as it did now, when he worried—the curve of his nose, the shape of his eyes, and their color—she'd search the whole earth for the shade of blue they owned, but knew she'd never find it.

She touched his face, her fingers tracing his blond eyebrows and down toward his mouth. "How am I supposed to just leave and get on with my life?"

His eyes glittered in the sunshine, hinting at wetness. A smile tugged at his lips, but went nowhere. In thundering silence, he drew her to him.

And just held her.

After a few minutes, Luke pulled back. "I need to ask you something. I've been warned that a story came out…an exposé of sorts, I suppose, about the Agency. Do you know anything about it?"

He had his game face on and she couldn't tell what he was thinking. Which was probably for the best. Panic gripped her as she wrestled with her conscience. If she told him the truth, she could very well lose him forever.

If she lied, she would lose him anyway.

Eventually.

"Did…did they say who wrote it?"

"I was hoping you could tell me."

"No. I don't know." She shook her head and walked a little further down the beach.

He caught up with her and pulled her to a stop. "What is it, Kris? What's wrong? If you had nothing to do with that story, then what's going on with you? Why are you running from me?"

Kristin pushed back hot tears and choked on emotion she had no right to quell. "I've told you. I don't want to leave. I'm just—terrified of the future. I'm not sure how I'm going to live without you."

His eyes crinkled into a smile that coaxed her heart out to dance. The warm ocean breeze blew about her face and caressed her cheeks. "Good. That's what I wanted to hear."

She buried the guilt of her lie and studied his smile instead. "I just said I'm not sure how I'm going to live without you and you're grinning like The Cheshire Cat. Are you that eager to be rid of me?"

Luke sobered, taking his hands from hers and running them down his face. "No." He put his hands around her face, drew her close and kissed her.

"You don't need to worry about how you're going to live without me," he said quietly. He fished a small object from the pocket of his khaki trousers and held it between his thumb and forefinger. "You won't have to."

Kristin's eyes flew wide. Her heart took up a reluctant beat and her throat dried up. "What is that?" she breathed, blood rushing away from her cheeks.

Luke dropped the ring into the palm of his hand and prodded it. "Looks like some kind of a ring if you ask me. A pretty good size diamond. Good cut, clarity…"

"Luke!" Tears blurred her vision. He lifted his head, his own eyes wet. For a long moment, she just stared at him, waiting until he could manage speech.

At last he cleared his throat, lifted her left hand in his, and took the ring in his right.

"We may have done things a little backwards, but I guess I'm wondering if you might want to get hitched."

Kristin choked on laughter, narrowing her eyes. "What kind of proposal is that?"

"A lousy one?" He raised an eyebrow and winked.

"Pathetic. Want to try again?"

Luke chuckled, dropped to one knee, his eyes holding hers, his smile broader than she'd ever seen it. "My dear Miss Taylor, would thou doest me the greatest honor…pleasure? Which is it?"

"Stop it, you dope!" Laughter burst from her and she pushed him backward, falling on top of him as he fell onto the sand. Luke kissed her, his own laughter filling her heart with new joy. She struggled up, wiping tears and sand off her face. "Where is it?"

"What?" He stretched out on the sand, a contented smile on his lips.

Kristin's eyes flared as she poked his chest. "My ring! Did you drop it?" Luke sprang up and onto his knees, a look of horror taking over his features as he scrabbled in the sand around them. Kristin let out a squeak, clapping a hand to her mouth. "You lost it? Luke!"

"Got it!" He held it triumphantly, grinning again. Kristin breathed a sigh of relief and put her hand out at once, not taking any chances.

"Not so fast, Madam." Luke shook his head, blowing sand off the stone.

"What?" Kristin slumped in the sand, folded her arms across her chest and glared at his wicked grin.

"You haven't answered my question."

"I don't believe I was asked one," she countered. "At least not properly."

His low growl indicated frustration, but he drew in a breath and reached for her hand again. "All right. Once more then." His stern look dissolved into a tender smile. "I love you, Kristin Taylor. I want to spend the rest of my life loving you, and keeping you happy. Would you please do me the honor of agreeing to spend the rest of your life with me, as my wife?"

"Hmm…" Kristin grinned back at him, enjoying the slight look of panic in his eyes at her hesitation. "I'll have to think about it. By the way, I hope that ring was bought legally."

"Kristin…" He took on a warning tone and she laughed, splaying her fingers over his.

"Okay."

"Okay, what?"

"I've thought about it."

"And?"

A lump rose in her throat as she nodded, watching his eyes light again. "I will, Luke. I will be your wife. Nothing would make me happier."

She held her breath as he slipped the ring onto her finger. A perfect fit. He put his arms around her, brought his lips to hers, and let her know his own feelings on the matter.

After a while, she sat back, studying him. Surely it couldn't be this easy. "What about your job?"

Luke took her hand in his, examining the ring on her finger. "I'm taking care of it."

"Luke…"

His smile faded. "I'm sorry. I can't leave just yet. But I will. I promise you, I'll be back in the States in another month, two at the most."

"Oh, Luke." This was more than she'd dreamed of. More than she'd ever hoped for. She wouldn't have to tell him. They'd go home, start a life together, and none of it would matter.

Off in the distance, the familiar buzz of helicopters sounded.

He tucked a strand of hair behind her ears. "Go home. Make plans. Just…nothing fancy, okay?"

Kristin shook her head. "I don't care if it's just you and me, and a justice of the peace." She fell silent, staring out at the ocean. "I've lost track of Teddy again. I'm not sure where he's gone. Have you heard anything about his company?"

"Not lately. But I'll find out."

"Thank you." Kristin ran the back of her hand down his stubbled jaw and wondered how a day could change from mundane to miraculous in a few moments. "You know, I may not have a job to go back to. Hayden's pretty mad at me. He may not recommend me to his successor."

Luke snorted, kissing her hard. "Well, if you can't work, you'll just have to write that bestseller you keep talking about."

"That was a joke, Luke." Kristin smiled at the determined look in his eyes. He really believed she could do anything. As if anyone would want to read a book about Vietnam.

Another round of choppers passed overhead, causing her heart to stick in her throat as thoughts of the casualties they carried filled her mind. A few more days and she'd never have to hear that sound again.

Chapter Twenty-Seven

*B*ack at her apartment, she found Jean Luc had left a package. Kristin read the article, flipping the pages with shaking hands. No real names, but enough information to make the boys at the Agency more than a little perturbed. She could hardly believe what she read, and certainly didn't recognize it as the initial story they'd worked on.

As much as she tried to convince herself the outcome wouldn't be as bad as she feared, she knew what Luke's reaction would be. He'd left on an assignment, but promised to be back in a day or so, and they would go out for dinner and celebrate the future before she left to go home.

Once he knew the truth, there would be no such celebration.

After showering and eating little, she poured her broken heart out into written words. She wrote for two days, taking only catnaps. The adrenaline pumping through her would not allow real rest. She had so much to say about what was going on here, what she was seeing, feeling… she felt an urgency to get it out of her system, written down before it was too late.

Before she was gone from this place and the tumult of feelings being here invoked.

It didn't matter whether anybody read what she wrote; she simply needed to give the words their freedom.

Her typewriter ran out of ink and she needed more paper. She pulled at her sweaty T-shirt and pondered asking one of the kids on the street to run an errand for her. Sometimes they were good—the ones she'd come to rely on—they'd take her money and get what she needed, confident she'd give them a few piastres on their return. Other times, kids ran off with her money and she never saw them again.

A door slammed down the hall and she looked up.

Luke.

She drew in a measured breath, forcing calm. She reached for the magazine Jean Luc had left for her and put it under a pile of papers. A moment later he burst into the apartment.

As soon as she saw his face, she knew.

"This was waiting for me on my desk when I went into the office this morning." He slapped the French news magazine down on the table in front of her. "One of your VC sources sold you out with some heavy persuasion. Care to explain?"

Kristin didn't need to pick up the magazine he'd thrown at her. Didn't want to touch it. She met Luke's condemning stare. And said nothing.

"You're not denying it?" He placed his hands down on the table and leaned in, stone-faced.

"No."

"You wrote this?"

"Some of it. Yes." She looked away, picked up a pencil and snapped it in half.

"You lied to me."

"Yes."

He backed off and paced the apartment. The distance between them provided a strange sense of relief. Eventually he stopped moving. "Do you have any idea what you've done?"

She swiveled in her chair, saw his eyes and knew the worst was yet to come.

"Your mole turned up dead. There will be retaliation. I've just spent hours trying to convince my superiors that you didn't get any information from me. And then I had to persuade them not to haul you in for questioning, which I have no doubt they'll do anyway. What the hell were you thinking?"

"That it would make a good story, obviously." Icy fingers pressed down on her, threatened to break her under the strain of finally facing the person she'd become.

She'd come to Vietnam with a head full of dreams and visions. Held lofty goals of becoming a journalist her father would be proud to work alongside. Somewhere along the way, in her quest for justice, retribution or whatever misguided ideals had driven her to this point, her real convictions retreated into the smoky shadows that covered this land.

In her place stood a stranger—a bitter, wounded soul.

Someone she no longer recognized when she looked in the mirror.

Someone willing to pay the highest price for the story she'd somehow believed would set her free.

It had done just the opposite.

"I need you to talk to me, Kristin." Luke took slow steps toward her. "There are two bylines. Who did you work with?"

She pushed away the tainted magazine as cold hands of guilt closed around her throat. Silently she shook her head.

The look of betrayal he shot her was the one she'd been desperate to avoid. "Don't give me that journalistic crap now. Who was it? Jean Luc?"

Kristin pulled trembling fingers through her hair. "It doesn't matter who it was." She let out a groan and covered her face with her hands. "I thought...I didn't realize the danger, and by the time I had second thoughts, it was too late."

"I'm not stupid enough to believe that," he spat. "Who were your sources?" Anger blazed through his eyes.

Kristin stood and went over to the window. The air was still and reeked of smoke and garbage. Traffic jammed the street below. Off in the distance, beyond the river, smoke inched upward in dark gray curls. "I can't tell you."

"Of course you can't." His eyes drilled her as she sat down again. "Why did you do this? Why risk everything for a story like this?"

It was a question she'd asked herself many times over the last few days.

"I wanted..." Kristin laced her hands together, pushed them outward and stretched, releasing the pressure in her back. She'd thought about what might happen should Luke ever discover the truth. She'd even convinced herself she could live without him.

The idea dissipated as she studied his face.

He was clean-shaven, his blond hair combed. His hard jaw was scratched and bruised. The cut above his eyebrow had been bandaged, presumably stitched. But the wounds within danced in the shadows of his eyes when he straightened and looked at her again.

And forced her to face the truth.

"I did it because of my father. He began this story before he died. A couple of years ago, my mother gave me his stuff, notebooks, papers. I've always wondered...whether the CIA had anything to do with his death. Not that it matters, I suppose. But I wanted to come here to finish what he started. I wanted to be different. To do something nobody else would."

Luke gave a low whistle. "Well, you've certainly accomplished that. Your accusations of internal brutality, secret killings...no wonder they were after you."

"There's nothing in that piece that isn't the truth." Defiance still spurred her on. "You know that. How do you live with yourself? How do you justify the things you get paid to do, Luke?"

He swore and stayed silent a long while before he met her eyes once more. "They can make things very difficult for me. Do you realize that?"

Kristin sucked in a breath. There was no room for regret...she'd done what she came here to do. Even though it was possibly the best story she'd written since coming to Vietnam, it would be her last.

Music from the radio in the apartment above theirs blasted through the window and made it impossible to think. Outside, the day spoke of normalcy. The sun continued its oppression, trees swayed in the gentle breeze. Spicy aromas wafted through the open window, strong enough to overpower the sewage, if only momentarily. Vile things she had found offensive only months ago were now part of her daily life. She barely heard the noise from the constant traffic below anymore. Sometimes she wondered if she'd ever sleep in silence and miss it. But today, the incessant honking and shouts pounded into her brain and blended with the music, telling her what a fool she'd been.

Luke slammed the window shut. "When did you start working on this?"

She shrugged, wiped her eyes and looked away. "Does it matter?"

"Yes. It does. I'd like to know just how long I've been played."

"It wasn't like that."

"Wasn't it?" His hard stare convicted her.

"I'm sorry," she whispered, winding her gold chain around her finger. "I'm a journalist, Luke. It was a good story. What am I supposed to say?"

Luke smacked his hand on the table, sending a glass flying. It shattered on the wooden floor. "We're in the middle of a bloody war! Just whose side are you on?"

"I'm not on anybody's side!" Kristin retorted. "I can't stand what's going on here. It's like everything is spinning out of control."

"You think?" Luke flexed the muscles in his shoulders, his eyes hard and unforgiving. "I don't understand you."

Ensuing silence threatened to break her. On his face she saw doubt, confusion, and unmistakable pain. He shook his head and moved away, bending to pick up the broken pieces of glass. She let him clean up the mess, unable to move.

When he finished, he stood before her, arms crossed over his chest. "Do you know what you mean to me? You gave me reason to want to live again. I never thought I'd get past the pain I carried when we first met. But I did. I dealt with it and pushed through it—for you—for us. So God help me, if you're going to stand there and tell me none of that was real—"

"It was!" Kristin went to him, grabbed his arms, desperation clawing, choking her. "Yes, in the beginning I was hoping to get information from you. I'd heard you were Agency and...well, I didn't like you all that much, if you recall. I figured I'd be long gone by the time this went to print anyway...but I didn't count on falling in love with you, Luke."

"But you still wrote it." He shook her off, went to the couch and sank onto it. Minutes stretched out by awful silence ticked by as he sat with his head in his hands. "What did you think would happen when this came out?"

"I don't know. I thought I could handle it." Kristin folded her arms, tears burning.

"I asked you what you were working on, Kristin, on more than one occasion."

"I know." She swiped moisture off her cheeks, filled with self-loathing.

"I don't trust many people, you know that. I've stayed alive a lot longer that way." He lifted a brow. "I suspected you were on to me a while back. I let my guard down. I let you get too close. I shouldn't have."

"Please don't say that."

Luke angled his head. His pain-filled eyes never left hers. "Since we're being honest, I suppose you should know that I asked Hayden to put us together. I wanted to keep an eye on you."

She pushed her hair off her face, tension thick as smoke filling the room and making it impossible to breathe. "You knew what I was doing?"

"I couldn't prove it. You cover your tracks pretty well. By the time I knew for sure…I didn't care. And I doubted you'd actually go through with it. Clearly I underestimated your tenacity."

"I'm sorry." Kristin stared down at her feet, desperate for a way out of the overgrown maze that had crept up around them. "What will they do now?"

He raised his hands, letting them fall slowly to his lap. "You've obviously done the research. What do you think?"

Kristin shook her head, pressing her fingers to her temples. This was her punishment. And she deserved every bit of it.

He got up, moved past her and stood, arms crossed. "They're sending me up north. I have to meet with some contacts, reassure them this thing isn't about to blow the lid off everything we've worked so hard to accomplish here. Damage control. I'm leaving within the hour. I'm not in a position to argue with them."

Kristin's throat constricted. "You're still playing the game."

"This isn't a game, Kristin!" Luke's eyes flared. "It's a war. And like it or not, there *are* two sides. I said you'd pick one eventually."

"That's not fair." More tears slid down her cheeks.

"Perhaps not. But it's how I feel right now."

"When will you be back?"

"I don't know."

"So where do we go from here?" she managed to ask.

He turned and stood before her, his face ashen. "At this particular moment, I have no idea. The only thing I know for sure is that it's a good thing you're getting out of Vietnam. I can't guarantee your safety anymore."

Luke paced the floor like he was planning a last, all-important mission. One she wasn't privy to. His chest rose and fell as he took deep breaths, until finally he straddled a chair and looked over at her. "I should have stepped in earlier, stopped this when I had the chance." The anger in his eyes was replaced by sorrow.

Confusion rode the waves of fear that crashed over her. "I feel like I've woken up in the middle of one of my nightmares, only I'm not dreaming anymore. It's like we don't even know each other."

"Maybe we don't." He flung one arm over his eyes and stayed like that for a while.

"Then talk to me." Kristin swiped at her eyes and cleared her throat. "What's a nice guy like you doing out here in the middle of hell?"

Luke gave a wan smile and shrugged. "You pretty much know my story. I work for the Agency, but I am a legitimate photographer. I'd only been working for the Government a few months when my family and I came here, I was still freelancing, trying to decide which direction I wanted to go. I came on assignment for Hayden, not for the CIA." He pushed a shaking hand through his hair, the past darkening his eyes. "When Marcia and Melissa were killed, I didn't have a reason to quit the Agency. I wanted to stay here—do anything I could to hunt down the enemy—anything that would help us win this war."

The truth hit her like a hail of bullets, pulling her downward into a bottomless ocean. She caught her breath and faced it head on. "You made it personal."

Her words seemed to sting, take him by surprise. Old grief flickered in his eyes. "It was personal."

Luke studied his boots. Kristin chewed on a fingernail and concentrated on a hole in the rug beneath her feet. "I didn't want to hurt you," she told him, barely trusting her ability to speak. "I put myself first, I know that. I shouldn't have lied to you. And I never intended for Jonno...for him to...I'm sorry. I know maybe that's not worth much to you right now, but I hope one day you'll be able to forgive me. After everything you've been through, you don't deserve any more pain." She went to him, waited until he raised his eyes to hers, then slipped the ring off her finger and held it toward him.

Luke got to his feet and closed his hand over hers. "What are you doing?"

Kristin shook her head, her throat too thick for speech.

He released a deep sigh, peeled her fingers back and took the ring between his thumb and forefinger. He tipped her chin and made her look at him. "Is this what you want?"

She lowered her gaze, unable to see through her tears. "How can we start a life together with all this between us?"

Luke shook his head and pressed the ring back into her hand. "I don't have time, Kris, they're waiting for me downstairs. I'm not doing this now."

"Luke…there's something…something else. I need to tell you…" Words refused to come. There was still so much anger on his face.

"Whatever it is can wait, Kristin. I can't stay. Just get yourself on that plane. We'll figure this out when I get home."

"All right." Defeat and cowardice dragged her down. "If that's what you want."

"None of this is what I want." He put his hands on her shoulders, stared at her for a while without, then drew her to him and placed his lips on her forehead. "I'm sorry. I have to go."

With trembling fingers, she undid the clasp of her chain at the nape of her neck. She took her father's cross in her hands and stared down at it. Then she fastened the cross around Luke's neck, ran her finger down the chain and over the carved symbol of the hope he cherished. She locked eyes with him and steeled herself against the agony of saying goodbye.

Somehow, some way, she had to believe God would keep Luke safe.

"Please…just…say you forgive me." Kristin waited, unable to stop her tears as his eyes shone with unshed moisture.

Luke threaded his fingers through her hair, pulled her face to his and pressed his lips against hers. "I'll see you, Kris."

"Luke…please…don't leave like this." Panic raced through her and she gripped his wrists. A horn's blast sounded from the street below.

He ran his hands over his face and let out a groan, pulled her to him once more and buried his face in her hair. "I'll try to get back to see you off." He kissed her again, then he let her go, striding out of the room without looking back.

Chapter Twenty-Eight

Kristin ran from the pile of clothes she'd been sorting through and reached the bathroom just in time. She vomited again. Sitting back against the cool tiled wall, she ran a towel over her face and groaned. Traveling like this would not be pleasant. Her heart refused to beat normally, hadn't done so for a few days, and probably wouldn't until she got home.

She traipsed from the bathroom into the kitchen, almost barreling into Caroline, who held a glass of water toward her, a smug smile toying with her lips. "You're pregnant, aren't you?"

Kristin took the water, stepped over piles of clothes in the bedroom, and lowered herself into a chair by the open window. Maybe if she ignored her, Caroline would go away.

"How far along?"

No such luck.

Caroline sank onto her bed and settled that nonchalant gaze on her that Kristin always found most infuriating. "Kris? Talk to me."

Kristin sighed and clenched her fingers around her glass. "It's probably just the flu."

Caroline's shocked expression transformed into a gleeful smile. She slapped her hands on her knees and laughed. "Oh, how the mighty have fallen!"

Kristin put the glass on the windowsill and covered her face with her hands. She tipped her head back, battling another wave of nausea. It wasn't the flu. She couldn't be a hundred percent sure, but wanted to wait until she got home to find out. "Caroline, that's not remotely funny."

"Of course it is! You know the lectures I've put up with from Luke! Honestly, the hypocrisy around here is just hysterical."

Kristin glared. "A little understanding might be more appropriate. And you're not the one who has to tell him."

"He doesn't know?" Caroline's laughter faded.

Kristin shook her head, fear overtaking her again. "Not yet. I tried to tell him before he left, but…I couldn't." Her heart picked up the unsteady beat she was getting used to. "I haven't been regular since I got here. It may be a false alarm, but…" Kristin shuddered at the thought, her eyes stinging. With their future uncertain, having a child didn't fit into the picture.

"You don't think this is a false alarm." Caroline went to her, pulled her hands into her own. "I'm sorry for being an idiot. Look, don't worry. Luke will be thrilled!"

"I don't know. He's furious with me. I'm not sure where things stand between us." Kristin sniffed, doubt prickling. She'd put her ring back on, but still wasn't sure what Luke wanted.

Caroline smiled and squeezed Kristin's arm. "Incase you haven't noticed, my brother is a little stubborn. Sure, you made a mistake, but it's done. He'll get over it, Kris. When he comes back, it will be like none of this ever happened. You'll see."

"I hope so." Kristin tried to smile. "This wasn't in the plan. Can you honestly see me and Luke as parents?"

"Yeah. I can. Luke was…he was great with Melissa." Caroline's eyes filled with sudden tears and she wiped them away.

Kristin ran a hand across the back of her damp neck. "I bet." She met Caroline's eyes. "Sometimes I…I can't help comparing myself to her, you know, to Marcia. Out here it's easy not to think about it, but I wonder… I'm not sure I'm going to measure up."

Caroline crossed the room and stood at the bookshelf at the far end, poking at the collection of books that had formed over the months they'd lived together. "Marcia wasn't perfect. I didn't know her that well, I was living in England with my mother, but she was nothing like you. She was from a wealthy family, spoiled, demanding. Luke couldn't do a thing without her approval."

Kristin gaped. "I can't imagine that."

Caroline grinned and flopped onto the couch. "They were pretty young when they met. He was different back then."

Kristin folded a few more clothes and glanced at her watch. "I'll see a doctor when I get home. Hopefully by that time, Luke will be on his way back."

"Don't worry about him, Kris."

"That's a little hard to do. If I hadn't written that story in the first place, he wouldn't be out there doing God knows what…" She took a deep breath and blinked moisture, willing tension out of her shoulders. She'd been shrouded by it the moment Luke left.

Caroline crouched before her, her blue eyes flashing. "Luke knows how to take care of himself. He wouldn't want you stressing out over this, or blaming yourself. So come on, chin up."

Kristin nodded and tried to look like she agreed. "I guess I'm a little scared. Being married and pregnant is one thing, but…I can't go home and tell my mother I'm having a kid, Caroline."

"Conservative?"

"Ultra. And very religious. This is hardly the kind of behavior a good Christian girl would indulge in, you know."

Caroline's laughter filled the small apartment. "Since when do you fit that description?"

Kristin rolled her eyes. "My mother and I don't get along that well as is, this will just be one more thing to put between us."

"She might surprise you."

"I doubt it." Kristin pulled her hair off her shoulders and felt sick all over again.

"So don't tell her. As soon as Luke gets back, you'll work all this out, get married and it'll be fine."

Something said it wasn't going to be that easy. "You don't know my mother. She can be quite intimidating when she wants to be."

A flicker of a smile brightened Caroline's features. "You, intimidated? The great Kristin Taylor who needs neither man nor God?"

Kristin shrugged and gave a wan smile. "Maybe I'm not that infallible after all."

Caroline rubbed a hand over her face and nodded. "None of us are, Kris. Everything will work out. Just worry about getting yourself home, and go from there."

"Why don't you come with me? We can get an apartment big enough for all of us; you can find work in Boston. Or we could even go to New York."

Caroline rose in one cat-like stretch and shook her head. "No. This is your time now. Yours and Luke's. He'll be there before you know it. You don't need a third wheel. I'll come home in another month or so. Or maybe I'll go to England and see my mother."

Kristin pushed herself to her feet, her heart heavy. She put a hand on Caroline's shoulder, smiling when she turned. "In case I never said it... thanks."

"For what?"

"For being my friend. Taking a chance on me when I got here. I wouldn't have met Luke if it hadn't been for you."

"Don't be so sure about that." Caroline's face brightened with her smile and she patted Kristin's cheek. "Some things are meant to be."

Kristin tugged on her hair and scanned the crowded airport once more. "He's not going to make it, is he?" She'd clung to a desperate hope that Luke would somehow get back to Saigon in time to see her off. Caroline shifted from one foot to the other, shook her head and lit another cigarette.

Mary Jo held Tuan on her hip. Kristin reached for the child. He flung his little arms around her neck and held on tight. "I should go. They've already called the flight." An uncomfortable knot formed in the pit of her stomach, combining with the nausea. Kristin tightened her hold on Tuan, as though he would somehow save her from the inevitable. "I don't want to leave."

"You don't have a choice." Caroline fixed her with a look that allowed no argument.

"Listen to me, Luke's fine, Kris. You'll hear from him soon. Now... please, would you get on the plane?"

Caroline's eyes were too bright and Kristin detected an edge of panic in her voice. Everything in her told her to stay, but an inexplicable force pulled her toward the doors that led out to the tarmac.

"Kristin, chèrie, are you coming?" Jean Luc and several other journalists were leaving today too. She nodded in his direction, her eyes burning.

Kristin hugged Tuan one more time, unable to stop her tears. "Be a good boy, Tuan. I love you."

"Okay, Missy Kris. Bye, bye."

She set the boy on the ground and turned to Bob and Mary Jo. The big man made no effort to control his emotions as he pulled her into a bear hug. "We'll pray for you honey," he said, his voice low and gruff.

Kristin turned to Mary Jo and choked back a sob. There were no adequate words to tell her friend what she needed to. "Thank you for everything. I'll never forget you. Next time you get back to the States, come see me."

Mary Jo smiled, her cheeks as red as her hair. She bit her lip as she pressed a parcel into Kristin's hands. "Just a little something to brighten up your new place. We love you, hon. Keep in touch, okay?"

"I will." Kristin nodded, her throat thick. Finally she looked at Caroline, desperation stealing her words. Sorrow and fear rendered her powerless to think, speak or move. "We haven't been able to get any word on Teddy. I wrote to tell him I was going, but I don't know if he got my letter. If you hear anything, if you run across him, tell him I've gone home."

Her future sister-in-law smiled and gave her a long hug. "I'll do my best to find him, Kris."

"Thanks. Come with Luke when he leaves, Caroline," Kristin whispered. "You should come home. Please."

Caroline laughed and tossed her long blonde hair over her shoulders. "I'll think about it. Go on, Kris. Get out of hell while you can." She pushed her toward the doors and Kristin went forward with heavy steps. She turned back for a final wave before boarding the plane that would take her from this country she'd grown to love.

Kristin huddled in her seat, her heart full as she watched the green hills beneath them grow smaller and smaller. Tears trailed down her cheeks. An anguish she hadn't thought possible rose within as she placed one hand against the cool plexi-glass of the round window of the airplane. As the plane reached its climbing altitude, she bade a final farewell to Vietnam, and the two men she loved more than anything.

Please God, keep Luke safe.

Keep Teddy safe.

And bring them home to me soon...

Homecoming.

Take the first step in faith.
You don't have to see the whole staircase.
Just take the first step. – Martin Luther King Jr.

Chapter Twenty-Nine

Boston, February 1968.

Kristin pulled her second-hand coat around her and pushed through the wind. Cement buildings blended into the gray sky and threw dark shadows over slush-covered sidewalks and the road between them. At the end of the block she spied the subway entrance. She trudged through the dirty snow, her feet wet and frozen, cheap boots doing little to protect them from the elements. Inside, she found a phone kiosk, came up with a few coins and dialed.

Kristin leaned against the dirt-encrusted glass door and listened to the dial tone. It was weird calling Mom at a different number, weirder to know her former boss was now her stepfather. And it would probably blow her mind to see them together. Not that it would happen any time soon.

"Thorne residence." Hayden's familiar voice made her smile.

"Hayden. It's me."

"Kristin." Relief rang through his voice. "How are things in Boston?"

"Not bad." Worse than bad. "Sorry I haven't called in a while."

"Well, we were getting worried. How's the job? They treating you okay? You found a place to stay?"

Kristin closed her eyes against the barrage of questions. The ratty hotel room she'd spent the last two weeks in made their apartment in Saigon look like a palace. Work had been a disaster. She couldn't get used to being back on US soil. Couldn't get her nerves under control. After a few days of jumping out of her skin every time the phone rang or a door slammed, enduring curious looks and careless comments that stung and exacerbated her already open wounds, she'd walked out.

"Um…it's not so great, Hayden. It's…hard." Her hands began to tremble and she shoved her free one in the pocket of her black pea coat. She ran a finger over the top of the phone box and slashed a line through the thick layer of dust. "I was thinking I might go to New York."

"New York? Okay. Well…" Hayden breathed into the receiver, muttered something under his breath and she heard papers rustling. "I can give you the names of some friends, they'll get you set up there. Are you sure you're okay? Maybe you should come out here, relax a bit before jumping back into work."

"No, I'm fine." She took down the names and numbers he rattled off and shoved her notebook back in her pocket.

"Any news on Luke?"

She'd known he would ask. He always did. But the question made her knees buckle just the same. Kristin's mouth went dry and tears came too quickly.

"Kristin?" Concern crept into his voice.

She squeezed her eyes shut and blocked out the pain. "No. I've been trying to call again, but I…"

Hayden released a low groan. "Oh, Kristin. I'm so sorry."

"Yeah." She sniffed and rubbed the top of her nose. "Can I talk to my mom?"

"Honey, you just missed her. She ran to the store. Listen, why don't you call back tomorrow? Talk to your mom and think about coming out here to us, okay? She can't wait to see you."

Kristin scowled at the man who waited to use the phone after her. "I gotta split, Hayden. I'll talk to you soon."

Through the darkness, she saw Luke's face before her. The image seemed so clear she could almost reach out and touch him. But as always, it soon faded into the black night.

Kristin lay back on the bed and closed her eyes again. Sleep was impossible. The nightmare she'd woken from rattled her and refused to let go.

Luke—walking away from her—his wife and child alive and laying claim to him. That image molded into another—Luke, motionless on a slab of marble. Then she only heard his voice, calling out from beyond any visible sphere—just calling her name. She'd bolted awake, trembling as sobs erupted.

Kristin shuddered and expelled the images from her mind. She pushed herself up, sat cross-legged, and buried her face in her hands. Any grief she'd previously experienced paled in comparison to the stranglehold these dreams possessed

She pulled thick blankets up around her and set her mind on rational thought. She couldn't fall apart. Almost out of money, she needed to make some decisions, for her and her baby.

Luke's child.

She hopped off the bed and paced the small hotel room. The early morning silence threatened, pulled her to places she didn't want to go. The sounds of Vietnam resonated inside her head—a worn-out recording she could not shut off. Kristin put her hands up to her ears and closed her eyes against the incessant hum of memory.

Dry heat engulfed her. She missed the humidity and sunny shores of Vietnam. The relentless chill of New England winter was depressing.

The radiator in the corner of the room gurgled and hissed and the windows rattled in the wind. She welcomed the sudden noise. Sometimes the guys next door partied or fought loudly with their girlfriends. Kristin didn't mind. She'd take the sounds of normal living over the screams inside her head any day.

She turned on her small transistor radio and allowed the music to soothe her. Every song they played dragged her back to the jungles and rivers of Vietnam. Wherever she went there, someone had a radio playing. Music became the one thing that bound them all, linked them to home, and carried them through the hell they lived.

And every song reminded her of Luke.

She stood at the window, pulled aside the thin drapes and watched snow fall. Thick puffy flakes swirled around each other. A silent magical dance that almost made her smile. Snowflakes covered the branches of the trees and painted the outside world white. First light poked through the half-drawn curtains, gray dawn rising over the tall pines that presided over the parking lot.

She left the window, crouched at the bed and reached for the green duffel bag she kept under it. With unsteady hands, she set the bag on the bed, settled herself beside it, and pulled out her treasures.

All the carvings Jonno gave her spilled onto the worn blanket. The folds of silk Mary Jo had pressed upon her at the airport, copies of all her newspaper articles, and the photographs. Luke's photographs.

Images of a life she'd known for a short time, yet become so immersed in she found it hard to remember she'd ever lived another. There was sporadic comfort in the memories. When she picked up the last picture in the pile, Kristin froze. Her tears burned like acid, emotion tightening her throat and stealing air from her lungs. It slipped out of her hands and fluttered onto the bed.

She retrieved the photo and her throat burned as she stared at the picture she'd taken of Luke on the beach at Long Binh. A sob worked its way upward as she traced the outline of his face with her index finger, lost herself in his gaze. Reaching deep into the depths of her memory, she listened for the sound of his voice.

Grief clawed at her like some beast from a dark and cavernous hole, desperate to pull her down into it and swallow her up in one gulp.

Kristin released a shuddering sigh and put her photographs away.

If this was God's way of punishing her, it was too much. No matter what sins she'd committed, she didn't deserve this kind of pain. Nobody did.

The batteries in her radio died and sent the room in to silence.

Silence. She longed for it and loathed it.

Kristin drew her legs up under her and rested her head against the headboard. She filled her lungs, exhaled and closed her eyes, trying to conjure up peaceful images—of beaches, the mountains, the children... but all she saw was blood.

Maybe she should have confided in Hayden, told him the truth, what she feared and what she couldn't face. So many conflicting emotions raged within.

She'd already seen the way returning Veterans were treated. It appalled her. There were no great homecoming celebrations; no cheering crowds welcomed them back. No parades given in their honor. They were met with silent stares, awkward conversation and sometimes, downright hostility.

These men who'd fought for their country, the women who'd served beside them in many capacities—who'd laid their lives on the line for freedom—treated like second-class citizens. It sickened her more than the nausea she suffered daily.

Her eyes came to rest on the pair of boots she'd kicked off earlier. They bore testimony to the roads she'd traveled—well worn and still scuffed with the red soil she'd left behind her a world away.

Everything about the life she knew here in Boston had changed. Nothing was the same. Or perhaps nothing was different and she was the one who'd changed.

Nothing could quell her memories—she couldn't get the sights and sounds of Vietnam out of her mind. It was all she could do to get out of bed each morning. The effort of survival sucked energy from her, like the leeches in the swamps she had waded through. Once attached to human flesh, they were almost immovable. She'd seen men screaming in pain while their buddies worked to get the things off them, using matches, sometimes knives, anything to relieve the pressure.

She found no such relief.

No, Hayden did not need to know the trauma she carried. Her haunted nights and desperate days were not his fault. She harbored no regrets about Vietnam.

And Mom…what would she tell her if she could? If only she could tell her mother what she knew of heroism. What she knew of gallantry and relentless courage. If she could just catch a glimpse of what it meant to lay down your life for another—to live each moment as though it were your last. If only Mom could know of the love Kristin had found there…

But her mother hadn't understood Kristin's reasons for going to Vietnam in the first place. She doubted she would comprehend the life-changing moments she'd experienced, but perhaps one day, she'd have the opportunity to share them with her.

Kristin scanned the room one last time. She slung her duffel bag over one shoulder, walked quietly down the hall and took the elevator down to the foyer. After she paid her bill, her heart clenched at the sight of the few dollars left in her wallet.

After trudging through snow over six blocks to the bus station, exhaustion began to take over. But she forced herself up to the ticket counter and pulled out her wallet.

"Where to, Miss?"

Kristin hesitated, staring at the man behind the thick glass. Then she nodded, her mind made up. "New York. Grand Central. One way."

Harlem Heights teemed with activity. Kristin passed slush-covered basketball courts crowded with players vying for space even in winter. Their shouts and whoops filled the air. Street lamps flickered on as dusk approached. Warm air swirled up through the manhole grids along the road. Brown apartment buildings loomed around her, clothes hanging from lines strung out on the balconies. Yelling, music and raucous laughter competed with the noise of the traffic on the street, while vibrations from a stereo pounded through her head. Smells of fried chicken, sausages and smoke from cigarettes tickled her nostrils.

For an alarming moment, she was transported back to the streets of Saigon.

She stopped, turned in a circle and tried to get her bearings.

Kristin squeezed her eyes shut, opened them again and glanced at the piece of paper she held. She spied a decrepit building that looked identical to the other four around it. But if the address was correct, this was it.

She maneuvered around the children sitting in the stairwell, catching the startled looks from the adults nearby. The elevator sat just inside a dimly lit foyer. Kristin took shallow breaths and tried not to gag on the putrid smell that permeated the air.

A gangly youth bounced a basketball at the foot of the stairs. "Elevator don't work."

She nodded her thanks, but discouragement swept through her. Fifteen flights? She squared her shoulders, shifted her bag, and stepped around him.

By the time she reached the fifteenth floor, Kristin was sure she would die from over-exertion. She'd always been fit, but walking up cement stairs carrying a heavy duffel bag was not something she would choose to do ever again.

Bicycles rested against the graffiti-covered walls of the hallway. Some apartment doors were propped open. Music and the sounds of televisions blared into the hall. All sorts of savory aromas filled the air, making her ravenous. Finally she found the number she looked for, and stopped in front of the apartment. She raised her hand and knocked.

The door swung open and a young woman with a baby on her hip stood before her. She looked Kristin up and down, narrowed her eyes and closed the door just a bit. "Whatchoo want?"

Fatigue and fear encased her, but Kristin summoned all the nerve she had left. "Are you Cassie? Cassandra Williams?" Kristin prayed she'd found the right place. She was too tired to take another step.

"Shoot." The woman's dark face broke into a grin that brought immediate tears to Kristin's eyes. "You gotta be Kristin Taylor."

Then woman's resemblance to Jonno rendered her momentarily speechless. Kristin smiled, relief washing away her fears. She shifted her bag from one shoulder to the other. "How did you know?"

The woman laughed, bouncing the baby on her hip. "Ain't no white women walking around here this time of day, honey. And last time I checked, the chicks from Social Services don't dress in jungle fatigues. Come on in. Shoot." She pulled the loaded bag off her shoulder, and Kristin felt twenty pounds lighter. Her arms tingled as blood rushed back into them. She followed Cassie inside.

"Eddy! We got company. Wake up!"

A burly man rose from a sofa on the other side of the small room. Kristin stepped back as he approached. Three other children seeming to range in age from about two to seven played on the floor. Toys spread across the thick rug like landmines. The kids looked up as she entered, and stared up at her through wide dark eyes.

"Mama, are we in trouble?" The biggest child scrambled over to Cassie and wrapped his arms around her legs.

"No, we ain't in no trouble. Hush." Cassie tousled the child's head and gently pushed him away. "This here's Kristin. She's a friend of your Uncle Jonno's."

"No kidding?" The man called Eddy straightened his bright striped shirt and heaved up his pants. Then he cleared his throat and extended a large hand toward her. "Guess that makes you family then. We sure heard a lot 'bout you, Miss Taylor." His grin chased off her trepidation.

Cassie handed the baby over to Eddy and faced Kristin again. Tears shone in her eyes. "I saved all your articles. Jonno wrote us about you, and his friend Luke. You were his family over there." She stopped speaking, her bottom lip quivering.

Kristin nodded, emotion clamping down speech. There was too much to say, no words adequate enough. But something unfamiliar began to settle in her soul.

Peace.

She'd made the right decision, coming here. "Your brother was a good man, Cassie. The best. I was honored to be his friend."

"He sure loved you, honey. I'm so glad you're here." Jonno's sister pulled Kristin into her arms.

For the first time since returning home, Kristin allowed herself to be held.

The mounting fear she'd tried to stave off since that awful moment when she'd realized Luke was missing, smashed through the fortress she'd built around her heart. The first sob broke, and her shoulders began to shake. Torrents of grief crashed over her, again and again, until she could not bear the weight of it.

Cassie ushered her to the couch, put strong arms around her and let her cry.

Chapter Thirty

$\mathcal{K}$ristin finally drew in a deep breath and wiped her eyes. She ran her hands down her filthy green jacket and took in her surroundings. Eddy and the children were gone.

Kristin met Cassie's questioning eyes. "Thank you."

Cassie only nodded, sat back and held tight to Kristin's hands.

"I'm sorry I didn't call first, but I only had your address. I didn't know where else to go. I couldn't stay in Boston—I—they—nobody understands. I thought you…I knew you would." She tripped over her words, unsure of how much to share.

"You don't need to explain." A glimpse of Jonno's grin appeared on Cassie's face. "I'm glad he told you where to find me. This ain't The Ritz, but you're welcome to stay as long as you want."

Kristin sank back against the cushions and rested her hands across her stomach. Over the last couple of days, before she'd made up her mind, she'd felt ill. Weariness settled over her and she forced her eyes to stay open. She saw Cassie's eyes veer to the ring on her finger, and the woman let out a low whistle.

"Honey, I missed that part. Where's your hunk at? I want to meet this guy. I heard he looks like Robert Redford."

Kristin swallowed hard against the answer. "Luke didn't…come home with me. I don't know where he is. He—he's missing."

"Sweet Jesus, have mercy. Oh, honey." Cassie placed her hand against Kristin's cheek. Her eyes were the color of toffee, warm and full of sympathy. She looked her up and down. "When's your baby due?"

Kristin blinked, surprise jolting her into alertness. "How did you know?"

Cassie's ebony cheeks rounded in a beautiful smile. "I got four kids, baby. I can tell."

Kristin nodded and frowned, trying to keep track of the dates. "I think I'm about two months along now, a bit more. I can't go home. My mother, well, she wouldn't understand. Luke and I...I...don't know what to do..." Speech grew difficult. Lucid thought failed her and she shrugged.

Cassie angled her head, her mouth closed and tight. "Are you keeping it?"

Kristin sat on a small bench on the balcony of Cassie's apartment, watching the late afternoon traffic on the street below. Music and cigarette smoke filtered down from the apartments above her. From here she could see the basketball courts. Spring brought warmer weather, and the courts were never empty. She wondered if any of the boys knew how good they were.

She reached for the notebook that was never far from her side, opened it and stared at the blank pages. The first half was filled with her incoherent ramblings, her last few weeks in-country. She'd drawn boxes around all the names, places she wanted to remember, people she longed to see again, and images she couldn't forget no matter how hard she tried.

The screen door squeaked and Cassie stepped out on the porch. "Thirsty?" She held a tall glass of water and Kristin took it.

"Thanks."

Cassie sat beside her and smoothed down the flowing skirt she wore. "Eddy took the kids to the park. Strange to have the place so quiet."

Kristin concentrated on the laundry hanging from the balconies of the building across the street. The poverty she encountered on a daily basis here stirred something in her and made her want to rise up against it, and do...something...anything. She just didn't have the strength.

"I'm sorry I woke you last night."

Cassie patted her arm and smiled. "No matter. I'm used to it by now. I just wish there was something I could do for you, honey."

"I know." Kristin leaned against the wall behind her and closed her eyes. Not that she'd slept all that well in-country, but she hadn't enjoyed a full night's sleep since leaving Vietnam. Doubted she ever would.

Cassie reached over and took Kristin's notebook, flipping through the pages. "You know, for someone who's supposed to be a writer, I don't see you doing much writing. You've been here a few months now and I don't think you've written anything new in this book. Does your stepfather know you're working the cash register down at the corner store?"

"No." Kristin drained her glass and set it down. Cassie and Eddy would have let her stay for nothing, but she'd insisted on contributing. Within a few months, she'd been embraced into a community she'd never known existed. She hadn't bothered to call the editor that Hayden had given her contact numbers for. "I can't write anymore, Cass. I'm done with that."

Cassie pushed the notebook into Kristin's hands and pierced her with a hard look.

"As my brother would say, 'that's hogwash'. I see you...the way you watch us...how you listen to the folks down the store when they come in just to talk. Maybe you don't want to go work in a newsroom, fine, but that doesn't mean you up and quit completely. You can't cut off the lifeline to your soul, baby. You gotta find something to write about. You need to find your way back."

Kristin smiled at her friend. "You speaking from experience?"

"Could be." Cassie returned her smile and rubbed her back as Kristin leaned forward and felt the baby move. She pressed down and felt the outline of a tiny foot. Sweat slid down her face and she sat up and wiped it away.

"What if nobody wants to hear what I have to say?"

"Then you keep knocking on doors until you find somebody that does." Cassie stood and went inside. Kristin heard noise coming in the direction of her bedroom. Her friend returned a few moments later, an old typewriter in her hands. She placed it on the small table on the far side of the porch and turned around, arms folded across her chest.

"Is this yours?" Kristin rose and ran her fingers across the keys. A strange tingling surged through her and brought a smile. She'd left her old Remington back in Boston in the care of friends.

"You ever hear of Ethel Payne?" Cassie sat again, brushing dirt off the wooden bench.

"Sure. I met her once at a party in Saigon." The young black journalist had been determined and committed to what she was doing and Kristin had admired her work for a while. They hadn't talked long, but Kristin was glad to have met her.

She pulled out a chair, sank onto it and looked at Cassie, avoiding the typewriter. Its tug was fierce and she feared she might give in at any moment.

"I wanted to be her, be a journalist. Travel the world," Cassie explained, her eyes filling with dreams of the past. "I wanted to go to college." She sighed, shook her head and smiled. "I had the grades too. I might have got a scholarship. But then Eddy came along, I got pregnant, and…here I am."

"Sorry." Kristin pushed hair out of her eyes and understood the regret in Cassie's words. Her friend nodded.

"You still have a chance, Kris. You can follow your dreams. It's not too late for you."

"It's not?" A faint tickle of hope started the slow march upward, gaining strength and momentum until it reached her mouth and tugged on her lips.

Cassie smiled back. "I'll go get you some paper."

Kristin jumped, let out a sigh and placed her hands over her belly. Eddy narrowed his eyes. He sprawled on the other end of the couch, wagging a finger at her. "Don't you go havin' no baby in here."

Kristin giggled and rubbed her taut stomach, willing the child within to settle. Cassie insisted it was a boy. Every now and again, the baby kicked. Hard. This week, the kicks were more frequent, more insistent. Somebody was growing impatient. Kristin longed to hold the child she already loved beyond comprehension.

In darker moments, she had considered giving the baby up for adoption. But she knew she'd never be able to live with that. Her child was all she had of Luke.

"Eddy, hush." Cassie yelled from the kitchen. "Kristin ain't having that boy yet. Now get in here and help me dish up."

After dinner, Kristin always read to the kids or helped them with their homework. Then she sat at their square dining-room table and wrote.

At first it was hard going. She was asking questions nobody wanted to answer. Giving people a glimpse into a side of the city nobody talked about. But then, finally, she'd found a small magazine willing to print her stories. They were well received and creating quite a stir. She was able to do a bit of freelancing here and there. It wasn't a full step back to gainful employment, but it was a start.

Once the baby arrived, things would get complicated. The three-bedroom apartment was already overcrowded. Money was tight and she was saving, but probably wouldn't have enough to pay her own rent for a while.

"Kris," Cassie poked her head around the bedroom door. "Telephone."

Kristin looked up. "For me?" She went into the kitchen and picked up the receiver.

"Kristin? Is that you? Are you there?" Her mother's familiar voice rang down the line and took Kristin's breath away. Tears flooded her vision as she nodded and tried to breathe.

"Hi, Mom."

"Sweetheart! Finally. Your letters never gave a telephone number. I've wanted to speak to you for ages but since you moved to New York you've hardly kept in touch…is everything all right?"

"Sorry, Mom." Kristin sank down into a chair, and closed her eyes. Beads of sweat began to form around her hairline. "I—um. I should have called. I'm staying with some friends…well, I guess you know that—how did you find me?"

A long silence set in. Her heart threatened to boycott her body as she waited for her mother's answer. Finally she heard Mom's voice again.

"Hayden called someone in Vietnam. A Colonel Douglas Maddox. Apparently you're engaged to his son."

Kristin shivered at the chill in Mom's tone, brushing tears off her cheeks. She focused on the colorful childish drawings covering the fridge. Cassie's kitchen reminded her of Mary Jo's…

"Kristin? Are you still there?" A frantic edge crept into her mother's voice.

"Yes, Mom. What were you saying?" Kristin clenched her fingers around the receiver and tried to pay attention.

"Hayden and Colonel Maddox put two and two together and figured out where you might be. Are you really in Harlem?"

"Yes." Kristin smiled at the incredulous look Mom would be wearing. She heard her let out her breath and waited for the next question. It didn't come. "Mom?" Kristin forced thought into speech. "Did Hayden say—has Douglas heard anything about…about Luke?" She put a hand against her damp forehead and held her breath.

Her mother's short sigh severed all hope.

"No. I'm sorry, darling. Nothing. He said…sweetheart, they've put him on the MIA list."

Light flashed before her eyes and Kristin bent over her knees. Cassie wouldn't appreciate puke all over her kitchen floor. She'd suspected as much, but to hear it…

"What about Teddy? Have you heard from him lately?"

"No." Mom's voice got stuffy, like she was fighting off a bad cold. "I'm sure he's fine." Dogs barked in the background on her mother's end and she heard a man's voice calling for them. "What's going on, Kristin? Why haven't you called? Your letters say next to nothing…I don't understand."

"I know." Kristin gathered her thoughts and tried to come up with some tangible excuse, but there was none. "I haven't been quite myself. I—I didn't want to be a bother…" Well, that was sort of true.

Her mother's sharp sigh said she wasn't buying it. "Nonsense. Come home, Kristin. Come up here to Vermont. I want you here."

"Mom…" Rubbing her swollen belly, Kristin swallowed hard and made up her mind. She was tired of running from the truth. "It's not that easy. I…" She drew in a deep shuddering breath and strained the next words out. "I'm going to have a baby."

Chapter Thirty-One

"Kris. Someone at the door for you." Eddy stepped out on the balcony, frowning.

Kristin heaved herself out of her chair and went into the apartment. It had been four days since she'd spoken with Mom. The rest of the conversation hadn't gone well. Just as well she'd decided to stay in New York. Somehow she'd have to manage.

She picked her way across the room, careful not to trip over the toys scattered across the carpet, got to the door and came face to face with an older gentleman she didn't recognize. Kristin narrowed her eyes, and sweat dripped down her back. There was no air to be had today.

He stood very straight and tall, dressed in jeans, and a navy polo shirt. Thick salt-and-pepper hair framed a handsome face. Under the umbrella of bushy eyebrows, a pair of sky blue eyes twinkled at her. "Kristin Taylor. We meet at last."

At the sound of Hayden Thorne's voice, her knees buckled. He drew her to him without a word, and simply held her as she cried.

Cassie came up behind her and put her hands on her shoulders. "Your mother called after you went to bed last night," Cassie explained. "She wants you to come home, Kris. I told her I'd talk you in to it."

"She's down in the car," Hayden added. "I didn't want her walking up all those stairs. So what do you say, Kristin? Ready to come home?"

Kristin turned, fear rising. Impossible. She shook her head. "I can't. I…"

"Come on in." Cassie ushered Hayden into the apartment and shooed children out of the way to give him somewhere to sit. "We won't be but a few minutes."

Cassie pulled her into the bedroom, sat her down, crouched at her knees and gave her the I-mean-business look Kristin so often saw her use with the kids.

"You gotta go with them, baby. Your Momma loves you."

"Cassie, I can't! I can't have this baby out there, alone."

Cassie's fierce expression softened into a smile. "Oh, girl, whether you like it or not, here or there, that baby's coming out. Won't it be better to have your Momma there beside you? Sugar, I know what you're heading to. I know what I'm sending you out to…" Cassie's luminous eyes grew wet. She cradled Kristin's hands in hers and squeezed.

"My eldest, Charlie. He was born before Eddy and I got married. It's a hard road, baby, no doubt. My Momma kicked me outta the house. We still don't really speak. Kris, you got your Momma down in that car waiting for you! She wants to take you home. You got no *idea* how lucky you are."

How would she cope being in a new home, a new town, with strangers—whispering—pointing at her behind her back—here she felt safe. They'd accepted her, protected her, and loved her. Even admired her for being in Vietnam. Out there, beyond this small community, the world would not be so kind. "I'm scared, Cass…"

Cassie nodded gravely. "I know you are. I told your Momma last night 'bout your fear. 'Bout your nightmares. She knows, honey. She's gonna look after you. But you listen to me now. You're a strong woman. I know you—the real you. The girl who went to Vietnam and wouldn't take no jive from nobody. *That's* the Kristin Taylor my Jonno wrote me about." Cassie smiled and stroked Kristin's hair. "She's still here, baby. You just gotta find her and bring her home."

Kristin stared at the frayed carpet, unable to speak. Her nose itched and her throat burned. "I don't know, Cass." When she raised her head again, tears ran down her cheeks. "I think I left her back there in Vietnam," she whispered. "With Luke."

For a long, terrifying moment, neither of them spoke. Finally Cassie clenched her jaw and blinked back her own tears. "You're gonna be all right, Kris. God's gonna take care of you."

Kristin wasn't so sure.

Cassie helped her pack her few possessions into the large duffel bag she still lived out of, and they hauled it through to the living room. Hayden stood as they entered, a victorious smile lighting his face.

Kristin shrugged, defeat cloaking her. "I guess I'm coming with you. Just—give me a minute."

She crouched as best she could on the floor near the children. In her hands, she held several of Jonno's stick figures and chuckled at their astonishment. She always let them play with the brightly painted objects, but they knew the priceless items were just on loan.

"You each get one. Remember your Uncle Jonno. Always." Her eyes moved to the framed photograph of Jonno sitting atop the television. Tall and proud in full Army uniform, a hint of his mischievous nature gleamed from his dark eyes.

She sighed and turned from the image, gave each of the children a long hug, then got to her feet. Eddy shuffled over and allowed her to hug him. He pressed a roll of bills into her hand, his eyes telling her there would be no argument. By the time she reached for Cassie, she could hardly speak or see through the veil of tears.

"You gonna be okay, girl." Cassie held her tight. Kristin inhaled her sweet vanilla perfume and wondered how much was left of her heart to break. Memories of saying goodbye to Mary Jo at the airport in Saigon assailed her. This moment mirrored the pain she'd felt that day. In some ways, it was worse.

She forced herself to step back, sniffed and slung her purse over her shoulder. "Thank you for everything. Come see me, okay?"

"You bet I will. I can't wait to love on that little boy, don't you worry 'bout that."

"You're so sure it's a boy. How do you know?" Kristin laughed.

Cassie grew serious, running a hand down Kristin's cheek. "You gotta listen to God when He speaks, baby. He's got a plan for you. For you and your boy. Everything's gonna work out. You'll see."

"Everything?" Kristin faltered, her throat burning again. "No, Cass. I don't think so."

"Don't you give up on that man of yours, Kristin Taylor!" Cassie's voice rose, defiance creeping into her eyes. "He needs you to keep praying for him. You got that?"

Kristin looked downward. Cassie's insistence that Luke was alive had become a sore point between them. But she wouldn't argue now.

Hayden carried her things down all fifteen flights. As she exited the building, Kristin blinked under the late afternoon sun's rays, casting a glance up and down the road. Across the street, a woman stepped out of an old Buick.

As soon as she met her mother's eyes, all hesitation vanished. Where she'd been, what she'd seen and heard, and what she now looked like—pregnant, bloated, disheveled and drawn—none of it mattered.

Mom held out her arms and Kristin ran into them.

She was home.

Chapter Thirty-Two

Vermont, Spring 1970, three years later.

Kristin stood in line at the checkout, her grocery cart half full. The conversation between the two older women just behind her reached her ears. As they intended.

"You know, the one I was telling you about."

"…who wrote all those awful stories about the war?"

"Yes, and those pieces about the coloreds, back in New York. And… unmarried…" The woman's voice dropped to a loud whisper. "Her poor mother."

"I don't know what gets into young people nowadays, Millie."

"Crazy to boot…"

"Well, most are. The ones that come back."

Kristin clenched her fingers around the plastic handle of her cart and pushed it forward. She watched the tips of her knuckles turn white. Crazy wouldn't justify what she wanted to do at that moment.

Gregory sat in the space at the front of the cart, dangling his chubby bare legs in the air as he pounded the handle with his fists. Kristin wiped sweat off her brow and envisioned plopping skinned turkeys into a vat of hot oil.

"Why you mad, Mommy? Why you mad?" Not yet three years old and he could already read her mind.

Just like his father.

Kristin's sneakers squeaked on the linoleum floor as she pushed the cart past the cash register and waited for the clerk to ring up her items.

Temptation goaded her to give a sarcastic answer the old hags would hear. *Because some adults have no manners, Greggy.*

"That'll be twenty-seven fifty, Miss." The young kid at the register watched her with a sour look. Not again…Kristin rifled through her purse. She only had a twenty, but she stalled for time.

A slow heat rose to her cheeks as she started to put some items aside. The women behind her began to snigger.

"I'll cover it." The man next in line after her stepped forward. Kristin snapped her head up. The two pennies she'd found fell from her hand and rolled on to the rubber belt. He picked them up and handed them back to her, passing the cashier a few bills. By the time she realized what he was doing, it was done. Her items were bagged and he'd paid for his and was pushing the cart toward the doors.

She'd mutely pointed to her car and they stood in the parking lot beside it and she was staring at him.

"Thank-you, I…guess I forgot how much I had in my wallet." Her cheeks heated again and she wanted to duck into the car, but the kind look on his face made her stay.

Familiar, somehow.

Deep brown eyes winked at her. "Happy to help. Hey, buddy," he said, turning his attention to Gregory, "what's your name?"

He looked to be about her age, a head taller, in faded jeans, a plaid shirt and a red bandana keeping his long hair back. Gregory smiled at him and she willed the tension out of her shoulders.

"Gregory."

Kristin rolled her eyes. He loved to be the center of attention.

"Nice to meet you, Gregory. I'm Josh." He tilted his head toward her, a smile set in place. "And you are?"

Kristin began to load the grocery bags into the trunk of her car. "Kristin."

"Got a last name, Kristin?"

"Taylor." She tried not to smile at the way he grinned back at her. A dimple poked through the scruff on his face when he laughed.

"You're Kristin Taylor?" He took the final bag from her, put it with the others and shut the trunk with a firm push. Dust flew all over him and Kristin cringed.

"Last time I checked. What's so funny?"

"Just kind of expected…something different."

"Sorry to disappoint you." She folded her arms and caught sight of the large wooden peace sign on a chain around his neck. Behind it she saw a glimpse of metal.

"Oh, I'm not disappointed."

She smiled politely. "Thank you. I've got to go." She'd spent a lot of time in Vietnam extricating herself from the advances of lonely soldiers and quickly learned how to discern between innocent flirtations and the not so innocent kind. She wasn't sure what vibes this guy was giving out, but didn't care to find out.

He laughed and fiddled with the strap of his watch. "Those biddies in there are gossip mongers. They talk about everyone. Truth rarely comes into play."

"You know them?"

"Grew up here. They go to my mom's church."

Kristin smiled. "Of course they do. They'll be talking about you next." She lifted Gregory out of the cart and kicked it onto the sidewalk while he scrambled into the car.

"They already do." His quiet chuckle soothed her frayed nerves, but she busied herself securing Gregory in the backseat. She straightened, brushed dirt off her cotton shirt and thrust her hands in the pockets of her denim overalls. "Thanks again, um, Josh. I'll pay you back if you want to let me know where to…"

"Nah, it was a few bucks. No need. But I uh—don't suppose you'd be interested in doing some work? I mean you probably already have a job…right?" He looked suddenly uncomfortable and Kristin arched an eyebrow.

"Wrong. There doesn't seem to be much out there for an unmarried mother, and a sympathizer to boot, who acts like she's three sheets to the wind most of the time."

Kristin waited for the pity speech, but his face remained impassive.

"Can you type?"

Kristin pursed her lips together.

He gave a sheepish grin and rubbed his jaw. "Stupid question, huh?"

Kristin waited, her nerves still on edge. He looked thoughtful for a moment. "I run a coffee house. On Arbor Street. Called Fresh Winds. Maybe you've heard about us. We're looking for someone to help us out with filing, put out some posters, write our newsletters, that sort of thing. I know it's not what you're used to doing, but…"

"A coffee house?" She'd heard about something out of California a while back, some hippie religious movement. She'd shown the article to her mother who had promptly thanked the Lord that no such thing existed in her town. A smile stretched her lips and almost made her laugh. "Wait a minute…you…you're not one of those Jesus Freaks are you?"

His face cracked with a wide smile and he tipped his head to one side. "Freak's kind of a strong word."

"Is this place like a…church? Because if so, I'm not interested."

He shrugged. "Church is what you make it. Why don't you come see for yourself?"

Kristin pushed her hands into the pockets of her jeans. She went to church on Christmas and Easter, and only to appease her mother. Sometimes, if they had a meal after service, she'd go with them. Free food was nothing to be sniffed at.

"How much would I get paid?"

He blanched and flashed another grin. "Not enough, that's for sure. But we could really use the help. You could bring your kid. We'd look after him."

Gregory banged on the window from the inside of the car and Kristin opened the door. "Stop that!" She pulled her keys out of her purse. "We as in all the other hippies at your coffee house church or whatever it is?"

He raised his hands and backed off. "Hey, if you're not interested, no sweat. I just thought it'd be something for you to do." His gaze was so intense she wondered if she had a sock stuck to her head or something.

"I have things to do. Plenty of things. I'm writing a book." Why in the world she'd suddenly decided to share that piece of information was beyond her.

"That so? What's it about?"

"Vietnam."

"Cool. Well, we could set you up in a room, when you're on breaks you could work on your manuscript without having to worry about your boy. Like I said, there'd be plenty of people around for him, kids too. What do you say?"

Cars sped by on the highway beyond the parking lot. The sun sent warmth through her tired soul. An odd sensation prickled through her. She almost didn't recognize it.

Hope.

"All right. I suppose I can come check it out. I'll stop by this week. But I don't want to be preached at."

He raised a hand and gave her another smile. "No preaching, I swear."

"You swear? Interesting. I didn't think you religious types did that kind of thing."

"I don't think you know our kind of religion, Kristin."

"I guess I don't." Gregory started squealing again. Kristin raised a hand, got into the car. "Gotta go."

"See you soon." He stepped back as she drove off. Kristin watched him in her rearview mirror. He turned and headed toward a car several spaces down from where she'd parked.

She'd finally gone insane. She hadn't even gotten his last name.

Kristin felt the tug of a smile, and then laughter tumbled out of her.

Josh-the-hippie-without-a-last-name. This was definitely the weirdest encounter she'd had since leaving Vietnam. She couldn't wait to tell Mom all about it.

The coffee house was more like a hole in the wall, but the minute she walked inside, Kristin felt at home. Josh and a few friends had purchased the old house a year ago and shared living quarters upstairs. They'd renovated the ground floor for their main meeting rooms and a couple of offices in back. The brick walls had been painted in psychedelic colors, with large DayGlo posters tacked up, interspersed with the work of local artists. The room was always warm and the strong aroma of coffee permeated her senses.

A few rustic tables and chairs invited patrons to sit and enjoy a beverage and company. People came and went as they pleased. Anyone was free to get up and sing, play guitar or recite poetry. Some nights they had something akin to a church service, nothing like the formal services Kristin had attended growing up.

Young people like her made their home here, some high school kids came by now and again to play ping pong or shoot hoops out back, and a handful of unemployed GIs wandered in and out on a daily basis. Kristin tried to avoid them at first, but their silent stares, eventual smiles and waves won her over. Like it or not, they connected her to Vietnam. To all she'd left behind and all she'd lost.

She spent her days writing, doing odd jobs and filling her time with whatever Josh asked of her while Gregory played nearby and ran in the small backyard with the other kids that frequented the place with their mothers.

The last couple of months were the best she'd had since returning from Vietnam. She just wasn't quite sure what to do with the days when she couldn't function.

Today was turning into one of them.

Wind howled outside the windows of the small back office, the old oak tree branches tapped against the glass panes in sharp succession. Rain pelted the roof and walls of the building, and thunder rolled in. Kristin turned up the volume on the small transistor radio on her desk, concentrated on the words she typed, and tried to shut out the noise.

Bap-bap-bap-bap-bap...enemy fire! Get down! Kristin, hit the dirt!

"No..." Kristin moaned, shook her head and plastered her hands to her ears.

Bap-bap-bap-bap-bap...boom!

She jumped back from her desk at the thunderclap and bolted from the room. Fear urged her on and she raced down the hall until she barreled straight into Joshua.

"Whoa!" He caught her in his arms just as another thunderclap boomed overhead. Kristin shook free and crouched on the floor, covering her head with her hands. She heard him let out a breath, and felt his arms come around her the next instant. He eased her into a sitting position in the middle of the hallway floor.

He crouched before her, holding her until she was able to look up at him. "Kristin, listen to me. It's just a storm. Okay? You're safe here, and nobody is going to hurt you. You're safe." He cradled her face between firm hands and held her gaze. "Do you hear me?"

Kristin slowed her breathing, but couldn't stop the trembling. That always took a while. She fought for air and exhaled, counting to ten in her head. She met Josh's worried look and fear melted into shame.

"What's wrong with me?" She forced the words out. "Do you think I'm really crazy, Josh? Because when this happens, I think I am. I don't know what to do. I'm scared...I'm scared to be alone with Gregory. I'm scared I might...that I'll...do something to him."

Her worst fears spoken, Kristin closed her eyes, drew her knees to her chest and bowed her head.

Silence enfolded them. The storm over, only children's laughter and the strumming of a guitar in the front room could be heard.

His hands closed around hers. Kristin lifted her head as he got to his feet, pulling her up with him. "You're not crazy. I get it. I know what you're seeing. The men, choppers circling, the sound of gunfire..."

She stared in disbelief. "How...?"

Josh smiled. "Come with me. I'll get you something to drink and explain."

They sat in his office. Kristin sipped hot coffee and enjoyed its soothing effect. She was suddenly reminded of Mary Jo. A smile tugged at the corners of her mouth.

"That's better." Josh grinned at her over the top of his mug.

Kristin lowered her eyes. "I had this friend in Vietnam. Mary Jo Granger. She and her husband Bob ran an orphanage. I kind of stumbled on the place, but we became friends. Whenever I needed a break, someone to talk to, I'd wind up sitting on her patio drinking tea. They were the best friends Luke and I..." She brought her mug up to her lips and swallowed.

Josh studied her through questioning eyes. "Gregory's father."

"Yes." Kristin placed her mug on the wooden coffee table in front of her, her fingers automatically circling the ring on her left hand. She studied the magazines on the table and tried to ignore the feeling of his eyes on her.

"You don't talk about him."

"There's not much to say."

"How long were you together?"

"Long enough." Kristin regretted the curt reply at once.

Josh smiled, seeming unperturbed. "Sorry. None of my business."

Kristin forced herself to meet his eyes. Kindness sparkled in them and remorse filled her. "No, it's all right. It's just…I don't talk about him because nobody asks."

"What happened to him?"

"He…went missing just before I came home." If there was anyone she trusted, it was Josh. "Luke worked for the CIA. I…wrote an exposé on the Agency. It came out just before I left Vietnam. They used an anonymous byline but…they found out it was me. I betrayed his trust." Anger and resentment quickly found their home in her voice and she shot him another apologetic look. "And now I guess I have to live through the hell of knowing that. Guess when I get to the real thing I'll know what to expect. Aren't you glad you asked?"

His shoulders rose and fell, but his smile remained. "What makes you so sure you're going to hell?"

"Here we go." Kristin grinned and put her hands on her knees as if to leave.

A dimple played in his cheek. "I'm allowed to ask. You're not obliged to answer."

Kristin sat back and tried to relax. In many ways, Josh reminded her of Teddy.

"I used to believe in God," she admitted. "But I'm not sure I do anymore. If you had any idea of the things I've seen…"

"Oh, I've got a pretty good idea." His voice trailed off and she watched his face change. He set his mug down and drew his arms across his chest. "Like I said, I get it." His unsettled eyes drew her. Kristin's pulse quickened the way it always did when she sensed a story in the making.

"I served two tours in Vietnam," he said at last. "Air Cavalry. Five-oh-six battalion—first division, Sergeant Brentwood at your service, ma'am."

He tipped an imaginary cap but his grin quickly faded. "I flew Hueys day in and day out. I watched men die right under me when I couldn't touch down long enough to get anyone out to save them. I don't need to tell you…you were there." He massaged his temples, his eyes hinting at familiar wounds.

Confusion nettled her. "Why didn't you say something before now?" Her voice came out as a hoarse whisper.

Josh lifted broad shoulders and let them fall again, his face taut with emotion. "Like you said, I don't talk about it because nobody asks."

Kristin nodded and gripped the sides of her chair. The room was closing in. "When did you get out?"

"A few years ago. When I came home, I spent some time in California, hooked up with a group down there, decided to see whether something like this would fly in Vermont."

Kristin knew she was staring. She couldn't help it. She'd been on so many helicopters. Wondered about so many of the pilots, if they ever made it out alive.

He gave a brief smile. "The answer is yes. You've seen me before. You rode with me about five times—you and Luke. I was at the end of my tour the last time I saw you."

Kristin dropped her head, tears stinging. The weight of the moment threatened to suck her under. That she would find someone like him, here, out in the middle of nowhere…someone who knew exactly where she'd been and what she'd gone through, and had gone through it himself.

"Do you ever see…hear…"

"Incoming chopper blades slicing through the dead of night? Sniper fire coming at me in the middle of a church service? All the time."

Kristin shuddered at his jovial expression. "What do you do?"

"I pray."

She let out a shaky sigh and laughed mirthlessly. "That figures." She tugged at her hair and glanced down at her watch. It was almost time to go, Gregory would be getting hungry. "I've tried praying. It doesn't work."

"Really?"

His curious tone made her laugh and she caught the mischief in his eyes. "Well, maybe you just have a better connection."

"Maybe so. But I'll give you the package deal for free any time you're interested."

"You like giving things away don't you, Joshua?" Kristin got to her feet, a comfortable feeling of friendship settling in some unfamiliar place within her soul.

"I have a good Teacher." He set his quiet smile on her once again and Kristin's cheeks began to tingle. She rolled her eyes to the ceiling in mock despair.

"Thanks for the coffee. And thanks for…sharing." There was too much she could say, but couldn't put into words.

"You're welcome." Josh rubbed his chin. "Any word on your brother?"

Kristin looked across the office out of the window. The sun's rays emerged from behind a cloud and lit the raindrops on the glass. After not hearing from Teddy for a few months, Hayden made some calls. And then they got the official word. Tears burned as she faced him and shook her head. "He's been put on the MIA list. First Luke, and now Teddy…I don't understand. Why would God allow this?"

To Kristin's dismay, all he did was shrug. She stared in surprise until he smiled and gave a short laugh. "Sorry, Kristin. Some questions don't have easy answers."

"Yeah." She'd heard that one before. In a very different place and time. "Well, thanks again." She wiped her eyes and got to her feet.

"Anytime. Oh, and Kristin…" He swallowed and veered his gaze for a moment. Then his eyes locked with hers once more. "Don't ever regret what you did over there. I read all your pieces. All the guys did. They pulled us through. You have no idea how many lives you touched with the words you wrote."

For a long moment, all she could do was stare at the floor. An unbidden smile flitted across her lips as she lifted her eyes to his. "Thanks, Josh." Whether he knew it or not, he'd just given her a priceless gift. Validation.

Chapter Thirty-Three

Vermont, Spring 1972.

K ristin stopped at the graveyard of the old church. She grasped the cold metal gate and pushed it open. Its familiar creak welcomed her, and she wandered in.

She settled on the gnarled wooden bench, studied the ancient headstones and gathered her thoughts. Winters in Vermont could be harsh and unforgiving. She longed for the warmer weather. One day, when she got back on her feet, she vowed to move to a warm climate.

At the rate she was going, she doubted "one day" would ever come.

When she'd first moved in with Mom and Hayden, Kristin never left the farm. Going into town often proved too difficult. The stares and whispers of strangers stung. Shame and guilt became her friends. Her mother tried to convince her nobody talked or thought the worst of her, but Kristin knew better. Being an unmarried mother in a small town bore scars.

Gregory Luke Taylor catapulted into the world a week early, howling his protest. Her mother went in with her for the delivery while Hayden paced the waiting room. He told her later he'd almost worn a hole in the rug.

From the moment she laid eyes on her son, she saw Luke. Each year the resemblance grew stronger. As much as she loved her child, sometimes, when she watched the little boy in slumber, his thick blond hair falling over his sweet little face, Kristin's heart ached.

Ached for all she had lost, and all her son would never know.

She feared she'd live with this pain for the rest of her life.

Once she began working with Joshua down at Fresh Winds, she'd seen a new side to the small town she now called home. Not everyone was cold-shouldered and judgmental. She'd made friends, good ones. Gregory was thriving, and she—well—she was getting by.

And Josh had a lot to do with that.

Kristin released a ragged sigh and pushed hair out of her eyes. He was a good man, a good friend. She enjoyed working with him and he encouraged her to press on with her writing, even through the days when she wanted to pitch her typewriter out the window. He hadn't pursued her in a romantic way, but lately she'd noticed lingering glances and the way her cheeks heated when he walked into the room. New feelings confused her, scared her.

Recently they'd been consumed with getting the Veteran center up and running. It had been Josh's idea, and Kristin jumped at it.

It gave her new purpose. To provide a place for the men to hang out—a safe environment where they could talk about their experiences without reservation with people who cared, and supported them, to receive help filling out paperwork and finding employment…it was long overdue. Thanks to Josh's persistence, despite the reluctant cooperation of the town council, it was becoming a reality.

Time heals all wounds. She'd heard the old cliché a million times. Yet she was beginning to believe it. Kristin was even beginning to feel she might belong in this community she'd once felt so ostracized by.

"There you are." Hayden's voice startled her and Kristin looked up, wiping her eyes. Her stepfather smiled, sat down beside her and patted her on the knee. "Beautiful day. Looks like spring is on the way. Summer will be right behind. Warm up that cold blood of yours."

"You say that every year around this time." She'd found a friend in him, a confidant. The fact that he'd known and worked with her father bonded them at once. Unlike Mom, who fretted over Kristin's sleepless nights and nervous condition, Hayden accepted it, and simply loved her through it.

Hayden laughed. "Probably. You're looking a little pensive. Everything okay?"

Kristin nodded, her throat suddenly thick. "It's Luke's birthday."

Time didn't heal *all* wounds.

"Oh, Kris." Hayden put an arm around her shoulders and Kristin leaned against him, inhaling Old Spice and motor oil. She smiled. It was good to have a father again. He could never replace Dad, but she'd grown to love him, and he doted on Gregory. Her mother had made a good choice.

"He'd be thirty-five," she whispered, kicking at the dirt under her feet. "I miss him so much."

He hugged her "I know you do. When you love someone like that, you never lose that love. Even though your mother and I found each other, I still miss my Joyce, and I know your mother misses your Dad. You just move on somehow."

Kristin wound her thumbs around each other and watched the sun sparkle through the diamond ring she still wore. "He's not coming back." The idea woke her in the middle of the night, threatened to snatch all new hope from her, but she battled on, and now the time had come to face the truth.

"MIA isn't the same as being dead, you know."

"Hayden…" Kristin drew in a breath. They'd had this conversation. Both Luke and Teddy were listed as MIA. No, their bodies hadn't been found, but she knew. Missing in action was the Army's polite way of saying "they're dead, we just can't confirm it."

"You know what your mother thinks…" Hayden seemed to hesitate and she let out a groan.

"Yes. I know what Mom thinks." Kristin kicked at the grass beneath her feet. "She thinks it's just as well that Luke's not coming back, that I need to move on with my life. With Joshua."

"She means well. She wants what's best for you and Gregory. We both do."

Kristin pulled her fingers through her hair. "I know. Josh is a good guy. You like him, don't you?"

"Sure I do." He sat back and studied her with a smile. "You two… uh…dating or anything yet?"

"No." She sat forward for a moment, so many images tumbling around in her mind. Saigon, Long Binh, the kids at the orphanage…somehow she had to find a way to put the past to rest. "Mom's right. I need to move on, Hayden."

"Good. So. How's that book of yours coming?"

His change of subject made her smile. "It's coming."

"From what you've shown me so far, I think you have a winner. As soon as you're done…"

"I know, I know. You'll be the first to read it." Kristin sighed. Sometimes her stepfather reminded her of Bob Granger. Hayden had a knack for getting to the heart of the matter, drawing out the tough answers whether she wanted to give them or not.

She missed the Grangers. They had no plans to leave Vietnam, but Mary Jo kept in touch faithfully. Kristin received pages of news in her friend's large handwriting, almost once a month, often with a few dollars tucked in, to go toward something for Gregory. Their generosity made her cry.

"I wish this war would end, Hayden."

"Things seem to be coming to a head," Hayden said. "I don't think it'll be long now."

"I hope not." She watched a couple of sparrows land on a nearby headstone. "I worry about Mary Jo, Bob…those kids. What's going to happen to them when the war is over?"

"I don't know." Hayden clenched his knees. "We pray and we keep trusting in God's plan. Even when we don't see it played out."

"I'm trying." She managed a smile. "I won't lie and say I'm ready to accept it all yet…but…I have more faith than I used to."

"I'm starting to see that." He gave a good-natured chuckle. "You don't argue with me nearly as much."

"Losing my edge I guess." She laughed. "I think Josh has softened me up a bit. And the guys…" Her eyes stung. The veterans she met with each week at Fresh Winds displayed courage she envied. They did their best to cope with all they'd seen and done…many came home with physical disabilities, all suffered emotionally. They were desperate to assimilate themselves into a life they didn't fit into anymore.

Kristin knew the feeling.

"Seeing the guys come back from Vietnam, so many of them have suffered so much, yet they still believe. They hold onto this faith…this intrinsic belief that God is still in control. That He hasn't let them down. It's a powerful thing to experience."

"God is about the only one who hasn't let them down." Hayden dry tone displayed his true feelings. "Some days I wonder where this country is headed."

"Probably best we don't know." It was difficult to put away her journalistic tendency to question everything, especially when it came to faith. Over time, she began to accept that maybe it wasn't about the knowing. Maybe it was more about trusting, and believing.

She sat back and studied her stepfather. For weeks now she'd been wrestling with the final pages of her manuscript, trying to come to terms with her time in Vietnam. Trying to come to terms with Luke's disappearance and God's role in it all.

"Did you ever doubt God's love for you, Hayden? Did you ever wonder if He really existed?"

He let out a long breath, and nodded, raking fingers through slowly graying hair. "Have I told you exactly how I became a Christian?"

"No." Kristin managed a smile.

A far-off look stilled his face and something else settled in, like sadness. "It was thanks to your Dad, actually."

"My father?" Kristin's hand automatically reached for her cross before she remembered she no longer had it.

Thoughts of Luke infiltrated her heart once more.

He smiled and nodded. "We were on assignments quite often together. I could never get him to shut up about two things; his family and his God. I didn't mind hearing about you, but I wasn't too sure about the Jesus kick I thought he was on. One night we accompanied a platoon on a particularly dangerous mission. Oh, I was a cocky son of a gun back in those days. Didn't need anyone. I felt invincible. I certainly didn't need God."

Kristin smiled and folded her arms. She could relate.

"Your dad and I split up. The Huey I was on got shot down. I was able to parachute out, and I landed in the middle of the bush, scared out of my mind and knowing for sure I was about to get a bullet in the brain. Or I'd have a heart attack and die before anybody could kill me."

"I've been there." If she closed her eyes, she would be back in the jungles of Vietnam, waiting for the gunfire to stop. The nightmares she lived with still sometimes showed up to taunt her during the day, often when she least expected it. She looked down at her trembling hands until the moment passed.

"You okay?" Concern layered the question.

"Yes." She drew herself up and nodded. "Go on."

"Well, that night I cried out to God. I'd been raised in the church, I knew the Bible, heard the Gospel. I just never accepted it. I always thought when the day came, I'd be able to bargain my way into Heaven." A smile came and went. "That night, I knew I needed to jump in feet first. I didn't know much about Jesus, but somehow, on that black night, I felt Him put His arms around me. All my doubts faded into the darkness. I put my faith in Him, and I fell asleep."

"What happened?" Kristin swallowed, her throat dry. She saw the VC stringing Hayden up by his bootlaces.

He laughed, slapping his hands on his denim clad knees. "Nothing. I got up the next morning and walked across a field, and found out I'd landed on the perimeter of a French base camp."

"Cool." Kristin grinned at the look of astonishment on his face.

He nodded, as though he still couldn't believe it, even after all these years. "You're not kidding. But I never forgot that night, and I determined in my heart that day, I'd live the rest of my life for God. I got myself a Bible, talked a lot to your dad, and by the time I came home, I was well on my way to a new life."

"And you've never looked back?"

"Oh, honey, I've had my moments, trust me. Nobody's perfect. But His grace is sufficient, Kristin."

"I guess." Kristin stared at the gray headstones around her. If only she could jump in and let her life raft go. But maybe believing was a day-to-day experience. For now at least, it would have to be. "Thanks, Hayden. I'll think about that."

"Can I say something else?" He took her hand in his.

She nodded.

"Ever since I brought you home, I've wanted to say this but haven't known how. Honey, I know you wrote that story, the CIA exposé. The one you told me you didn't. And I know...I know you think that somehow, Luke's disappearance is related to that. So you hold yourself responsible."

"Hayden." She jerked her head up, her throat tight.

He held up a hand. "Hear me out. Kristin, it wasn't your fault. You say you need to move on with your life, and that's great. I couldn't agree more. But you won't be able to if you don't let this thing go. Will you do that?"

"I don't know how," she whispered. "How do I forgive myself?"

"You know what Luke would say?" He sat back and stared at her through serious eyes. "He'd say stop wasting time worrying about what you can't change. Kris...he worked for the CIA. He put his life in jeopardy day in and day out. He knew that. So did you, at the end. Whatever happened...and we may never know...you need to know he was fully aware of the possible consequences. And he wouldn't blame you, Kristin. I think you know that. It's time to let it go."

A cooling breeze drifted around her as she sat in silence. Her eyes moved to the far end of the graveyard. For an instant, she thought she saw a figure, standing just off to one side of the graves, his arms folded across his broad chest, his blond hair lifting in the wind.

And he was smiling.

Kristin inhaled fresh spring air and pressed back tears. She looked at Hayden and nodded. "All right. I'll try."

No matter how early she arrived at the Fresh Winds, Josh was there first. This morning she knew he'd definitely beat her. She was an hour late already.

She pulled off her lightweight spring coat as she walked down the hall, pausing outside the room Josh used for an office. He was there, his dark head bent over a stack of paperwork, brow furrowed in concentration. She knew he'd much rather be outside shooting hoops with the neighborhood boys. He hated this part of his job, but, like everything Joshua Brentwood put his hand to, he did it well and without complaint.

"Taxes?"

He raised his head at the sound of her voice, a smile chasing off the intent look. "The devil's invention." One eyebrow rose in question. "You okay?"

Kristin walked around the room, straightening the chairs, picking magazines up off the floor. "Gregory took forever to get ready this morning. He lost his shoes. Again."

"You should tie them to his ankles at night."

"Sure." She laughed, imagining poor Gregory tripping over his shoes the next morning.

"Maybe when he starts school, it'll get easier," he offered, looking hopeful.

Kristin rolled her eyes and sat down. "I can't believe he'll be ready for that soon."

He pushed his hair out of his eyes and studied her in silence. "You seem a little preoccupied. And you're not usually this late."

"I know. I overslept this morning, it wasn't just Gregory." Kristin's nerves got the better of her. She looked down at the bright blue shag rag under her feet and searched for courage. "I…um…finished my book. Hayden's reading it."

Josh gave a slow whistle and a wide grin. "That's great news. How do you feel?"

She let out her breath and allowed a smile. "Good. Like…a chapter of my life is over. Not that I'll ever forget, you know, but…it's done."

"Well, we should celebrate." He stood and went to the corner of the room where he kept a flask of coffee, poured two mugs and handed one to her. "To your bestseller."

"I don't know about that." She laughed anyway, met his eyes, and nodded again. "Anyway. I wanted to tell you something."

"Okay." He leaned back in his chair, steepled his hands and waited.

"I've been doing a lot of thinking." She let the words come. "Luke's not coming back, Josh. I know that. I've made peace with it. I'm ready to move on." She gripped her mug and waited for the lump that always formed in her throat when she talked of Luke.

It didn't.

He sat forward, put his elbows on the desk and rested his chin in his hands. His eyes never left hers, but they sparked with new light. A quiet smile played on his lips. "Are you sure?"

Kristin put her mug down and nodded. "Yes. And please don't say it's about time."

He didn't. Instead, he rose, rounded the desk and pulled her up into a long hug. He drew back, holding her at arm's length. "I know that wasn't easy for you."

"No. But I can't live the rest of my life looking down the road. That's not fair to anyone." She searched his eyes for anything that would tell her what he was thinking. Maybe she'd been off base, picked up on the wrong signals.

His lips curled upward in an attractive smile. "I don't suppose it'll come as any great shock if I say I'm really glad to hear it."

"No." So she hadn't been wrong.

Something in his expression changed and Josh grew serious. His eyes locked with hers and she saw a flicker of new hope in them—a different kind of hope. He reached for her hands and laced his fingers through her own. "I won't rush you."

"I know. But I don't...I can't promise you anything..."

"I'm not asking you to. We'll take it slow, see where things go. I'm not generally impulsive by nature, Kristin." His words tugged at a sudden memory. Something tapped at her heart, almost in warning, but she couldn't be sure. His lazy smile returned and brought a glow to his cheeks. "Maybe dinner and a movie once or twice a week. And lunch at your Mom's on Sundays."

Her eyebrows shot up. "Lunch with my mother? Are you trying to kill me?" Kristin gaped.

Josh laughed, pulling her in for another hug. "Just kidding. No lunch yet. What are you doing on Friday night?"

"Well, I'll have to check the calendar." She teased him, enjoying the way his mouth turned downward. She poked his chest and smiled. "I don't have anything planned, silly. Why?"

"I thought we could...you know...do that dinner and a movie thing."

"Don't waste any time, do you?"

"Too soon?" His grin faded as his eyes roamed her face.

"You're serious. You're asking me out."

Josh nodded, a look of exasperation creeping over him. Kristin smiled and pushed away the last thread of doubt. "Then I guess we have a date."

Chapter Thirty-Four

Vermont, February 1973.

Valerie entered the living room and pulled up short. Kristin stood at the wide glass window at the front of the room and watched the two warriors outside do battle. Valerie moved a little closer and took in the scene.

They each hid behind huge mounds of snow, waiting for the most opportune moment to strike. Gregory used his ammunition often, but Josh was more astute, able to sense the cold missiles headed in his direction and duck before they reached their target.

She grinned at the frustrated look on her grandson's face as he came out of hiding and raced toward Josh's side of the battlefield, hurling snowballs as fast and far as his little arms would allow. Josh charged and met him halfway, grabbing him in a full tackle and tossing him easily to the ground. The two Border Collies raced around the pair, barking at their shouts and squeals.

Valerie put a hand on Kristin's shoulder. "He's a good man." Once she'd gotten to know Joshua, her initial reservations slid away. And, after months of her not-so-subtle hinting, he'd even cut his hair and most days appeared clean-shaven.

Kristin shifted, her shoulders tightening. "He is. So why am I standing here still thinking it should be Luke out there?"

Over the past year, since she and Joshua began dating, Kristin had made a valiant effort to move beyond the past. Valerie knew that. And Josh, bless his heart, had been patient, more than patient with her. They got along well, remarkably so, considering Kristin's quick temper and his slow-as-molasses reaction time.

Kristin had slowly ventured out of her shell. She laughed and smiled more, and took time to look after herself instead of devoting every waking hour to her son. Valerie had Joshua to thank for that. He pointed her daughter to the bright side of every situation, encouraged her in her new faith, and pulled her through the days when memories still paralyzed her. And he'd become a father to Gregory.

But he wasn't Luke Maddox.

And as much as she hated to admit it, Valerie wasn't sure Joshua could ever be enough for her daughter.

"Josh asked me to marry him."

Valerie allowed the words to sink in and breathed a silent prayer of thanks. "Honey, that's wonderful!" Kristin said nothing, just continued to stare out the window. Valerie squeezed her shoulder. "You are going to say yes, aren't you?"

Kristin went to stand before the fire. Valerie watched the way she set her jaw and sensed the wall going up around her heart. She pulled an afghan from the couch and tucked it around her daughter's thin frame.

"I don't know." Kristin's voice was low, noncommittal. Tears shone from her eyes. "I thought I'd accepted it, Mom. Thought I could go on, knowing he's not coming back…but some days…I can't."

"Luke isn't coming back." Regret seared her at once and Valerie wished she could take back her harsh words.

Kristin narrowed her eyes. "Do you think Teddy's dead too? Have you given up on your own son?"

"Kristin, stop." Valerie bit down on her trembling lip and blinked back tears. Teddy wasn't dead. Couldn't be. Yet…it had been too long.

"I'm sorry," Kristin whispered. "I shouldn't have said that."

Valerie tried to rally and wiped her eyes. "Do you think I don't want to have hope, Kristin? I'd love to believe that Teddy's alive, that he's coming home, but I have to be realistic. We have to let it go, honey. That man out there loves you, and he loves Gregory. You'll have a good life with him. You deserve to be happy."

"I *was* happy."

Valerie's heart ached at the tremor in her daughter's hands. That she should have to suffer like this seemed so unfair.

Kristin met her eyes and drew her lips together. "I never told you this, but…I wrote a story, a few months before I left Vietnam. It was something Dad had started before he died—I found it in all his notes and files you gave me—it was about the CIA. Luke…"

Valerie knew what was coming but said nothing, waiting for Kristin to find her voice again.

"Luke worked for the Agency. Things…happened…he suspected I was doing something, but I lied to him. More than once. You can imagine how he reacted when the story did come out. He…was sent up north and we didn't get the chance to resolve things. I feel responsible, Mom. Hayden says I need to forgive myself, that it's not my fault, but…I haven't been able to move past it."

Valerie felt the weight of Kristin's confession and accepted it. Somehow she'd always known that Kristin's reasons for going to Vietnam had more to do with her father than anything else. She put her arms around her daughter and hugged her.

Tears streaked Kristin's face. "I loved him so much, Mom. I didn't mean to hurt him…I just…I made the wrong decision. It's hard to let it go, not knowing for sure that he forgave me for doing it. And I honestly don't know that I can love anyone the way I loved Luke. Is that how you felt after Dad died?"

"Oh, yes." Valerie nodded, memories of dark days and lonely nights flooding through her. "It was a very long time until I thought I might be ready for another relationship. Not until I met Hayden."

Kristin nodded, her face impassive. "I feel like a part of me is missing." She pressed a hand against the window. "Is it fair to Josh? Can I really love him like I'm supposed to?"

"It'll be different." Valerie chose her words carefully "Maybe not like it was with Luke, but sweetheart, he makes you happy. He loves you. And I know you love him too, don't you?"

"As best I can. He says it's enough."

"Then let it be." Valerie smiled and rested her hand against Kristin's cold cheek. "You deserve a future, honey, a good man to love you, a father for Gregory."

"I know." A small smile inched up the corners of Kristin's mouth. "When I first found out I was pregnant, I was terrified. And then Luke was gone…I didn't know what I was supposed to do…I wished…for it to be a mistake. That's terrible, isn't it?"

"No." Valerie rubbed Kristin's back. "Understandable under the circumstances."

Another tear slid down her pale face and Kristin wiped it away. "I wouldn't change it now. As hard as it is, being a mother, I'd do anything for Gregory. Without him, I don't think I would have had any reason to go on."

Valerie released a slow breath, her throat tight. "Come, sit." She untied her apron and led Kristin to the couch. Her daughter put her head in her hands and sighed.

"I'm so tired. If I could just sleep, maybe I could think straight."

Over the past few years she'd grown used to hearing Kristin up at all hours, midnight, two in the morning, pacing her bedroom or working on her book, the rat-a-tat-tat of her typewriter going a mile a minute. Some nights she didn't get out of bed, but her muffled cries floated through the silence of the house.

"Sweetheart." Valerie gently pulled Kristin's hands from her face, and clasped them in her hands. A bare smile crossed her face. "I owe you an apology."

"For what?" Kristin raised an eyebrow.

Valerie drew in a breath. It was time. "You know I never wanted you to go there, to Vietnam."

"You made that pretty clear, yes." Kristin sat back against the couch and her stubborn look returned. Valerie nodded, ignoring the lump in her throat and the fear that came with it. Things needed to be said.

"I was terrified of losing you. I saw so much of your father in you, and I thought…I thought it would happen all over again. What I didn't see was your dream. I didn't see your love for writing, for going after a story, and telling it in a way only you could. It wasn't until I met Hayden that I truly understood that. And it was only then that I really saw how talented you are."

Kristin gave a bleak smile. "If I'd tried to put myself in your place, to understand what you were going through, I might not have gone."

"No. You would have gone. You *should* have gone. I just wish…I hate what you went through, Kristin. I hate seeing you in so much pain." Anger took her breath away. Valerie glanced down at the floor and gathered her thoughts. "I do sometimes wish you had never gone to Vietnam. But we can't change the past. We need to focus on the future." She smiled and ran a hand over her daughter's head.

"Believe me, I know what you've been through. I know what it's like to give your heart and soul to a man and know you simply cannot live without him. And I also know what it's like to wake up one day and find yourself pregnant."

Kristin sat up and stared, her eyes widening. "What?"

Valerie ignored the hammering of her heart and nodded. "Yes. Your father and I were young. Reckless. But oh, we loved each other. Not that it made it right. We found out early enough, and we got married. My parents never questioned why the rush. And I never told them." She gave a short laugh. "I'm sure they figured it out after you came along. So you see…" Valerie smiled and wiped the tears from Kristin's cheeks.

"I understand you better than you know. Had your father not stood by me, I would have been alone. But I would have done everything in my power to keep you and protect you. I'm so proud of you, honey, the way you've coped, looking after Gregory on your own. I should have told you this earlier, when you first told me you were pregnant. But I was scared for you, and I didn't know how to say it. I'm sorry if you ever thought I judged you or that I was disappointed in you."

Kristin let out a sob and Valerie put her arms around her. Her eyes went to the photographs on the mantle and found Kristin's high-school graduation portrait. A younger version of her daughter sat proud in cap and gown, filled with hope and excitement as she stepped over the threshold of youth into an exciting new world. Had she known then all Kristin would endure, she might have tried to stop time.

Finally Kristin spoke. "Thank you for telling me." A softer look came over her and a half-smile lifted her mouth. "In spite of it all, I don't have any regrets. I loved Luke, and I'm not ashamed of that. Gregory is a part of him I'll always have. And I'm not ashamed of the stories I wrote or the position I took. Dad always taught me to stand up for what I believe in. I think I did that."

"I think you did too. And I…I should have tried harder, to understand you. To believe in you. Can you forgive me?"

"Oh, Mom. I love you. I don't know what I would have done if you and Hayden hadn't come to New York to find me." Kristin hugged her again and Valerie held tight.

"You would have been fine. You're a survivor, Kristin Taylor. I think you forgot that for a few years, but I see your spark coming back. And I think…you're beginning to heal, aren't you?"

"It's not easy. But most days are pretty good now." Kristin gave Valerie a girlish grin that pulled her back to Kristin's childhood in an instant. "Maybe I'm just having a bad day."

"Well." Valerie stood and took a moment before she spoke again. She moved across the room, picking up toys as she went. "Why don't you get away for a few days, take a little trip? We'll keep Gregory with us and you can have some time alone. I have a friend who owns a bed and breakfast up in Stowe. I'm sure she'd have you."

"All right." Kristin nodded, seeming to like the idea. Valerie smiled. Perhaps there was hope to be had after all.

"Am I interrupting?" Hayden poked his head around the door. Valerie waved him in. He entered the room, two letters in hand. "Kris?"

"Yeah?"

Valerie saw her daughter stiffen her resolve as she waited for Hayden to speak. These days, opening the mailbox was much like waiting for a hand grenade to detonate. She or Hayden tried to reach the box before Kristin came home. But if the sparkle in her husband's eyes was anything to go on, this time it wasn't bad news.

Hayden cleared his throat and held up the first envelope. "The editor I sent your manuscript to wants to publish your book." Before Kristin could get a word out, he held up the second envelope, his face split with the widest smile she'd ever seen him wear. "And…you've been nominated for the George Polk award for foreign reporting."

Chapter Thirty-Five

The seven o'clock news blared from the television through the first floor of the rambling farmhouse. In the kitchen, Kristin put the last pot away and dried her hands on the dishtowel and wondered if she dared talk to her mother again about the possibility that she might need hearing aids. Kristin was packed and ready to leave for Stowe in the morning, still riding high on the astonishing news of last week. Her rewards were bittersweet.

The one person she would have loved to share them with was gone.

When she returned from her trip, she prayed she'd have the answers she needed.

Kristin caught Gregory watching her from where he sat coloring at the kitchen table. His expression was often far more serious than any four year-olds should be. She grinned and stuck her tongue out at him. He mirrored her, letting out an enthusiastic belly laugh that squeezed at her heart. His eyes widened a moment later at the loud shriek from the room next door.

Kristin sprinted into the living room, Gregory close behind. Her heart raced at the look of horror on Mom's face. "What?"

Mom and Hayden leaned forward on the couch, glued to the television. Her mother raised a shaking hand, tears pooling in her eyes as she pointed toward the screen.

"Teddy," she whispered.

Kristin frowned. A few years shy of sixty, Mom possessed more energy than a baby foal, yet sometimes gave Kristin cause to doubt her sanity. Like now.

Kristin bit her tongue and turned her attention to the black and white images in front of her. The well-dressed news reporter stood in front of a large airplane in stark contrast to the row of straggly-looking men filing past her as she talked.

The broadcast was covering *Operation Homecoming*—the release of American prisoners, arranged after the signing of The Paris Peace Accords last month. The war over, Americans kept in captivity in prisons across Vietnam for years were finally on their way home. People had been talking about this for weeks.

Kristin planted her feet to the floor and forced herself to view the broadcast.

A lump formed in her throat as she took in the gaunt expressions of the men who walked across the tarmac. As they boarded the jetliner that would fly them back to American soil, some waved and smiled. Some just stared, showing no hint of emotion whatsoever.

Although she couldn't say she knew any of them, she recognized the haunted expressions. Sometimes, even now, almost six years later, Kristin knew she wore that same look.

"He was there, Kristin! I swear to you, I saw my boy! I saw Teddy!"

"Mom, please…" Blood rushed in her ears. She cast a glance at Hayden, but he merely shrugged. Of course he wouldn't know Teddy. They'd never met.

For a moment the faintest glimmer of hope caused her heart to skip a beat. But she pushed it back and gripped cold reality.

Kristin drew her lips together and turned to her mother. "We just talked about this. Teddy's gone and so is Luke. I've accepted it and I'm moving on, just like you want me to. So you need to do the same. Don't talk yourself into believing something that's just not going to happen!" She marched across the room and turned the knob of the television, sending the room into silence. Her heart pitched hard and she searched for calm that seemed out of range.

She waited a minute, ran her hands through her hair and slowly turned to face them. Gregory backed up toward the couch, eyeing her like he would a ferocious dog.

Kristin's erratic pulse decelerated. "I'm sorry. I shouldn't have yelled."

Hayden cleared his throat, got to his feet and moved to where Gregory stood, held out a hand and grinned down at him. "Come on. Papa needs some help in the barn."

Gregory scampered up at once, running over to give her a hug before heading out of the room with Hayden. In the time it took them to pull on coats and boots, Kristin slowed her breathing but jumped as the screen door slammed behind them. The dogs barked out in the front yard.

She sank into an easy chair. Her thoughts swirled, she couldn't think. Hot tears clouded her vision and she blinked them away, self-loathing curling around her heart.

"I'm sorry, Mom," she whispered. "I just hate seeing you have any false hope. You've coped so well. Much better than I have."

Her mother set her jaw, and a far away look crept into her eyes. "I know my son, Kristin. Mark my words, he's coming home."

"Fine, Mom. That's great." Defeat moved in and Kristin failed to keep the tremor out of her voice. She rose and headed for the door. "I need some air."

"Kristin?" Her mother's voice stopped her as she reached the door, left her no choice but to face her again. For a long moment, silence ran between them. A slow smile lifted her mother's lips for just an instant before her serious gaze returned. "If you've 'accepted it', if you believe Luke is dead, that he's not coming back, if you're even thinking about marrying Joshua, I just have one question for you."

"What, Mom?" Kristin exhaled, spent and shattered.

"Why do you still wear Luke's ring on a chain around your neck?"

Kristin stood at her dresser, fiddling with the items strewn over top of the white crocheted doily, her mother's words ringing in her ears.

"Why do you still wear Luke's ring...?"

Joshua probably wondered the same thing.

He'd told her the night he'd proposed that he wanted to give her time. Once she'd made her decision, he said, they'd choose a ring together.

She reached for a shell from her collection, picked it up and turned it over in her hand, held it up to her nose and sniffed. If she closed her eyes, she'd be on the beach at Long Binh. She put the shell back in place. Her fingers hovered over the cluster of wooden stick figures. She couldn't bring herself to touch them anymore and so they sat unused, taunting her. Reminding her of the friend she'd never see again, and the life he'd lost.

Framed photographs took up the rest of the space on the dresser. Pictures of Luke, and the guys she traveled with and written about. Candid shots of Jonno, Caroline and Doc sat in frames of many sizes.

A wry grin chased off her frown as she wondered what the PTA would say about the image of her sitting on the hood of the Jeep holding Luke's M-16.

Enough.

Her sigh was one of defeat, but she knew it was time. God wasn't so far off these days. He'd seen her through the worst, carried her to this point. And now He'd brought another man into her life. A good man. Josh loved her. She would love him and do her best to make him happy. They would build a life of their own, provide a stable home for Gregory.

Kristin pulled open her top drawer, shoved aside papers and socks, and began dropping her treasures into the drawer. She left out a few pictures of Luke for Gregory. She foraged in the drawer once more, retrieving a small velvet box.

"I guess I'm wondering if you might want to get hitched."

Luke's face swam before her. His eyes shone with bright anticipation that day on the beach. He'd stared so intently she thought for a moment that he believed she might say no.

She wondered then if he ever really understood the depth of her love for him. She prayed he had, and that it had carried him through to the end.

Kristin undid the clasp of the gold chain she'd put her ring on some months ago, and slid it off, put it back on her finger, admiring the beauty of the stone, and the miracle of the moment in which Luke had given it to her. He'd taken her completely by surprise.

He always had.

Tremulous fingers closed around the gold band. Tears warmed her cheeks but she ignored them. She twisted the ring off her finger and placed it into the box, determination snapping the lid shut. She put the box on the pile of photographs she'd put away, pushed the drawer shut, crawled into bed, and wept.

It was late when they turned into the gates of the farm the day Kristin returned from her few days in Stowe. Josh and Gregory met her as she reached town, and they went out for pizza. Kristin smiled at the sleeping figure of her son in the backseat. Tomorrow was Saturday. No harm done. She'd sleep in too. She shut off the engine and got out of the car.

Josh pulled up behind her and she waited for him as he stomped through the snow toward her.

All the lights were on in the living room. She frowned. "What time is it?"

"About nine-thirty." Josh opened the passenger door. Kristin stepped back to give him room. Hayden and Mom never stayed downstairs past nine. They rose at the crack of dawn and turned in early. "What's wrong?" Josh straightened and pushed the car door shut, Gregory in his arms.

Kristin shivered and tried to ignore the strange feeling of foreboding. "Nothing. I'm just surprised they're still up. Through the front window she swore she saw people in the living room. As she neared the door, she heard voices. Perhaps it was the television, but she didn't think so. They either had company or Mom really did need those hearing aids.

Kristin squinted across the yard. On the far side of the drive she could just make out the shadowy silhouette of a strange car. She hadn't noticed it on her way in. Mom and Hayden didn't entertain much, but perhaps some friends had dropped in.

"Are you planning on standing there all night, babe?" Joshua hissed from behind. "This kid weighs a ton."

Kristin shot him a feigned look of annoyance and pushed the door open. She stamped her boots on the mat, kicked them off, hung up her coat and made her way into the living room. "We're home What are you..."

Kristin stood in the doorway and stared, her feet stuck to the floor. All rational thought abandoned her, along with every breath of air.

Mom and Hayden sat together on the loveseat near the fire, and shot to their feet as she spoke.

They did have company.

Chapter Thirty-Six

Kristin shut her eyes, afraid to open them again. Because she knew what she saw wasn't possible. Insanity had finally defeated her and celebrated by creating a severe hallucination.

Her brother stood at the far end of the room, and began walking toward her.

And Luke stood right behind him.

Kristin let out a strangled cry, gasped for air and stared at the two men in front of her.

In the dead of night, with sleep out of reach, she had imagined this moment. Imagined the elation she would feel as she ran into Luke's waiting arms. But those dreams had not included Joshua. And she could never have dreamt up the confusion on Luke's face as he looked past her.

In that one instant, the world she knew and had come to accept, spun into a different reality.

"God in heaven." Josh's quiet intake of breath behind her shook her to her senses. She'd shown him pictures of Teddy and Luke. It wouldn't take much to put together what was happening.

Yet still she struggled with the truth in front of her.

She couldn't bring herself to move. Shock seeped through her veins and sent her heart racing. Blood rushed in her ears and hot tears scalded her unbelieving eyes.

Kristin stared at Teddy, opened her mouth, but no words came. Silence thickened the air and strangled speech. The dogs whined, but soon put their heads down again.

"Hi, Sis." Her brother's wide smile jolted through her like a bolt of electricity. "Are you just going to stand there or do I get a hug?"

A faint buzzing sounded in her ears, and her vision blurred. She looked beyond him to make sure she hadn't been seeing things—hadn't just thought she'd seen him—but Luke still stood there, unmoving, piercing blue eyes glued on her.

Luke.

Kristin took a faltering step towards him, and then her knees gave out.

Teddy caught her and drew her into his arms. They sank to the floor and she buried herself in her brother's embrace. The first sob broke the dam and she was pulled down under a torrent of emotion. Relief, anger, grief, fear, awe, elation, she was suffocating beneath the barrage. Every emotion she'd ever felt was back with reinforcements. She heard Luke speak, but she couldn't focus. Strong cords wrapped themselves around her and left her without air. Her mind became a swirl of revived and overpowering feelings. It took all of her strength to raise her head and look at her brother. Luke crouched on her other side, concern narrowing his eyes.

"You were dead," she whispered, gasping, hyperventilating. Her eyes moved to Luke. The tears would not relent. "You...I thought—" She gasped again.

"Shh...it's okay." Teddy stroked her head and smiled, giving her his old nonchalant shrug. "Sorry we couldn't let you know sooner."

Disbelief reined. She reached a hand up to touch Luke's scruff-covered cheek, a strong tremor ripping through her. "It's really you. Oh my God, thank you." His silence terrified her. She needed to hear his voice, had to know for sure she wasn't really hallucinating.

"Hi, Kris." A brief smile crossed his face as he drew closer, rested his forehead against hers for just a moment and released a shuddering sigh. Then he captured her eyes once more and Kristin felt her world tilt again. The sorrow within them said all he couldn't. He rose and left her, going to stand before the fire.

Tears blurred her vision as she tried to focus on her brother. She wasn't going insane. Oh, he was so thin! She felt his ribs poking through the flannel shirt he wore as she hugged him once more.

Kristin tried to breathe normally. "When? How? I don't understand..."

"Sweetheart, sit." Hayden came up behind her with a chair. Mom followed with a glass of water. Kristin sank into the chair and put her head in her hands trying desperately to stop crying. Teddy crouched at her side, placed a hand on her knee and waited until she lifted her head again.

"I know it's a shock. We were released over the weekend. They had reporters and TV crews there. We flew back home, they held us for a few days debriefing—took longer than we wanted. Luke got a special visit from the CIA boys before we left Vietnam, but I had to stand in line with the rest of the guys back here. But we finally got here."

The volley of information hit hard and fast with little time for comprehension.

"Released?" she squeaked. "What are you talking about? Released from where, Teddy?" Nausea worked upward and Kristin swallowed. She took in his sunken cheeks and thin frame and a sob ripped through her.

Please, God, no.

"Hanoi."

The atrocious word slapped her and she recoiled. She drew in long breaths and tried to think. "No. That's not possible…you…both of you? You were together?"

Her brother nodded, tears pooling. "They got Luke in '68, me in '70. Sorry we didn't write."

Only Luke seemed to appreciate Teddy's sense of humor.

"In '68? But that means…you…" She swiveled and met Luke's eyes at last, and saw pain flash through them.

"Yes." He pushed his shoulders back, ran a hand down his face and nodded. "That's why I never made it back to see you off. I got a little tied up."

Teddy gave a half laugh that petered out with the look of horror her mother shot him.

Kristin refused the truth. It wasn't possible. They couldn't have been POW's.

She knew what they did to prisoners.

A muted cry snaked out of her as she raised her head again. Joshua still stood near the doorway, holding Gregory, his face ashen, like he'd had too much rice wine.

"Josh," she whispered, not knowing what else to say.

"I'll take him upstairs," he said quietly. Kristin let out her breath and struggled to her feet.

"Wait." Luke spat the word out.

Kristin spun around at the sound of his voice. Tension put her down a foxhole, waiting for the first air strike. Luke's questioning gaze rippled through her entire being. One look told her he was fully aware that Gregory belonged to him.

Luke folded his arms across his chest. Uncertainty spread across his face as he looked from her to Joshua. But then he fixed his eyes on Gregory.

Kristin guarded her heart and mind and prayed through the silence, powerless to do anything else as Luke moved past her to where Joshua stood. He stood beside him and stared at his son. A small smile curved his mouth upward. When he raised a hand toward Gregory's blond head, Kristin moved.

"Please don't wake him up." Her harsh whisper fell like incoming fire.

Luke lowered his hand. "I wasn't going to."

Joshua sidestepped him and left the room. Kristin's heart lurched over the precipice of reason at the agonized look he wore. Luke mirrored Joshua's expression.

"Who is that?" He sounded like he had a bad case of laryngitis. Eyes of the most dazzling blue—eyes she'd thought she'd never see again except in the face of her son—held questions she didn't want to answer.

"He...he's..." Fog rolled in again. A strong arm came around her shoulders and Hayden hugged her to him.

"Joshua Brentwood. He's been a good friend to Kristin."

"I see." Luke shifted, narrowing his eyes.

"Luke, please...I..." Speech became impossible again. Kristin lost herself in the sight of him, taking in everything. He stood as tall as she remembered, his hair just as blond, but long and unkempt. The lower half of his jaw was covered in a beard that glinted with flecks of gray and gold. The jeans and deep blue wool sweater he wore looked new.

The truth staggered her. She wasn't dreaming. This was really happening. Luke was alive!

"Please…" Kristin stepped forward, unable to quell the urge to go to him, touch him.

He took a step backward and held up a hand. "Don't." His eyes searched the room until they landed on her brother.

"It's okay, Luke." Teddy was at his side immediately. Luke inhaled, in and out in controlled movements. Kristin watched helpless and beaten, tears springing to her eyes.

Joshua returned, hesitating in the doorway, as though assessing the situation. Her racing pulse picked up speed and she thought she really would faint this time. He crossed the room in three swift steps and put a protective arm around her.

Teddy came forward. "I'm Teddy." Her brother extended a hand toward Josh, unsmiling. Luke stiffened behind him, his eyes blue chips of ice. Teddy glanced at him and hesitated. "And this is Luke. Kristin's, uh…Gregory's… uh…father."

Joshua nodded, his jaw set, his eyes hooded. "Glad you both made it home. God is good."

Teddy cleared his throat, mumbled some reply. They stood like statues for what felt like an eternity. Kristin could only stare at them, still not sure what was real.

"Why don't you all sit?" Her mother got up. "I can make tea."

Luke thrust his hands into the pockets of his jeans, his mouth drawn. "No. Thanks. I need to get some air." He concentrated on Teddy. "Can we…take a ride?"

"No. Wait." Kristin felt herself slipping off the cliff, about to crash onto the rocks below. "You can't leave," she whispered. "We'll make some tea, have something to eat. We can…"

"Honey, it's late." Mom approached, her frozen smile said not to argue. "Maybe we should get some sleep. Luke, you and Teddy can have the guest room. I'm sure in the morning…"

Luke cleared his throat, glanced at Kristin and shook his head. "Thanks, Mrs. Thorne, but I…don't think I should stay here."

Valerie lifted an eyebrow and went to stand beside her husband. "Where will you go? The nearest hotel is miles away."

Luke didn't answer, just left the room in long strides.

"I'll be back," Teddy chased him down and Kristin followed, desperation clinging to her like a swamp leech.

"Wait, Luke!" She stopped in the hallway, her heart racing. Teddy pulled on his coat and groaned, shaking his head. Luke was halfway out the door. "Luke! Please, don't go."

Luke paused long enough to turn in her direction. Torment screamed from his eyes. He blinked under the dim light, his jaw twitching. "I'm sorry. I...can't handle this right now."

"You don't understand..." Scalding tears coursed down her cheeks as she stared at him. Guilt tightened its hold and laughed as it shook her.

Luke gave her a long, lingering look, his eyes too bright. "Don't I? I've been gone five years, Kris. That's a long time. You don't need to explain. I get the picture." He walked out of the house, closing the front door behind him.

"Where is he going?" She twisted the bottom of her sweater and stared at Teddy, fear clawing.

"I don't know. I'll...try to stop him." Teddy leaned in and kissed her cheek before tearing outside after Luke.

Kristin returned to the living room, numb. Josh, Mom and Hayden huddled in a small group by the fire, talking in murmurs.

"Did you know they were coming?" She wasn't sure who to address the question to. Her mother rushed to her and hugged her tight. "Sweetheart, come and sit down."

"No." Kristin stepped back and folded her arms. "Just...tell me. How did this happen?"

Mom swiped tears and sniffed. "We got a call at the beginning of the week, after you left for Stowe. I...we...didn't want to give you the news over the phone. And we weren't sure how long it would all take for them to get here. Then..." She put a hand to her head, her face a mixture of sorrow and joy. "Teddy called from Colonel Maddox's house late last night. Told us they were coming up here. We tried to reach you this morning, but you'd already left."

Kristin waved her off, took small, faltering steps until she reached the couch and sank into it. She put her head in her hands and tried to breathe normally.

Panic exploded the effort.

"What am I supposed to do? Dear God, what do I do?"

She didn't realize she had spoken out loud until she looked up and found Josh staring at her, surprise clouding his eyes. His sigh filled the room and told of defeat. "I…uh…think I'll go home. I'll call you tomorrow."

Kristin nodded, but couldn't speak. Much as she wanted to reassure him, she didn't know how. As Josh turned to go, Teddy returned, his face flushed. His thick down jacket hung open, snow dripped from his hair.

"Where's Luke? Did you find him?" Kristin settled an expectant gaze on him.

He shrugged his shoulders, worry creasing his forehead. "He took off in the car we rented. Wouldn't let me go with him. I don't know where he would go. He was…uh…pretty shook up. Snow's really coming down."

Joshua strode out of the room, the front door slamming shut behind him. The lights on the side tables rattled. The noise roused the dogs. They barked only once, shut down by Hayden's sharp command.

Kristin groaned and sank against the cushions, her throat constricting. Out of the corner of her eye she saw the questioning look Teddy aimed at their mother. Mom shrugged and dabbed her eyes with a tissue.

Hayden puffed out air and moved toward the door. "Dear Lord, help us all," he muttered. "I'm going to let the dogs out."

Teddy shifted where he stood, still in his boots. A pool of moisture spread onto the rug around them but he didn't notice. "You're not…Kris, you're not married to that guy are you?"

"No." She let out a cry and shook her head. "Not yet."

Chapter Thirty-Seven

At around four the next morning, Kristin gave up on sleep, pulled on jeans and a sweatshirt and padded downstairs. She rummaged in the kitchen as quietly as possible and put on a pot of coffee. Mom and Hayden wouldn't be up for another hour or so.

When the coffee perked, she filled her mug and sat, staring numbly at the clock on the wall.

"Hey." Teddy wandered in, disheveled in a pair of gray sweats and navy sweater.

Kristin managed a smile, still reeling from the shock of having him in the same room. "Did I wake you?"

He helped himself to coffee and joined her at the oak table. "No. I heard you get up. I'm not sleeping too well, not used to a real bed yet." He chest rattled with a cough and he stretched his thin arms high over his head.

"You should see a doctor." Purple shadows circled his eyes and told a story she wasn't ready to hear.

Teddy waved a hand. "Seen one, but knowing Mom I'll have an appointment by the beginning of the week." He cradled his mug. "As soon as it's a decent enough hour, I'll call Colonel Maddox. Maybe Luke went there."

"You think he would drive all the way back to Doc's? Doesn't he live in New Jersey?"

"Yeah. Who knows?" Teddy shrugged. "I don't think he was expecting that last night, Kris. To see you walk in with someone else."

"Well, I wasn't expecting to see him, so I guess we're even."

Teddy grinned and took another sip. "Colonel Maddox says they don't hear from you. Caroline's home now, did you know that?"

"She wrote a while back." Kristin swallowed hot liquid along with remorse. "How is she?"

"She looks pretty good to me, but then I have been locked up for a few years." Teddy's grin broadened and Kristin couldn't stop a smile. Her brother hesitated, as though unsure of what to say. "I think they felt like you shut them out when you came home, that you didn't want them to be a part of your life or Gregory's. Is that true?" Confusion riddled his question.

She fingered the quilted material placemat in front of her and wrestled with the past. "In a way. They stayed in-country a long time after I left. Hoping for word of Luke, I imagine. Doc called when he came home last year, but I—I couldn't see him. I'd moved on. It's just..."

"Easier not to. Because he would remind you of Luke." As always, Teddy understood her. "They told me they've never met Gregory."

It wasn't an accusation, but Kristin felt the weight of it. "Not yet. I assume you were the one who told Luke about him?" It was the only answer that made sense.

Her brother nodded. "I thought he knew. He…he was pretty rattled when I told him."

"I wanted to tell him before I left, Teddy, but I—never got the chance." She looked away for a moment, hating the guilt she still dealt with.

Teddy fiddled with the handle of his mug, his clear eyes never leaving her face. "Kris, I'm so sorry you had to be here all alone. I wish…"

"No." She reached for her brother's hands. "I managed. And, eventually, I realized that God was looking out for me. I'm starting to believe He's got a plan for my life after all. Well, up until last night, that is." She fought doubt and confusion once again. "I wish I knew where He was going with the plan right now, Teddy. I've never been more confused."

Teddy searched her face in silence. "Do you love him?"

Kristin turned from the question. Her eyes burned, her chest sore from the effort it took to keep this insufferable emotion in check. She watched the first streaks of light stretch across the horizon of the fields beyond the kitchen window. "I've always loved him."

"I was talking about Joshua."

She caught his knowing smile before it disappeared. Anguish tore into her flesh like a bullet, systematically shredding what was left of her heart. How was it possible to love two men at the same time, in very different ways?

She didn't have the answer for that one.

When Teddy took himself upstairs to shower, Kristin went to the phone. She knew the number by heart and dialed it often.

"Whoever you are, this better be important."

Tears stung at the sound of the voice still heavy with sleep on the other end. "Hey, Cassie. Sorry I woke you."

"Kristin? Girl, is that you?"

"Yeah, it's me." She leaned against the counter and closed her eyes. "Cass, I need your help. I don't know what to do. Luke's home."

"He's not there." Teddy hung up the phone with a defeated sigh. "Colonel Maddox and Caroline are leaving now, they should be here by afternoon. Hopefully we'll find him before then."

Kristin cleared the breakfast table, the dishes clattering in her trembling hands.

Mom rose, put a hand on her arm and shook her head. "I'll do it. You sit."

Kristin obeyed, thankful for her mother's understanding. "Where would he go? Teddy, what did Doc say?" A frantic edge crept into her tone as she slumped in her chair. Teddy took a seat opposite her and glanced at Hayden.

"He said they own a cabin, maybe an hour or less from here. He thinks Luke might have gone there. I took down directions." He pushed a piece of paper across the table.

Hayden read the scrawled letters with a grunt. "Yes. I think I know where that is."

"But he said it hasn't been used in years. It's not winterized and it's all locked up. Luke wouldn't have a key."

Teddy's furrowed brow made Kristin smile. "Luke wouldn't need a key."

"Right." His eyes crinkled as a sudden chuckle escaped him. "Well, we can drive up there if you want. There's no phone."

Kristin's mind raced with confusing thoughts. Saturday. "Gregory's going to a friend's house to play. I can go. I think I should go alone."

Her mother joined them at the table and cast a worried look in her direction. "No, sweetheart. I don't think that's wise. He looked so...rough."

"Mom." Kristin scowled, annoyance tempting her to lash out. Mom had plenty of reasons not to want her going up there alone, but Luke's appearance wasn't one of them. "He's not going to hurt me. I'll be fine."

Mom looked to Teddy for approval. To Kristin's surprise, her brother shook his head.

"I think it's better if I go with you." He raised a hand at his mother's short intake of breath. "All I'm saying is, he's had a shock. We're just back and...it's hard...you know? He's not crazy or anything, Mom, he's just..."

"He's not going to forgive me, is he?" Kristin knew what Teddy wanted to say.

What he couldn't say.

Luke had spent the last five years holding on to life with the goal of returning to her. When Teddy told him about their son, he'd no doubt found even more reason to stay alive, dreamt about coming home and being a family. And she'd shattered that dream the minute she'd walked into the room with Joshua. The look on his face said it was like losing his family all over again. Only this time, right in front of his eyes.

"I think..." Teddy rested his chin on his hands, his gaze unwavering. "He's going to need some time. We're all going to need time, Kris. You can't go barreling in there and try to put things right in a couple of hours. You don't even know what it is you want."

Kristin left the table.

What did she want?

She paced the kitchen, listening to the sounds of Saturday cartoons filtering through the hall from the living room. She'd have to talk to Gregory. Soon. But she needed to talk to Luke first.

She turned on her heel, desperation overriding diplomacy. "I just want...to see him, Teddy. I need...to...see him."

"All right." Teddy rose and went to her, the depth of understanding they'd always shared still there, shining for her in his eyes. "Then we'll go."

Chapter Thirty-Eight

*L*uke paced the front room of the cabin, clenching and unclenching his fists, trying to get the image of another man holding his son out of his head.

The moment had yanked him back to the torture chambers of Hanoi.

He hadn't known what to say, who to look at first. None of them had. The shock on Kristin's face would be forever seared in his memory.

Luke kicked at the worn-out brown shag carpet and punched the air. Mixed emotions raged all night, churning within him like waves predicting a coming storm. In the back of his mind, where lucid thought dozed, he'd sometimes reasoned that she would move on with her life, find someone else. But to know…to see for himself…he wasn't able to process that yet.

He picked up a stray cushion from the couch, hurled it across the room and cursed as it knocked over the lamp on the table.

Clearly, she'd believed he was dead.

Why wouldn't she?

Whoever this Joshua was, Luke knew he was more than just the 'friend' Hayden tried to explain him away as. The look on the guy's face last night told the whole story.

Luke muttered prayers and tried to make sense of his thoughts as he righted the lamp and chucked the cushion back onto the couch. Hunger gnawed at him. He'd left the farm in such a hurry that by the time he reached the cabin he hadn't given any thought to the fact that there wouldn't be any food or water.

And it was a good thing there was no alcohol to be had.

He'd filled a large pot with snow the night before and set it in front of the fire to melt. At least he now had fresh water. He grabbed a mug from the shelf above the sink, filled it, and drank deeply.

Wind rattled the old windows, jarring his thoughts from the state of the cabin. Luke glanced outside. Snow came down in gusts of white, swirling every which way, mirroring his emotions.

He released a deep sigh and forced calm. Being cooped up in here for too long wouldn't do much to preserve what was left of his sanity. He took measured steps through the small kitchen into the living room. He'd go back to the farm later, once he figured out what to say, how to handle whatever news she would give him.

A loud rap on the door jolted him. One of the neighbors must have seen his car and come to investigate. He made his way over to the front door, opened it a crack.

Luke took one look at them and rolled his eyes to the ceiling. "What are you doing here?"

"Open up!" Teddy yelled above the wind. "It's freezing out here."

Luke muttered under his breath and stepped aside. Teddy fell into the room, his arms laden with grocery bags. Kristin followed, carrying something wrapped in a colorful dishtowel. Whatever it was, it smelled good. Hunger overpowered his anger and he kicked the door shut and stood back. "How did you find me?"

"I called your Dad." Teddy veered his gaze and looked around the room.

Luke groaned and shook his head. "Great. He and Caroline are probably already on the way. Thanks, Preacher."

Teddy grinned, shaking snow from his hair. "The weather isn't the greatest. You've got a few hours to get cleaned up before they arrive. Where's the kitchen? Mom sent food."

Luke nodded toward the hall. "Through there." Kristin moved past him without a word, and Teddy followed. Luke sauntered after them. "I didn't get the impression your mother liked me."

Kristin set her parcel down on the square table in the kitchen and unwrapped it. Luke moved in, getting a whiff of whatever was in the brown casserole dish.

She glanced his way and he recognized hesitation in her eyes. "My mother can't stand to see a man starve to death. It's a breakfast Frittata. Do you have plates?"

They'd even brought two flasks of coffee. Luke threw some cutlery onto the table, found some plates, blew dust off them and they dug in. He and Teddy wolfed down almost the entire dish before he realized Kristin hadn't eaten any of it.

He settled his eyes on her when she wasn't looking his way. Which was often. In fact she seemed to be making a concerted effort not to look at him.

Teddy pushed his empty plate away. "How'd you sleep?"

"I didn't." The fork he held slipped from his hand and clattered onto the plate. Kristin startled, staring up at them through wide doe eyes. She cleared her throat and reached for more coffee. She could hardly pick up the Thermos. Luke's hand came over hers and she pulled back at once, searing him with that deer-in-the-headlights look again. He managed to right the Thermos before any spilled out. He took her cup and filled it for her.

Concern for her nudged his conscience as he watched her cradle the mug with both hands. She was more jumpy than the guy picked to walk point.

After a while she rose and began to clear their plates. Teddy stood to help but Kristin waved him off. He sank down again with a yawn.

"There's no water," Luke told her as she turned the tap.

The Corelle plates crashed into the sink. "Good. Then I don't have to wash up."

Luke grinned at her backhanded answer. He didn't want to, but couldn't help it. Memories skipped around him, teasing and taunting, reminding him of better days.

He wasn't ready for this.

He ran a hand over his face and saw Teddy watching him. "What are you looking at?"

Teddy folded his arms on the table and fixed him with his most annoying now-it's-time-for-the-lecture look. Luke had received many of them over the years, and wasn't in the mood for one this morning. "Don't start with me, Preacher."

Teddy raised a hand. "Luke, you can't stay here. There's no electricity, no running water. It's below zero out there, and they're predicting snowstorms for the rest of the weekend."

"Where do you suggest I stay then?" Luke narrowed his eyes. He noticed Kristin had put her coat back on. She moved to the doorway. "Leaving so soon?"

She shook her head. "Can we go in there, by the fire? It's freezing in here."

"Help yourself."

They bolted for the next room. Luke rubbed his eyes and tugged on his sweater. Wimps. It wasn't *that* cold. He watched his breath hang in the air as he exhaled. A wry grin moved across his mouth. Okay, maybe it was.

Luke made his way back to the living room. Teddy threw another log on the fire. Kristin huddled on the couch under the blanket Luke had discarded. She lifted her head as he approached, but her eyes veered away at once.

Every time he looked at her, he lost a little more hope.

How would they survive this?

Luke grunted at the ache in his legs, lowered himself into the wooden rocking chair in front of the fire, and let out a deep breath. He drew his lips together and stared at Kristin.

She raised her head again and finally made eye contact. Her hair was longer and hung around her face. Her skin seemed to have lost the healthy glow he remembered. The dark shadows that circled her eyes told him she didn't sleep much either.

An unexpected smile worked its way across her mouth. Luke felt it clear to the tips of his toes. Her eyes lit with their old sparkle for just a moment, a hint of color touching her cheeks.

Lord help him, she was so beautiful.

Teddy sighed—loudly and with much aggravation. "This is stupid. Come on back to the house with us. Mom's fine with it. She and Hayden insist."

Luke dislodged the lump in his throat and coughed. "I'm not so sure that's best."

Kristin's mouth turned downward into the scowl he remembered all too well. "You can't stay here and freeze to death."

"No. That would be too convenient I suppose." He cracked his knuckles and took in the flash of pain that swept across her face, but steeled his heart against it.

"Shut up, Luke." It was a promising comeback, but it fizzled too quickly. She seemed to have lost the tenacity she possessed in Vietnam. The spark he'd once loved about her had been snuffed out. Time had changed her.

Changed them all.

She stared at the fire and worked on chewing a fingernail. From where he sat, Luke had a clear view of her left hand.

The ring he'd given her all those years ago was no longer there.

But no new ring replaced it.

Silence skipped around the room and mocked him. At this rate he'd send her running into the guy's arms. Good going, Maddox.

The wind picked up and screamed its presence, howling through the tall pines and lashing the windows. Kristin shivered and pulled the blanket tighter around her thin shoulders.

Teddy coughed and shifted from one foot to the other. "Um…I think I'll get some more coffee. Anybody…nope…okay." He beat a hasty retreat into the kitchen.

Luke smothered a grin. Tact had never been the kid's strong point.

Kristin made a shaky sound that resembled a muffled sob. He watched her wipe her eyes and slowly shift her position back toward him. For a long moment, all she did was stare, as though she still couldn't believe what she saw.

Luke sat back and had to catch his breath. He was having trouble with the idea as well—that he was out of Hanoi—home—with Kristin less than four feet away.

He ached to hold her. Take her in his arms and tell her how much he loved her. How he had longed to see her again.

Luke pushed down desire and prayed for self-control. Much as he wanted to ask her about this Joshua fellow, it could wait. He leaned forward, put his elbows on his knees and rested his chin between his fingers. "Tell me about Gregory."

Another smile lit her features and took him by surprise. "He's great. He's doing really well. He...um...he likes to read. Books, magazines, newspapers—the back of the cereal box." Kristin's eyes glowed with new light. "He's too smart for his own good, talks non-stop, has a definite stubborn streak and a rather explosive temper."

Laughter scratched his throat. "Must take after his mother." His smile broadened at the flush that crept into her pale cheeks.

"Actually, he's always reminded me of you." Kristin's tone softened and her eyes grew wet. She lowered her head. Her hair fell over her shoulders and hid her eyes. She placed her hands palms down on her knees and he saw her stiffen as she drew in a breath. The flames from the fire cast an orange glow across her face. When she brought her head up again, tears streaked her cheeks. "I thought you were dead, Luke. I really did."

Luke inhaled and nodded, clenching his fingers together. "I gathered that."

He pushed himself out of the rocker and walked the length of the room. Familiar anger hammered at him, demanding retribution. Luke turned back to face her and prayed for wisdom before he let himself speak. "I'm not trying to make things harder on you, Kris. Really, I'm not. But I found out I had a son when I was locked up in Hanoi and couldn't do a bloody thing about it. I was in there five years, and spent the last three just keeping myself alive...asking God to keep you safe, protect you and Gregory until I could come home. Sending another man to take my place wasn't quite what I had in mind."

She got to her feet, met him where he stood, and took hold of his hands. A look of panic ran across her face. Her fingers were cold, but her eyes lit with fire. "Joshua could never take your place, Luke! Gregory's known about you since he was old enough to understand. He's got pictures of you all over his room. He asks me to tell him stories about you—about us—all the time." She let him go and dragged her fingers through her hair. "He knows more about Vietnam than most adults I've met, poor kid." Kristin moved away from him and stood before the fire.

Fresh silence was punctuated by the odd crash coming from the kitchen. Luke couldn't imagine what Teddy was doing. Probably chasing mice. He'd always enjoyed the sport in Hanoi.

When she faced him and spoke again, her eyes pleaded understanding. "Luke…he needs you in his life. He needs his father. I want you to be a part of his life."

"Just his?"

Kristin lowered her gaze. "It's complicated."

The soft-spoken words ripped at his heart. Luke pinched his eyes with his thumb and forefinger, took deep measured breaths. He forced himself not to go to her, grab her, and shake her to her senses.

"I guess it is. But maybe we should talk about it."

"We will. I just…I don't know what to say right now."

"There's a switch." He brushed past her, picked up the last log in the tarnished copper tub and hurled it into the fireplace. The wood cracked and hissed and he turned in time to see Kristin jump back and let out a cry. Even with the distance between them he saw her hands shaking. His anger melted away.

Something was very wrong.

She looked so helpless, so fragile standing there, staring at him through wide eyes, fearful. Almost childlike, as though she didn't understand what was happening any better than he did.

Luke closed the gap that separated them and pulled her against him. He didn't think about whether it was a good idea or not. Gut reactions always preceded rational thought when she was involved.

She crumbled the minute his arms came around her. Luke shut his eyes against the sounds of her stifled sobs and held her trembling body close. He breathed in the smell of her, her hair, the perfume she'd always worn—the way she fit into his embrace like the last piece of a puzzle—old feelings surged through him like the morning tide, woke him from the nightmare that had been his life and slowly unlocked the chains around his heart.

This was the moment he'd dreamed of. Holding her again. Feeling her arms around him. Whatever came next didn't matter. If this was all he could have, right here, right now, he'd take it.

She lifted her eyes to his, blinking through tears. Her hand shook as she placed it against the side of his face. Luke threaded his fingers through her hair and allowed his lips to touch her forehead. He wondered if he still had the right to kiss her the way he really wanted to.

The agonized look she wore told him he didn't.

"I thought you were dead," she whispered.

Luke managed a smile and drew back, the feel of her hand against his skin scorching him. "I wish you'd stop saying that. It's morbid." He took another step back, his pulse racing. If he didn't put some distance between them he'd be in trouble. And she'd be out of here quicker than a grenade charging out of an M-20.

"So." Luke swallowed, and ran a hand over his hair. He hadn't planned on asking her—not today—but something urged him on. He had to know. "When did you find out you were pregnant?"

Chapter Thirty-Nine

Kristin fought the urge to run from the cabin and floor the truck back to the farm. Being in Luke's arms, seeing a flicker of hope in his eyes as he'd walked toward her and pulled her against him made her want to forget everything.

The feelings she'd locked away years ago had somehow escaped. Resurfaced the minute she'd laid eyes on him again, and now clamored for recognition.

She floundered for words and tried to think clearly. She'd lived through explosions, dodged bullets and spent nights under fire not knowing if she'd make it to morning. The fear she'd conquered then seemed laughable compared to the terror Luke's blazing eyes evoked.

If she made it through the next minute, she might survive this.

"Kristin?"

She hesitated, the temptation to lie great. But it would be pointless. He could do the math. And she wanted whatever relationship they would have from this point forward to be based on the truth, nothing less.

"I didn't know for sure before I left Vietnam, but I was pretty certain."

"And you chose not to tell me?" Anger flared in his eyes.

Kristin folded her arms and glared. "No. I was going to tell you...I tried to tell you that day, before you left...but...you were so angry."

"What are you talking about?"

"The day you found out about my story, the day you left. Remember? I was going to tell you then, but you had to go...you said whatever it was it could wait."

"I remember." His sharp intake of breath ignited every nerve in her body. "God, I'm sorry."

"I wouldn't have kept it from you, Luke. I've lived with the regret of not telling you that day for all these years. I hope you can believe that."

The crackling of the fire dominated the musty room. Kristin fought against the sorrow trying to pull her heart to pieces. She made herself look at him, and willed him to say something.

Luke moved past her and went to stand at the window at the far side of the room. Kristin felt all breath leave her body. She sank onto the worn couch and put her head in her hands. Tears ran unchecked down her cheeks.

Eventually he took slow steps back to where she sat. Kristin raised her head and took in the anguish chiseled into his features. "I suppose it doesn't matter now." He raised his hands and let them drop to his sides. The tendon along his jaw line pounded. "I tried to come back, Kristin. I knew the way I left that day was wrong. I couldn't let you leave without telling you that I forgave you. I walked off the job to do it. I was ambushed just outside the DMZ. Didn't even see them coming."

Kristin felt powerless to move, pinned under his tortured gaze. "You… you were coming back?"

A sad smile lifted his mouth. "Yeah. I was coming back."

She sat there and watched the flames. A cold wind ran through the cabin, took all feeling with it and left her wanting, raw inside. His face bore scars that told more than she wanted to imagine. And in his eyes she saw a different kind of pain. "When they listed you MIA, I didn't want to believe it. Couldn't believe it. I spent a long time waiting, hoping, praying that one day you'd come home…and then I met Josh."

Luke backed off and sat opposite her. "And lived happily ever after."

Irritation picked at wounds she'd thought were well on the way to healing. "I know you're angry…"

"Angry?" He shoved his fingers through his straggly mess of hair. "Who says I'm angry? What do I have to be angry about? All this time, I hoped I'd have a family to come home to. Seems that's not the case. But perhaps it's as much as I deserve."

"Why would you say that?"

Luke shrugged. "Everything I did over there. The decisions I made…"

"That's ridiculous, Luke. This isn't some way of God punishing you. Or me. It's just…" Kristin squared her jaw. "I thought you weren't coming back."

"You thought wrong." Luke rested his hands behind his head. "And if memory serves me correctly, we were still engaged when you left Vietnam. So pardon me if I'm not overjoyed at the fact that you've found someone else to share your life with."

Bitterness dripped from his words and she refused to accept it. "Do you think this is easy for me, Luke? You want me to just tell Joshua to take a hike because you're back now and I don't need him anymore? That's not right."

Luke drew in a breath and stared. "You always did have a rather strange view of what was 'right', didn't you?"

"If you're going to bring up that story, don't. I can't—"

"Can't what, Kris? Justify it?"

"I can justify it all right…but I won't rehash it. You know why I wrote it and you know what it cost me…what it cost us both. Besides, I thought you said you'd forgiven me." She couldn't look at him. Couldn't bear the pain on his face a moment longer.

"I have." He breathed out a curse. "I've had a lot of time to mull it over."

"Luke—"

"Look…" He waved a hand, eyes flashing in the dimly lit room. "I don't want to fight with you. When can I see Gregory?"

"Whenever you want." She almost whispered the words, unable to trust her voice. "Just…let me talk to him first. Okay?"

"Fine. Go talk to him. I'll be there later." He pushed to his feet, strode past her and disappeared into a darkened part of the cabin. The slamming of a door shook her to the core.

Kristin stared into the flames, watching them die down. The room grew cold. Numbness settled in again. She crumpled to her knees and gave her sobs their freedom.

She jumped as Teddy's arms came around her and he held her close.

Kristin raised her head, her throat burned so badly she could hardly get words out. "That didn't go so well."

"I heard." He smoothed her hair down and attempted a smile. As always, Teddy would try to make her feel better. "He's angry right now, Kris, but it'll be okay. You'll see."

Kristin shook her head, grief plowing over any joy she felt at having them home. "I'm not so sure, Teddy. This is all my fault." The thought seeped into her consciousness the minute she'd heard where Luke had been.

If she'd told him that day…insisted that he listen…perhaps he would never have left Saigon.

Never been captured.

"I'll talk to him." Teddy sounded tired and unsure of himself.

Kristin gripped his hands. "Don't. Let's just go. Please…" She struggled to her feet, her hands trembling as she fiddled with the zipper of her coat. She shot a furtive glance down the hall. "He said he'd come back later, to see Gregory." She had no strength left. It was all she could do to make it out to the truck.

She and Teddy arrived back at the farm to see another unfamiliar car parked at the side of the house. It had to be Doc and Caroline.

Delectable aromas filled the house. Apple pie, banana loaf and fresh bread made Kristin's mouth water. Mom must have been in the kitchen all morning. Whenever she was upset or angry, she baked.

They entered the house, removed coats and boots, and took slow steps into the living room. Her mother and Hayden sat on the couch. Coffee and pie had already been served.

"Kris!" Caroline reached her first, drawing her in to a long hug. "It's so good to see you."

Kristin managed a smile and wiped back tears as Doc embraced her next.

"Hello, Kristin. How've you been?"

She didn't think he expected an answer so she didn't give one. She found a chair and sat, drew her knees up and wrapped her arms around them and tried to make sense of the past twenty-four hours.

Hayden and her mother returned to their afternoon chores. Teddy hovered, sitting, getting up, and then sitting again. He seemed unable to keep still.

"How is Luke?" Doc directed the question at Teddy, his eyes filled with worry. Kristin saw her brother shrug.

"He's upset." Teddy shrugged, his eyes hooded, his mouth drawn. He looked on the verge of tears and she grew concerned.

Caroline snorted and sent a scathing glance her way. "Of course he's upset! Who wouldn't be upset? He gets home after five years of hell and finds out…"

"Caroline, enough." Docs' sharp warning reverberated around the room.

Kristin closed her eyes for a moment. In the past she would have retaliated without a second thought. Found some smart remark and hurled it back at Caroline. Not today.

Teddy cleared his throat. "He'll be okay. I don't know—he—I don't know…" He flashed her a look that hinted of anger and left the room.

Kristin stared after him, a chill running down her spine. She'd suddenly turned into the villain here, and there wasn't a thing she could do about it. Fresh emotion burned up her throat.

"I'm sorry I snapped at you. Are you all right?" Caroline pulled her long blonde hair over one shoulder, crossed her legs, and stared unabashed.

"No." Kristin chewed on her thumbnail. "No, I'm not all right, Caroline."

"What did Luke say? Is he planning to hold vigil in that cabin indefinitely?"

"No. He…" Kristin pressed trembling hands to her knees. "He's coming back this afternoon. To see Gregory."

"Assuming you'll allow him."

"Caroline! That's not fair." Kristin snapped her head up, grappled with the truth as it threatened to strangle her.

"You cut us off, Kris. I sent you letters and you never wrote back to me, not once. I didn't know where you were until Dad told me. And you haven't seen him since he came home—he hasn't even met his own grandson. So don't talk to me about fair!"

Doc cleared his throat, studying her with that quizzical expression she'd forgotten. "That's in the past now. Kristin, we know you haven't had an easy time of it. Your mother told us. How you can't sleep—your paranoia—honey, you're not alone. It's common behavior for men in battle, and for the men and women who've seen and heard the things we have. They call it by different names, shell shock, battle fatigue, but the symptoms are the same. We just need to figure out how to treat it."

"Common behavior?" Kristin laughed, acid churning in her stomach. "That's a comfort. The next generation being raised by a bunch of deranged psychopaths."

Awkward silence ruled. Kristin tried to clear her head, not ready to think of what came next. Her gaze moved to Caroline, taking in the fancy clothes and careful makeup that didn't quite conceal the dark circles beneath her eyes. "Can we start again? How've you been?"

Caroline shrugged, a smile flirting with her lips. "Surviving. I came home about six months ago. I've been in Paris. I…well…I ended a bad relationship and decided maybe it was time I went back to the States. I'm in New York now, working for NBC. I've sworn off men forever."

"I'm sorry." Kristin managed a smile as she caught remnants of her old friend in the mischievous grin that came and went too quickly. She turned to Doc, and her heart swelled. Despite the shock and pain seeing them brought, she had missed him. Missed them both. Time had left streaks of gray in his hair and new lines around his eyes. "How are you, Doc?"

"I've been okay. Bought a house in New Jersey, tried to find something meaningful to do with my retirement. I've been working on opening a Vet center. I'm sure you've seen how the boys are treated once they get home. They need somewhere to go, someone to talk to. People who understand."

Kristin nodded, and watched the flames rise and fall in the fireplace. "We've set one up here too. Nobody really does understand. Unless you've been there, you have no idea…" The wood popped, crackled and sent sparks flying, and she almost jumped out of her chair.

"It's just the fire," Caroline said needlessly.

Kristin rested her head in her hands and closed her eyes, willing her frazzled nerves to stillness. She'd accepted her lack of control over these knee-jerk reactions a while ago, but still recoiled with embarrassment.

"How is he, Kristin?" Doc asked. "Your boy?"

Kristin faced him and caught his pained expression. The dogs began to bark and she heard a car door slam, Gregory shouting goodbye. She smiled for what felt like the first time in forever, and got to her feet. "See for yourself."

She went to the front door, waved her thanks to them for bringing Gregory home, and ushered him in out of the cold. He struggled out of his coat and boots, and she crouched before him, running a hand over his blond hair.

He grinned, his snub nose shining. "We made a snowman. I got to put his hat on. Mr. Dan helped me. Then Tommy's brothers came and knocked it over. So we pounded on 'em."

Kristin widened her eyes, unable to stop a grin. "Well, I can understand that, but maybe 'pounding on 'em' wasn't quite the right thing to do, huh?"

Gregory set his jaw and folded his arms, a very familiar stubborn look coming over him. "They were mean."

"Okay." Kristin laughed as she pulled him in for a kiss. She wouldn't argue the point now. "Listen. We've got some visitors. I want you to meet them."

"Who?" A look of consternation crossed his face and she grinned again. Patience was something he did not yet possess. Genetics said his chances of ever doing so were fairly low.

"Well, they're family. Your family." Kristin let out her breath, feeling the sharp sting of tears. Only now did she realize what she'd robbed her son of, estranging herself from Doc and Caroline.

"Papa and Gramma is my family. And you."

Kristin nodded, choosing her words. She didn't know how he'd react to what she had to say. "That's true. But, remember I told you, you have another Grandpa, and an Auntie…" And a father… Excitement surged and took her by surprise, but she quelled it. She couldn't think about that just yet.

Gregory narrowed his eyes, as though he didn't quite believe her. He bit down on his bottom lip and cocked his head to one side, pulling on the straps of his denim overalls.

"Lemme see." He pushed past her and marched into the living room. Kristin followed, praying all the while. Her fears were unfounded. She smiled as she watched him stride right up to Doc. He stared up at the big man, his hands on his hips.

Doc widened his eyes, but then his face broke into an amused grin.

"Blimey." Caroline stared in clear astonishment.

Kristin knew what they both saw. Gregory was a miniature image of his father in every way.

For the first time since giving birth to him, the thought didn't hurt.

"Hi. I'm Gregory Luke Taylor." Gregory announced himself in a strong clear voice. "Are you really my Grandpa?"

Doc's familiar laughter filled the room and broadened Kristin's smile. He leaned over, placed his hands on Gregory's shoulders, met his grandson's inquisitive gaze, and nodded. Tears glistened in his eyes. "I believe I am, son."

"Watcha crying for?" Gregory's voice lowered a notch, his eyes moving to Kristin.

She came closer, put a protective hand on his back, and cleared her throat, willing back tears of her own. "He's just very happy to meet you, Greggy. That's all."

"Oh. How come?"

More laughter overrode the serious moment. Caroline came to them and crouched before Gregory, shaking her head. Wonder shone from her eyes. "Hi, Gregory. I'm your Auntie Caroline."

"I've got a picture of you." Gregory's smile grew wider and he raised his head to look at Kristin. "They're here!" he whispered. His excitement did not surprise her. Although she hadn't kept in touch, they talked often of Luke and his family. Sometimes at night, if Gregory woke and couldn't get back to sleep, he'd ask to hear 'the stories'. Lately, since Joshua, he'd almost stopped asking. She wondered now how her son would take Luke's sudden appearance.

Kristin led him to where she had been sitting, and put him on her knee, holding him close. Caroline and Doc sat opposite them, clearly unable to take their eyes off the child who bore so much resemblance to Luke.

She couldn't put it off. "Sweetheart, I have to tell you something."

Gregory swiveled to face her, his blue eyes filled with anticipation. "Is it about my Daddy?" His intelligence never ceased to amaze her.

Kristin nodded, brushing his hair off his face, anxious thoughts threatening to sour the moment. She drew in a breath and nodded again. "Yes, it is. Gregory, your father…" What? She struggled to find the right words.

"Is he coming home too? For real?" Hope shone from her son's eyes as he stared up at her with all the innocence of childhood.

Kristin smiled, gave a small shrug of her shoulders. "Yes."

Chapter Forty

Later that afternoon, after a late lunch, they sat around the kitchen table and Gregory set an inquiring gaze on her.

"Is my Daddy coming now, Mommy?" Excitement bubbled from him and she had to smile. But she didn't miss the frown that creased her mother's brow. Doc and Hayden chuckled, but Teddy and Caroline exchanged a worried glance.

Kristin pushed her fingers through her hair and drew in a breath. "I think so, sweetie. Soon." Tears pricked her eyes. She got to her feet and cleared her plate. She left the room, unable to take the stifling tension one more minute. Upstairs she took a long hot shower, dressed and brushed her mess of tangles until she was satisfied she didn't look like she'd just come off the field.

Later, while Hayden and Mom napped, Doc dozed by the fire and Caroline read. Teddy sat on the floor with Gregory and played with his collection of Matchbox cars. The two became friends for life the minute they set eyes on each other.

Kristin couldn't relax. She paced the length of the long room, glancing at the clock every few minutes. She fiddled with the buttons on her blouse, smoothed down her woolen slacks until her damp palms left marks on them, and ran her fingers through her hair about a million times. When the dogs raced for the door barking, she froze.

Doc sat up with a grunt. Caroline put her book down and Teddy looked up.

Kristin moved to the window and saw Luke unfolding himself from the small rental car.

"He's here." She wasn't altogether comfortable with the way her heart jumped at the sight of him.

Teddy started for the door, Gregory skipping after him, his eyes bright. Kristin reached out and grabbed his shoulder. "Greggy, wait. Let him… catch his breath." She turned to the door, not knowing what to do. Her racing pulse gave her little choice but to sit.

What was wrong with her? It was like she was back at The Rockpile. Gregory obeyed reluctantly. He scrambled on to her lap and she held him close, burying her face in his soft blond hair, holding his hands in hers. Teddy and Luke's voices filtered through the room from the front hall.

Gregory gave a little gasp and tightened his hold on her hands. Kristin felt his heart going a mile a minute. She raised her head, and saw Luke standing in the doorway.

Teddy inched past him and took a seat near Caroline. Doc gave him a slap on the back, but Luke only had eyes for his son.

He crossed the room with slow steps until he stood in front of them. Crouching to Gregory's eye-level he settled his steady gaze on him.

The barest of smiles tugged at Luke's mouth, his sigh just audible. "Hi, sport." His voice caught and tears shimmered in his eyes.

"Hi." Gregory pushed his back into her and she kissed the top of his head. She couldn't see his face, but felt his hesitation in the way his fingers gripped hers.

Luke's eyes traveled over every inch of his son, his worn expression replaced by a look of utter fascination and awe.

"Are you my Daddy?" Gregory's small voice broke the silence.

Luke nodded, a smile starting. Two tears ran down his sallow cheeks. Gregory swiveled and looked up at Kristin. "He's crying, like Grandpa Douglas."

"I know, baby."

Gregory pressed a finger against her wet cheek. "You're crying too."

"Yes." She nodded, somehow able to find a smile. Gregory faced Luke again. For a long moment, all she heard was her son's steady breathing and Caroline sniffing from across the room.

"I'm named after you. Gregory Luke Taylor. Did you know?"

Luke wiped his eyes, cleared his throat and nodded. "Your uncle told me." With a trembling hand, he stroked Gregory's blond hair. The tender expression he wore reminded Kristin of the way he'd looked at Tuan and the other kids at the orphanage.

"And I'm four if you didn't know. I'm going to be five in October. Which is kinda a long ways away. You can come to my party if you want."

"Thanks." Luke's smile broadened and fresh tears filled his blue eyes.

Gregory tilted his face upward and met Kristin's eyes. "Can I give my Daddy a hug?"

Kristin nodded, set him down on the rug and watched her son put a hand on Luke's shoulder. "Mommy says when you're sad, hugs are best." He put his little arms around Luke's broad shoulders and squeezed.

Luke enfolded him in an instant, and she saw him break, no longer able to fight the emotion she knew he'd been wrestling. He held Gregory close and just shook his head, over and over again. Kristin gave way to the enormity of the moment and allowed her own tears to fall unchecked.

Gregory finally wiggled out of Luke's embrace. "Wanna see my room? I gots all sorts of cool stuff up there. And I'll show you my model planes too, and I gotsa train set and trucks!" His cheerful voice lightened the heaviness in the air. He skipped over to Doc and grabbed his hand. "You come too, Grandpa!"

Luke straightened, his face split wide with his smile. It disappeared when he caught her looking at him.

Kristin brushed away her tears and smiled anyway. "I think you're a hit."

Luke raised an eyebrow, an unexpected grin spreading across his flushed face. "You had me believing you." The gleam in his eyes filled her with new hope.

She widened her eyes and shrugged. "About what?"

"Come on! Come see my room!" She watched Gregory try to pull Doc to his feet, then went to Caroline and pulled on her hands as well, talking non-stop all the while.

Luke raised his eyes to the ceiling, tipped his head back and laughed. The low familiar sound sent warm waves of recognition tumbling through her. Kristin crossed her arms and scowled. "What's so funny?"

Luke glanced at Gregory and shook his head. "You letting me think the kid takes after me. That motor mouth belongs to you, Taylor."

Kristin flushed under his teasing gaze and swallowed. Air was in short supply all of a sudden.

They could have been the only ones in the room.

Luke turned from her and joined Gregory in the doorway. Doc and Caroline followed. Teddy went too, even though he'd been given the grand tour yesterday.

Kristin leaned back against the couch and stared at the fire. The sparks she'd felt moments ago had nothing to do with the flames jumping in front of her. When she'd locked eyes with him, it took a minute to realize what was happening. The feeling was so familiar, yet not. Somewhere in the recesses of her soul, something woke. She could not deny what she felt.

What she'd always felt.

Just what on earth was she supposed to do about it?

Kristin made her way downstairs earlier than usual on Monday morning. She wanted to have some quiet time, try to figure out what to do with the mess her life had suddenly turned into. Having Luke under the same roof made her more than nervous.

If she didn't get some sleep soon, her mother would have to commit her.

They'd all stayed up talking well after midnight last night. Everyone had gone to church for evening service, even Luke. The day passed quickly with the guys playing with Gregory outside most of the time. Hayden and Mom went to bed first, but the rest of them sat around the dining-room table swapping stories, sharing memories, and remembering Vietnam.

Luke and Teddy began to relax, their weariness lifting. She knew nothing would ever completely erase the nightmares they suffered, but she hoped and prayed for healing to come quickly.

God *had* taken care of them. Protected them. Even answered her own prayer—the one she'd half-heartedly whispered on the plane, high over the mountains of Vietnam.

"Please God, keep him safe. Keep Teddy safe. And bring them home to me soon..."

And...eventually...He had.

Kristin stopped short in the doorway of the kitchen. Luke stood at the counter fumbling with the new automatic drip machine Hayden had bought her mother last Christmas. Surprised to see him, she stayed where she was and watched him undetected.

He wore jeans and a red-and-blue-striped rugby shirt, his feet bare. His wet hair had been tied at the back of his neck with an elastic band. She'd never seen it this long and wasn't at all sure she liked the new look. And she didn't care for the beard either. Not that her opinion mattered.

Luke's grunt smacked of annoyance as he stepped back, scratched his head and poked at the machine again. His frustrated mumbling brought an unbidden smile. Like her, Luke did not function well without his morning coffee.

Releasing her breath, she forced herself forward. Running back up the stairs would have been easier. "Need some help?"

He swiveled, his face contorted with concentration. "What in hell's blazes is this thing?"

Kristin laughed and moved in. He stepped aside as she put it together, poured the right amount of water into the proper compartment and spooned coffee into the basket. In a moment, she'd pressed the button and the machine began to sizzle, hot brown liquid drizzling into the glass carafe. "Meet Mr. Coffee. He's become a very popular guy around here."

Luke arched a blond eyebrow, rubbing the scruff on his chin. He tucked an errant strand of hair behind his ears and grinned. "Mr. Coffee, huh? Guess I have been gone a while."

Kristin pulled a face and retrieved two mugs from the cupboard. A glance at the clock told her Mom and Hayden were already out and about. She had about forty-five minutes before waking Gregory. "Is Teddy still asleep?"

Luke nodded. "He usually tosses for three hours, then conks out for another three."

Kristin put the mugs on the counter and stared out the window at the white fields beyond the fence. Two black horses ambled across her line of vision, and she smiled.

They'd become closer than brothers, Luke and Teddy. How she wished it had been under different circumstances.

Slowly, she turned. Luke's eyes settled on her in an instant. And Kristin finally allowed herself the luxury of studying him.

A jagged scar ran from the corner of his eye across to his ear. Another less visible line showed at his hairline. His eyes were troubled and hinted at unspeakable subjects.

Kristin knew the physical scars he bore paled to what he carried on the inside.

Her gut twisted and she veered her gaze. She fiddled with the radio on the counter. Music soon filled the room and excused conversation.

When the coffee finished brewing, she poured it and offered a mug to him. She saw his eyes move to her trembling hand as he took it from her. He cleared his throat and stepped back to let her pass. Kristin sat at the table and cradled her own mug, inhaling the strong aroma.

Luke pulled up a chair and sat opposite her. "Are you all right?"

His soft question pieced her heart. She shrugged. "What's your definition of all right?"

A smile slid across his mouth and he toyed with the cross around his neck.

Her father's cross.

The fact that he still had it surprised her. That he still wore it seared her.

"It can't have been easy for you, having Gregory, being on your own."

"No." She met his eyes again and warmed to them. He set his coffee down and rubbed his jaw, looking thoughtful. Kristin lifted her chin and shook her head. Her hardships were insignificant compared to what he had endured. "I can't complain, Luke. I was fortunate. God blessed me in many ways."

"Is that so?" Surprise moved across his face and his eyes brightened.

Kristin blinked back tears and found her voice again. "For a long time after I came home, I was very angry. I didn't understand what had happened to you. It was just one more thing to add to my list of reasons to hate God. I hated that He took you from me, left Gregory without a father. I thought maybe it was His way of punishing me."

Luke sighed and shook his head. "God doesn't work that way."

"Oh, I know that now." She smiled, letting the warmth of the mug she held infiltrate her cold skin. "I'm definitely back on speaking terms with Him, even though I still don't understand it all, and I still have questions."

"That doesn't surprise me." Luke flashed a knowing grin that made her smile.

"I wasn't in much shape to know what to do with a child. I made a lot of mistakes." Kristin studied the table, unable to look his way. "Still do."

"You're doing fine. He's an amazing kid."

She shrugged. "When I first came home, I tried to go back to work. I couldn't—it didn't work out. I didn't want to tell my mom that I was pregnant. I left Boston and went to New York. I went to stay with Cassie, Jonno's sister." Kristin looked up and blinked under his startled expression.

"You did?" Luke grinned, a subdued laugh escaping. "Jonno would have loved that. Did you learn how to make that cornbread he was always talking about?"

She wiped her eyes and nodded. "Not as well as Cassie does, but I do a fairly good imitation." The past didn't seem quite so harsh now. The words tumbled out easily as she told the rest. "So that's how we ended up here. She says hi by the way."

"You've talked to her?"

"Yesterday."

"And what words of wisdom did she have for you?"

Kristin managed a brief smile. "One day at a time, baby, one day at a time."

He nodded, taking another sip, capturing her in the sea of his eyes. "I should call Bob and Mary Jo. Let them know…are they still in-country?"

"Yes. I have the number."

Luke nodded. "I hear you have a book coming out. And the Polk Award?"

Kristin sucked in a breath, drumming her fingers on the table to the tune of her hammering heart and the song from the radio. "Yeah. Don't know why they picked me."

His hand came over hers and stilled it. She flinched but didn't pull away. Didn't look at him either. If she did, she'd lose the little composure she had left.

"You do know why." He squeezed her hand and she raised her eyes to his. "I'm proud of you, Kris. I always believed in what you were doing. Even when I couldn't show it."

His admission flooded her senses and she took a minute to acknowledge it. "Really? After everything I…"

Luke shook his head, his eyes clouding over. "I thought we did this already. There's no sense rehashing the past. Let's move on."

"How?"

His smile did nothing to quell her floundering sense of place and time. "That, love, is the sixty-four thousand dollar question." After a few moments Luke spoke again. "I'm sorry, Kris. It wasn't supposed to be like this."

"No," she whispered. "No, it wasn't."

Luke removed his hand and cleared his throat. "So what are you doing with your days when you're not writing?"

She drained what was left of in her mug and nodded. "I help out at a coffee house, Fresh Winds. Josh and some friends opened it a few years ago. And a new Vet center just opened in town, so I'm volunteering there too with…um…when I have time."

"I see." He raised an eyebrow, his mouth drawn. A hint of color tinged his cheeks. For a long moment, he stayed silent. "So. This guy…Joshua. Is he a good man?"

Kristin sat back. "Yes." Good enough to give her time to process the last forty-eight hours without pushing and demanding answers. But she owed him some. Soon.

Luke let out a shaky sigh, his eyes growing wet. "How long have you known him?"

"A couple of years." Luke's tortured expression pushed the knife deeper. "We were friends and then…"

"Teddy told me that Joshua asked you to marry him."

"Yes." She inhaled at the blow she dealt.

"I don't see a ring."

"I haven't given him an answer yet."

Luke rubbed his jaw, his eyes glinting. "If you're expecting me to fight for you, I have to be honest, I don't think I have it in me."

Kristin recoiled at the declaration, blood rushing to her cheeks. "Are you telling me I *should* marry Joshua?"

"I don't know, Kristin. This wasn't the scenario I dreamt about in Hanoi, okay?" Luke shrugged and pushed his mug away. "But, despite how I've been acting the past couple of days, I'm not an idiot. Five years is five years. I can't change what happened. If he makes you happy, if he's good to Gregory…if you love him…and you want to marry him…then I guess you should."

"And you…you'd be okay with that?"

Luke sat forward, his eyes glinting under the overhead light. "Tell me what I'm supposed to do here. Do I just step back and watch you live your life with some other guy, with the occasional visit from my son on weekends?" Anger and frustration crept into his tone. His hand slammed onto the table.

"That's the kind of life *I* had, Kristin. After my parents divorced, we spent all our time flying from one city to the next, bouncing between houses. That's not what I want for my son. Our son. So no, I'm not okay with it. But I don't think I have a whole lot of choice in the matter. Do I?"

Tears spilled onto her cheeks and she swiped them away. "Do you think I'm doing this to hurt you? I just…I need to do the right thing."

"Back to that."

He studied her so intently she wondered how long she could endure it. "What do you want, Luke?"

"What do you think?" He snorted as he pushed back from the table. His empty coffee-mug tipped over and rolled in her direction. Luke righted it with a trembling hand. "If I asked you right here, right now, to break things off with him, to give us another chance, what would you say?"

Kristin's vision blurred as she took in the pain on his face. She pressed her lips together and somehow couldn't give an answer.

"That's what I thought." The tremor in his voice tore at her heart. "All right. I do want to stick around here though. I'll look for somewhere to

297

stay and find a job. I want to get to know my son. Do you have any objection to that?"

"No. Of course not." Her reply sounded forced, as though she couldn't wait to see the back of him. "I want you to be part of Gregory's life. But we're going to have to find some middle ground. I can't live with you glaring at me every time I turn around."

He narrowed his eyes, his jaw hard, twitching ever so slightly. "Who's glaring?"

Kristin shook her head and got to her feet. "I need to get Gregory up. Have a good day, Luke."

Chapter Forty-One

Two weeks later, Kristin walked through Fresh Winds, hoping to get some writing done.

"Kristin?" As she passed Josh's office, he called out to her. She headed back that way and stopped in the doorway.

"What's going on?"

Josh stood at his desk, packing things into cardboard boxes.

"Come in." He lifted a box to the floor, unsmiling. "Shut the door." He released a quick breath as they sat in the two armchairs at the far side of the room. Silence prowled around them as Kristin searched his face, trying to read him.

"A job opportunity came up for me in Florida. I've decided to take it."

She stared, sudden fear snaking through her. "Without talking to me?"

"I'm talking now. Kristin, I…" His voice trailed off and he looked away. When he looked her way again, his eyes were wet. "I can't do this anymore." He let his hands rise and fall in one slow movement. "I knew the minute Luke showed up that things couldn't be—wouldn't ever be—the same between us. I hoped I was wrong. I tried to convince myself we still had a future. But I'm not stupid. I knew it was over that night. I should have done this a lot sooner."

"Joshua…" Kristin breathed out his name, tears stinging.

Josh raised an eyebrow. "I'm not sure why you haven't talked to me about it, about Luke being home, how you really feel about it. I thought we had a better relationship than that…I don't know…maybe you haven't figured it all out yet. But I have. And I don't want to live my life knowing I was your second choice. Neither one of us deserve that."

Kristin straightened in her chair. "Luke and I...we can barely stand to be in the same room together. You've seen that. And he's...different. He's been through so much."

"Do you still love him?"

It wasn't a hard question, but the answer remained out of reach.

Kristin bent over, put her head in her hands and drew in a deep breath and prayed for the strength she needed to really listen to the reason she was coming up with more excuses than the military when a mission went south.

She raised her head, pushed her hair back and frowned, tears blurring her vision. "He doesn't love me."

Josh's quiet laugh chilled her. He shook his head, a tiny smile pulling at his lips. "If you truly believe that, Kristin, then you really did spend too much time in the trenches. But that's not what I asked you. I asked if you love him."

"I..." Tears trailed down her cheeks and she made no effort to wipe them away.

"Josh, I'm so sorry," she whispered. "I had no idea that this..."

"Of course you didn't." He rose and went to her, extended a hand and pulled her to him. Kristin stood for a long time in his arms before they said goodbye, her thoughts swirling. Nothing made sense any more.

And nothing felt safe.

Luke sipped his coffee, ignored the not-so subtle looks the young waitress kept sending his way, and watched Gregory down his milkshake. He'd already polished off a huge burger and a plate of fries and asked for more. Luke hated saying no, but he recalled the last time he'd allowed Gregory two burgers. His second-hand pick-up still held the slight stench of vomit.

Kris had not been amused. She'd blamed it on his driving too fast. Nothing ever seemed to please her. Luke tried—worked odd jobs wherever he could find them—did whatever necessary to provide for his son. The work he put his hands to held little meaning.

He hadn't yet been able to pick up a camera.

All his efforts to do the right things seemed wasted. Joshua Brentwood cornered the market on popularity in this town. Luke tried to master the jealousy that seethed whenever he thought of Kristin with Josh, but each day it grew harder. He always ended up snapping her head off for no reason.

Luke sighed, remembering better times. If Jonno were here to see this—the way they shot smart remarks and snide comments at each other—oh boy. His friend would have more than a few words to say on the matter, no doubt.

"Daddy?"

Luke's mouth curled upward. Two months in and he still wasn't used to that, but he loved the sound of it. "Yeah?"

Gregory wiped a hand across his mouth, leaving a chocolate stain on his shirtsleeve. "Can you take me to my swimming lesson next week? It's on Thursdays."

Luke frowned at Gregory's earnest expression. "I thought you did that with Joshua." Luke did his best to stay out of the man's way. He'd been good about checking with Kristin whenever he wanted to do things with Gregory. The last thing he wanted was to step on any toes. Besides, no way could he justify beating up a Jesus Freak.

Gregory yawned and shook his head. "Josh had to leave." His little brow furrowed as he stared into Luke's eyes. "Mommy is taking me now. But I want you to. Can you, Daddy?"

"Well...I guess so. It's just for next week, right?" He hadn't remembered Kris saying anything about Josh going anywhere. Then again, he didn't pay much attention when she talked about him.

"Nuh-uh." Gregory shook his head and slurped. "For like forever. Oh, and we're gonna need a coach for T-Ball too."

Luke cleared his throat, his greasy lunch sitting heavy in his stomach. "Josh left town?" Come to think of it, he hadn't seen the guy around for a while. "When?"

"I don't know. He hatta go to Florida. He left...um...I dunno." Gregory rolled his eyes and poked his cheek with a grimy forefinger. "But he sent me a postcard. I gotsa picture of Mickey Mouse. I could show you if you want."

"Sure." Luke drew in a breath and let it out slowly.

Kristin hadn't said a word.

"Okay, Greg, I'll be there on Thursday." Luke checked his watch. "It's getting late. We should get you home."

"Okay." Gregory held his gaze, pinning Luke to his chair. "Daddy?"

"Yep?"

"Can you come live with us?"

Luke clamped his mouth shut and shoved down his emotions. "Why'd you ask me that, sport?"

Gregory shrugged and huffed out a sigh. "Just 'cause. Mommy's sad. I think she was happy you came home, but it'd be better if you lived with us. I don't think she'd be so sad then." He drew in a breath and leaned over the table, his eyes getting rounder. "Don't tell. But one time, before, you know, you came, she gave me a bunch of old pictures to keep, all for me. But then Josh left and she took 'em back. I still got lots of you, so it's okay, but—I don't know why she wants them if they make her sad. She sits on her bed and looks at 'em a long time, and cries. I'm not supposta watch though, Grandma says its leavesdropping."

"Eavesdropping." Luke's smile didn't stop the tears from pricking his eyes. He blinked them back and nodded.

Okay. He had the lay of the land now. Maybe it was time he and God did some more business.

And then it would be Kristin's turn.

He rose and took his son's hand in his, grinning down at him. "You ever heard of the CIA, kiddo?"

Luke stirred from sound slumber and listened. Someone was at the door.

"Go away!" He found sleeping in the afternoons a lot easier than trying to make it through the night. He hadn't managed to get full time work yet, so allowed himself a slightly erratic schedule. Thankfully he had enough in savings to last for a while.

He groaned again at the persistent knocking. Teddy had probably lost his keys again. Luke rolled out of bed, pulled a blanket around his body and went to let him in.

"For cryin' out loud, Preacher! Hey…" He stepped back and stared. "Kris."

Kristin stood in the hall, looking like she wished the floor would just swallow her up whole. "Maybe I should have called."

"No, it's fine. Is Gregory okay?" Luke pulled at his beard and tipped his head to one side. His pressure rose as his mind raced ahead with worst-case scenarios.

"Yes. He's at school. I'm just on my way to pick him up. I…" She stood on her toes and looked past him into the apartment. "Do you have company?"

"Do I what?" Luke glared at her and then looked down at the blanket he held around his chest. A grin slid his lips apart. "No. I was sleeping."

"Sleeping?" Disapproval furrowed her brow. "It's the beginning of April. You still haven't found a job?"

Luke gritted his teeth. "Unfortunately not all of us can be published authors and Polk award winners."

Kristin shook her head and swiveled on the heel of her shoe.

Luke grabbed her wrist. "Stop. I'm sorry. Come on in. I'll get dressed."

He scrambled into jeans and a t-shirt and tried not to imagine what she was doing here. When he made it back to the living room, Kristin held an invitation-sized envelope toward him. "You're probably busy but…just take it."

He couldn't.

Maybe Gregory had got it wrong. What if Josh hadn't left, just had to go somewhere on business and…

"It's not going to explode, Luke." She waved it at him again.

Luke's mouth twitched as he slit open the envelope. "If this is an invitation to your wedding, you wasted your time. I'm not coming."

"It's not."

He scanned the fine script and gave relief about thirty seconds. Then he met her eyes. "The awards ceremony. Trying to fill the empty place at the table?" The moment the words were out, he wanted to snatch them back.

"I guess I deserved that." She lowered her gaze, fiddled with the strap of her purse and turned toward the door again.

"No, you didn't." He placed a hand on her shoulder. "Kris, wait."

"I can't be late," she mumbled, ducking out from under his grip.

Luke pushed a hand through his hair and tried to smile. "I'm sorry. I just...you took me by surprise." And if there were an award for the biggest jerk in town, he'd be first in line. "Are you sure you want me there?"

Kristin stared him down, her eyes too bright. "We're spending the weekend at your dad's. I thought...I didn't want you to feel left out. And it would mean a lot to Gregory if you were there. But you don't have to come."

Luke scratched his head and tried to decipher the mysteries locked behind her eyes. She looked tired. And stressed. "Do you want me to come or not? Because it doesn't matter to me—I can be there—if you want." Just as soon as he sewed his tongue back together.

Kristin pressed her lips into a thin line and gave a shrug. "It's not an invitation to the White House, Luke. Come, don't come. It's a peace offering, okay? Take it or leave it."

"Sorry. I'm tired." He suffered another scathing glance.

"Aren't we all."

"So you...uh...must be looking forward to it. It's a pretty big deal." He attempted civility, floundering for the right words. He never knew what to say around her anymore.

Kristin sighed and screwed up her nose. "I'm not, actually. I don't do so well in crowds. And I have to give a speech."

"Well, that shouldn't be a problem for you." He grinned but she didn't seem to appreciate the joke. "I mean...I..."

"Forget it, Luke." She held up a hand and shook her head. "I have to go."

Chapter Forty-Two

"Anybody heard from Luke?" Teddy sat opposite Kristin at the round table, spinning his dessert spoon. Gregory, beside him, tried to imitate the trick. Kristin didn't have the energy to stop him or answer her brother's annoying question.

Caroline shook her head and glanced at the program again. "Kris, you're last. How'd that happen?"

"They probably figured I'd lose my nerve and skip out." Kristin's stomach rolled and she pushed her plate of food away. "I can't do this."

"Yes, you can." Everyone at the table spoke at once.

Cassie laughed and slid an arm around Kristin's shoulders. "Baby, I didn't drive through all that construction to haul your bootie out of the ladies room, but I will if I have to."

"She'll be fine." Hayden's look said she better be.

Kristin smiled and reached for her water glass. She'd been shot at, dodged hand-grenades, survived enemy fire, and childbirth. How hard could giving a speech in front of a few hundred people be?

Somehow she sat through all the awards and speeches until they called her name. She walked to the podium on trembling legs, her mouth jammed with cotton. As the presenter made his introduction, she anchored her gaze on the table just a few feet away from her.

Mom, dabbing her eyes already, Hayden beaming like this was as much for him as it was for her—Caroline, Doc, and Teddy with Gregory on his knees—all cheered her on with wide smiles. And Cassie and Eddy. It was so good to see them again, to have them here to celebrate this moment.

She avoided looking at the empty chair and stepped forward to receive her award.

"Thank you." Kristin cleared her throat and scanned her notes. "This is truly an honor." She paused and glanced up. The doors to the dining room had opened, wait staff clearing tables as quietly as they could. She tried to extricate the lump that kept forming in the back of her throat and drew in a breath.

"In nineteen-sixty-seven, I hopped a plane to a faraway land I'd only heard about through newspaper articles and television reports. I was just a few years out of college, had little money and no job. And I was—still am—a woman trying to do a man's job. Or so they told me." Laughter rippled through the audience and Kristin took a moment to read her typed out papers.

"I went to Vietnam to honor my father's memory, to finish what he started. I thought…" She hesitated, staring over the sea of people once more. "I thought that was the reason I was supposed to be there. To grow as a journalist, begin my career in the very place my father died years before."

A figure moved through the open doors at the back of the room. Kristin watched Luke take a few halting steps inside. He looked straight at her, flashed a quick smile and stood still.

"But it wasn't." Anxiety slid away. She gripped the podium and steadied her voice. "I believe I went to Vietnam so I could learn how to live. And love." Murmured approval buoyed her on, but it was the light in Luke's eyes that gave her real courage. "During my time there, I was privileged to work alongside many talented journalists. I learned from them, laughed and cried with them. We tried in vain to make sense of the quagmire we'd landed in. I'm not sure any of us ever did. And I know we still bear the scars of the inner battles we fought while we watched young boys losing their fight every day."

Kristin swallowed and her throat grew thick again.

She wasn't going to make it.

Her eyes sought Luke's.

He nodded and moved in, slowly making his way through the maze of tables until he stood behind Teddy. Gregory swiveled and Kristin heard his gasp of delight. Luke placed a finger to his lips, and a hand on his son's head, his eyes never leaving hers.

Kristin gathered new strength and pressed on. "I would like to dedicate this award to the memory of my father, Malcolm Taylor, and to all the amazing, courageous men and women who lost their lives in Vietnam. But I can't take credit for this honor alone." She pushed her notes to one side, focused only on Luke.

"For most of my time in-country, I was fortunate enough to be paired with an exceptionally talented photographer. Many of my articles are partnered with his work. When we first met, I thought I knew everything. He quickly set me straight." She wiped an errant tear from her cheek. "His courage under fire amazed me, his devotion to the things he believed in astounded me, and his dry wit annoyed the crap out of me." She waited a brief moment for the quiet laughter from her colleagues and family to die down. "By the time I left Vietnam a year later, I wasn't sure I knew anything at all. And I didn't know whether I would ever see him again."

Kristin tasted salt on her lips as she gripped her plaque in one hand and held it at shoulder level. "Luke Maddox, this is for you. You showed me how to accept things I couldn't change, work on the things I could, and you encouraged me to do the best damn job I was capable of or die trying. And through it all, you stood by me...even when I let you down. You showed me how to live. You taught me how to love." She locked eyes with him and finally smiled. "And if it's okay with you, I'd like to sign up for a few extra lessons."

Applause rang in her ears as people got to their feet.

The room began to close in with the noise and familiar waves of panic swirled around her as she hurried off the stage and down the steps.

Luke stood at the bottom.

He stepped forward, two fingers pointing to his eyes. "Right here, love, look right here." Before she could get a word out, he pulled her into his arms and crushed her against him. "You're okay. I've got you. Just breathe."

Pressed against him, she did as he instructed, and began to relax at last. Laughter stuck in her throat. "I can't."

"It's okay, Kris. You'll be fine." Luke tightened his embrace and she smothered a giggle.

"No, I mean I really can't breathe. You're squishing me."

He put some space between them in a hurry. "Sorry." Luke gave a sheepish grin. "Better now?"

Kristin wiped her eyes and mustered a smile as she took in the sight of him. "I thought you weren't coming."

He shrugged, ran a hand down his damp face and pulled at the knot of his tie. "Sorry. I got stuck in traffic. Nice speech."

"We should probably sit," Kristin whispered. "People are staring."

Luke's grin told her he didn't care, but he took her hand anyway and led her back to the table. A few excruciatingly long minutes later, it was over and her friends and colleagues crowded around to congratulate her.

Kristin finally managed to escape the still noisy dining room and ventured out into the hotel lobby. She cast about for a glimpse of her family, and her eyes landed on Luke.

He stood off to one side, in the far corner of the room, facing the window. His blond hair was now short and tidy, his face clean-shaven at last, and when he turned, as though he'd sensed her presence, his eyes sparkled in a way that made her doubt her ability to walk across the floor toward him.

"You disappeared," she accused.

Luke smiled and lifted his shoulders. "I don't do so well in crowds either."

"I don't think I've ever seen you in a suit." She brushed some lint off the navy double-breasted sports coat, stood back and nodded her approval.

Luke pushed up a smart green-and-blue-striped tie and winked. "Take a good look, Taylor. It won't happen often."

She clutched her purse and plaque to her chest and glanced down at the silk dress of deep emerald she'd bought for the occasion. "I don't suppose combat gear would have gone over too well."

"Probably not." Luke stepped a little closer and tucked a stray curl behind her ear. After much debate, Caroline convinced her to wear it down. "You look beautiful."

Nerves pelted her stomach as she watched the dimple in his cheek come out to play. "Where is everybody?"

"They went back to Dad's. Are you all right?"

Kristin nodded, her heart still jumping at the realization of what his presence here meant. "I met the editor of *The New York Times*. He offered me a job."

Luke raised an eyebrow. "Really?"

The apprehension on his face made her smile and gave her the answer she needed. "Yeah. He thinks I should move to New York, wants me to start right away."

"I see." His jaw began to twitch as he ran a hand through his hair. "What did you tell him?"

"Well, I thanked him, obviously." She tipped her head and grinned. "Then I told him I'd have to talk to my partner about it, but not to hold his breath, because he probably wouldn't be that keen. And since we have a son settled in school in Vermont, it's not the best time for us to make a move."

Luke's broad smile affirmed her decision. And the opportunity to free-lance was still on the table. But she'd never make the mistake of putting her career first again.

"Let's go outside." He pressed a hand to her back and guided her through the doors out onto the terrace.

Kristin took in the view of the city, the tall buildings, the noise and hustle on the street below, and suddenly longed for the green mountains of Vermont.

He led her to a secluded area and indicated a white wrought iron table and chairs. "Sit, if you want."

She shook her head, wandering across to check out a flowering plant. "That was harder than I thought it would be. Talking about Vietnam." Sorrow washed in again, engulfed her, and covered her with familiar remorse. There was still so much they would have to work through, so much still left unsaid.

"I think it always will be."

Kristin met his eyes. "I don't know how you survived it, Luke."

He shrugged and walked a few paces, his heels tapping on the concrete. When he turned back to her, he wore a thin smile. "By the grace of God, Kris. That's how."

"Do you…think about it…all the time?" Kristin choked on the words and decided to sit after all. She knew Teddy had days when he couldn't leave his apartment. She'd wondered how Luke coped, but hadn't dared ask.

"I'm working through it. Nothing happens by accident, Kristin. God didn't watch me get captured and go 'Oops!' He had a reason for it."

She stared at him in wonder. "I can't accept that. What good came out of it?"

Luke joined her, propped his elbows on the table, rested his chin on his hands and just looked at her. "Do you remember I once told you some questions don't have easy answers?"

Kristin saw a depth of wisdom in his eyes she didn't recognize. "Yes." She remembered all too well.

Luke nodded, his face grave. "We may never know why things happened the way they did. But I don't think that matters. What matters is how we grow through the struggles we're given. At least that's what I'm trying to do."

She let go a tired sigh. "The whole what doesn't kill you makes you stronger philosophy?"

"Something like that."

She'd spent many hours of solitude over the past years, praying, pleading for the kind of understanding Luke seemed to possess. Kristin flinched as she recalled the hours she'd railed at God—begging Him to bring Luke back to them.

The reality of her answered prayer crashed through the high wall around her heart once again. Tears pooled in her eyes and she lowered her head. For the first time since she laid eyes on Luke that tumultuous winter night, Kristin felt peace.

Yet she still wrestled with her own guilt, and she didn't know what to do with that.

"I'm really not used to you being so quiet, Taylor. It's kind of unnerving." Luke's soft laugh chased off her melancholy thoughts.

Slowly she raised her head to look at him, wiped her cheeks and shrugged. "Some days I don't have a lot to say."

"Forgive me, but somehow I find that hard to believe." New lines creased the corners of his eyes as he smiled. He placed his program down on the table, flipped it over to the back page, pulled a pen from his jacket and drew two horizontal lines, followed by two verticals.

He made the first mark.

X's and O's. Or, as he always liked to correct her, naughts and crosses. *Proper English, please.* They'd spent a lot of time together in Vietnam just waiting around. Waiting for rides, waiting for calls to be patched through… hanging out in the mess hall at the 24th, taking a breather. Wherever they were, the pad and pencils would come out, the battle declared.

Luke's eyes sparked with challenge. Kristin grinned and snatched the pen he waved. With a shaking hand, she made an O in the middle of the block.

Luke groaned and smacked his forehead. "You always did that."

"You could have taken it," she retorted. "You didn't."

Several minutes later Kristin drew a line through her O's and put down her weapon. "You've lost your touch, Maddox." She shot him a tentative smile.

He sat back and raised an eyebrow. "Hardly. I let you win. As I recall, you can be a rather sore loser."

The relaxed moment moved into a minefield. Kristin got to her feet and left the table. She walked to the railing and stood staring at the slow moving traffic below. Inhaled a deep breath and willed fresh tears away. A moment later Luke stood behind her. His very presence still set her nerves on edge.

"Kris, it was just a joke. I didn't…mean to upset you." He cleared his throat. "Seems I'm pretty good at doing that these days."

Kristin shook her head. "It's not the stupid game. It's just—you. Me." She choked on her words and faced him, desperate to get this done. "I never expected you to forgive me for what happened, for what I did. But I need to tell you how sorry I am." She shrugged at his look of confusion. "I should have told you I thought I was pregnant. I shouldn't have let you leave that day without telling you. It's my fault you were captured. I know I can't change it, but I don't…I don't know how to live with it."

The first sob sent tremors through her as she gave way to emotion she'd held at bay for so much time. She buried her face in her hands and struggled to regain control.

Luke let out a muted groan and pulled her to him.

When her sobs subsided, Luke placed a hand under her chin and tipped her face upward. She had no choice but to meet his anxious eyes. "Is that really what you think? That I ended up in Hanoi because of you?"

"Yes." She stared at him in anguish, remembering that awful afternoon in Vietnam like it happened yesterday.

"You're wrong, love." His eyes were desperate and pleaded with her to believe him. "It could have happened any time. Anywhere. And I never blamed you for it."

Kristin steadied her breathing and accepted his words. "Caroline said that," she whispered. "She said you'd never blame me."

"My sister knows me too well." Luke gave a wan smile, lifted his shoulders and let them fall. "Caroline also thinks I've been acting like a moron. That I'm an idiot, pig-headed and stubborn."

Kristin raised an eyebrow, forgotten humor reviving her shattered spirit. "Is that all?"

His sheepish grin confirmed her assumption. He laughed, took a moment, then let out his breath in a shaky exhale. "Well. There were other more descriptive nouns…" Luke ran a light finger down the side of her face. His touch sent a familiar shiver of delight through her.

He searched her face, his eyes filled with questions. "Did you mean what you said in there?"

"Every word." Kristin sniffed and rested her hands against his chest, felt the beating of his heart and lost herself in the past. If only they could move beyond the shadows of yesterday. "Do you wish you'd never gone there, Luke? To Vietnam?"

Luke held her gaze but pain slashed his face. Kristin's heart ached for him, for all he'd suffered, all he still did. But then a quiet smile touched his lips. That wonderful smile she'd waited so long to see back when they first met, and thought gone forever.

Until right now.

He cupped her face between his warm hands, threading his fingers through her hair, and shook his head. "If I hadn't gone to Vietnam, I'd never have met you." He brushed the tears from her cheeks with the base of his thumbs. He hesitated for just a moment, then drew her closer. In a slow movement, he brought his lips to hers. And then, at long last, he kissed her.

Luke's eyes were misty and his face more solemn than she'd ever seen it. "I miss you, Kris. I miss us." The deep passion and sincerity on his face told her he meant it.

Kristin slipped her arms around him and melted into his embrace the way she always had, and everything in her surrendered to it. To him. "I miss us too."

He tightened his arms around her, touching the tip of her nose with his. "I love you, Kristin Taylor. I always have. And if I have to live my life without you in it, I'd rather go back to Hanoi."

"Oh, Luke, don't say that." Kristin pressed her fingers against his lips. She basked in the deep love for her still shining in his eyes. "I thought this would never happen. I thought I'd destroyed us."

"No." Luke's firm kiss denied it. "You could never do that. We're a team, remember?"

"I remember." Fresh tears flooded her eyes, but his smile warmed her heart and it soared to new heights. She was in Luke's arms, at last.

And he still loved her.

For the first time since returning home from Vietnam, Kristin felt safe.

"I never stopped loving you." She beamed at the revelation and relished the peace it brought.

Victory danced across his face as he swept her off the ground. She squealed and he put her down, sobering. "I thought you'd given your heart to someone else for a while there." His teasing tone held a serious edge.

Kristin shook her head, tracing the outline of his jaw with her fingertip. "You can't give away something you no longer own, Luke. I left my heart with you, in Vietnam. Don't you know that?"

He kissed her again, slow and lazy. When he pulled back, his eyes twinkled with familiar mischief. "Speaking of belongings…" Luke cleared his throat, reaching into his breast pocket. He held a small black velvet box in the palm of his hand. "I believe this belongs to you." He flipped the lid and Kristin gasped at the sight of her diamond ring.

She narrowed her eyes. "Where did you get that, Luke Maddox? Have you been snooping in my room?"

His grin preceded a deep chuckle. "No. Gregory found it for me."

Kristin's mouth fell open. "That's despicable! What are you teaching him?"

"I made it very clear it would only be this one time…don't give me that look. But come to think of it, I do think he has a future in the Agency."

Kristin rolled her eyes and shuddered. "What has he told you?"

Luke's gentle smile stripped away all fear. He reached for her hand. "We can talk about that later. Right now, I need to ask you a question."

When he dropped to one knee, her tears fell again. She couldn't stop them. Didn't even try. Luke's eyes were bright as well, but in them she saw her future.

"Yes." She blurted it out and laughed at his astonished expression. "You don't have to ask. I'll marry you tonight if you want me to."

"Well, in that case…" Luke stood and put his arms around her again, kissing her long and hard, igniting the fierce passion that always ran between them. He let her go and took the ring from its box, lifted her shaking hand in his, and slipped it back into place on her finger. "Still a perfect fit."

Kristin nodded, wiped her tears away and took a long look at the symbol of a promise she'd believed lost forever. It now shone with the assurance of a new beginning.

She raised her eyes to Luke's, brushed her hand over his hair, and leaned in to kiss him. "Teddy once told me something I've never forgotten. He said you can't change the past, and you don't know what tomorrow holds. The only day that really matters is today."

Luke nodded. "Yesterday's Tomorrow." He brought his lips to hers once more and held her close. "May we spend them all together, however many God grants."

THE END

Thank You!

Writing is a solitary profession, but an author needs a support system. I'm beyond grateful to have so many amazing people in my life and I'd be lost without them.

To all my wonderful friends in my writing communities – Jenness Walker, Becky Yauger, you guys have been there from the start and somehow you're still cheering. Beth Vogt, Jennifer Major and all The Spice Girls – thank you for listening, kicking my butt when I need it, and holding my hand through this crazy publishing journey. I'm so grateful for each one of you. My can't-live-without friends at home, LeeAnne, Debbie, Rochelle, Cathy K. – you guys keep me somewhat normal, thank you forever.

Rachelle Gardner, my amazing agent and wonderful friend, thank you for still loving this book! I'm so blessed to have you and the Books & Such ladies in my corner.

Mick Silva, editor extraordinaire - you took this story to the next level, and actually made the process fun. Thank you for believing in this book and in me.

Dineen Miller – what can I say? The cover? Spectacular. You rock, girl.

My family - Dad and Vivian – your ongoing support, love and encouragement means more than you know.

Pam – my awesome sister, I cherish your love and the relationship God has given us. Thank you for being there for me always.

Mom West, Pete, Lynn, Bonnie and all the Canada clan, so glad we're family.

Sarah and Randy – watching your love story unfold makes me want to write romance forever. It's been a joy to witness your first year of marriage. May God bless you with many more.

Chris and Deni – your beautiful music inspires me every day. Keep creating your magical sounds, you bring the world much joy.

And my husband, Stephen – I couldn't do this without you beside me. I want to spend all my tomorrows with you.

My God who is ever faithful, whose mercies astound me every day. Thank you for giving me this gift and the ability to pursue it.

Author Notes

Researching The Vietnam War was a fascinating process. Here are some of the books and websites that I found extremely helpful. *War Torn: Stories of War from the Women Reporters who Covered Vietnam,* Tad Bartimus, Tracy Wood, Kate Webb, Laura Palmer, Edith Lederer and Jurate Kazicakas. Random House (August 20, 2002).

On Their Own: Women Journalists and the American Experience in Vietnam, Joyce Hoffmann. Da Capo Press; 1st Edition (June 24, 2008).

A Piece of My Heart: The Stories of 26 American Women Who Served In Vietnam, Keith Walker. Presidio Press (February 5, 1997).

Fire in the Lake: The Vietnamese and the Americans in Vietnam, Frances FitzGerald. Back Bay Books (July 17, 2002).

Shrapnel in the Heart: Letters and Remembrances from the Vietnam Veterans Memorial, Laura Palmer. Vintage; 1st Vintage Books Edition (November 5, 1998).

The Cat From Hué; A Vietnam War Story, by John Laurence Public Affairs; New Edition Edition (December 17, 2002).

American Experience Vietnam Online: http://www.pbs.org/wgbh/amex/vietnam/

506th Infantry Regiment (Air Mobile—Air Assault): http://www.506infantry.org/

93rd Evacuation Hospital: http://members.tripod.com/~msg_fisher/93evac.html

24th Evacuation Hospital, Long Binh, Vietnam: http://www.24thevacuationhospital.org/314

About the Author

 Catherine West is an award-winning author who writes stories of hope and healing from her island home in Bermuda. *Yesterday's Tomorrow* won the INSPY for Romance in 2011, a Silver Medal in the Reader's Favorite Awards, and was a finalist in the Grace Awards. Catherine's second novel, *Hidden in the Heart*, was long listed in the 2012 INSPY's and was a finalist in the 2013 Grace Awards.

When she's not at the computer working on her next story, you can find her taking her Border Collie for long walks or tending to her roses and orchids. She and her husband have two grown children. Catherine is a member of American Christian Fiction Writers and Romance Writers of America, and is represented by Rachelle Gardner of Books & Such Literary Management. Catherine loves to connect with her readers and can be reached at Catherine@catherinejwest.com

Catherine's Website – http://www.catherinejwest.com

Made in the USA
Charleston, SC
22 November 2014